RIVER
RATS

ANDY GRIFFEE

RIVER RATS

Orphans
Publishing

This paperback edition published in 2022 by Orphans Publishing
Enterprise Park, Leominster
Herefordshire HR6 0LD

www.orphanspublishing.co.uk

A Cataloguing in Publication record for this book
is available from the British Library

Paperback: 978-1-903360-40-8

Printed and bound by Clays Ltd, Elcograf, S.p.A.

To Will and Ella

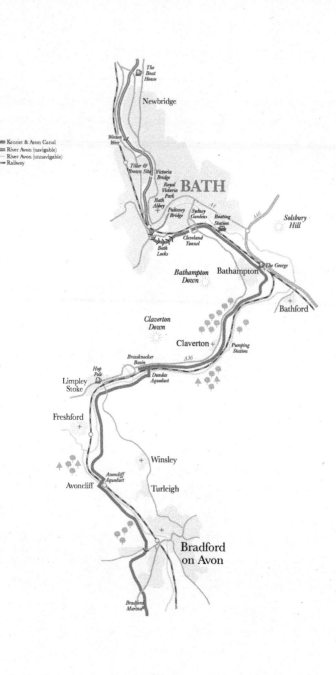

Kennet & Avon Canal
River Avon (navigable)
River Avon (unnavigable)
Railway

The Boat House

Newbridge

Weston Weir

Tiller & Brown Slit

Victoria Bridge

Royal Victoria Park

BATH

A 4

Bath Abbey

Pulteney Bridge

Sydney Gardens

Boating Station

A 46

Solsbury Hill

Cleveland Tunnel

Bath Locks

Bathampton Down

Bathampton

The George

Bathford

Claverton Down

Claverton

Pumping Station

Brassknocker Basin

A 36

Hop Pole

Limpley Stoke

Dundas Aqueduct

Freshford

Winsley

Avoncliff Aqueduct

Avoncliff

Turleigh

Bradford on Avon

Bradford Marina

A man is leaning against the ancient stones of Bath Abbey, with one leg bent at the knee. His relaxed posture conceals the violence of his thoughts. It has been raining for the past hour and the small square is empty of the tourists and buskers who fill it during the day. The handful of people braving the downpour are hurrying past in the dark with their heads bent to the ground. Most barely give the man a second glance and, even if they choose to look at his tall frame for a moment longer, his face is completely hidden by a motorcycle crash helmet. Through the raised visor, his eyes remain fixed on the entrance to the city's Pump Room opposite him. The chatter of a function taking place inside the imposing Georgian building reaches him each time the doors open. He is indifferent to the coldness of the stones or the rain soaking his thick leather jacket. A puddle is slowly spreading around his heavy-duty biker boots.

The watcher stiffens slightly as a middle-aged man in a bow tie, dinner suit and unbuttoned raincoat emerges with another man and a woman. Their faces are easily visible in the bright light of the chandeliers shining through the large windows. The quarry smooths his mane of swept-back silver hair, briskly shakes hands with his male companion and kisses the woman on her cheek. The couple link arms and walk away as the man puts up an umbrella and then, clamping it under the crook of one arm, frees his hands to light a small cigar. He blows smoke into the night air, buttons his raincoat and sets off at a leisurely pace along the side of the Abbey. The biker falls into step ten metres behind, sniffing the trail of cigar smoke as he passes the metal portico of the former Empire Hotel on their left. The man in front stumbles slightly in his highly polished dress shoes as he steps off a wet kerb to cross the road. On the other side, he stops to look into the window of one of the shops that line each side of Pulteney Bridge. The biker slips into the doorway of another shop and waits patiently. The helmet still hides his face but, beneath it, his thin lips curl into a satisfied smile as he watches the man turn right into a dark doorway. It is just as he anticipated. This entrance leads to a passageway with stone steps that drop down to a riverside path below the ancient bridge.

The man stops at the bottom of the steps, loosening his bow tie and enjoying the view of the three U-shaped shelves of water that form the city centre weir. Its smooth undulations are spotted by rain, but the reflection of the streetlights high above creates a glossy black sheen. He takes one last puff of his cigar and then throws the stub into the water.

The man remains at the river's edge, looking up at the three strangely different roof profiles on the tall building on the opposite bank and does not seem to hear the rubber-soled boots descending the steps behind him. Nor does he hear a bag filled with ball bearings being pulled out of a jacket pocket. But a slight disturbance in the air makes him turn his head just milliseconds before the cosh cracks viciously against it. It is a fatal move. The weapon crashes into the pterion, the side of the forehead where four different bones join together at the skull's weakest point. The blow ruptures an artery and he immediately crumples to the ground at his attacker's feet.

The biker quickly scans his perimeter as he was trained to do. It's late and he is still alone but he knows that he needs to move fast. He pulls a black wallet from his victim's inside breast pocket and then removes a mobile phone from the other. A trickle of blood is leaking from one of the man's ears. The biker hesitates. Then he quickly pulls off a glove and places two forefingers on the man's blood-smeared neck. He waits for a moment, frowns and then replaces the glove. All this time his eyes are raised towards the stone balustrade of Grand Parade opposite and above him, in case a passer-by chances to stop and glance down. He looks again at the prone figure before suddenly stooping to lift it under both arms so that the chest is balanced on top of the metal rail. Then he quickly transfers both his hands to the man's ankles and flips them upwards with a grunt so that the body somersaults into the water. There is a splash and he watches as the current sweeps the body away, headfirst and face down into the centre of

2

the weir. It is followed by the upturned and floating umbrella. The body dips and levels out three times over the shelves of water and is then pushed further into the darkness of the river beyond. The umbrella momentarily snags but then breaks free and follows the same route.

The biker checks that the cosh, wallet and phone are safely in his pockets and quickly scans the ground around him. The CCTV camera on the bridge has been hanging uselessly by its wires from a bracket since he dismantled it two hours ago. The biker takes a small metal canister out of a trouser pocket, turns to face the stone wall and sprays some markings onto it in four small and jerky movements. Then he heads briskly back up the steps to street level, taking them easily, two at a time without losing breath. Two giggling girls, arm in arm and dressed for a night out, are entering the passageway just as he is leaving it. They fall silent at the sudden appearance of the tall broad-shouldered man in his bulky leather jacket, boots and helmet and shrink back to let him pass. He turns right and across the bridge towards the long, broad expanse of Great Pulteney Street, which stretches away in front of him. Glancing at his reflection in the window of a chemist's shop as he leaves the bridge, he drops his visor again. Several builders' skips are stationed along the wide expanse of pavement and he tosses the paint canister into one as he passes. He empties the wallet of its cash and credit cards. As he passes the next skip, without breaking stride, he extends an arm and drops the wallet and the phone, which join the rubble and plasterboard already half-filling its depths.

CHAPTER ONE

The familiar damp fug of the launderette greets me as soon as I push open its doors. The chemical smell of the soap powder and the noise of the big revolving drums are somehow comforting. You get to be a regular customer of these places when you live full-time on a narrowboat. It's awkward getting through the two narrow doors with a huge bag of dirty laundry over one shoulder and with Eddie pulling me excitedly by the lead. He enjoys our fortnightly trips to do the washing – mainly because the woman in charge spoils him with a regular supply of gravy biscuits from a jar under her counter. But this afternoon she's absent. The only other customer is a large woman with thick red hair tied back in a ponytail wearing a long shapeless purple cotton dress. She has two children with her. The tumble dryers are stacked on top of each other and she is reaching up to empty the contents of one of them into a big bag similar to mine. 'Doggie dog dog,' squeals the smaller of the children, a boy who I estimate to be about four years old. He's wearing faded dungarees over a clean white T-shirt and holds out both his arms as he comes rushing towards me and Eddie. Eddie obligingly strains at his lead to greet the boy, but his mother catches him by an outstretched hand and yanks him back to her.

'For God's sake, Noah, just stay still, will you?' she snaps. 'I need to get this stuff out.'

I dump my bag on the floor and drop to one knee to hold Eddie by his chest. 'It's okay,' I say. 'He's terribly friendly.'

The girl, who seems to be a couple of years older than her brother, and who is also dressed in dungarees, tugs her mother's dress. 'Can I say hello to the dog, Mum?'

'I asked first,' protests her brother.

'No, you didn't ask,' says the girl bossily. 'He didn't ask, did he, Mum?'

I'm not wholly at ease with children, mainly through lack of practice. My ex-wife Debbie and I couldn't have our own and it became one of several issues that led to our divorce. The financial settlement had left me just enough to buy the narrowboat I live on. However, these two look pretty acceptable. Their clothes are inexpensive but clean and well ironed and their hair is well brushed.

'You could give him a biscuit, if you like,' I say. 'I know where some are hidden behind the counter.'

The woman's head snaps round to give me a furious look. It looks as though she is about to talk to me but then thinks better of it. She bends down to lift the boy under his arms and places him firmly on a plastic chair. Then she points to one alongside it.

'Juno,' she says firmly to the girl, who extends her lower lip in disappointment but moves obediently to sit on the chair.

'Just sit there quietly, both of you,' says the woman. She gives me a glare, as if daring me to find fault with her parenting skills and turns back to her task.

I give the kids a wink and a shrug as they sit there, their legs swinging above the floor and their big eyes still fixed hungrily on Eddie. I tie his lead to a table leg and move over to load one of the big washing machines. When it gurgles into life I return to Eddie and the newspaper I had bought on our walk here. The woman has filled one bag now and is leaning with one hand against another dryer, willing it to finish its cycle.

'I'm bored, Mum,' the boy whines. 'I want to go home.'

'Be quiet, Noah.' The woman darts another suspicious look at me before going on. 'I've told you both lots of times, you must never speak to strange men. I'm very cross.'

'We just wanted to say hello to the dog,' says the girl in a quiet voice. Then she looks at her mother, looks at me and makes a decision. 'What's his name?' she asks me directly.

'Eddie,' I reply and bend to ruffle his wiry brown head. At his name, Eddie obligingly wags his tail. 'He's a Border Terrier.'

But the woman is already advancing towards me, her purple dress billowing and a red fingernail pointing at my face. 'You don't talk to my children unless I say so, okay?' She is close enough for me to notice the slight gap between her two front teeth and the lines of tiredness that fan out from her blazing eyes.

I shrug. 'Only trying to be friendly.'

'Well, don't,' she snaps, folding her arms in front of her. 'Or don't you think I have the right to say who my kids can talk to? Whether they can approach dogs that they don't know?'

I sigh in exasperation. It seems like this woman has been spoiling for a fight ever since I struggled through the door. 'Okay, okay. You don't want them to talk to me or pet the dog. That's up to you.'

'Yes. It is,' she says with obvious satisfaction before turning back to her dryer, which is now slowing to a stop.

The children remain silent and watch as their mother yanks open the machine's door and stuffs its contents into a second bag. She puts one bag over each shoulder, grunting with the effort.

'Come on, you two, back to the boat – it's tea time,' she says, marching towards the narrow entrance doors and pushing both open simultaneously.

The boy hops off the chair and runs in her wake but the girl moves slowly and dips down to pat the top of Eddie's head as she passes.

'JUNO!' Her mother is outside on the pavement looking back inside the launderette. The girl jumps guiltily and runs to join her.

Boat people, I think to myself. Just like me. The Kennet & Avon Canal, which stretches eastwards out of Bath, is home to a motley population of boat owners who have chosen it as their permanent way of life. Many have no doubt done so out of financial necessity, like me, but others are embracing an independent, off-grid culture that chimes with their characters or circumstances. When you walk along the canal through the outskirts of the city and beyond, there's always something to see – a shack erected on the towpath and filled with books to swap, like a miniature library; weird and wonderful homemade sculptures; or wind vanes that pop up along the bank. Most of the boats have dogs who manage to find a spot to lie down among the bits and pieces that are piled up on the bow, stern and roof. Their owners bring their faces up close to rain-streaked portholes from the darkness of the interiors and eye passing hire boats with a mixture of wariness and disdain.

I pass a solitary hour with the paper before I can unload my clean, dry clothing into a bag. Its heavy weight drags uncomfortably across one shoulder. I doubt my ability to shoulder two at the same time in the same way as the short-tempered mother. At first, I'd found it interesting that launderettes could survive, let alone thrive, in a city where the price of property is comparable to London. Many of the elegant Georgian mansions may now be divided into apartments, but they remain far above the purchasing power of most mere mortals. Presumably, their owners can easily afford their own washing machines – and probably even the staff to operate them. However, having lived in Bath for a few months now, I know that the honey-coloured stone facades which spread up and across its hills hide a stark rich–poor divide. If you care to look, and most tourists don't, there is no shortage of shapeless forms slumped on makeshift beds in vacant doorways or cross-legged beggars with messages scrawled on cardboard. There is no shortage either of drink- or drug-addled regulars, shouting and fighting with each other in some of the city's squares. At times, especially after dark, it's easy to imagine the violence and danger that must have co-existed with the great wealth and privilege of the nobility who arrived in their private carriages to take the water and dance under the guiding presence of Beau Nash during the eighteenth century.

As I head home along the canal, my mobile pings to indicate an incoming text and I stop at a bench to call it up. It's from Nina.

Arriving JJF Friday at 5pm. Be there!

Eddie has been quivering with excitement for most of the day. He knows that any sustained effort to clean and tidy the interior of *Jumping Jack Flash*, the narrowboat I call home, must chronicle an imminent visit by Nina – the love of both our lives. It's only Wednesday and, as Nina won't travel from Salisbury until Friday, I will have to put up with his tightly wound anticipation for another couple of days. In truth, his mood matches my own. I can't wait to see her small, slim form curled up on the recently acquired sofa, which is now a feature of the saloon that merges into the galley at the bow of the boat.

My passion for Nina, unlike Eddie's, remains unreciprocated. The dog is definitely the winner in mutual displays of demonstrative affection. But we have become very firm friends in the wake of our shared experiences at a particularly emotional time in both of our lives – widowhood for her and a painful divorce for me. Nina now rents an apartment near Salisbury Cathedral, which has given her some much-needed private space away from the suffocating concern of the family and friends she shared with her late husband. She comes to Bath for a couple of weekends each month and we walk Eddie on the hills surrounding the city, or weave in and out of the busy streets and lanes of its centre. We go to the cinema, try out new restaurants or simply chill out on the boat, reading, cooking and taking on board too much alcohol. She knows how much I would like to take our friendship to the next level, but she has made it clear that she isn't ready for an intimate new relationship. I cling to the hope that she may be ready one day and so, in the meantime, we enjoy each other's company.

When I make it back to *Jumping Jack Flash*, I gratefully empty the laundry into a pile on my double bed in the centre of the boat and set off again to give Eddie a proper run. The scruffy little dog charges ahead of me to the stern and jumps down onto the level stretch of lawn at the bottom of my landlord's terraced garden. I attach his lead and we walk up into the green spaces of Sydney Gardens. As I walk, I run through the meals I am planning to cook for Nina and the stock of spirits that I keep in the bar-shelf, which I had specially made and mounted on the wall of the saloon. Nina often matches me drink for drink when it comes to whisky or gin, but I calculate there's enough to last until she leaves again on Monday.

Eddie is eagerly on the lookout for the park's resident population of grey squirrels. The grass is still damp from the rain that fell yesterday evening and throughout the night, but today is typically warm and sunny for early July. I look fondly around the pleasure gardens, which are effectively my back garden while I am on my current mooring. I have read that the builders of the Kennet & Avon Canal were forced to pay handsomely to invade the serenity of these gardens, first opened in 1795. But the elegant tunnels and ornate iron footbridges of the canal now just add to the interest and beauty of the little park. The canal company even sited Cleveland House, its mansion-headquarters, above one of the tunnels and used a trapdoor in the tunnel roof for its clerks to exchange paperwork with the boats passing below. I like the way the gardens and the canal evolved together, and I spend too much time idling on its benches, quietly watching the world go by. Bath may be a busy tourist honeypot at most times of the year, but I have found it a place of reflection and relaxation after the madness of last year. As I breathe in the warm pine-scented air, I hope that Nina, Eddie and I will continue to enjoy our peaceful sojourn in one of Europe's most beautiful cities.

The noise of a high-speed London to Bristol train shatters the calm as it passes through the deep railway cutting that bisects the gardens. I take it as my cue to move on and Eddie eagerly pulls me out of the park, past the grand frontage of the Holburne Museum and onto the broad straight length of Great Pulteney Street, which heads into the city centre.

I smile to myself at the thought of Nina's text message as we make our way towards an appointment with a pint of beer at the Boater. She's never lost the ability to bark no-nonsense orders at me ever since our first day on the boat. Nina overheard me on the phone in a canalside pub remonstrating with a mate over his non-appearance as my crew, and having earlier witnessed my extreme incompetence as a boater, she volunteered to take his place to assist me. Although I am the owner of *Jumping Jack Flash*, the captain–crew hierarchy of our relationship was firmly established from her first day on board – with her very much in the senior role.

The pub is one of my favourites at the moment, a short stroll from the boat and slightly grandiose with its classic Georgian façade and tall ceilings. Its wooden interiors are full of maritime paraphernalia and it spreads over three floors. A bearded and waistcoated hipster is behind the bar and, as usual, he takes my order with studied nonchalance before coming around the counter to make a fuss of Eddie and give him a couple of biscuits.

The weather is too nice to stay in the gloom with the current crop of late afternoon locals and foreign tourists. Eddie leads me down a flight of steps and through the Cellar Bar with its graffiti mural aimed at giving it an urban, arty edge. The Boater boasts one of the largest beer gardens in the city and the sunlight temporarily blinds me as I emerge through the lower back doors onto the terrace. I find an empty table, put my glass of London Pride down and loop the handle of Eddie's lead under a leg of the bench. Across to my right is a short flight of steps up to a railing and the door of a stone stairway and passage that leads up to Pulteney Bridge. In front of me is the U-shaped weir. It must be one of the most photographed scenes in the city and perhaps even the country. It's a lovely peaceful spot to take in the view with a quiet pint.

CHAPTER TWO

At this time of year, trees form a partial canopy over my mooring, keeping the early morning sunlight from flooding the boat's interior before I am showered, breakfasted and almost human after two mugs of strong coffee. I throw some ham and tomato sandwiches together while Eddie quickly clears a bowl of dog food. Stuffing my lunch into a shoulder bag, I head out. Eddie runs ahead of me to the small garden shed where I am allowed to keep my bicycle and scratches at the door. My refusal to lift him into the wicker handlebar basket is met with good grace. Instead, he positions himself near my rear wheel for his morning run to work. I am slightly late this morning so I take the most direct route across to the canal towpath, past a short flight of locks, alongside some allotments and behind a hotel with its large, reed-fringed pool of water. This leads to Widcombe Lock, where the man-made order of the canal connects with a wide bend of the River Avon. Eddie's scampering trot easily keeps pace with me. I swing left, looking down at the river where a few boats are clinging to its steep sides. The back of Bath Spa train station comes into view, two dissected brightly painted rowing boats hanging vertically as slightly eccentric decorations. We are approaching a busy roundabout and road junction, so I stop and scoop Eddie up into the basket. He sits upright, his nose in the air and his little ears twitching as he takes in his surroundings. I turn right across a pedestrian bridge and we make our way past the front of the station to the offices of the *Bath Chronicle*.

This venerable local newspaper was founded in 1760 and has gone through myriad titles in its time. It was a daily paper until a decade ago and, although Bath is a relatively small city, it never had a problem filling its pages on six days of the week with the comings and goings of 85,000 citizens. Then advertising budgets began to switch to the internet and readers began to get their news there too. The paper changed ownership, joining ever larger newspaper groups, which tried to exploit their economies of scale whilst eyeing the financial bottom line with a clear-eyed ruthlessness. Reporters, sub-editors and photographers left without being replaced, the large city centre building that housed the newsroom, print-room and offices was sold, and now the paper only hits the streets once a week, every Thursday.

The *Chronicle*'s current editor is an extremely stocky thirty-two-year-old New Zealander called Ben Mockett. He is passionate about the Kiwis rugby team and played a great deal of the game himself during his twenties as a hooker. Like most hookers, he is broad and squat with a blunt and closely shaven head, which largely dispenses with a neck in order to emerge directly out of a pair of powerful shoulders. Like most hookers, he barely bothers to repress a ferociously combative and competitive attitude to life. Ben's face captures this pugnacity in jaw muscles which are constantly clenching and unclenching, narrow challenging eyes separated by two deep furrows and a squashed boxer's nose.

I banged on his door shortly after arriving in Bath and, although he wasn't hiring, my timing was lucky. A bout of flu had swept through his few remaining staff and he was struggling to get the paper out that week. I was shown to a desk with a computer and Ben hovered aggressively behind me as I wrestled an assortment of copy and pictures into four well-organised pages. Since then, I have been called in at almost no notice to work two or three shifts a week. I am sometimes urged to make myself scarce, in the event of a visit by the group editor or someone from head office. I assume that Ben is somehow paying me from a budget that isn't labelled 'staff salaries'. Truthfully, I don't much care how he funds me as long as he does.

The work is much more straightforward than the sub-editing I used to do for a national newspaper in another life, even if the money is barely a fifth of what I earned in London. Everyone does everything on the *Chronicle*, including Ben, but I enjoy the occasional variety of writing or subbing copy, or dashing out of the office on my bike to get some pictures on my smartphone or to interview someone. After *Canal Pushers* was published, Ben chose to temporarily forget my freelance status and made a big thing of its author being on the *Chronicle*'s staff. I was the subject of a centre page spread, complete with pictures of me and Eddie on board *Jumping Jack Flash*. I am almost always hired to work on Thursdays, when there is usually an all-staff, all-morning scramble to assemble the front page and pages two and three with the latest news before the print run begins at lunchtime. If no obvious lead story has presented itself during the previous seven days, this is often a test of creative thinking and editorial ingenuity. Today, however, this clearly isn't going to be a problem.

Eddie bounds into the almost empty office and runs over to Ben, stretching up on his short legs to say hello.

'Hi there, little fella,' says Ben affectionately, ruffling the stray wisps of fur on the dog's head. 'About time, Mr Johnson,' he adds, turning to me and looking at his watch.

I gesture around the newsroom, still empty apart from the two of us. 'I'm ten minutes early, Ben.'

He rubs his hands together in glee. 'Whatever. We've actually got a bloody decent lead story for once. Sit down, log on and go to work, mate.'

Eddie sips some water from his bowl and curls up in a small dog-bed under my desk while I slip him a biscuit out of a drawer to reward his good behaviour. I click on the file holding the contents of the front page. Ben has clearly been busy. I read it through from start to finish before starting to worry about editing it, designing the page and coming up with some headlines. Ben scoots off into his corner office, but I am in no doubt that he will also be using one of his screens to watch my work proceed in real time.

It seems that the body of Mr Rufus Powell, president of Bath's Georgian Fellowship and a widely known and well-respected magistrate, has been found floating just below the city centre weir yesterday by an early morning runner. Mr Powell was last seen alive on Tuesday evening, when he attended one of the Fellowship's formal dinners at the Pump Room. He left at just past midnight. A post-mortem was being carried out and his family had been informed. Mr Powell was sixty-three years old and married with one teenage daughter. The facts were few and far between, but the circumstances of his death and his status in the city meant that Ben was right – it was indeed a 'bloody decent lead story'. Ben had padded it out with an account of the dead man's distinguished and successful career. Mr Powell had run his own architectural practice in London, where he had specialised in work on the capital's historic buildings, before selling the business when he turned sixty and retiring to Bath. Having joined the Georgian Fellowship, he had been quickly elected as vice president and then president whilst continuing to sit on the bench at the city's magistrates' court. Ben had secured expressions of shock and tributes from the city's member of parliament, council leader and mayor, which he had woven into the story.

A subsidiary file contained a brief account of the Georgian Fellowship. It always had a membership of 100 people, no more, no less – and existed to protect and champion Bath's status as a World Heritage Site. It scrutinised every planning application and would weigh in with powerful objections if it thought that any scheme would compromise the city's history or overall aesthetics. If necessary, it would also mount campaigns to save the architectural legacy of John Wood the Elder and Robert Adams from any modern eyesores which threatened to appear on the horizon. The group had acquired real status and power over the years and the city planners needed to think long and hard before deciding to lock horns with it. It seemed that Rufus Powell had become a particularly active officer of the Fellowship in a short space of time and Ben had combed the paper's digital archive in order to list a number of schemes over the past three years which he had attacked or, in far fewer cases, championed. Judging by the volume, the man was probably still working full-time, but without pay, on the Fellowship's activities rather than enjoying a quiet retirement in the West Country.

I pull up a striking colour headshot of the dead man and decide to place it squarely in the centre of the front page. The man in the picture looks serious and intelligent with probing eyes under a thick mane of silver-grey hair swept back from his forehead. The set of his jaw suggests a deliberate refusal to smile for the camera as well as an attempt to convey a message along the lines of, 'I have seen something of life and will not compromise on the things I believe in.' It is not the face of a man which would give much hope to criminals facing him in the dock, I think. I decide to add the thinnest sliver of a black border around the edges of his picture. A hand thumps hard onto my right shoulder while a plastic cup of machine-made coffee appears to my left on the desk. I look up from my screen, suddenly aware that most of the other desks in the newsroom are now occupied.

'Great stuff, Jack. Got a minute?'

I tell Eddie to stay and follow Ben into his tiny office, where he clears some review books from a chair in front of his desk and ushers me into it.

'So, Jack – any ideas?' His small but solid frame is almost bouncing in his chair with excitement.

'Err... about what, Ben?' I take a sip of the dreadful coffee and wince.

He links both hands behind his head and looks at me smugly. 'Jesus, Jack, you're the expert. The Canal Pusher. D'you think we've got a live one here in Bath?'

I rest my elbows on his desk, hold my forehead in both palms for a few seconds and give an audible sigh. Ben is referring to the sociopathic serial killer who ambushed solitary individuals on the towpaths of the Midlands canals and drowned them with his fishing net. The 'Canal Pusher', as the media had dubbed him, had stalked Nina and me as we travelled on *Jumping Jack Flash* and been keen to add me to his

16

tally of victims. Fortunately, Nina had come to my rescue and he was now serving several concurrent life sentences in a high-security prison. My financial position had improved considerably after I wrote a book about the killer and had it serialised by a national newspaper.

'He was arrested, Ben – remember? He's in prison.'

'Yeah, sure,' says Ben impatiently. 'Not the same guy, obviously. But a copycat killer?'

I take another sip of disgusting coffee, this time to disguise my thoughts. The truth is I have been worried by the prospect of such a scenario for some time, and especially after publication of my book. The trouble with true crime stories is that there's always the possibility they might inspire more true crimes. What if I have given someone else the idea? I instinctively try to reject the notion.

'Oh, come on, Ben,' I say. 'There's no evidence at all that Rufus Powell was deliberately pushed into the water. No witnesses and, as yet, no postmortem results. How can you even begin to go down that route?'

Ben folds his arms across his belly. 'But it could be true, right? And here I am, with the country's leading authority on deliberate drownings sitting opposite me. Am I right?'

I shake my head, but I already know it will be almost impossible to dissuade him. Ben Mockett is sitting in his first editor's chair and he is in a hurry to move on, to run bigger and better newspapers. Now he has glimpsed a mother lode of stories stretching ahead of him for weeks. He is already imagining the scary headlines, the national press descending on his patch, the increase in circulation and the unalloyed excitement of leading the career-enhancing coverage of a huge running story. It would take a rubber mallet to the forehead to calm him down at this moment.

'Yes, Ben, it could be true but so could lots of other things. Let's wait and see before we set this particular hare running. People turn up drowned all the time. Look at those warning signs on the river.' I gesture out of his window and down towards the Avon. 'Five deaths in five years here, between 2009 and 2014, they say. It happens.'

'Yeah, and what if they weren't accidents, either?'

I sigh and shake my head.

'You can't be serious? You're willing to risk starting a mass panic on the basis of one drowning and no evidence whatsoever.'

'Not yet,' he concedes grumpily. Then he points a finger at me. 'But if there's even the slightest suggestion that Powell was murdered, then we're going big with it and you, mate, are going to be in the front row of our coverage.'

Eventually, after some minor disagreements, the first three pages are finally approved by Ben and whisked off via a secure internet cable to the edge of town printworks, where 10,000 copies will soon be coming out of the rear entrance to be loaded onto a fleet of small vans. This is usually the signal for the *Chronicle*'s handful of editorial staff to decamp to a nearby pub for a largely liquid lunch. The afternoon will be a much less frenetic affair, as everyone works through the more mundane content that will begin to fill the interior of next week's paper. This Thursday, Ben is so excited that he decides to lead the exodus himself and four of us trail in his wake to the Dark Horse on Kingsmead Square. I think Ben likes it because it has a series of prints on the wall called the 'Heartless Bastards'. He shoulders his way to the centre of the underlit bar, where a wooden eagle is about to land on its prey with outstretched wings.

'Okay, kiddies, what'll it be?'

I concede that the other three are all in their early or mid-twenties but reflect that I must be at least ten years older than Ben. Nevertheless, he's buying and I'm not about to argue with that. Samantha, Tom and Caroline are all white, well-spoken, upper- or middle-class products of humanities degrees who are on their first proper jobs. Their parents could afford to subsidise the exploitative internships they needed to do before securing one of the declining number of vacancies in journalism. If anything, the industry is even less diverse now than it was when I first muscled my way into it – without a degree and with a working-class chip on my shoulder. They are all thin and tall with great hair, great teeth and great skin, and they are all chronically overworked by Ben, who terrifies them. They each have a portfolio of job titles, covering most sections but crucially including 'multimedia journalist', which means they are expected to write for the newspaper as well as the website, sub their own copy and take their own photographs, as well as undertake any specialist duties for their additional roles. Tom, for example, is the *Chronicle*'s 'Business and Property Correspondent', and Sam may also occasionally boast a byline describing her as 'Community Correspondent', whatever that means.

However, these human Swiss Army knives do not have their versatility matched by high wages as there is widespread competition for their jobs. Fortunately, this relative poverty continues to be supplemented by their parental allowances and so they can still afford to live in mid-priced rental apartments and shop for food from an upmarket range of supermarkets or Bath delicatessens. Pints are pulled and distributed and we make our way into the bar's dark red-painted cavern with leather Chesterfield sofas all around its walls. Ben takes a huge swallow of his drink before wiping his mouth with the back of a hand and burping with satisfaction.

'So, Jack,' he says. 'Powell's death. What do you think?'

The others look at me expectantly.

'Have you noticed how often you begin a sentence with the word "So", Ben?' I ask, in an attempt to distract him. 'And you always end a sentence on an upward inflexion, even if it's only two syllables.' I make my voice go higher on the final syllable of 'syllables' to make my point and Caroline can't help giggling – even though the youngsters all talk in exactly the same Antipodean way.

'So what?'

This time they all snigger as Ben repeats the same verbal tic. He squares himself belligerently, bangs his glass down on the table and glares at his staff.

'What's the matter? Don't you want a decent bloody story for once?' They all take a drink and avoid meeting his eyes. 'So, Mr Worldwide Canal Pushing Expert. What *exactly* are we watching for?'

I really don't want to encourage Ben's fantasy story or turn our lunch break into an extended editorial discussion, but the others are looking at me with respect and anticipation. I find it's sometimes hard to disappoint the young. I feed Eddie a crisp under the table before I reply.

'Well, firstly, suicide by drowning is very rare but it can't be discounted. There might be a suicide note or something to indicate intention.'

Ben snorts with disgust, dismissing the idea out of hand.

'We'd know that by now,' he says. 'And he's not the type, is he?'

'Maybe,' I concede. 'But who knows? Rufus Powell could have had marriage or financial problems that we don't know about. If it was an accident, then he might have had a heart attack and fallen into the water. Or he could have been full of drink – or drugs. He could have stopped to have a pee and just lost his balance. He'd been at a dinner all evening.'

Ben snorts again in disbelief. 'Yeah, and he could have been legless and pushed in – just like you were by the Canal Pusher.'

'Were you really?' asks Caroline breathlessly. She is a very recent recruit and wide-eyed surprise seems to be her default setting.

I ignore her question. 'True,' I nod at Ben. 'Most of the Canal Pusher's victims were in that state. It makes it easier to make sure they drown, and it makes it harder for the post-mortem to identify any marks or bruises on the body.'

Ben takes another long swig of beer in satisfaction and thumps his half-empty glass down again.

'But that still doesn't mean Powell was pushed in,' I add quickly. 'Maybe, if there's evidence that he was attacked first, or robbed. Or if we suddenly see a spike in the number of people being fished out of the river or the canal. Or if we get a smoking gun – someone seen arguing with him on CCTV or even an eye-witness.'

The others are shifting their attention between me and Ben like spectators at a tennis match. He rubs his hands in glee.

'Please, God, any and all of the above,' he says, draining the remainder of his pint in one go. The others have barely touched theirs. 'Now then, Mr Bloody Expert, it's your round, mate.'

CHAPTER THREE

Our lunch break continues for more than an hour and a half as Ben holds court with a lengthy analysis of Bath Rugby Club's current form, their off-season signings and continuing failure to build a decent permanent stadium. There is barely a sign that he has knocked back four pints in ninety minutes. I match him for two rounds before switching to halves. Caroline slips away after the first round, muttering something about a pre-arranged phone call. The remaining two bravely switch to tonic water in spite of their boss's sneering dismissal of them as 'lightweights'. By the time we get back to the newsroom, a few copies of the first edition have been delivered and a hush descends as everyone reads them from cover to cover. The front-page headline reads: **CITY CHAMPION FOUND DEAD.** I'd originally drafted 'Heritage Chief Found Dead', but Ben likes alliteration to a fault. Then he had demanded that 'Found Dead' was changed to 'Found Drowned'.

'You can't say that, Ben,' I'd argued. 'You don't know how he died.'

'He was found in the river, wasn't he?'

'Yes, but you won't know that he drowned until we know the post-mortem results. He could have been shot or strangled or just had a stroke for all we know.'

Ben had reluctantly conceded the point but demanded that I increase the size of a photograph of the spot on the river where the body had been found. I now notice that he had also added an unnecessarily mysterious caption: 'How did Rufus Powell die at this spot on the River Avon?'

Ben stomps out of his office at four o'clock, shrugging on his jacket as he passes. 'I'm going to try to see the cops,' he announces to the room. 'You can all bugger off home in an hour and not a minute before.'

When the time comes, Eddie stretches gratefully and follows me out of the building. I check ahead to make sure the reception desk is clear but as we are crossing the lobby a Welsh voice gushes, 'Ah, there he is, the little sweetheart. I've got a little something for him, Jack. Just wait there a second, will you, darling?'

Petra Williams has somehow materialised from under the counter. So much for checking the coast was clear.

'I was just taking my heels off for the walk home.' She ducks her carefully coiffeured mane of blonde hair back under the counter and emerges with a dog biscuit. 'Here it is. Come to Mummy, Eddie.'

Obediently, I lift Eddie up to the height of Petra's chest where he snaffles the treat out of a hand adorned with bright pink talons and countless bangles.

'Thanks, Petra,' I mutter. 'Very nice of you.'

'Ah, it's nothing really. He's such a lovely boy.'

Unnervingly, Petra is staring directly at me rather than Eddie when she says this. The rest of the staff have decided that the twice-married receptionist has a bit of a crush on me but has decided to lavish her affection on Eddie for the moment as some kind of deferred sign of intent. It's all quite scary and I refuse to rise to the bait when Tom teases me about my 'Petra-dish'.

'Well, we must be getting on. I've got a friend coming to stay for the weekend.' I have stopped short of saying girlfriend or partner because Nina isn't, and so Petra automatically assumes my visitor is a man.

'Ah, that's nice, Jack. Must be lonely, living on that boat of yours. You know you can come to my place for some home cooking at any time, don't you? You and Eddie, of course. I've always said that.'

'Yes. Yes, thanks, Petra.' Eddie is pulling hard on his lead towards the door and for once I am quite sanguine about it. 'Well, I must be getting off. See you next time I'm in.'

'Toodle-oo,' says Petra, waggling bejewelled fingers.

I unlock my bike, put Eddie in the basket and head into the city centre where I collect two steaks from a good butcher, ingredients for a marinade, some vegetables and a couple of decent bottles of red wine. The city centre is still crowded with shoppers, summer tourists on guided tours and office workers like me, who are making their way home. Although I'm tired, I feel the need for some air after the lunchtime drinks and the stuffy heat of the newsroom. And so I set off, backpack crammed full of provisions, pedalling fast along the old Midland Railway line, which has now been reinvented as the Bristol and Bath Railway Path. Eddie seems to be enjoying the cool breeze as much as me as we head out of town. I cross under the A4 onto some river meadows, where I stop and let him wander about for a while. Then we remount my bike and swing onto the path that heads back into the city alongside the River Avon.

We pass the smart modern frontage of the Boathouse pub, with its first-floor balcony and continue past Bath Marina's small community of boats. A second pub, the Locksbrook Inn, comes up fast but I ignore the example of a large number of Lycra-clad cyclists who are drinking in its beer garden and pedal on past the weir which helps to control the height and speed of the river in the city centre. Various small factories and industrial units back onto the narrow river path and I'm slowed down by other cyclists and pedestrians. The vegetation on the riverbank is growing fast but I can still see the water at most points and, in one place, as I slow to edge past a man jogging with a three-wheeled pushchair, small fish loitering near the surface. The sun is still warm on my back and I am enjoying this extra burst of exercise. Nina will be arriving tomorrow; my bank balance is in modest credit and all feels right with the world.

Nina continues to be the focus of most of my waking thoughts – and many of my sleeping ones too. I am that cliché, a middle-aged and divorced man who has lost his heart to a younger woman. She is the widow of an army officer who died while fighting in Afghanistan last year. I didn't know it then, but her offer to help me handle the 64-foot-long narrowboat was made, in part, to allow her to escape the suffocating sympathy of her friends and family. But it was hardly a safe sanctuary as we became caught up in a tussle with the press, a drugs gang and, ultimately, the serial killer who became known as the Canal Pusher. We escaped all of them eventually, but I could only do this by sacrificing *Jumping Jack Flash* to a cilling – deliberately parking the boat's stern on the stone ledge of a lock and tipping her so steeply that water rushed into the interior and sunk her.

After extensive repairs, I had brought my boat south from Worcester to Bath alone while Nina made a new life in Salisbury. It had been a slow trip that largely spanned the transition of winter into spring. However, the experience gave me a lot more confidence that I could handle the boat competently in most circumstances and I quickly settled into the rhythm of life on board my newly fitted-out floating home.

As I cycle opposite a vast former industrial site, which stretches along a slight bend in the river and fills most of the land between the Lower Bristol Road and the Upper Bristol Road, I notice some new signs on the tall wire fence that encloses the entire site: 'Danger – Keep Out'; 'Acquired for Development'. The buildings on the site look basic and huge, with none of the elegance of the riverside warehouses nearer the city centre. Towards the far end of the site is Victoria Bridge, an elegant stone and iron structure for pedestrians, painted green, and I can see five or six boats moored near it on the far bank. As I get closer, with a jolt of surprise I recognise two children on the bridge as the brother and sister from the launderette. They are playing with a kitten that's leaping up and down with paws outstretched in an attempt to catch the string they're dangling.

The black iron railings either side of the bridge look quite widely spaced and are potentially large enough for a child to slip through. I bring the bike to a stop, pick Eddie up out of the basket and carry the bike and dog up some steps and onto the bridge to take a closer look. There is no sign of their mother. The little girl called Juno sees me first and quickly scoops the kitten up when she sees Eddie straining in my arms.

'Don't worry,' I say. 'I've got him. He won't hurt your kitten. Where's your mummy?'

The girl is still hugging the kitten tightly and doesn't reply but the little boy points backwards at the boats below the bridge.

'Mummy says we mustn't talk to strangers,' says Juno, and now her brother nods his head vigorously in agreement before putting a thumb in his mouth. 'I'm going home now. Goodbye. Come on, Noah.'

I watch quietly as they run to the far end of the bridge where more steps lead down to the towpath.

I count four boats moored to scaffolding poles that stand vertically in the water. Each is fixed to the bank by another horizontal pole. The arrangement allows the boats to rise and fall with the level of the river. The boat farthest from me has another smaller fibreglass river cruiser moored alongside it, so there are five boats in total. There are some more industrial buildings alongside the moorings, but the tall wire fence is set back a little to create a narrow access path from the bridge. The fence continues past the end of the suspension bridge, where there is a metal gate for pedestrians fitted into it. Presumably it was one of a number of entrances for the workforce at one time, but now it is fixed with a hefty chain and padlock. The fence continues along the riverbank for a considerable distance.

The second furthest boat in the row is painted cream and black with a large off-white awning partially rigged over its stern. As I'm watching, a woman appears from the boat's entrance hatch with a bucket of water, which she throws over the side. I immediately recognise her as the children's red-haired mother. She is wearing a baggy cotton dress similar to the one she wore in the launderette, but this one is pink. She ducks back down into her boat. Its roof is littered: three bicycles, two of them child-sized; ramshackle solar panels; a pile of logs and kindling;

greying plastic chairs; various containers. It's clear the boat hasn't been moved for some time and there are no plans for an imminent departure.

Two more canal boats are moored between this one and the bridge. Her immediate neighbour's boat is a much wider and longer vessel with a smart blue canopy over the stern. Its solar panels are neatly embedded into the roof alongside a new-looking satellite dish and stove chimney. Otherwise, its roof is clean and clear of any clutter. It has a mixture of polished metal port holes and rectangular windows along its length, which I estimate to be seventy feet. It is an immaculate-looking craft and I suspect it is almost new.

It's certainly a contrast to the other three boats on the mooring. The hull of the one furthest from me is streaked with rust and grime and its superstructure is badly in need of paint. It has logs, odd scraps of wood, an old lifebuoy, a pair of oars, a long steel ladder and a motley collection of dying plants along its roof. It has the smaller grey-white river cruiser moored alongside it. This, too, has seen better days and there is green moss visible around its windows, and two fenders hanging down its side, which are black with mould. The fifth boat, the one nearest me, is largely hidden under a massive grey-green canvas that stretches across the full length of its roof and seems to be hiding the windows as well. Its dirty condition suggests a cheap and not very cheerful repair aimed at keeping the rain out.

The children are now in the stern of their mother's boat with all their attention focused on the kitten. Their excited chatter reaches me across the water. As I watch them, a middle-aged woman in a black business suit and inappropriate high heels emerges from the stern of the largest and smartest-looking boat. She is holding a briefcase carefully in two hands as she totters down the wide metal gangway. Her shoulders are hunched, and her body language suggests anger and frustration as she climbs up the steps and strides past me across the bridge.

I suppose I must have registered this little cluster of boats before on my recreational cycle rides out of the city, but I haven't paid them any attention. Now my interest is piqued. These boats appear to have permanent moorings near the centre of a city where such things are very rare and expensive.

My idle musings are interrupted by a furious voice.

'Just who the hell are you and what are you doing near my children again?'

CHAPTER FOUR

The childrens' mother has appeared at my side and is standing, legs akimbo and a hand on each hip. Her mass of red hair is no longer contained in a ponytail and curls out in all directions. 'Who are you and what do you want?' she demands again.

'I'm sorry?'

'You heard me. You were in the launderette yesterday and now you just happen to turn up here. This is our home, you know. Are you a friend of Ted? Is that it? Did he hire you?'

'Who's Ted?'

She narrows her eyes at me as though she is trying to work out if my bafflement is genuine.

'I don't know anyone called Ted,' I say. 'Yes, I was at the launderette and then I was cycling past and saw the children again, on the bridge – on their own. I just stopped to make sure they were all right.'

'Why wouldn't they be all right?' she snaps. 'My kids are properly looked after. Are you from the council?'

'What?' Now it appears she thinks I may be from social services. 'No... no... look...' I fumble in my back pocket for my wallet.

'Now then, Linda, what's all this about? Can I be of assistance?'

A tall, elderly white-haired man has appeared on the bridge. He has a slight stoop but has raised his head to stare at me with a pair of bright blue intelligent eyes.

'This guy's following me and the kids around. He was in the launderette yesterday trying to talk to them and now he's popped up here. He tried to talk to them again. They told me,' she says with satisfaction, as if this justified her hostility and suspicion.

'Look, I've told you. It's a coincidence. I live on a boat too and so I use the launderette all the time.' I turn to address the elderly newcomer. 'And I was just cycling past today when I saw the kids on the bridge. On their own. I stopped to make sure they were okay.' I take my press card from my wallet. 'Look. My name is Jack Johnson and I'm a journalist. I work on the *Chronicle*. This is my dog Eddie and we live on the canal.'

'A journalist?' spits the red-haired woman. 'What d'you want with us then?'

She snatches my card, peers at it crossly and then hands it to the elderly man, who brings it up close to his nose to read it.

'I'm afraid I left my reading glasses on the boat,' he apologises.

I sigh. 'Look, I don't want anything. I'm just saying that's who I am. I don't know anyone called Ted. I'm not a social worker and it's purely a coincidence that I'm here talking to you again.'

The elderly man steps forward and offers his hand. 'I am Professor Arthur Chesney, owner of the good ship *Nautilus*.' He indicates the smartest and largest of the boats below. 'I'm pleased to meet you, Mr Johnson.' His grip is strong in spite of his thin wrists. He must be easily in his mid to late seventies, possibly even in his eighties, and is dressed smartly in a collared shirt, narrow-striped tie, sleeveless cardigan and tweed trousers.

'Jack, please,' I say.

'And this lovely lady is Mrs Linda Symington, mistress of the good ship *Maid of Coventry* and mother of two delightful children whom you've already met, Juno and Noah.'

I proffer my hand, which Linda accepts with reluctance and then quickly releases.

'Call me Jack. Pleased to meet you both.'

'And this is Eddie?' says the professor, bending to ruffle the dog's ears. 'What a splendid-looking hound. A Border Terrier, isn't he?'

I immediately warm to the old gentleman. Most strangers take one look at Eddie's otter-shaped face and dishevelled fur and assume he is some kind of mongrel rather than the proud descendant of a breed of determined fox-hunting terriers from the English–Scottish borders.

Another man emerges from the towpath by the boats and up the bridge's stone steps to join us. I am nearly six feet tall, but this man must be another six inches closer to heaven. His bulky frame is draped in a pair of sleeveless oil-streaked denim overalls, which are stretched across a wide expanse of chest and a generous belly. He also has a pair of huge workman's boots on. His puzzled eyes flit between Linda, the professor and me, as though he is unsure how to break into our little gathering.

'Ah, Danny,' says the professor. 'Welcome. May I introduce Mr Jack Johnson who just happened to be passing. He lives on a narrowboat too and is a journalist with the *Chronicle*. And this is his dog, Eddie. Jack, this is Danny Fairweather who lives on *Otter*.'

Danny extends a massive ham of a fist and shakes my hand with vigour. He has a beaming smile which quickly changes into a look of confusion.

'You're not with them, then?'

I notice he has a slight Irish lilt to his voice. 'Who's them?'

'Them,' he replies, looking at the other two as if to reassure himself that it's me who is being a bit slow. 'Did that woman call round on you again too?' he asks his neighbours.

'Yes, she did.' The professor has an air of exasperation. 'And I told her once again that I am not prepared to co-operate. I have tried to be polite, but I had to ask her to stop bothering me again.'

I think that it is hard to imagine this well-spoken elderly gentleman ever being anything other than polite and courteous.

'Aye, well I wish she'd leave us alone too,' says Danny. His eyes have begun to water and for one moment I think he is going to cry. 'It's a lot of money, right enough, but I've told her this is our home forever and we won't be moving on – even if I could with *Otter*'s engine in the state it is.'

'Well,' adds Linda fiercely. 'I told her in no uncertain terms that she can stick her money where the sun don't shine. And now I need to get the kids' tea.' She shoots me one last suspicious look. 'Can't stand around here chatting all day like some people.' She marches off and Danny trails sadly in her wake. The professor and I watch from the bridge as they both return to their boats and duck down inside.

'I assume all that has something to do with the woman I saw leaving your boat?' I say. 'Whoever she was, she seemed in a pretty bad mood.'

The professor sighs with frustration and nods in the direction of the industrial site behind its fencing at the end of the bridge. 'A company has bought all of this land and the buildings on it. It appears that their redevelopment plans do not include our small community and they are trying to pay us to leave the moorings. We, on the other hand, have been very happy here and are refusing their blandishments.'

I immediately smell a possible story. 'That sounds interesting. D'you think it might be helpful to have some local press coverage?'

The professor purses his lips. 'I assume that any agreement with them might include some kind of non-disclosure clause,' he says, thinking aloud. 'However, as none of us has signed any agreement and we don't plan to, I cannot see any harm in giving you the background. I would need to get all of my neighbours to approve before you published anything. I fear we would find anything that disturbed our peaceful existence in this little backwater to be unwelcome.'

'Agreed,' I say, stretching out my hand to shake his for the second time. 'Off-the-record and nothing to be written without your consent.'

'Would you care to look around *Nautilus*, Jack?'

'I thought you'd never ask,' I reply with a grin.

CHAPTER FIVE

As we approach the professor's boat, I give a little whistle of admiration. 'She's a beauty,' I say, gauging the length from stern to bow where the name *Nautilus* has been elegantly painted in gold and black. 'She must be the full seventy feet?'

'Indeed,' nods her owner. 'Pretty well the maximum length to get through most locks.'

'She also looks slightly wider in the beam than standard, too?'

'Correct again,' says the professor. 'Thirteen feet across. I wanted a bit more room for my collection, as you'll see inside. I bought her a couple of years ago, when I stepped down from my chair at Bristol University.' He leads the way onto the stern and down some steps into the boat. 'I was Professor of English Literature there for quite a while. Then, when I retired, I decided to sell my house in Clifton and decamp onto the water. I had quite a lot of cash and I'm afraid I got carried away. She's too big for me to take very far on my own – not that I want to.'

The professor maintains his commentary as we move into the gloom of the interior but, by now, I am well and truly distracted by what I am seeing. The whole boat has the trappings of a very exclusive gentleman's club in Pall Mall. Beautifully carved, made-to-measure wooden bookcases along each wall are interspersed with port holes, gold-coloured wall lampshades and oil paintings. Metres of books stretch the length of the boat from floor to ceiling. An occasional small leather armchair or antique side table do nothing to diminish the sense of spaciousness. Towards the end of the room is a leather-topped desk with a green-glass lamp and a chair facing back towards the stern. Beyond this is a door into a generously sized bedroom with more bookshelves on either side followed by a well-equipped shower room which leads on to a very modern granite-topped galley with a dining table, three chairs and a brown leather button-backed sofa.

'Of course, I had to get rid of a lot of my books, but it was a cathartic exercise and I've managed to keep the cream of my old library. Tea, or something stronger?'

'I'm astonished,' I admit. 'This isn't a boat – it's a work of art.'

The professor laughs with genuine pleasure. 'Ah, my dear boy... too kind. Of course, I had to work very closely with the boatyard to get what I wanted. And then I needed some help getting her here. But I adore Bath and of course I still have some old academic chums in Bristol – although they're starting to die off at an alarming rate. This location is perfect for me. I prefer the river to the canal, you know. It feels more attuned to nature's rhythms. I also keep a little car in a garage near here – although the rental is ruinously expensive. Now, would you like tea... or whisky?'

I could tell he was hoping for the latter by the way his hand hovered over a kettle but quickly moved on to caress an unopened bottle of eighteen-year-old Hakushu.

'If that's the whisky you have in mind, I'd be a bloody fool to settle for tea.'

He gives a little chuckle. 'I'm a seventy-five-year-old bachelor and I can afford to indulge myself occasionally,' he says, reaching for two generously sized crystal glasses. 'This is quite delicate. They say that's due to the impact of the distillery's location. It's seven hundred metres above sea level, you know. I visited it once, during a conference in Japan. Quite, quite wonderful. I still remember the cherry blossom.'

The professor pours two meaningful measures, gives one to me, swirls his and gives it a good sniff. I do likewise. 'Sharp green apples,' he pronounces. Then, without asking, he adds a splash of water to each glass from a little jug and motions me back to the library. We amble past the bed which is hidden by velvet drapes that hang all around it. He settles behind his desk and I take a small comfortable chair facing him.

'Your good health,' I say, raising the glass.

'And yours, Jack,' he replies. Silence descends as we admire the pale gold colour and roll the wonderfully balanced liquid around in our mouths.

'Quite a spicy finish,' says the professor with approval.

'I've never had it before,' I admit. 'I feel very honoured. It's so refined.'

'You're young enough to still be enjoying the big, peaty malts but I prefer something a little subtler and more complicated these days.'

The sound of city centre traffic is a very remote buzz in the distance. I take another sip before standing to look at some of the book spines nearest me.

'You must borrow any you wish,' says the professor. 'I do so enjoy it when other people can get pleasure from my collection. Some are quite valuable modern first editions, but I have never been let down and they have always been returned.'

I pick out a hardback copy of *The Old Man and the Sea* from some shelves devoted to American literature. It is a British edition, printed in 1955, and contains some sumptuous black-and-white etchings which look as though they have been done on scraperboard.

'Ah, Hemingway. Have you read it?' says the professor looking over my shoulder.

'No, never,' I confess.

'He's a writer who usually appeals to journalists.'

'Because he was a newspaperman himself?'

'Perhaps. But also because he elevated the spare prose of the journalist into a literary form of art. Short, sharp sentences. Few adjectives. I don't think I would have liked his company very much in person, but I do admire his dictum: *Grace Under Pressure*. Of course, he rather undermined that when he blew his own brains out – just as his father did.'

I replace the book carefully, but the professor takes it back out again and gives it to me.

'Borrow it. Books should be read.'

'Doesn't the damp damage them?'

'I have a dehumidifier. Of course, it uses a lot of my battery and so I have to run the generator quite frequently and that means topping up with diesel rather more often than I would wish – although the solar panels also help. I take the boat down to the jetty at Bath Marina for fuel but going through the lock and turning her round to come back is getting a bit much for me. It's a shame we haven't yet managed to run a mains supply onto the towpath.'

'Let me know any time you need a hand,' I say, catching sight of Eddie who is moping by the stern door with his ears down. 'But first, tell me about the offers of money you've been getting to move off these moorings.'

'Ah yes,' says the professor, taking another mouthful of whisky and waving me back to my seat. 'The other residents and I bought the right to moor here from the site's previous owners, Tiller & Brown. Their factories had been here for decades, but business was drying up and money got tight. I had the good fortune to know their managing director, and I knew they needed to raise some cash to pay the wages and so we all managed to drum up £20,000 each in return for these four permanent moorings. It was an enormous sum for the others, but it remains a wonderful bargain. That was two years ago. The only other permanent moorings on the river are down at Newbridge, by Bath Marina and the fuel jetty. They are all occupied, and all the others on the river at Bath are temporary visitor moorings.' He points vaguely upstream, around the bend of the river. 'And they are strictly enforced.'

'So, then the firm stopped operations and sold the site?'

'Tiller & Brown specialised in very heavy engineering but lost out in the end to German and Japanese know-how. The receivers auctioned the site and it was snapped up by a company called Andropov Developments Ltd. I don't know very much about them or what their plans are, but their representative – the lady you saw leaving *Nautilus* – has visited several times to try to persuade us to leave.'

I take a sip of the wonderful whisky. Another example of Japanese know-how. 'But why don't they want you here?'

The professor shrugs. 'Who knows? They will only say that we don't feature in their plans for the site. But of course, we aren't really part of their site. We're part of the river. Perhaps we are just a little too scruffy to fit in with their aspirations.'

'I don't think you could possibly say that about *Nautilus*. May I ask how much they are offering?'

I am genuinely interested. I was incredibly lucky to find my own permanent mooring in the centre of Bath. It is costing me more than £2,000 a year in rent but it is easily possible to pay £6,000 a year for a permanent mooring.

'They started at £25,000 for each mooring and they raised it to £30,000 today.'

'Not a bad profit in two years,' I observe.

'But still far less than you would pay to stay somewhere for the rest of your life,' responds the professor. 'Although perhaps not in my case. But I don't particularly need the money and I like it here. I don't think I would enjoy being in a marina – a little too suburban for me.'

'And the others?' I ask. 'They don't look as though they're particularly well off?'

'Ah, let's see.' He holds up a thin, white hand and unfurls a bony finger in turn as he describes the other boat owners. 'There's the redoubtable Linda and her two lovely children. She has had a troubled past and the mooring is something of a safe sanctuary for her. Juno is settled in school and Linda has several cleaning jobs in homes near the park, which keep them all fed and clothed. She's a good mother but fierce with strangers – as you may have noticed?' I nod in agreement. 'Appropriately enough, I think she has something of Chaucer's Wife of Bath about her. "Her hosen weren of fyn scarlet ree" and even the slight gap in her teeth, "Gat-tothed was she". But for God's sake don't tell her I said so.'

I laugh and promise not to.

'Then there's Danny, who you also met. He's a simple soul and lives on *Otter* with his daughter Tammy. She must be sixteen or seventeen. His boat is in very poor mechanical condition and he'd have difficulty moving it anywhere else. And even if he used the money to have his engine repaired, he is desperately keen not to be forced to keep moving on every fourteen days. He makes ends meet as an odd-job man, but money is very tight.'

The professor unfurls a third finger. 'There's a sweet young couple called Esther and Fred who live on the little fibreglass river cruiser moored up alongside *Otter*. They pay Danny when they can for the privilege – sort of a sub-let, if you like. But I believe the woman from Andropov Developments has also offered them money to move on and so I imagine they will be very tempted to do so before she finds out that they haven't actually got a contract to moor there.'

'There's me, of course, and then my immediate neighbour next to the bridge is a chap called Bill Francis.' The professor now has all five fingers extended. 'Bill is... how shall I put it? Bill's a bit of a character. He used to be a professional jockey and heaven knows how he makes a living now. I suspect he likes a flutter with varying degrees of success. He seems to vanish for extended periods and we seldom know whether he is on board his boat or not, under that huge bit of canvas that covers it. It must be pitch black inside, but none of us have ever been invited on board. He has asked us to deny all knowledge of him if anyone comes asking. And that is our merry little floating hamlet in a nutshell.'

'Really interesting,' I say. 'Well, I'll keep my ears open about what the new owners are planning to do with the site.'

'And you won't write anything without our permission?'

'Scout's honour.' I hand the professor a business card from my wallet. 'Here's my mobile number. I'd better get going. I have a friend coming from Salisbury tomorrow and need to get my boat ready for her.'

'How charming,' says the professor, putting his empty glass down on the desk. 'I never married. Came close a couple of times but it was not to be.'

'I got divorced last year... ' I concede '...and my friend is just a friend.' It may be the whisky, but I can hear the wistfulness in my voice.

There is no way I am leaving a drop of the eighteen-year-old Japanese nectar in my glass and so I swallow the remains without shame. 'Wonderful drink and you have a very beautiful boat, Professor.'

We both stand and as he follows me back through the library, I feel his hand on my shoulder. 'It has been very nice to meet you, Jack. Perhaps your lady companion would like to visit me too? I am always pleased to make a new acquaintance.' His bright blue eyes are twinkling with a mischievous intelligence as we shake hands.

'Well, she certainly appreciates a good single malt – as well as a good book. We may take you up on that.' Eddie leads the way down the gangplank and off the magnificent floating library. 'And thanks for the Hemingway.'

I recover my bike, secure my backpack, wave goodbye to the professor and decide to let Eddie stretch his legs a bit on the return trip. As I cross the little suspension bridge I see Danny dangling a fishing rod from the stern of his boat. A black-haired teenage girl is sitting on the roof of the boat. She is wearing a frayed pair of denim shorts and her very white bare legs and feet are dangling over the side. Danny looks up and gives me a hearty wave as I cycle past, but the teenager's attention is wholly fixed on the mobile phone she is holding in both hands just inches from her face. Eddie and I rejoin the riverbank path at the opposite end of the bridge and head back to *Jumping Jack Flash*.

CHAPTER SIX

'Ahoy there, anyone at home?'

Eddie gives a bark of recognition at the loud Essex-accented voice of my landlord. I slip out of bed, pull on a pair of baggy, paint-spattered shorts and emerge into the warmth of another sunny day.

'Gawd, look what the cat's dragged in.'

I yawn, rub my bare chest and blink in the sunlight. 'Morning, Robert.'

Robert Anderson is tastefully dressed as usual in his trademark off-duty pale red chinos, an expensive-looking blue linen shirt, leather loafers and a sickeningly healthy golden tan. He has been on holiday in Mauritius for a fortnight and is now sitting on a well-carved wooden bench at the end of his garden with one bare ankle resting on a knee.

'Decent cup of coffee here if you want it.'

When Robert isn't on expensive holidays, he divides his time between his eighteenth-century Bath mansion, a townhouse in Greenwich and his office at Canary Wharf. When he's in Bath he often wanders down his steeply sloping rear garden for a chat with his floating tenant. I step over onto the grass and gratefully grab the blue-and-white striped china mug off the arm of the bench, and sit beside him. We sip in companionable silence, looking across the canal at the occasional jogger, dog-walker or cyclist as they pass by. Eddie has jumped between us and is sitting upright with his back against the bench and his front paws bent down in front of him like a canine teddy bear.

At forty-four, Robert is only two years younger than me but there is a financial chasm between us. I do words, he does numbers – and very effectively. Robert may sound like a market stall owner from Chelmsford, but in fact he is a trained accountant, joint director of a private investment fund and last time I looked him up on the *Sunday Times* Rich List, he had an estimated personal net worth of £50 million. An estate agent drinking buddy told me this house in Bath is probably worth £7 million. All this means that the mooring fee I pay is significant in my terms but probably smaller than Robert's monthly wine bill. However, the presence of me and Eddie provides his home with additional security and he seems to enjoy my company when he's around.

I had registered the sign saying '*Private – No Mooring*' on the other side of the canal shortly after arriving in Bath. Vacant moorings like this are rarer than hens' teeth in the city so I tracked down the front door of the impressive house and banged on it. An ability to knock confidently on the doors of complete strangers is part of every journalist's essential skillset. It was late morning and a slightly worse for wear Robert answered the door in a silk dressing gown. A very beautiful but dishevelled young woman hovered behind him, getting ready to leave the house. I expected to get short shrift but I had actually caught him in a very good mood. I suspected it might have something to do with the young woman. She kissed him and left and he invited me in. We hit it off over the remains of a bottle of champagne and then opened another. It turned out that a number of large Bath homes were being targeted by burglars at the time and he liked the idea of a sentry at the bottom of his garden who would pay him for the privilege.

We quickly settled on a monthly mooring fee and an agreement to cook a boozy dinner for each other occasionally. We usually alternate the venue for these dinners between his vast chrome and black granite kitchen and my tiny galley and he sometimes has another house guest when it is his turn to cook. His companions of both sexes always boast the looks of professional models.

'It's like that guy Woody Allen said, doubles your chances of a date on Saturday night,' he'd told me during a dinner on *Jumping Jack*

Flash, guffawing loudly. 'But don't worry, Jack – you're not my type. No offence, mate.'

He also found it hilarious to discover I had a 'continuous cruising licence' – 'just like me!' he had roared. But my private mooring now means I don't have to keep moving on every fortnight. I can just about afford to pay Robert because of the royalties and the newspaper serialisation fees that I earned from my written account of the activities of the Canal Pusher. This windfall is now being regularly topped up by income from my freelance shifts on the *Chronicle*.

'How was the holiday?' I say eventually.

'Ah... it speaks! Not bad, although I was a bit bloody bored by the end.'

'Yeah... must be hell in that private villa with the private beach and the private staff waiting on you hand and foot.'

Robert chuckles and rubs Eddie's head fondly. 'You know what the man says – hell is other people. What have you been up to?'

I tell him about the death of Rufus Powell, but Robert seems uninterested. He perks up however when I mention my meeting with some of the boat people and the potential development of the former Tiller & Brown site on the Avon.

'So... things are starting to move there, are they? We had a look at that site but we were worried about ground pollution and, to be honest, I didn't want the hassle. It can take years to get planning permission in this city. I seem to remember it's more than thirty acres. That's a hell of a lot of real estate in a place like Bath. Whoever's behind it will need to have very deep pockets.'

'I think they're called Andropov Developments Ltd.'

'Name doesn't ring any bells,' he says, throwing the dregs of his coffee into the canal and running a hand through his thick straw-coloured hair. 'Let's look them up. Come on, you lazy bastard.'

The climb up the garden terraces always leaves me slightly breathless but Robert, who has a well-equipped gym in his home, takes it in his stride. I am still in my shorts, barefoot and bare-chested, which feels very underdressed for the palatial splendour of the Anderson residence. I pad after Robert across the polished wooden floors and up a sweeping cantilevered stone staircase to a first-floor study with two huge sash windows at the front of the building. He swivels into a high-backed chair behind an enormous desk made of black glass and chrome. I hover behind him as he brings a wafer-thin computer to life and uses a wireless mouse to access a private research company's website.

'I pay a small fortune to these guys, but it saves me a lot of time and effort,' he says. 'It's surprising how many companies pay someone to keep a deliberately low profile for themselves on the usual search engines.' He quickly finds a summary description of Andropov Developments Ltd. It has a small number of links to further information. Robert clicks through to the Companies House website while I look over his shoulder.

'Right then,' he says. 'Looks like it was only registered six months ago. Says it's into residential and commercial property development. No trading figures yet but says the company's main asset is the former Tiller & Brown site, Bath.'

'Does it say who's behind it?'

Robert makes a few more clicks with his mouse. 'Directors and sole shareholders are Anthony and Sebastian Andropov. Could be a father and son or brothers, I guess. Never heard of them.' He moves out of the Companies House site and onto a link that brings up a photograph credited to some kind of luxury goods magazine. It shows two men in their mid to late twenties holding flutes of champagne at a drinks party. They look slim, fit, expensively suited and booted and identical in every way. Their thick dark hair has been cut to exactly the same style and length and even their wrist watches look identical. They are handsome and close shaven, but their Hollywood smiles fail to reach their eyes, which are hard and business-like. They have slightly pouting mouths which seem to suggest an overwhelming satisfaction with themselves and each other. 'We may be indistinguishable,' they seem to be saying, 'but we are distinguished masters of the universe.'

Robert expands the caption to full screen and I read it out loud.

By our Social Diarist, Petronella Webb

Anthony and Sebastian Andropov (l to r) were among the more eye-catching guests who enjoyed the sponsor's latest vintage at their Soho House bash. At first, we thought the champagne had given us double vision! These identical 25-year-old twins are the sons of Russian oligarch and gas billionaire Victor Andropov and his English ex-wife, Caroline. The couple divorced when the boys were at Winchester College. They graduated in Business Studies at Oxford and the charming Anthony tells us they are now going into property development with their new company, Andropov Developments Ltd. Sebastian is clearly the strong silent type, but I'd be happy to take either home – or even both!

'They've done very well for themselves to buy the old Tiller & Brown site,' observes Robert. 'That would have cost tens of millions even without planning permission. Daddy must be bankrolling it.'

'Just look up the site for me, would you?'

Robert closes his research company's website, and a few seconds later locates a commercial estate agents' site. A map appears with a round border drawn on it. It stretches between the two main roads, across both banks of the river and along beyond the suspension bridge behind the boat moorings.

Robert is looking at it greedily. 'Bloody hell. I'd forgotten how big it was. They'll get a few thousand homes on that.'

'If they get planning permission,' I observe.

Robert looks back up at me. 'And that's never a sure thing in this city,' he says. 'But you don't spend out on a site like this without being pretty sure of your ground. And, although it's expensive and time-consuming, it is getting a bit easier these days. The government's desperate to build more homes. It's actively encouraging brownfield development. And councils don't like to spend lots of money on lawyers fighting planning appeals against well-funded developers. It'll all depend on what they want to build and their relationship with the local movers and shakers.'

I put my empty coffee mug on the polished glass of his desk.

'Heathen,' he complains as he logs off, moves the mug onto a slate coaster and pushes back his chair. He looks me up and down and sniffs. 'You'd better go and get dressed. Is the lovely Nina coming down this weekend?'

'Yep – today.' I can't help giving a silly grin.

'In that case, matey, I'd also recommend a shower. You have a whiff of canal water, dog fur and sleep-sweat about you.'

I head off with Eddie after setting the next date for our monthly dinner. Back on *Jumping Jack Flash*, I run the engine for an hour to charge the batteries for the weekend, spend an hour on a cryptic crossword and then focus on brushing and mopping the floor, wiping down all of the surfaces, and folding away my clean clothes. I grab a sandwich lunch before stripping off to jump into the tiny wetroom for a thorough soaping and shampoo. Afterwards, I spend another half hour wiping it down, scrubbing at my congealed spills of toothpaste and making sure the loo is spotless. All of this housekeeping activity sends Eddie into another frenzy as he knows it signals the imminent arrival of his beloved Nina. I am still not expecting her for a couple of hours but just as I begin to get dressed, I hear Eddie's high-pitched yapping move up into a frantic fifth gear. There are only ever two reasons for him to do this. The first is when he discovers a squirrel hiding at the base of one of the trees at Sydney Gardens. The second is when he claps eyes on Nina.

I haul on some boxer shorts, black jeans and a sweatshirt and head for the stern hatchway. Sure enough, Nina is on her knees on the platform by the tiller, laughing as Eddie jumps all over her, his tongue flicking in and out like a lizard as he attempts to make contact with her face. It gives me a few moments to admire her properly. Her coal-black hair has been given a short Audrey Hepburn crop that suits her short, slim build. She is wearing a pair of tight white trousers cropped just under her knee, a pink rugby shirt and white trainers.

'Hello, you,' I say. 'You're early.'

'Jack!' She stands and gives me a brief but tight hug and accepts a kiss on each cheek. 'My lunch was cancelled so I got away early. Great to see you.'

I quell the jealous thought of who might have joined her for lunch and carry her weekend bag on board, where I boil the kettle and we settle down with two mugs of tea in the open bow seating area. Eddie immediately claims her lap. The little dog had previously belonged to a homeless young man who had been one of the Canal Pusher's victims on the Stratford Canal. I'd met the lad shortly before his death and, unable to bear not knowing what had happened to the scruffy dog he'd had with him, Nina had eventually tracked the dog down, rescued him and then left Eddie with me as a permanent companion and crewmate.

'So, what's been happening?' I ask. 'Apart from the new hairstyle – which suits you brilliantly by the way.'

'Thanks. Not a lot really. I was only here three weeks ago.' It has seemed an age to me but I reluctantly concede the point. 'Alan's life insurance has come through, so I might start looking around for somewhere to buy rather than continue subsidising my landlord's mortgage.'

'Makes sense,' I say, although I would very happily let her live on the boat with me rent-free, if necessary. I know how this suggestion will sound. I decide to compromise. 'Or you could look for somewhere to buy here in Bath? It's more expensive than Salisbury, but you'd be bound to make more money in the end. House prices just keep going up and up here. It's like a mini London.'

'Hmmm ... it's a thought. And I'd be able to see lots more of Eddie then.' I try to smile graciously at my rival who is still sitting smugly on her lap. 'I might look around for a job, too.'

'I thought you were enjoying the hospice?'

Nina has been volunteering at a hospice in Salisbury for several months now and has been deeply moved by the charity's outstanding care for people at the end of their lives. During her last visit she proudly showed me pictures of herself fulfilling a dying horserider's last wishes by leading a small pony into an in-patient's room to be fed carrots.

I also suspect her work at the hospice has some kind of connection with her husband's death and the grief which followed it. It may be helping to fill a void or simply reassuring her that death hasn't exclusively singled her out for widowhood and that it can even be a comforting release.

'I do love it there. I really do. But I just feel I ought to knuckle down. The money won't last long, especially if I use it to buy somewhere else. And my army widow's pension won't stretch that far either.'

I suspect Nina is also refusing financial help from her well-heeled family, but she seldom talks about them. She is still mending fences after fleeing at the height of her grief last year. It was an escape that attracted national newspaper interest and prompted a nationwide missing person's search while she was hiding out on my boat. I'm sure I am still *persona non grata* with Nina's mother.

'And the bereavement counselling?' I ask tentatively. Nina's husband had been killed in action barely months after their wedding and I had witnessed the desperate rawness of her grief at first hand.

'Oh, you know.' Her hands flutter nervously. 'The hospice has been great. And so has Dawn. I can say things to her that I can't say to... to friends.'

I assume that means yours truly, among others, and feel an enormous wave of sadness that she is reluctant to open up herself to me. But then, I tell myself, I haven't had the training and, up until now, most of my conversations with the friends and family of dead people have been aimed at securing the best possible quotes for the ensuing stories. Perhaps I am not the natural choice after all.

'Dawn is suggesting that I join a group session. She says it'll be a safe space. I might give it a go.'

'Sounds like a new dawn...' I say, as cheerfully as I can.

Nina groans and throws a cushion in my face. Eddie barks excitedly in approval. 'Anyway, enough about me. What's been happening in your life, Mr Johnson?'

For the second time that day, I describe the sudden death of the magistrate and president of the Georgian Fellowship and this time I touch on my editor's eagerness for there to be a new 'Pusher' at large.

'A copycat?' she asks incredulously.

'I know. It's ridiculous,' I say. 'So far, there's absolutely no evidence that Rufus Powell was pushed in or even suffered a violent death. He probably had a heart attack after wining and dining too much and ended up falling in the water. But that's Ben for you. He's desperate for a long-running story that gets him noticed by the big boys.'

I fetch her yesterday's newspaper from inside the boat and she reads the front page while I acknowledge the friendly greetings from passers-by on the towpath opposite.

'Intriguing,' she says. 'It looks like it's all being made to sound mysterious when at the moment it's just unexplained. And what else has been happening in JJ's exciting life?'

I tell her about the small community of boats moored by the entrance to the old Tiller & Brown site, the professor's amazing library boat and about how I'd met Linda and her two children.

'And this Linda,' she says with a smile. 'Is she very pretty and was she bowled over by your charms?'

I shake my head, refusing to play her game. It's deeply frustrating when she teases me about being attractive to other women without showing any sign of sharing such opinions.

'Quite the opposite, actually. She seems to think I'm spying on her for some reason, or that I'm some kind of threat to her kids. But the really interesting thing is that the new owners of the big old industrial site next to their moorings are trying to pay them to leave.' I tell her what Robert and I had discovered that morning about Andropov Developments and the Andropov twins, Anthony and Sebastian.

'Thirty thousand pounds sounds like it would be a lot of money to most of them,' observes Nina.

'Sure,' I say. 'But twenty thousand for a life-long mooring is a great deal. It can't be much fun being there in December when the river is in full spate, but they seem to be very happily settled. There's another thing...'

'What's that?'

'The professor has the most amazing single malt whisky on board and he's invited you to meet him.'

Nina laughs, showing her white and even teeth. It has become one of my favourite sounds in the world. 'Then we mustn't disappoint him, must we?'

CHAPTER SEVEN

The following morning, I hear Eddie snuffling around in Nina's twin-berth bedroom at the bottom of the hatchway steps. The treacherous little dog quickly abandons his basket on the floor by my bed for Nina's bed when she is on board. I link my hands behind my head and decide to enjoy a brief lie-in until my guest gets up. Motes of dust float through the boat's interior in the wide pipes of sunlight formed by the portholes. They add to the quiet and cosy atmosphere that I find so calming. I can't imagine for one second trading in *Jumping Jack Flash* for a bricks and mortar mortgage now. When it's warm and sunny, it is easy to forget some of the privations of canal life during the colder months.

At one stage last winter, my journey south had been delayed as ice held the boat prisoner. The same month, I witnessed two retired and elderly liveaboards being transferred to an ambulance with suspected pneumonia. Afterwards, the doctor lamented the paucity of insulation between the boat's metal hull and its interior and the inadequacy of heating a 65-foot-long boat with just one solid-fuel stove. The all-pervading dampness can also be dispiriting at times, but amnesia kicks in on warm July days like this one.

My diesel-run radiators and solid-fuel stove can quickly warm the whole boat and wet clothes dry nearly as quickly as a wet dog in front of them. I feel as though my current city centre mooring could not be bettered and commiserate with fellow boat owners who are forced by the Canal and River Trust's boat licence support officers to keep moving on in order to meet the conditions of their licence and their mooring. There is also a constant dispute between the Trust and some boat owners about how far they should move each time. There are more than 34,000 boats overseen by the CRT and each year a handful are ordered to leave the waterways due to licence issues. However, my mooring at the bottom of Robert's garden means there is a canal-width of privacy from the towpath and the gongoozlers – pedestrians who stop to peer in through the windows of moored boats. And the restricted access to my mooring, through the garden via a locked door at the side of Robert's home, means it is also much less likely to attract thieves or vandals.

But I'm still not sure how long I shall stay in Bath and sometimes the urge to start travelling again is overwhelming. I've still only scratched the surface of the UK's 2,200 miles of canals and I spend many quiet hours studying maps of the network and planning future journeys. Robert is a convivial landlord and has never mentioned putting any kind of time limit on our arrangement. But in truth, I admit to myself that it is conveniently close for Nina to visit from Salisbury and it is these visits that have become the most important moments in my life. I am in no hurry to make them less frequent by putting even more of a physical distance between us. And in the meantime, I hang onto the hope that my feelings for her will be returned one day. These well-worn musings go around and around the same tracks in my mind without ever being resolved.

'Morning!' Nina's grinning face has poked around her bedroom's swing door. 'Are you decent?'

'Sort of,' I say yawning and pushing my frustrations to one side. I sit up in bed, adjust a pillow behind my back and pull the duvet up to my midriff. She pushes her way through the swing door with Eddie close behind. She is looking fabulous in a pair of pink cotton shorts and a black vest and she sits on the bed alongside me smelling of toothpaste and soap. She opens her laptop and balances it on her raised knees.

'Here. Look at this.'

I peer over at her screen and see it is open on the BBC's local news website for Bristol and Bath. She reads out loud.

'A murder investigation has been launched into the death of prominent Bath magistrate and heritage campaigner, Rufus Powell. The body of Mr Powell, who was president of the city's Georgian Fellowship, was found in the River Avon beyond Pulteney Weir on Wednesday morning. Detective Inspector Mary Kerr has revealed that the 63-year-old man suffered a serious head wound before he drowned. "A post-mortem has shown that Mr Powell suffered a fractured skull consistent with a vicious attack. Moroever, he was not dead when he entered the water," said DI Kerr. CCTV footage is being checked and anyone with information is asked to contact Avon and Somerset Police. It is thought that Mr Powell was returning home after leaving a Georgian Fellowship function at Bath's Pump Room after midnight on Tuesday night/Wednesday morning. "There seems to be clear evidence that a serious crime has been committed," said DI Kerr. "Mr Powell's wallet and mobile phone were missing. We are not ruling out theft as a motive, although we are keeping an open mind." Mr Powell, a retired architect, was a strong champion of Bath's architectural heritage. He was married with one daughter.'

'Bloody hell,' I say. 'That changes things a bit. Ben's going to be unstoppable.'

'A mugging that got out of hand?'

'Maybe. The poor bastard.'

At that moment my phone starts ringing. The display tells me it's the editor of the *Bath Chronicle*. 'Didn't take him long,' I mutter. I press 'speaker', so that Nina can hear both ends of the conversation.

'Talk of the devil. Hi, Ben.'

'Jack, mate, have you seen the news about Powell?'

'Yes, I've just been reading it.'

'So, I need you in work now. I want a think piece. Five hundred words. "Is there a Bath Pusher Serial Killer at large?" Do a fresh picture of yourself on your boat, will you – for a photo by-line?'

'No.'

There is a momentary silence. 'What?'

'I said no, Ben. It's far too early to write that kind of scare story. Okay, it's a murder investigation. But where is there any kind of proof that a serial killer is to blame?'

'It's murder, Jack. He was bashed over the head and ended up in the water. It could easily be someone copying your Canal Pusher.'

'Ben, Keith Tomlinson pushed people in and drowned them with a specially strengthened fishing net. He didn't bash them over the head first and take their wallets and their mobile phones. This could easily have just been a mugging that went wrong. It was dark. Rufus Powell had been drinking. He probably looked prosperous. Who knows what happened?'

'Yeah, sure, anything could have happened... including maybe someone read your book and had the same idea,' says Ben nastily.

I feel my hackles rising. Nina puts a warning hand on my arm.

'Ben, why don't you leave my book out of this? You're clutching at straws and it's irresponsible. You'll scare people witless without any good reason.'

'Look, Jack. It's legitimate speculation. Our website will carry this story whether you do it or not and it'll be in Thursday's paper unless something else happens... like another murder, maybe. I'm asking you to come in and write it.'

'And I'm saying I won't do it.'

'Okay, mate. Is that your final word?'

I can sense Nina's growing concern and her hand has tightened on my arm, but I avoid her eye.

'Yes, it is, unless some more evidence comes out that makes it a responsible storyline.'

'Okay. In that case don't bother coming in again. I think we can manage without you from now on.'

'Ben... be reasonable...'

The line goes dead.

'Fuck!' I throw my phone onto the bed in frustration. 'Can you believe that guy?'

'Jack. You needed that job,' says Nina in a quiet voice. 'Call him back.'

'No way. He's a jerk. I'll manage.'

She gets off the bed, leans against the far wall and gives me a long, level look.

'Seriously? You can't live off your book forever and this mooring isn't cheap. You'll probably have to move somewhere else without the *Chronicle*'s money.'

'Yeah, well,' I say sulkily. 'What's that to you?' And then, because I'm an idiot, I add sarcastically, 'Oh sorry, yeah, I'm sure you'd miss Eddie.'

Nina shakes her head but says nothing, which makes me feel worse.

'Look, Nina, I'm just not going to write that kind of crap,' I say firmly. 'Are you taking Eddie out? I need a shower.'

'And you need to grow up,' she says angrily, before banging back through her door.

I wait until she has left before I begin my own angry banging about the boat. I shower, dress, and make some tea and toast. Was I right to mount my high horse? Nina was quite right. I do need the cash from my three shifts a week at the paper if I am to avoid eating further into the money that I have saved from my Canal Pusher book and newspaper articles. I am already nibbling into these savings to meet Robert's monthly mooring fee. As one young dreadlocked liveaboard once sadly observed to me, as he puffed on a fragrant roll-up, 'Alternative lifestyles can cost a lot of bread, man.' But I'm certain that I am in the right. It's lunacy for Ben to jump to one particular serial killer theory at this stage. If only he had never read my book. If only I hadn't written it.

CHAPTER EIGHT

There is an uneasy truce between us after Nina returns. She has brought a couple of takeaway coffees, which I accept as a peace offering. Neither of us want to spoil our precious weekend and so we agree to take Eddie for a long walk in the sunshine. Sparsely scattered florets of cumulus cloud are drifting lazily across a startlingly blue sky. The weather should hold fine and dry. We briefly debate the merits of catching a bus out to the Mendips but, as usual, the boss has her own firm opinions and we settle on an afternoon walk along the riverbank, after spending some time in the city centre as tourists. We take a detour into the indoor market at Green Park Station, the disused terminus for the Somerset and Dorset Railway, with its high semi-circular glass ceiling and ironwork. It is bustling with people but we find an empty metal table and enjoy two more freshly brewed cups of coffee before meandering around an old vinyl record shop. The couple of rockers running it are wearing matching tour T-shirts with badges identifying them as Chris and Deborah. They nearly persuade me to buy their favourite album, Pink Floyd's *Wish You Were Here*. Nina teases me for it and it's true: I do keep meaning to buy a record player for the boat. Nina buys a smart new leather collar for Eddie from one of the many stalls. Then we head further into the heart of the city and happily wander around the crowded streets and lanes, taking in the busy atmosphere and deciding where we shall have lunch.

Nina usually wants to tick off some of Bath's must-see landmarks each time that she visits and so we head uphill, past the shops lining

Milsom Street, turn left and make our way towards The Circus, the first circular street in Britain. This is one of her favourite spots. We now have a game where I must tell her at least one new historical fact about Bath each time she visits. I have a small library of books about the city on the boat and I diligently do my homework in advance. This time, I tell her how the majestic trees on the grass mound in the centre of The Circus had previously been the site of a small reservoir that gravity-fed water into the basement kitchens of the thirty-three imposing houses around its perimeter. I tell her how Tobias Smollett, the author, said this open basin was 'liable to be defiled with dead dogs, cats, rats and every species of nastiness which the rascally populace may throw into it, from mere wantonness and brutality.' She laughs at the idea as we turn into Brock Street, heading for the imposing cliff-like curvature of the Royal Crescent.

'That's so typical of you,' she says, linking one arm in mine while Eddie trots happily along on her other side. 'You're always more interested in the seamy underbelly of Bath than its glories.'

I have to confess that it's a fair observation. Despite its grandeur, the city has always been a social melting pot where people came to indulge in a bit of gambling, lewdness and debauchery. I expect it was the same in Roman times for the city they called Aquae Sulis. The bacterial contamination of its supposedly healing spring water seems a very good metaphor for the place to me. We saunter along to the centre of John Wood the Younger's Royal Crescent, where Nina rattles off the differences between the Doric, Ionic and Corinthian columns. You can take the woman out of the head girl, but you can't take the head girl out of the woman.

We are walking past the five-star splendour of the luxury hotel at Number 16, in the centre of the great sweeping terrace, when I see a beautifully polished powder-blue Bentley Mulsanne parked below the raised pavement. I stop to stare.

'She's a beauty,' I say.

'Yes, about as long as *Jumping Jack Flash* – and a lot more expensive,' observes Nina drily. She doesn't really get cars.

'They've probably both got the same turning circle,' I agree, laughing.

Suddenly, Nina pulls me to the right, past a smartly dressed young doorman and into the Royal Crescent Hotel itself.

'What are you doing?' I ask in panic.

'Don't worry. It's my treat,' she grins, 'seeing as you're unemployed and destitute.'

I let the comment pass and we make our way through the antique-laden opulence of the hotel's ground floor and outside onto the immaculately trimmed rear lawn. We are politely ushered to two canvas deckchairs, which flank a small wooden table. Nina orders without consulting me.

'Two very dry gin martinis, please, both with lemon twists.'

It is barely twelve noon, but I surrender in delight as her finger searches the list of brands and she settles on a gin made in Bristol called Psychopomp. Eddie is brought a complimentary dog biscuit along with our olives and crisps and we sip the ice-cold concoction from classic V-shaped glasses.

'I've got something to tell you, Jack,' says Nina.

'And the drink is to soften me up first?'

'Well, no,' she says thoughtfully. 'I bought you the drink because you were sacked this morning.'

'I resigned,' I say untruthfully. 'On a point of principle.'

'You were sacked.'

I just shake my head. I really don't want to spoil the moment by reopening our previous argument.

'I told you I was thinking about getting a job, didn't I?'

'Yep, you mentioned it yesterday,' I say cautiously. 'In Salisbury?'

'Well... maybe not in Salisbury.'

'In Bath?' I ask hopefully.

She looks at me warily. 'I've sort of been offered a job abroad and I don't really know what to do.'

I feel shock, dismay and anger all in the same moment. I've put my entire life on hold in the hope of being with this woman for my remaining days and she's seriously planning to leave the country? What the fuck? I go to drain my drink but find the glass is already empty. How did that happen?

'An ex-Army friend of Alan's is working for a big financial firm in Dubai,' continues Nina, who is eyeing me nervously. 'He's been in touch and says there's a job for me if I want it. It's to do with customer relations and schmoozing the movers and shakers out there. The salary is ridiculous and there's a company flat I can have, in a complex near a beach. Or I could buy somewhere, as an investment. I'm sorry, I'm rabbiting on but I'm just not sure what to do. It's a big step.'

I try to calculate what she's really saying. Is she telling me that she is moving on in more than one sense? I swallow hard and wonder if I can trust my voice not to be too strangled.

'What's the timescale?'

I think this is an innocent enough question, but my tone is terse and she tightens her jaw and gives me a look that is all too familiar.

'What? Well...' She pauses, and then, 'Do you know what, Jack? Congratulations would be nice. "Wow, Nina, that's amazing... and exciting... good for you. You'll be great." But you're just thinking of yourself, aren't you, Jack?'

'No... no. Not at all,' I stammer helplessly, then decide the only course of action is to backpedal as fast as I can. 'Of course, it's exciting. Of course, I'd be incredibly gutted not to see you so often. I'm sorry, but of course you'd be brilliant at it. What an opportunity. Go for it.'

'Really?'

'Of course,' I say, not meaning a single solitary word.

'I'm a bit scared,' she confesses. 'And anyway, it's not in the bag yet. I've got to do some kind of interview over the internet with their marketing director.'

'Maybe I can help you rehearse for it?' I say. *And maybe I can help you to bugger it up*, I think to myself grimly.

'Dear Jack.' She smiles sadly and finishes the remains of her drink.

'Just one question,' I reply. 'Do they have canals in Dubai?'

She laughs. 'I expect so – but they'll be inside some kind of shopping centre or massive hotel.' We appear to have navigated the conversation onto safe ground for the moment.

'Another?' She waggles her empty glass at me.

Although sorely tempted, I shake my head.

Nina grins. 'I like to have a martini, two at the very most...'

I rush to finish the quote. 'Because after three I'm under the table, and after four I'm under my host.' Dorothy Parker's quip has become a well-worn, shared joke whenever we drink our favourite cocktail – only this time it stabs me in the gut. 'Ah... if only,' I add, somewhat pathetically.

'Are you sure you don't want me to have four?' she replies teasingly.

'Pay the bill, you hussy.'

After the eye-watering expense of the two drinks we decide to economise and picnic in Royal Victoria Park. Then we doze for an hour with Nina resting her head on my chest and Eddie resting his on her stomach. My mind is still racing with the news that Nina may be moving abroad, but eventually I doze until the noise of children playing and the chimes of an ice cream van bring us both back to consciousness. Mouths dry from the gin and our siesta, we quickly empty a bottle of water between us.

'Come on,' I say. 'Let's call in on Professor Chesney so I can introduce you.' We walk down through the park, through a children's playground, across the busy Upper Bristol Road and on to the riverside path. The sprawl of the Tiller & Brown site opens out before us with its high fencing, unwelcoming signs and huge redundant buildings. Nina whistles.

'Gosh, it's huge. And right on the edge of the city centre. It must be worth a fortune.'

'With planning permission, it'll be worth a lot more.'

We swing left and walk past a range of new flats and Victorian houses that have been converted into apartments, until we get to the elegant little Victoria Bridge. As we cross to reach the cluster of moored boats, Nina suddenly grabs my arm.

'Jack. Look!' She has swivelled 180 degrees and is staring back across the suspension bridge and beyond the stone tower at its end. I follow her pointed arm. Now we are at a distance from the riverbank homes, we can see that some have white sheets or wooden boards hanging from their windowsills. A variety of messages have been crudely painted in black on them. One reads: '*Boat Trash – Go Home!*' Another says: '*Sail Away Scum*' whilst another simply says, '*Eyesore.*' The largest appears to be two sheets stitched together and it hangs across the gap between two windows. '*RIVER RATS*' is painted across it in capital letters at least a metre high. We both just stand in silence. I am shocked by the aggression of the display and its sudden appearance. Nina has a hand to her mouth and her eyes are wide open.

'It's horrible,' she gasps. She hasn't even met the professor, Linda or Danny yet, but the nastiness of the signs has clearly stunned her.

'Yes. It is, isn't it?' says a voice behind us.

We turn to find Linda standing in the centre of the bridge with her hands on her hips and her two children hiding behind her. She is like a lioness guarding her cubs and her home, an impression reinforced today by the bright yellow of another long cotton dress and her mane of red hair. 'Bloody disgraceful, that's what it is.'

I introduce the two women, who shake hands. Then Nina bends down to say hello to Juno and Noah and encourages them to give Eddie a pat. Linda is watching her closely. I hope that Nina's presence will make Linda less suspicious of me and that seems to be the case already. Either that, or the professor has put in a good word.

'They appeared this morning,' she explains. 'They must have put them up during the night. We don't know what's going on. You expect a bit of muttering about our coal fires or the noise when we run the engines to charge up. But they're a bit of a way off. The river is quite wide here. And we haven't had any fuss up to now. We're careful with our rubbish and everything else. We don't play loud music.' Linda now sounds more sad and puzzled than angry. 'We really do try to be good neighbours.'

'It's horrid,' says Nina.

'Aye, well,' says Linda briskly, 'there's no need for you to concern yourselves. It's our problem and we can sort it out. I just don't understand why no one has said anything to us.'

'Er, actually, we were just going to call on the professor,' I say.

'Right. He said he enjoyed your visit. He's in at the moment.'

Nina gives Eddie's lead to Juno, who holds it self-importantly while Noah skips behind in jealous frustration as we all descend to the towpath. Professor Chesney is sitting in a folding chair on the bank by the stern of *Nautilus*, his head protected by an elegant panama hat with a green-and-white headband. He carefully marks the place in his book, closes it, rises and raises his hat in old-fashioned courtesy as I introduce him to Mrs Angelina Wilde.

She corrects me quickly. 'Nina, please.'

'I am delighted to make your acquaintance, Nina,' he says warmly.

'Likewise,' she says. 'Jack's told me all about your amazing boat.'

'What do you make of the signs?' I ask the professor. He takes off his reading glasses and his watery eyes peer sadly across the river and up at the neighbouring buildings.

'A great pity,' he says. 'And rather baffling. We really aren't sure what has prompted this ... this sudden campaign. Linda and I have been talking about going over to try to see what the problem is, but I think we need a moment of calm reflection first.'

I suspect that the professor fears Linda's no-nonsense belligerence might inflame the situation further. This is confirmed when she snorts in disgust. 'They need a good talking to, they do. Bloody outrageous. "River Rats" indeed.'

'As I say, it is rather baffling,' says the professor. 'We haven't had any complaints and yet this certainly seems to have been co-ordinated in some way.'

'Unless...' I hear myself saying. The others all turn to look at me. 'Unless this is in some way connected to the financial offers you've had to give up the moorings.'

'Financial offers,' huffs Linda. 'Bribes, more like.'

'The same thought had occurred to me,' admits the professor. 'Proving it, however, may be an altogether different matter.'

Some more chairs are brought out and a cold bottle of Chablis is opened by the professor. The children have found an old tennis ball and are throwing it for Eddie to fetch. But the peacefulness of the scene is overshadowed by the rash of ugly messages glaring down on us from across the water. I tell them what Robert and I have discovered about Andropov Developments Ltd and the Andropov twins who own the company.

'But surely, we can't matter that much to men of such wealth?' says the professor.

'It's hard to believe,' I say. 'But what else could be behind all this?' I ask, indicating the signs.

'We don't know, do we? But you're going to find out,' says Nina firmly.

'I am?' I ask, slightly startled.

'You are,' says Nina. 'You're a journalist, aren't you? And it's not as though you've got a job any more.'

'Ouch.'

'What's happened, Jack?' asks the professor with a look of concern. After a brief explanation, we spend the next half hour discussing the death of Rufus Powell and the possible reasons for it. This naturally leads on to the story of our encounter with the Midlands Canal Pusher and before we know it, Linda is looking at her watch and announcing it is five o'clock: 'Time for tea, kids.'

'Aww, Mum. Can't we play with Eddie for a little bit longer?'

I offer to let the children walk Eddie with me to their boat, the *Maid of Coventry*. When I return, a couple of minutes later, the professor turns to me and there is a naughty twinkle in his eye. He and Nina have been having their own private conversation.

'Jack, my dear boy, I have a proposal.'

'I'm all ears.'

'Might I invite you and the charming Nina to dine onboard with me this evening?' I see Nina smile and nod at me. 'And whilst I am showing her my boat, would you be so kind as to fetch a couple more steaks from the Green Park supermarket? I am afraid I have only shopped for one.'

Before I can answer, the other two are on their feet and folding their chairs. It is clear I have no real input to the proposal, other than to carry out my orders. They disappear into *Nautilus* with Eddie, so I turn to set out on my shopping errand. As I am passing the stern of the boat moored closest to the bridge, there is a rustle of movement and a corner of the huge canvas sheet is suddenly lifted from inside. The head and shoulders of a thin man pop up; he looks quickly left and right, like a weasel emerging from its burrow. His face corresponds with the image. He has a long beak of a nose and deeply furrowed lines running down hollow cheeks. He narrows his eyes at me suspiciously.

'Who are you? What do you want?' The voice is nasal, the tone aggressive.

'Hi. I'm Jack Johnson. I'm just visiting the professor on *Nautilus*.' I move towards the man with an outstretched hand, but he quickly looks left and right again before ducking down below the canvas once more, just as suddenly as he appeared.

Shaking my head in bafflement, I move off again. I remember the professor mentioning the man as Bill Francis, a former jockey with a suspected gambling habit and an anxiety to avoid strangers. Did he suspect that I was a creditor calling to demand full and final settlement of his gambling debts? He'd certainly vanished quickly enough, even after my explanation. The occupants of this little floating community were turning out to be an intriguing bunch.

CHAPTER NINE

Vince Porlock is seriously pissed off. The previous five hours of his Saturday afternoon have not been particularly enjoyable and someone, somewhere is going to pay for it. His three overlapping chins, covered in greying six o'clock stubble, are wobbling with rage as he steps out of Bristol's main police station. He smacks his metal walking stick angrily against an upright of the handrail. The resounding clang attracts the attention of two uniformed officers who are mounting the steps at the same time. He gives them a hard, uncompromising stare, which they return as they stop to watch the fat man's grey ponytail and the back of his wide badge-festooned denim waistcoat slowly descend the steps, one at a time, to street level. A large skull-and-crossbones stitched into the centre of the badges looks back at them menacingly.

First and foremost, Vince is seriously pissed off with himself about his afternoon at the police station. His brains must have been scrambled. Of course, he now realises, he should have told the woman detective inspector and her sergeant to piss off and come back with a warrant if they wanted to talk to him. But he hadn't been thinking straight when the marked police car had pulled up onto the drive outside his large detached home. It wasn't as if he gave a toss about his stuck-up neighbours in the posh suburb of Bristol where he lived. They could get stuffed. Rather, it was his rapid mental inventory of what the cops might discover in his house at that precise moment.

There was the briefcase in his loft filled with fifty thousand unused US dollars. It belonged to some American biker friends and the money was waiting to be laundered into sterling – in return for a generous handling fee, of course.

And then there was his man from the docks at Avonmouth, sitting politely in Vince's sitting room where he had just opened the first of three parcels packed with a white powdery substance. The parcels had been smuggled through the port in the door panels of three new imported cars. It had taken Vince more than a year and several trips to Amsterdam and Berlin to set up this new supply chain and he wasn't about to take unnecessary risks with it.

So, he had almost laughed with relief when they had asked him to go to the station with them 'to assist with our inquiry' into the death of a magistrate in Bath. He didn't have a bloody clue what it was all about, but he wanted them off his doorstep and away from his home and its incriminating contents as quickly as possible. Not that they'd have got past him and inside the house in a hurry. His 'weight issues', as his doctor nervously called them, were handy when it came to parking all of his twenty stones in a doorway and refusing to budge. Vince is also pissed off because he'd had to kick his heels for two hours in a shitty little room at the station while he waited for his solicitor, Guy Redhouse, to disentangle himself from a court hearing. Vince and his boys provided the lawyer with a lot of business and he expected better customer service from the expensive and slippery, smooth-talking bastard.

However, Vince's annoyance reached stratospheric levels after the lawyer finally arrived and the police eventually got around to telling him the reason for their 'little chat'. He quickly realised it was to do with his son Clive, otherwise known to Vince as 'The Idiot'. Clive Porlock was currently serving a one-year prison sentence after he got a bit over-excited during a ruck with some anti-fascist protesters in Bath. Vince's Bristol Bulldogs had been hired to provide a bit of extra muscle and moral support for a right-wing anti-immigration group who had decided to hold a march and rally in the city one Saturday afternoon in September. It didn't pay much, but it made for a nice ride out for the lads and gave them a chance to let off steam. But 'The Idiot' had got a bit carried away and buried his fist in the face of one particularly annoying little twat who had been screaming into a loudspeaker. It had taken fifteen minutes, four officers and a taser to get his son into the back of the police van. The victim's glasses had broken on impact and splinters of glass had entered one eye. His sight had only just been saved after several hours of surgery. Guy Redhouse had managed to prevent the case being bumped up to Crown Court, but the magistrates had still thrown the book at Clive, giving him the maximum sentence that they could within their powers. Vince was quite phlegmatic about it all. Prison will be part of his son's further education and he'll be treated with a bit more respect by the other Bulldogs when he comes out.

Nevertheless, Vince had not been happy to learn that the senior magistrate responsible for Vince's imprisonment had been killed during some half-arsed mugging. He still remembers his son laughing in court, calling the magistrate an obscene four-letter word and telling him to watch his back as two court officers manhandled him back down to the cells.

Well, the culprit obviously couldn't be Clive. But it could easily have been one of his mates. He wondered if his son had actually ordered a revenge killing. Fair enough, thought Vince. An eye for an eye and all that. But why did the stupid sod feel it necessary to spray the logo of the Bristol Bulldogs onto a wall of the bridge where the cops thought the attack took place? Everyone knew the sign, with its two back-to-back capital Bs, signified the largest and most notorious Hells Angels' gang in the West Country. And now he was going to have to put up with the cops asking questions and disrupting his business interests as they tried to find out which one of his lads had carried out this particular bit of creative freelance work.

The thought of having to go and visit his son in prison didn't improve Vince's mood. It wasn't so much the killing that bothered him. It was the lack of discipline. An initiative like this should always come to him for approval. Vince's thoughts are interrupted as the gleaming chrome of a Harley Davidson motorbike, complete with sidecar, pulls to a halt at the bottom of the station steps with a deep-throated roar and an idling rumble. Its rider is a tall, well-built young man in a black leather jacket festooned with chains and a fringe along both arms, oil-streaked denim trousers and big biker's boots.

'Mr Porlock! Vince! Wait a minute, will you?' Vince turns to see his solicitor jogging towards him, both sides of his blue, double-breasted suit jacket flapping out sideways.

'What is it?' growls Vince. 'My lift's here.' He is still pissed off about the lawyer keeping him waiting at the station for so long.

'We'll need to get together properly,' says Redhouse breathlessly. 'On our own. We need to talk things through.'

'Like I told them. That man's death is nothing to do with me,' shrugs Vince. He's in a hurry to give some orders and do some urgent tidying-up at home in case the cops come calling again with a search warrant.

'Vince. The sign left on the wall? The broken camera at the scene and the CCTV picture of the biker up on the street? And what about the threat that Clive made to the dead man?'

Vince shrugs again and sniffs. 'One of the lads might have been a bit naughty. But like I told them, it's nothing to do with me.

'Yes, well,' says Guy Redhouse uncomfortably. 'I think I'd better call around tomorrow. Get all our ducks in a row, you know. See what Clive has to say for himself. The police aren't going to let this one go.'

Vince leans forward and tightens the knot of the lawyer's expensive silk tie. 'Start your meter ticking over, you mean.' But then Vince dismisses him with a flutter of a podgy hand covered in a spider's web tattoo. 'Go on. Run away. I'll see you tomorrow. Got things to do now. Urgent things.'

The young biker is standing back respectfully, waiting with the door to the sidecar open. Bob-the-Prospect is halfway through his apprenticeship and has two back-to-back capital Bs painted on the front crown of his open-faced crash helmet. But he won't be allowed to have it tattooed on his chest until he is accepted by Vince as a Full-Patch member of the chapter.

He takes Vince's walking stick, helps him to squeeze his considerable bulk into the little cockpit and then reunites him with the stick.

'Where to, Vince?' he asks, straddling the bike.

'The Archangel, you dipstick.'

'Right you are,' replies the young man cheerfully before kicking the bike's engine into action.

The Archangel is one of the Bristol Bulldogs' favourite drinking establishments – and so it consequently receives very little custom from anyone else who lives in the same run-down district of Bristol. This doesn't worry the landlord, who moved down from the Peckham chapter several years ago. There are more than one hundred Bristol Bulldogs and they easily get through enough drinks to keep him in business – even after breakages. Two lines of powerful motorbikes have been parked on the large tarmac apron in front of the pub for much of the day. It is only early evening, but the Archangel's interior is already crammed with about fifty men of all ages and a handful of women. A wispy fog of cigarette smoke clings to the pub's mustard-yellow ceiling. Word has spread like wildfire that the cops picked up Vince from his home and speculation is rife.

'The Big Man's here!' A woman in matching denims and bottle-blonde hair is peering out over the top of the frosted glass that lines the pub's windows. The landlord immediately turns down the volume of a heavy metal track and conversations come to an abrupt halt.

Bob-the-Prospect pushes open both pub doors and steps aside as Vince waddles awkwardly through them. The doors are closed behind him and he stands still, both hands resting on the handle of the stick in front of him. He slowly looks left to right in the silence, registering who has answered his urgent summons and who has unwisely decided that they have other priorities. Then his delicate little mouth snarls, 'Right, you bastards. Which one of you has been a naughty boy, then?'

CHAPTER TEN

There is a church bell tolling somewhere, calling the faithful to a Sunday morning service, but I won't be one of them. The remnants of the bottle of Hakushu had been emptied between the three of us after a shared bottle of red over dinner. The professor held his liquor well and just seemed to become more erudite and carefully spoken as the evening progressed. He clearly adored Nina and the feeling was obviously mutual, as she spent most of our weaving walk back to *Jumping Jack Flash* extolling the professor's virtues and those of his boat. I might have been a tad jealous if he hadn't been in his seventh or eighth decade.

I stretch, yawn until my jaw cracks and check my watch. It is nearly ten o'clock and Nina bursts through my door on the stroke of the hour. She's in her running gear – trainers, shorts and a vest damp with sweat. She has clearly broken our pact to sleep in and decided to run off any debilitating effects of the night before. At least it means Eddie has already been out, keeping pace with her usual route through the park or along the river, I imagine.

Once again, she is holding her laptop and once again she settles herself onto the outside edge of my bed while Eddie tries to give me a good morning face-wash. I swallow a pint of water that I had the foresight to prepare the night before and pull myself upright to rest my back on the wall.

'Ugh... turn off those bloody bells, will you?'

'They're getting ready to hold some kind of community fete in the park,' she announces excitedly. 'There are posters up by the bandstand. It kicks off at one o'clock.'

I had envisaged a quiet, lazy day comprising a couple of pints in a pub, a Sunday roast, newspapers and an afternoon snooze. A community fete does not particularly appeal.

'And I've been doing some digging while you've been festering in your pit,' she says. 'Look.' She thrusts the computer onto my lap and I try to bring my eyes into focus.

'What am I looking at?' I ask hopelessly.

'Oh, for God's sake.' She snatches the laptop back and starts navigating around the screen. 'I've been searching to see why those horrible signs have gone up, and look.'

She thrusts the laptop back under my nose once more. I can see she has settled on a Bath councillor's website. There is a glossy photograph of a slab-faced man with a boyish side-parting smiling unconvincingly at the camera under a banner headline that reads: 'Councillor Robin Claverton. Fighting for your interests, night and day.' Underneath is a selection of clumsily designed boxes for text, each indicating his stance on Brexit (pro), Defence Spending (pro) and Immigration (anti) plus a variety of local issues including an unreliable bus timetable, the need for an extra pedestrian crossing on the Upper Bristol Road, the need to balance the demand to develop new homes versus maintaining allotment sites and the difficulty of getting children into their nearest school.

'Look,' says Nina again, eagerly, scrolling to a small box at the bottom of the page.

I am proud to be tackling the eyesore of the boat people who are living on the River Avon near Victoria Bridge. Residents have complained to me about the flotilla that is moored opposite their lovely homes. These RIVER RATS pay no council tax but enjoy all of the advantages of living in the centre of our lovely city. Enough is enough. They should never have been allowed to buy permanent moorings at this sensitive site and we shall be collecting a petition to have them moved on. Residents object to the appearance, noise and pollution created by these boat owners. Join the fight and meet me by the bandstand at Royal Victoria Park between 1pm and 4pm this weekend to sign our petition.

'Bastard!' I exclaim. 'He must have organised the banners.'

'Bastard,' Nina agrees. 'And don't you see? He's going to be at the community fete in the park that I saw on my run.'

'I could do with a cup of tea,' I say in a gravel-filled voice, 'and a quiet afternoon.'

'Oh, for God's sake, Jack. We need to meet this man. We need to persuade him to lay off the professor, Linda and the others. Come on, get up. You can make yourself a cup of tea while I'm in the shower. And then you can have a shower yourself – you smell of stale whisky.'

I groan but nod in agreement. Anything for a quiet life. But I find the motion to be quite painful between my eyes. 'Plenty of time till one o'clock,' I mutter.

Nina goes for a shower and I return to a horizontal position and am quickly asleep again. An hour and a half later, Nina begins banging about noisily in the galley. The smell of bacon and the whistle of the kettle eventually persuade me into the shower and I'm soon feeling slightly more human. We take our tea and brunch rolls into the bow and stretch out on benches opposite each other.

'It can't be coincidence, can it?' says Nina. 'A local councillor starts up a campaign against the boat owners, immediately after they refuse a developers' bribe to give up their moorings?'

'I doubt it very much,' I say. 'But as the professor said yesterday, proving it is another matter.'

'Well,' says Nina, and I immediately recognise the stubborn line of her jaw. 'All they have to do is keep refusing the money and ignore this stupid campaign. They can't force them to move, can they?'

'I don't know. Probably not. Andropov Developments wouldn't be offering them money to leave if there was some kind of legal loophole in their contracts with Tiller & Brown. But this isn't really our fight, is it?'

It seems to me to be a fair point in favour of the pub lunch and lazy afternoon, but Nina is having none of it.

'Jack Johnson. Shame on you. We need to help these poor people. And anyway, it's got the makings of a great story hasn't it? I thought you were a journalist?'

'I was,' I concede. 'But I'm not sure I am at the moment.'

'Bollocks,' she says. 'Once a journalist, always a journalist. That's what you always say, isn't it? Ben will come crawling back when you bring this story to him.'

I shake my head doubtfully. 'I think he's a bit preoccupied with the idea of a Bath Pusher.'

'Who's that then?' demands Nina. 'Someone who pushes people into baths?'

'Presumably they're all roll-top and stand-alone with ornate feet in this city?'

'Perhaps we should call him the Bath Plunger?'

We both snort with laughter. Then we lock up the boat and head for the park, where a small temporary fence is circling the stalls and we are forced to hand over two pounds each at a manned entrance gate. Inside there's a tombola piled with bottles, a face-painting booth, a fortune-teller's tent and a lot of stalls selling bric-a-brac. A fire engine is parked in one corner for children to clamber around and a large marquee is offering tea and cakes for sale. It's a classic English fundraising fete of the kind that springs up in its tens of thousands across the country each summer. This one seems to be raising money for some kind of local residents' association.

'There he is,' says Nina, gripping my arm and nodding to a stall in the centre of the space covered with a Union Jack flag and pieces of paper. A tall beefy man is standing behind it in a cream summer jacket and blue-striped shirt. I recognise him from his picture on the website. He is not quite fat, but something about his stoutness reminds me of an overweight child. His slab-like stature and carefully side-parted thick black hair gives him the look of a playground bully. He fixes a wide welcoming smile as we approach and stretches out a hand to me.

'Good afternoon. Isn't this sunshine lovely? Councillor Robin Claverton, at your service. What a lovely little dog.'

I shake his outstretched hand. 'Hi, Jack Johnson, from the *Bath Chronicle*.'

'Nina Wilde,' says Nina.

Councillor Claverton ignores her completely and fixes two greedy eyes on me.

'Ah. Her Majesty's press. Welcome, welcome. I don't think I've seen you before.'

'I'm national press really,' I lie. 'But I'm freelance and I work for the *Chronicle* too,' I say, semi-truthfully. Somehow, I forget to tell him that my current employment status is questionable on both counts.

'Well, as you see, I am fairly new on the council, but I'm already at the heart of the community and making myself available to my constituents,' he says grandly. 'Feel free to take a leaflet. Or even a photograph,' he adds eagerly. Nina picks up one of the leaflets. Its capital letters shout 'RIVER RATS GO HOME'. She scans it, curls a lip in disgust and passes it to me without saying anything.

'Ah yes. This is a new cause I've taken up on behalf of some residents. Perhaps the *Chronicle* might be interested in a feature about it? These boats on the Avon really are a terrible eyesore. They should never have been allowed permanent moorings in this particular location.'

I pull a small leather notebook out of my back pocket and hover over it with a ballpoint pen. 'So, can you tell me which residents came to you with complaints about them?'

He frowns. 'No. No, I don't think that would be fair, do you? There might be reprisals by these boat people. There were several complaints, though, so I'm doing what I can to support their campaign.'

'Have you any comment on the signs that have appeared in some windows overlooking the boats? They seem pretty provocative and nasty.'

'Really? I don't think they are at all. I'm happy to see residents getting involved in trying to improve the appearance of their community and feelings are running quite high, you know.'

Nina puts both hands on her hips. 'That applies to anyone who chooses a different lifestyle to you or looks a little bit different, does it? Is that why you're anti-immigration too? You're not just indifferent to difference, are you? You're hostile to it.'

Claverton's bulk seems to increase as his face reddens and he towers over Nina. 'I don't know who you are, missy, but I think you need to watch your mouth.'

I step forward with the notebook again to deflect his focus. 'So... just for the record. Have you tried to speak to the boat owners about the residents' so-called concerns?'

'So-called concerns,' he repeats angrily. 'They have genuine concerns and it sounds like you two have got a bit of an agenda going here.'

'It's you who's got an agenda,' says Nina. 'And maybe it's something to do with Andropov Developments? Doing their dirty work, are you, after their bribes didn't work? What's in it for you then?'

I do a double-take of frustration at Nina. I had planned to ask the councillor whether he'd been in communication with the Andropov twins, but not so bluntly. Nina's full-frontal attack seems to prompt Claverton to turn from pop-eyed rage to icy calm. We aren't likely to get any fresh information now. He carefully squares off a pile of leaflets without speaking and then moves around from behind the stall to loom over us. We are just a foot apart now. He has dropped his voice to barely louder than a whisper.

'I don't need to tell you that remarks like that can land you in a lot of trouble. Write them down, why don't you? I'll enjoy cashing in at the *Chronicle*'s expense in a libel court. Now, I'm afraid you are both spoiling my afternoon so why don't you just piss off?'

Nina is boiling now. 'You're a bigot... and a bully... and... '

Claverton turns his back on her and waves a hand dismissively over one shoulder. I decide to have one last go.

'Look, Councillor Claverton, all we're trying to do is... '

But at this point, Nina pushes a pile of the politician's leaflets off the table onto the grass. Claverton splutters in outrage while Nina thrusts Eddie's lead into my hand, turns on her heels and storms off. I think about picking up the scattered leaflets but quickly abandon the idea and try to follow Nina, who is already striding through a group of children and their parents queuing at the ice cream van.

Claverton is bellowing behind me. 'That's right. You take her away and get her house-trained. I'll be talking to your editor about this.'

Eddie and I catch up with Nina after breaking into a run. I hold her elbow and steer her firmly to a park bench when she sits down and crosses her arms furiously. There are tears of frustration and anger swimming in her black eyes.

'Well, you weren't much good!' she snaps at me.

'No, it was you who weren't much bloody good,' I snap back. I stay standing. 'You put his back up before I could ask a question.'

'You heard him,' she says. Our raised voices are prompting passers-by to turn their heads towards us. 'The bastard! He supported those signs. He probably suggested them in the first place.'

'Yes, and that's all we got, Nina. We don't know who the residents are. We don't know whether he's been in touch with the developers. We don't know what he's planning to do next. I could have kept him talking. But you had to wade in. Anti-immigration? Hostile to difference? Jesus!' I hold both palms upwards in frustration.

Nina looks up at me. Her lips are still compressed in anger. 'What's this all about, Jack?' she asks suddenly.

'What the hell does that mean?'

'Is this about me getting a job in Dubai?'

I don't believe what I'm hearing. I just shake my head at her.

'Is it?'

'So, guess what, Nina? Believe it or not I'm actually quite good at my job. I know how to ask questions and get answers. So, no – it's not about you deciding to piss off to the Middle East. It's about you dragging me out to meet this guy and then torpedoing any chance of finding out anything useful at all.'

It's my turn to stride off and I pull Eddie along in my wake without looking back. I am fiercely disappointed in her. How dare she assume that all my motivations can be tracked back to the single source of my feelings for her? How dare she presume to understand my overwhelming frustration at her impending decision to leave the country? Even as I have this thought, I realise that there may be more truth to it than I probably care to recognise. I'm still completely thrown by her plan and what it means for our relationship – such as it is. Perhaps my anger at her did in fact come from somewhere deeper than annoyance at a botched interview? I can feel Eddie putting up real resistance now and whining, so I stop and stare down crossly to see him turning back towards to Nina, who is hurrying to catch me up.

'Jack. Jack, I'm sorry.' She looks down at the ground. 'I know I screwed it up. I'm sorry. He just made me so mad.'

I can't bear to prolong a fight – not with her at any rate. 'Well... I do have to concede, he does seem to be one very arrogant prick.'

She gives a little giggle. 'Yes, he does.'

'Well,' I say, 'it's still Sunday afternoon and it's a glorious day. I refuse to let arrogant pricks like Claverton prick our bubble. How about we go win something for Noah and Juno?'

Nina links her arm in mine. 'Good plan, Batman.'

CHAPTER ELEVEN

We walk back through the park and stop to fish for plastic yellow ducks bobbing in an inflatable paddling pool. After spending five pounds on countless attempts, we finally end up with two oversized teddy bears. I tuck one under each arm and Nina takes Eddie's lead as he seems keen on tearing the toys to pieces. Then we cross the main road and cut through on the Midland Bridge Road to the river. The path is busy with families having an afternoon stroll, enjoying the sunshine and picking early blackberries. As we approach the moorings I laugh and point to Linda's boat, but Nina has already seen the Jolly Roger waving from a broomstick handle above the roof. The pirate skull and crossbones flag is a clear gesture of defiance and brings a smile to Nina's face too. 'It's good to see they're fighting back.'

'Typical Linda,' I say. However, when we turn at the end of the bridge, we can see that two new sheets have appeared below two fourth floor windows. One reads 'Bath for Bath Ratepayers' and the other simply says, 'Spongers'.

'It's getting worse,' says Nina.

'Jack! Hey, Jack.'

I look down onto the riverbank and see the huge frame of Danny bearing down on us.

'I thought it was you, so I did.' His huge smile is full of crooked and yellowing teeth, but it is the genuine article. Danny is someone you can't ever imagine acting with cunning or guile.

'Hi, Danny,' I say, whilst he pumps my hand again enthusiastically. 'Nina, this is Danny Fairweather. Danny, this is my friend Nina Wilde.'

He enthusiastically shakes Nina's hand, then says, 'Could you give me a hand, Jack?' He nods vaguely in the direction of *Maid of Coventry*.

'Sure, what is it?'

'Noah's buggy ended up in the water last night. Linda's asked me to fetch it out but it's just out of reach. I need someone strong to hold me.'

I put the teddies on the ground, carefully out of Eddie's reach as Nina holds him on a very short leash. As Danny and I make our way onto Linda's boat she emerges to watch. Danny picks up a boat hook from the roof and edges along the gunwale, the narrow ledge running the full length of the boat. I follow closely behind him until he stops and points to the water. I can just make out the pushchair below the surface.

'You hold onto my belt, Jack, and I'll give it a stretch with the boat hook.'

I look at his generous build and quickly arrive at a better idea. 'No, I'm lighter than you, Danny, let me have a go.'

I take the pole with its metal hook on the end, let Danny get a firm grip on my leather belt with one hand and the handrail with the other, and then I lean outwards. It takes four splashes of the boathook, with my arms extended as far as possible, before it catches on the buggy. I pull, and Danny pulls me, and we get it up onto the roof with considerable effort. It looks a bit of a mess but may just about be salvageable. We edge back to the stern.

'How did that end up in the water?' I ask.

'Kids, I expect,' says Linda. 'We didn't hear them, but it happened during the night.'

Danny nods sadly. 'Aye, and the prof lost his chimney too.' I look back at *Nautilus* and, sure enough, the detachable little chimney which was connected to the professor's solid fuel stove is no longer poking out of the roof of his boat.

'Does this happen often?'

'Now and then,' says Linda. 'We're easy targets after dark and the local kids think it's a laugh. Little buggers.'

'Have you lost much stuff, Danny?'

'Bits and pieces. Nothing last night, though.'

There is a cough from the riverbank where Nina is struggling to hold two oversized teddy bears and restrain Eddie.

'Oh yes, Linda. We won a couple of teddy bears at the park. I thought Juno and Noah might like them?'

Linda looks dubious and I suddenly realise they might not be the best presents for the cramped interior of a narrowboat. But it's too late. The children have heard their names and appeared in the hatchway.

Juno squeals with excitement. 'Look, Mummy, look. Can we keep them, please, Mummy? Can we?' Noah is jumping up and down.

Linda smiles. 'Yes,' she says to the children, then turns to me. 'Thank you. I think they could do with a treat.'

The children clap excitedly and rush to collect their booty from Nina as Linda orders them to say thank you politely. The children manhandle the bears down into *Maid of Coventry* with some difficulty, and a helping hand from their mother, and their voices drift up from the boat's interior.

'My bear's called Harry,' says Noah.

'Of course he is, just like your best friend at nursery,' we hear Linda say, laughing.

'And mine is called Lucy,' says Juno.

'Harry and Lucy,' says Linda, emerging outside again with a smile. But it freezes as she looks across the water at the flats with their signs. 'I just need to give the kids a bit of tea and then we'll be going. Come along inside if you'd like a cuppa.' Nina follows Linda into the boat, but Danny holds my arm to stop me.

'Why d'you think they're being so nasty to us, Jack?' he says, his eyes watering and his face a picture of dismay.

'I honestly don't know, Danny... but we're going to find out.' I'm not sure if he has heard me as he remains silent and stays staring up at the signs, his hand still gripping my arm.

'Er... the professor tells me you live with your daughter?' I say, if only to move things along. 'I saw a girl with you last time I was here. You were fishing. Was that her?'

Danny comes out of his reverie and claps his hands together.

'Tammy. Lovely girl. Come and say hello.'

Somehow, I am pulled along in Danny's wake. Of all the boats in the group, *Otter* is undoubtedly the scruffiest. You can barely see its roof under the pile of bits and pieces that cover it. Its metal hull is chipped, rusting and festooned with river weed and its windows are filthy.

'Sorry for the mess,' Danny calls out cheerfully as we descend into the darkness and oppressive heat of the interior. 'Too busy working to get much else done. Tammy. Tammy! Come and say hello to Mr Jack here.'

The living quarters of the boat are chaotic; every surface is covered with bits of equipment, empty bottles, cardboard takeaway boxes, silver foil and tools. An engine has been dismantled and its parts seem to be spread throughout the boat. A small pool of oil is leaking across a table and another is doing the same in the shower tray. The contrast with the clean and carefully ordered luxury of *Nautilus* could not be greater.

I give a slight start as I realise someone is sitting immediately to my left in the gloom of the galley, where a sink is piled high with unwashed pots, plates and cutlery.

'This is Tammy,' says Danny in delighted tones. 'Say hello, sweetheart.'

'Lo,' says Tammy, looking up at me from her phone with no hint of a smile. She has a silver ring through one corner of her upper lip and another through her left nostril. She doesn't extend a hand and, unsure of contemporary teenage greeting etiquette, I don't either. It's hard to make out what she's wearing as so little sunlight is penetrating the windows, but it is black. Her hair looks unnaturally black too.

'Jack's a friend of the professor and Linda,' says Danny, who doesn't appear fazed in the slightest by his daughter's surliness.

'So, Tammy,' I say, feeling about a hundred years old, 'what do you do?' God, now I sound like someone on a royal visit. She curls the lip with the ring in it as if to say, 'Is that all you've got?'

Danny steps in. 'Tammy finished school last year, didn't you, love? Now she helps me on the boat.'

She scowls as if to indicate that she takes issue with her father's reply but can't be bothered to explain why.

'Great,' I say meaninglessly. 'Well, great to meet you, Tammy. So, I think there's going to be a meeting about the signs...' I add in a desperate attempt to fill the awkward silence. Danny seems blissfully unaware of it. 'Is it just the two of you on the boat?' I ask, starting to back out the way I came.

'Yes, that's the truth of it,' says Danny. 'Tammy's ma died five years ago, and we bought the boat with her life insurance.'

I look at the engine's innards spread far and wide around me. This DIY fix isn't going to be completed any time soon. 'Why don't you take the cash offer for the mooring and get someone to fix it for you?' I ask.

Tammy looks up and seems to take an interest in the conversation for the first time. 'Good question,' she mutters, to herself more than anyone else.

'Tammy, we've been through all this,' says Danny pleadingly as she scowls at him.

'I'm sorry,' I say. 'I didn't mean to interfere.'

'Tammy doesn't much like being in one place,' admits Danny. 'But we can't really move on – not in this state.' He gestures helplessly around him.

'But we could if you took the money, Dad.'

'And then what? What do we do when it runs out? We just start being moved from pillar to post again – like the last time.' I am horrified to see the gentle giant's eyes have filled with tears again. 'We spent your grandma's money on a permanent home for both of us, Tammy, love. We can stay here as long as we want now. That's a good thing isn't it, love?'

But his appeal falls on deaf ears. This is obviously a rerun of a conversation they have had many times before.

'It's good for you, not for me,' she says sadly. 'Thirty thousand pounds! It's a fortune. We'd have proper cash instead of the pennies you earn.'

Danny seems angry for the first time. 'They can take their money and –'

But I don't find out what they can do with their money as Tammy pushes past Danny and me up the stairs, like a drowning woman swimming for the surface and air to fill her lungs. Her father watches her go and sadly shakes his head. His anger has subsided as rapidly as it came.

'Sorry about that, Jack. She misses her mammy and I don't really know what to say to her. It's her age, so it is.'

I shrug, embarrassed on his behalf, and we follow Tammy's route back through the boat and out onto the stern platform. There's no sign of the teenager when we emerge blinking into the light. The aggression of the signs hanging from the homes opposite is striking. Danny sees me looking at them again.

'It's a crying shame, it is,' he says. 'We aren't doing any harm. Why can't people be left in peace?'

I pat him awkwardly on his shoulder.

'Don't worry about it, Danny. You're not going anywhere, are you?'

'That's the truth, Jack, that's the truth. I was fed up having to be on the move all the time. Three years we had of it. "Move along. Move along. How long you staying? Move along." That's why we paid to stay here in the end. It was a stretch, but too good to turn down thanks to the professor, bless him. I couldn't afford a house for me and Tammy.' A single big fat tear rolls down his weatherbeaten cheek and halts, suspended and glistening, in the stubble of his cheek. 'I'm not going back to that life and Tammy's just going to have to get used to it.'

I pat him again on the shoulder.

'Well,' I say awkwardly. 'We'd better see if the others are ready for this meeting.'

'Ah, just in time,' says Linda loudly. She is on her stern with Nina and the two children and closing her hatchway with a very solid steel padlock.

CHAPTER TWELVE

I look around at the little group assembling on the towpath, and do a quick mental headcount. There are five boats in total and there should be nine occupants: the Professor, Danny and Tammy, Linda and her two children, Bill and the two others I haven't met yet. Tammy is still missing. Bill is as small as I imagined, a furtive and twitchy individual dressed in tracksuit bottoms and a dirty quilted jacket. He is loitering awkwardly on the fringes of the group, drawing heavily on a roll-up and darting glances all around him. There are also a thin and pale young man and woman in their early or mid-twenties, who I take to be the owners of the small fibreglass river cruiser that is tethered to Danny's boat. They have similar buzz-cropped hairstyles and are standing shyly to one side, hand in hand. Linda climbs off her boat, nods to the others and sets off in the lead with a child holding each of her hands. I fall into step with the professor, who is striding out with apparent ease despite his walking stick.

'It's a bad business,' he says glumly as we walk along. 'More signs went up this morning.'

'We saw. I hear you lost your chimney pipe during the night?'

'Vandals. It's a perennial issue.'

'You don't think it could have been connected with the campaign against you?'

The professor shrugs. 'I wouldn't have thought so... it just happens occasionally. It's annoying, but we have learnt to live with it.'

'Where are we going?' I ask.

'The Old Green Tree. I pop in there occasionally and the landlord has said we can use his front bar.'

I know the pub; it is tiny but famous for being unspoilt and having a good range of real ales. I've tried and failed to get in there on days when Bath's rugby team is playing at home. Hopefully, it will be quieter today. When we arrive, the landlord has been good to his word and the small front bar, with its thin swirly-patterned green carpet and dark wood panelling, is empty and waiting for us. It provides a welcome coolness after the summer heat of the city centre. A door opens onto the side of the bar and a woman with an Eastern European accent takes our orders. Linda sits in a corner, with Noah and Juno on either side of her quietly tucking into crisps. The others are ranged around the walls. The professor pays for all of the drinks without any fuss and settles himself at a small round table with a pint of bitter in front of him. Apart from the children's lemonades, everyone is drinking beer. Tammy has materialised from somewhere and is now sitting next to her father.

'Right,' says Linda. 'Tammy, shut the door, love. This is Jack and Nina,' she says to the room. 'Jack's a reporter on the *Chronicle* and he lives on a boat on the canal.' This last fact seems to cement my good credentials and the others all give me a friendly nod. 'I think you've met most of us,' continues Linda, 'except for Fred and Esther, and Bill here.'

The little man gives me a shifty look. 'We've met very briefly,' I say, reaching over to shake his hand. He takes it but I notice he looks everywhere except at me whilst doing so.

'I'm Nina,' she says, offering Bill her hand too. 'Jack's friend.'

'Bill,' he mutters.

'And this is Fred and Esther who are tied up to Danny's *Otter*,' continues Linda. The couple nod at us and take a simultaneous sip of their drinks. 'Now we all know why we're here and we need to decide what we're going to do about it.'

I put my beer down. 'Before you start, Linda, perhaps the group would like to hear what Nina and I have found out?'

'Good idea,' says the professor.

And so I explain that Andropov Developments Ltd have bought the land from Tiller & Brown's creditors. I say I have no idea how much they paid for it, but that they are almost certain to apply for planning permission to build thousands of new riverside homes on the site. The others are all familiar with the story so far, so I go on to tell them about the identical Andropov twins, who now own Andropov Developments Ltd, and how they are probably being financed by their Russian billionaire father. I tell them that I assume it is their company which is now offering the group £30,000 each to move away.

At this point, I notice the young man putting a reassuring hand on his girlfriend's leg. The couple are remarkably thin, but in a fit and lithe way, with prominent tattoos covering most of their arms and, through a frayed hole in the denim, I can see tattoos on her leg too. He raises his arm for permission to speak, like a polite sixth-former. I pause, and he coughs nervously.

'Esther and I want to... er... I'm sorry, but we want to tell you that we've thought about this long and hard and we've decided to take the money.'

'We're very sorry,' says Esther quietly. 'Especially to Danny and Tammy who have let us stay alongside them.' She looks directly at the father and daughter. 'You've been good neighbours to us both.'

Fred looks around the little group. 'I feel as though we're letting you all down. But our boat isn't worth anything really and what they're offering is a lot of money to us.'

Especially if they hadn't shelled out for their mooring in the first place, I think to myself. I'd do the same in their position. The room goes quiet. Then Linda gets up and swoops across to the couple where she envelops them both. Noah and Juno scurry after their mother and push themselves into the group hug too.

'Don't you be silly, my loves,' she says. 'You must do what you think is right, but we'll miss you.'

'And, well,' stammers Fred, 'all this business with the people opposite. It's tipped the balance for us.'

'We might even be able to afford a new boat,' Esther says.

'Or at least get some proper work done to ours,' adds her boyfriend.

'You go with all of our best wishes,' says the professor, raising his glass to both of them so that all the others follow suit. Danny hasn't said anything yet and I imagine his thoughts are dominated by the loss of Fred and Esther's occasional payments for the right to moor alongside him.

'Have you any more to tell us, Jack?' asks the professor. All eyes turn back to me again.

'Nina discovered that a local city councillor seems to be running the campaign against you,' I say.

'He's called Robin Claverton,' Nina tells them. 'He has leaflets prepared and he's trying to get people to sign a petition to get your moorings scrapped.'

'He can't do that,' says Linda.

'I can't see how he can,' I agree, 'but I'm not a lawyer. Nina and I tracked him down to Victoria Park this afternoon where he had a stall. We... well, Nina confronted him but he refused to say which residents had complained about you and he pretty well denied any connection with Andropov Developments. To be honest, he seems to be a nasty piece of work.'

'Councillor Claverton certainly hasn't had the courtesy to speak to us yet,' says the professor. 'Perhaps we should invite him to do so? We could try to have a civilised conversation with him over a cup of tea.'

I look around the room as the professor speaks. Linda's children are starting to fidget; Danny and Tammy are completely quiet, but watching and listening closely to the discussion. The young couple are also sitting quietly, slightly embarrassed by their continuing presence. Bill takes a big swallow of beer, wipes his mouth with the back of his hand and then wipes his hand on his jacket before he speaks.

'I won't pretend the money wouldn't be useful. It would sort out a few outstanding debts, like.' It's easy to picture Bill as the jockey he once was, his thin lips compressed in fierce determination, his long, lined face mirroring that of the horses he rode. He looks craftily around the room before he goes on. 'But it would be stupid. We've got somewhere free to live forever now. It'll take more'n a few banners to make me move on.'

Fred and Esther flinch slightly, and somehow the sentiment rings hollow, but the professor nods approvingly. 'Well said, Bill. For the record, I shall not be taking the money either. I am too old to begin moving *Nautilus* around and I am very happy living on the Avon.'

'Nor us,' says Danny. Tammy gives her father a sulky look.

'And nor me,' says Linda firmly, cupping her arms around Juno and Noah. 'So, what are we going to do about this Claverton and his campaign? Apart from asking him round for a nice cup of tea, I mean.' She smiles apologetically to the professor who clearly takes no offence.

'Well, I do very much like your pirate flag,' says Nina and the others all laugh while Juno claps her hands. Linda is delighted and gives Nina an affectionate look.

'And that begs the question,' says the professor, 'are we better lying low and hoping this all blows over or do we want to draw attention to ourselves?'

'We don't yet know exactly what Andropov Developments are planning to do with the site,' says Nina. 'It'll probably be a huge housing scheme. That's where the big profits are, and Jack can dig around and try to find out more.' I look at her, but she avoids my eye. 'If we're going to see off this so-called residents' campaign, we need to prove a connection between Councillor Claverton and Andropov Developments. Jack can work on that too.'

I shoot her another look but it seems that my one-woman employment agency is on something of a roll.

'A bit of publicity might flush them out, or at least get you some more public support. Jack can write an article about all this for the *Chronicle*.'

'That would all be very helpful, Jack, thank you very much,' beams Linda. 'And I'm sorry if I was a bit rude when we first met. I had my reasons. And thank you, Nina.'

Nina nods happily in sisterly conspiracy. I decide not to mention my current unpopularity with the *Chronicle*'s editor, nor the extremely unlikely prospect that Ben will be willing to commission a story from me about anything other than his fictional serial killer.

'Very well,' says the professor. 'That's the plan. In the meantime, I think we need to support each other and keep talking.' They all nod and the meeting comes to a natural end as I head to the bar to get another round of drinks.

'I'd love to stay for another but these two need their bed,' says Linda as she picks up Noah and takes Juno by her hand. 'Say goodnight, kids.' The children shyly wave to everyone and Linda heads off.

'She's a good mum,' says Danny fondly.

Pictures of RAF fighter planes from the Battle of Britain decorate the little bar room. I muse that they are particularly appropriate for witnessing what has turned out to be a council of war and, just like then, the odds between the two sides seem far from even-sided. As I wait for the pints to be pulled for the 'happy few', Danny looms behind me with six empty glasses clenched in his huge hands. I look behind him to count how many pints I need to order. Fred and Esther have fled. Tammy is chatting quietly to Nina and the professor is in a reverie of his own.

'Has Bill gone?' I ask, wondering if he has just slipped out to the loo.

'Yes, he's gone.' Danny gives a knowing wink. 'Said he had to see a man about a dog.'

The Wolf is deliberately wearing dark colours – a plain navy blue baseball cap, a black roll-neck jumper, black jacket and black jeans. He has threaded his way on foot through a housing estate to a metal bridge that crosses the Avon, upstream of Weston Lock and its adjacent weir. The riveted dark metal base of the bridge uses a pier of concrete blocks to span the gap in the middle of the river. Indecipherable graffiti decorate the concrete that supports the bridge. It is a dark and lonely spot with just the blank rear walls of factories and industrial units lining the river path at this point. He glances at the luminous dial of his military diver's watch: 11.30pm. He leans back against the concrete blocks which are embedded into the riverbank. He wants a cigarette, but his army experience tells him it will ruin his night vision and risk attracting attention to himself in the darkness. Instead of reaching for the pack in his shirt pocket, he pats his waistband in the small of his back. The bulk of the handgun is reassuring. He will not be taking any risks now that the man Powell is dead and the police are treating it as murder. But that doesn't stop him being angry with himself. He had been told to deliver a message that Powell would take very seriously. If only the man had not turned his head. He looks up at the riveted horizontal girders that form the base of the bridge. There is a short gap between each one. He counts five in and sees the small spot of fluorescent white paint on one of the rivets. He scans the path in both directions and listens intently, but the only sound is of faraway traffic.

The Wolf reaches into a jacket pocket and pulls out a small plastic package secured by an elastic band. He checks the seal is still secure and then, scanning the path once again, reaches up to the fifth girder by the white spot and slides the package onto a small shelf facing the water. Then he turns and quietly jogs back through the quiet and empty streets to his motorbike.

CHAPTER THIRTEEN

It's a grey beginning to the week. Cloud has moved in overnight and the temperature has dropped considerably. Nina and I are both wearing sweatshirts and long trousers as we demolish coffee and croissants in the bow of *Jumping Jack Flash*.

'What time are you going?' I ask. Nina usually leaves on a Monday mid-morning train after her weekends with me. She peers at me thoughtfully over the top of her mug.

'I was thinking I might hang about a bit longer, if it's okay with you? It's all getting quite interesting.'

I am quietly delighted. The unusually tense moments and harsh words of the weekend are still hanging over me. But I try to play it cool. 'Sure. Of course. That's fine. I'll need to get some more shopping.'

'Let me do that,' she says. 'Look, Jack, I've been thinking...'

'Uh-oh.'

'I know you don't want to write anything to support Ben's serial killer theory. But why don't you go and tell him about the campaign against the boat people? It's a good local story, isn't it? And you told them you'd try.'

'Um. I think it was actually *you* who told them that.'

Nina chooses to ignore this observation. 'Go to see Ben and see if you can talk him round. I'll keep Eddie with me.'

I shrug in acquiescence. 'I *was* planning to try to see him today,' I admit. 'But he can be very stubborn.'

Nina shakes her head in mock sympathy. 'Poor Jack, surrounded by stubborn people. Go on, get off your arse.'

'I'm not begging for my job back.' Even as I say this, I realise how childishly stubborn it sounds.

Nina looks as though she is about to say something but bites her lower lip and moves to wash up the breakfast things instead. She is soon out of the door with shopping bags and Eddie. I smarten myself up a bit and saunter to the *Chronicle*'s offices. Petra raises one eyebrow and one index finger when she sees me coming through the front doors. The finger indicates that I shouldn't just sweep through the turnstile that leads to the newsroom by using the electronic pass that I still have in my possession.

'Hang on, Jack, darling,' she says in her sing-song Welsh accent. 'I'd better give Ben a ring first.' She picks up her phone and mouths a silent 'sorry' at me. It seems that I may still be *persona non grata* and she is under specific orders. After a very short conversation, she tilts her head to one side and adopts an overly dramatic whisper: 'He'll see you in the conference room, Jack, love. Good luck.'

The conference room is a grandly titled but modestly sized meeting room off main reception where reporters can quiz anyone who comes in off the street without admitting them into the inner sanctum of the newsroom. Ben's definitely sending me a message. I head for the room and take a chair. He keeps me waiting for fifteen minutes but eventually kicks the door open and walks in with an armful of paper printouts.

'Jack, mate,' he says without a smile. The 'mate' isn't said with any kind of friendly intent. He sits opposite me, rolls his shoulders and squares his frame as though he is about to crouch, bind and engage with me in a rugby scrum. 'So, I imagine you'll be interested in this.'

He slides an A4-sized picture across the table to me. It is a very grey and grainy photograph of a figure in a full-face crash helmet who is walking side-on to the camera. It looks as though it could be located on Grand Parade, the road at street level above Pulteney Weir, but it is raining and dark and the face of the man, if it is a man, is completely hidden. His hands are thrust deep into a bulky jacket's pouch pockets and his shoulders are stooped.

'A suspect?' I ask.

'The Pusher,' he answers excitedly. 'Police released the picture this morning. All the usual crap of course, *"we just need to eliminate this man from our inquiries"* blah blah blah. But it's him, Jack.'

'Even if it is,' I say cautiously, 'he's pretty anonymous.'

'Well, anonymous or not, he's all over the front page this week along with our theory that we've got a copycat of the Canal Pusher at large.'

I try to correct him. 'Your theory, Ben. Not ours, not the police's and definitely not mine.'

He bangs the table angrily with a clenched fist. I see Petra looking anxiously through the glass.

'JESUS, Jack! How did you ever earn a living in this game? You should have been a bloody lawyer. If it bleeds, it leads. You know that. If you're not here to help us, then why exactly *are* you here?' He looks pointedly at his watch. 'I don't remember inviting you.'

'I've got another story for you,' I say.

'Yeah, well, I'm a bit preoccupied at the moment,' he says, putting the picture back on top of his pile of papers and gathering them together. 'Send me an outline by email if you like.'

'Just give me five minutes now, Ben. Please. It's a good story.'

He sighs with exasperation but sits down. 'Five minutes max. I'm busy on a real story.'

I tell him about the little community of boats owners who are being offered money to leave their moorings by the new owners of the Tiller & Brown site and the residents' campaign which is being stirred up by a local councillor. But I am doing a bad job of selling it as anything other than a minor local spat and I can see his frustration mounting until he bangs the edge of the table decisively with both palms and stands up.

'Sorry, Jack. Bit of a row between some boat owners and some flat owners. Afraid it doesn't float my boat. No pun intended. No one dead.

Unlike a prominent city father, Mr Rufus Powell, and maybe some other people in the past and some other people in the future. I've got one of the girls digging out previous drownings from the archives.'

'But what about the developers?'

'What about them?' asks Ben. 'We know the site's been sold and young Tom's expecting a planning application any day. So, they don't want a load of scruffy old boats at one of the main entrances to their prestige new site. Big deal.' But then he seems to be struck by a sudden thought and he sits back down with a glimmer of a smile.

'What is it, Ben?' I ask suspiciously.

'Well, I may have one bit of work you can do. We can agree it'll take three days if you like, starting tomorrow.'

'Go on.'

'Mrs Powell has said she'll give us an interview,' he says happily. 'She's had the nationals banging on her door. They've all been told to bugger off, but she trusts us, and so we can flog it to everyone else just before we run with it. Nice little earner,' he laughs, rubbing both palms together vigorously. 'And good for our reputation.'

He means his reputation.

'We'd want to get a picture of the two of you together at her home,' he continues. "Author of *The Canal Pusher* meets drowned man's widow." Let's aim for a thousand words as part of a centre page spread with a short news story selling it on the front.'

It's almost fun to plunge a six-inch nail into his rapidly expanding balloon. 'No thanks, Ben.'

His mouth gapes open. 'No?'

'No. I'm not doing anything to help you pour petrol on your serial killer theory. And by the way, I really wouldn't use that headline unless you've been told that he died by drowning – which you haven't.'

'Yeah,' he snarls, leaping back to his feet and pointing a stubby forefinger at me. 'Well actually, we know now that he wasn't dead before he went into the water, don't we? So how else did he die? And you know what you can do, mate? You can piss off back to your boat with your crappy little story and you can forget about ever working here again.'

The raised voices must have easily carried to Petra, but she still jumps when Ben kicks the door open and storms back to his office. I give her a shrug of resignation and head back outside.

Nina is waiting for me on the boat and I tell her briefly about our exchange. I anticipate sympathy, but her response surprises me.

'You had the chance to comfort that poor widow, Jack. How could you say no? That's just terrible.' Eddie is sitting on her lap and she is fondling his ears agitatedly.

'I wasn't being asked to comfort her, Nina. I was being asked to interview her and support Ben's bloody stupid copycat Pusher theory.'

She shakes her head firmly.

'No, you didn't need to do that, Jack. You know you could have just done a straightforward, sympathetic interview with her. She might not have anyone else to talk to. I think you're being selfish.'

I try counting to ten but barely make it to five. 'Selfish? No, Nina! What would be selfish would be writing any old crap just to stay in a job. Have you any idea how far out on a limb Ben is with this serial killer nonsense? It's not enough that a magistrate has been killed – probably due to an everyday mugging that went wrong. He has to start a wholesale hue-and-cry just to flog more papers and get himself noticed. Well, I'm not having anything to do with it.'

'Never mind Ben,' Nina snaps back. 'I'm just saying you had the chance to speak to Mrs Powell and you blew it. And you didn't persuade Ben to run a story about the boat people and so you blew that too.'

Eddie's ears are pinned back in unhappiness at our raised voices. 'Blew it? Why in hell's name do I need to speak to Mrs Powell? What can she add to anything? If anyone knows anything about blowing interviews, it's you. You did a pretty good job with Councillor Claverton. And by the way,' I add, my blood well and truly boiling by now, 'I don't remember *you* wanting to do many newspaper interviews when you'd just been widowed, even though the entire national press was on your trail and yours truly was keeping them at bay.'

Silence. A long silence. Nina deliberately places a miserable-looking Eddie onto the floor.

'Nina...' I begin.

She shakes her head at me and speaks quietly but firmly. 'We've had more cross words with each other this weekend than we have ever since we met,' she says. 'What's going on, Jack?'

I decide to lay it on the line. What's the point of keeping it to myself anyway? 'I thought we were friends – maybe more than friends. But you just announce that you're going off to work in Dubai. Just like that.'

'And that's what it all comes back to, doesn't it, Jack? It's nothing to do with Ben or Rufus Powell or the boat people or anything else. It's all to do with your hurt pride.' She stands up. 'Well, I think maybe I should be getting back home after all. I'll get the first train in the morning if that's all right with you.'

'Nina... '

But she is gone – up and out of the hatchway and striding up the steep steps between the terraces of Robin's garden and leaving me to stew in exasperation.

As the afternoon progresses the mugginess of the morning becomes ever more oppressive. Eddie is agitated, matching my own mood. He tries to settle, circling and scratching the floor or the sofa, but after just a minute or so he sighs heavily and trots to the hatchway to sniff the air. The onboard barometer shows that the pressure is falling fast and there is still no sign of Nina by four o'clock when I hear the first drum-rolls of thunder in the distance. Outside, on the towpath, the number of joggers and dog walkers is markedly reduced as the timpani of thunder gets louder and nearer.

I hear the rain hitting the metal roof of *Jumping Jack Flash* before I see it. The hatchway cover has been open, anticipating Nina's return, but now I quickly slide it shut and close the doors into the bow's seating area. Through a porthole, I see fat, single, heavy drops of rain pockmark the canal water. The sun can no longer be seen; dark, ragged clouds cover the whole sky. Within a matter of minutes, the single drops are replaced by sheets of storm rain, thrown down with enough force to make the surface of the canal look like a bubbling torrent. At times, the savagery of the summer storm creates a shining plastic curtain that almost prevents me from seeing the far towpath. I pray that Nina has found somewhere sensible to shelter. Eddie is curled up in his basket, his chin is resting on his paws, and his liquid brown eyes are filled with tragedy. I turn on the internal lights of the boat to brighten the gloom.

And then the flickering flashes of lightning begin. Some last for seconds at a time as the kettle-drum thunder continues to roll across the sky above the city. I pull down a half-read novel but find it impossible to concentrate – partly because of the storm and partly due to my thoughts constantly returning to the argument with Nina. I still don't regret refusing Ben's request to do the interview with Mrs Powell – but maybe I shouldn't have reminded Nina of her own widowhood. I definitely don't want her to go home tomorrow.

The storm passes away until eventually the thunder is silent and the lightning only a faint flicker away to the east. A light steady rain continues to fall for an hour or so and then, thirty minutes after it stops, I hear the hatchway sliding open. Nina appears, her clothes dark with water and her short hair so wet that it looks freshly cropped. She doesn't smile at me and I assume from this that her plans haven't changed. The storm outside may have passed, but the atmosphere between us remains highly charged.

'You need to dry off. Have you eaten?'

'Yes, thanks.'

'What time's your train tomorrow?'

'Six o'clock.'

And that's it. For the rest of the evening we avoid sharing each other's space as much as is possible within the confines of a six-foot ten-inch-wide floating corridor. I give Eddie a last stroll around Sydney Gardens and Nina's light is already out by the time I return. Her blanket is pulled up over her head.

'Goodnight, Nina,' I say, after locking the hatchway door from the inside. There is no reply. Let her sulk, I think to myself. It's clear that she has no desire for a proper relationship with me and the sooner I come to terms with that the better. I decide to stay in my bed in the morning and let her slip away to catch her early morning train on her own.

CHAPTER FOURTEEN

I get very little sleep and I can tell from the tossing and turning next door that Nina is restless as well. In the early hours of Tuesday morning I study the wood-lined ceiling of the boat and begin to think about life after Nina. If I have no job to keep me in Bath, it will be too expensive to stay on at Robin's mooring and I begin to think about where else I might travel with *Jumping Jack Flash* – ideally somewhere that I might pick up some work. I have nothing calling me to any particular part of the country. Both my parents are dead and I was an only child. I have some distant cousins, but they are too distant to call on. My oldest and best friend is an actor who travels all over the country himself. I don't want to try to pick up my pre-divorce life. I have few remaining connections and, I realise uncomfortably, I have come to regard Nina as 'the still point in my turning world'. Without her, I shall be figuratively and literally adrift – and probably very lonely too. It isn't a very cheering thought.

It is five o'clock when I hear Nina moving about in her little forward cabin. The railway station is barely ten minutes away and so I assume she must be going for one of her very early morning runs. She likes to pound along the towpath or riverbank just as the sun is coming up and the mist on the water is beginning to dissipate. Sure enough, I hear Eddie scamper out after her with an excited yap – a sure sign that she is squeezing in a run before catching her early train back to Salisbury.

Thirty minutes later, however, I am checking my watch. If Nina is to catch the six o'clock train, she is beginning to cut it fine. Then my mobile vibrates with an incoming text. It is from Nina.

> Urgent. Come quick. Linda's boat drifting.

I pull on yesterday's clothes and hurry to get my bike out of the shed. It'll be the fastest way to get to the moorings. I curse the fact that I'm starting on the side of the canal without a towpath and need to do a detour in the opposite direction first. If Linda's boat is drifting on the river, Linda and the kids could be in real peril. As I skid on the gravel past Bath Bottom Lock, I can see that the Avon is flowing pretty fast this morning. Yesterday's thunderstorm will have raised the river level upstream and I assume some floodgates have been opened overnight. I hurtle over the pedestrian bridge behind the railway station and race on along the edge of Green Park towards Victoria Bridge and the moorings. Soon I can see across the river and, without slowing, I register that *Maid of Coventry* is missing from its berth between *Nautilus* and *Otter*.

The absence is like seeing a missing tooth in a familiar face. I have a queasy feeling in the pit of my stomach. Where has Linda gone? Has she decided to take the money and abandon the little group after all? No. Nina's text suggests that something else has happened. I pedal on, up onto Victoria Bridge, and that is when I see them. The cream and black paintwork of *Maid of Coventry* is just appearing from around the bend further downstream, motoring back against the current and towards me. Linda is at the tiller with Nina standing next to her. Danny and Tammy are in the bow of the boat. There is no sign of the children.

I push my bike down the slope and along the path to Linda's empty mooring where the professor and Fred and Esther, the young couple from the river cruiser, are all standing with anxious expressions.

'What happened?' The professor, who is wearing a purple dressing gown over striped cotton pyjamas and leather backless slippers, shakes his head despondently.

'The mooring ropes were untied and they drifted out into the river. I didn't hear a thing,' he says in self-recrimination.

I squeeze his arm. 'It's not your fault. But hell's teeth, they could have been killed.'

He nods. 'The weir. There's a safety rope strung across it, but I doubt it would have stopped them going over with the current like this.'

I mentally picture the fast-flowing weir, which is on a wide stretch of the Avon alongside Weston Lock. The lock allows boats to navigate their way past it safely. The prospect of Linda's boat, with her and the children on board, being swept sideways over the storm-swollen weir, probably overturning in the process, fills me with horror. Fred has moved to one end of the empty mooring and Esther to the other. Linda throttles back and expertly brings her boat into the gap before hitting reverse and then neutral. Her face is deathly pale beneath the unbrushed chaos of her red hair. It is the first time I have seen her looking scared and vulnerable. Danny throws the bow mooring rope over to Fred while Nina throws the stern rope to Esther. The young couple fix them firmly to the metal mooring stakes, which I notice are still hammered deeply into the bank. If the stakes weren't pulled out and the ropes weren't cut, it suggests that someone had simply untied the boat and allowed it drift out into the current – or perhaps even given it a helpful push.

Linda cuts the engine and there is something awful about the silence that follows. No one speaks. The ugly slogans hang menacingly above the scene. Then Linda's shoulders begin to heave, and she crumples onto a seat by the tiller with her face in her hands. Nina is up alongside her in seconds with one arm around her shoulder. Danny and Tammy climb down onto the towpath and we congregate at the stern of the boat. I register that all of the boat people are there except Bill. There is no sign of life on board his boat, although with the huge tarpaulin covering it, it would be difficult to tell if he was there or not.

The professor breaks the silence. 'Delayed shock, I think. I'll fetch some brandy.' He heads back to *Nautilus*. Nina breaks off from hugging Linda, gives me a grim look and then ushers her down into the boat. I watch through a window as the two children hug Linda tightly, their eyes wide open at seeing their capable and confident mother reduced to tears.

'What happened?' I ask the group. Danny, who is standing with his arms round Tammy, is the first to respond.

'I got a call from Linda,' he says. 'I couldn't make her out at first. She was screaming and shouting something about the boat. Well, I looked out the back and saw that *Maid* had slipped her mooring. That woke me up good and proper, I can tell you.'

Tammy is looking exhausted, dark-eyed and white-faced. She is holding on to her father's arms. The professor slips past us with a bottle of brandy, which he takes into Linda's boat.

'Linda told me her boat was stuck up against the bridge above the weir. So I woke Tammy, grabbed some ropes and ran downriver,' Danny continues. 'It was awful. Linda's boat was sideways on up against the bridge. She couldn't start the engine and the force of the water was pushing it hard up against the pier in the middle of the river. The kids were clinging onto her for dear life at the stern. Then Nina was running towards me on the towpath. I didn't know what to do but Nina led the way. We climbed up onto the bridge, ran halfway across and then Nina climbed over the rail. The *Maid* was right below us. She jumped down onto its roof. That took real courage, I tell you. I tied one end of the rope round the bridge and threw the other down to her.'

Danny was giving his account calmly enough in his gentle Irish lilt, but I could well imagine the terror of the moment: water rushing past in the dawn light, the furious sound of the weir in their ears, the boat powerless against the fierce current. *Maid of Coventry* must have struck the concrete pier almost exactly at her midpoint. Otherwise, the current would have spun her backwards or forwards around the concrete pier and onwards over the weir.

'Well, once we had the boat tied firmly to the bridge it all calmed down a bit. Tammy jumped down then too and we fixed another rope in place so there was no chance of it being pushed on towards the weir any more. I managed to get myself on board and we got ourselves straight and shipshape. I tried to start the engine, but the key just kept clicking. So I gave the starter motor a bash with a bit of wood and that freed up the solenoid. That got the engine going and we used the bow rope to pivot the *Maid of Coventry* from the bank and get her pointing back upstream. Shaking like a leaf, Linda was. Not surprised. Could have been terrible. Terrible.'

'Wow. Well done, Danny – and you, Tammy. You were real heroes.'

Danny looked embarrassed, and Tammy was shuffling her feet. 'Aye, well so was your Nina,' says Danny.

'But the question is, how did the boat come to be adrift?'

'For sure, we don't need to look too far for an answer to that one,' says Danny bitterly as he stares across the river at the signs hanging from the windows of the buildings on the other side.

'If they'd gone over that weir it would've been murder or manslaughter,' I reply.

Tammy is shaking as if the extreme peril of the situation has suddenly struck her. Danny wraps one of his big arms around her. 'It's all right, love, you were great. I'm very proud of you.'

'And none of you heard anyone on the towpath this morning?' I ask. They all shake their heads as the professor emerges from Linda's boat. It appears that Linda has also given her account of the near-disaster to him and Nina.

'She only woke up when the boat crashed into the bridge,' he says, shaking his head in disbelief. 'It must have been terrifying, especially with Juno and Noah on board.' Then he pulls the lapels of his dressing gown tighter across his thin chest. 'I'm cold. I must get dressed. Jack, a word, if you please?'

I follow the professor back down into *Nautilus* where we move through the rows of books to his desk. He retrieves a cheap bottle of blended whisky and pours two glasses.

'Medicinal,' he says, looking at the bottle with ill-disguised contempt. 'At this time of day, it's the only excuse.' I'm not sure whether he's talking about the brand of whisky or the early time of day, but we both swallow it quickly without water.

'This is a serious turn of events, Jack,' he says, slumping into the green leather and wood chair behind his desk.

'I agree. This goes way beyond slogans and petitions.'

'I believe we need to notify the police.'

'I agree. And maybe this will force the *Chronicle* to take a bit of notice,' I add, although I still think there's only a fifty-fifty chance of changing Ben's mind.

'Well. I shall see if Linda and the others will talk to the police. We mustn't be tempted to take the law into our own hands, even if we are able to find out who did this terrible thing.'

I leave the professor to get dressed and head back to the *Maid of Coventry*. Nina is now standing on the towpath with Danny and Fred and I realise for the first time that she has Eddie with her.

Nina hands him over to me. 'I had to leave him on the bridge when I jumped on board, but he followed us back along the riverbank because he's a clever little dog, aren't you?' She nuzzles her nose into the fur on his neck.

'I've been hearing about your heroic rescue.'

She looks up at me, suspicious after the awkwardness of the night before, but then she sees that I am totally genuine.

'You were brilliant, Nina,' I say, giving her a hug. 'Well done. Jumping down onto that boat took real guts. You almost certainly saved their lives. How's Linda?'

'The brandy has helped a bit, as well as talking it all through,' she says. 'But she's in shock and she's exhausted. I've told her to try to get some sleep and I've asked Esther or Tammy to look after the children – but Linda's taken Noah and Juno in bed with her at the moment.'

I pull her slightly away from the others and drop my voice.

'The professor is going to call the police – if Linda agrees.'

'Makes sense,' nods Nina.

'Er, I'm afraid you've missed your train,' I say, checking my watch. It is now almost eight o'clock, although it seems an age since Nina left for her run.

She looks at me and then at the boat with Linda and her children somewhere safely within. Then she tilts her head up at the signs across the river. 'I think I'll hang around a bit longer, if it's okay with you? These guys could really do with our help.'

'Stay as long as you want,' I reply.

It is unspoken, but I think we both feel chastened by the scale of this morning's life-threatening events compared to our weekend spats.

'D'you know what?' I say. 'I think we should get some breakfast and then have a little wander around the front of those houses.' I look at them again and try to get a fix on the flats displaying the signs. 'It would be interesting to have a little chat with the people who have joined Councillor Robin Claverton's residents' campaign.'

'Occasionally – just occasionally mind – you come up with a good idea,' says Nina.

CHAPTER FIFTEEN

Fed, showered and feeling a little better after our sleepless night and traumatic early morning, we return on foot to the small cluster of streets on the bank opposite the boats. They span the gap between the river and Upper Bristol Road where it borders Royal Victoria Park. But from this point, it is impossible to pinpoint the flats with the banners facing the moorings. The frontages of the tall Victorian homes and their neighbouring apartment blocks bear little resemblance to what we can remember of the view of the rear of the buildings. It may be that we are going to have to do door-to-door inquiries, and that will depend on someone admitting us through the shared front doors.

As Nina and I ponder this dilemma, standing and staring up at one particular apartment block, Eddie sitting patiently on his lead between us, a testy voice from behind addresses us.

'Excuse me, please, you're blocking the dropped kerb.' A shiny red mobility scooter is parked in the road, and sitting on it is a slight and elderly Asian woman wearing a bright green sari under a green waxed cotton jacket of the type favoured by gamekeepers. Her finely spun white hair is immaculately coiffured above a face that, although lined with age, is still finely sculpted and elegant with high cheekbones. The wire basket on the front of her scooter contains two full shopping bags.

'Oh, I'm so sorry. We didn't hear you there,' Nina says politely, and we hurriedly clear a space for her to drive up onto the pavement. 'My friend and I were just trying to find out which residents are so upset about the boats that are moored in front of these flats.'

'Were you indeed?' says the woman. Her green eyes stare sharply over the top of a small pair of round wire-framed glasses. 'And why, may I ask, is that?' Her pronunciation reminds me of the professor. It is a cultured and educated voice and each word is beautifully enunciated.

'We're friends with the people who own the boats,' I say. 'And there was rather a shocking incident early this morning.'

'Yes, I've seen both of you before.' Nina and I exchange puzzled glances. 'What kind of shocking incident?'

'One of the boats drifted down towards the weir,' says Nina. 'There was a woman and her two children on board. We think it may have been deliberately untied from its mooring.'

The elderly woman momentarily covers her mouth with the outstretched fingers of one hand. She seems genuinely shocked. 'In that case, you must come inside for tea and tell me all about it,' she says. She holds out her hand. 'Mrs Rani Manningham-Westcott. My late husband was the Honourable Mr Justice Manningham-Westcott,' she adds proudly.

A concrete ramp leads up one side of the steps to the front door of the apartment building in front of us. Mrs Manningham-Westcott zooms up it confidently and brakes at the top, where she waves a key fob at a panel to unlock the door. It swings open automatically and she moves her little joystick forward to glide into a large tiled foyer. We follow her inside.

'I would prefer the character of an older house but the space and facilities in these newer places are so much more convenient.' She manoeuvres across to the lift and presses the button for the fifth floor. Clearly Mrs Rani Manningham-Westcott leads an independent life in spite of her mobility problems.

Once in the spacious hall of her apartment, she parks the scooter, picks up two sticks and walks with difficulty into her kitchen. I am directed into a large sitting room while Nina follows her with the bags and I hear her telling Nina where to store the shopping and where to find a biscuit for Eddie. Although the flat is quite modern, it is full of highly polished antique furniture and oil portraits, including one of a serious looking judge in full wig and regalia that hangs in prime position above a marble mantlepiece. I walk to the large rear window. A camera with the barrel of a telescopic lens is on a tripod pointing directly down and across the river at the five moored boats. I put my eye to the viewfinder and the stern of *Nautilus* leaps into focus. The clarity of the image is astonishing. To my right there is a side window. Its louvred shutters are folded open and it overlooks the roof of a neighbouring Victorian house. It is slightly lower than Mrs Manningham-Westcott's flat and a metal fire escape zigzags down its side.

Our hostess eventually emerges from the kitchen with Nina, who is carrying a silver tray with a china teapot and three sets of matching cups and saucers. Mrs Manningham-Westcott settles herself in a high wing-backed chair next to the window with a sigh of relief and asks Nina to pour. We take seats facing her.

'So, you are Mr Jack Johnson?' she says. 'Nina has told me a little about you and your friends from the boats.'

'Do you know why your neighbours have suddenly begun this campaign to have the boat owners moved on?' I ask, taking a sip of the fragrant Earl Grey.

'Oh yes,' she says. 'It's all because of that odious man, Robin Claverton. He came knocking on my door asking me to sign his ridiculous petition. Do you know, I can all too easily picture him as one of Mosley's blackshirts! He stood there stammering and stuttering when he saw I was an Anglo-Indian. I sent him packing very quickly.'

'So, you don't mind the boat people?' asks Nina.

The old lady points at her camera. 'My dear, I find them an endless source of fascination. I detest television. Apart from my books and the wireless, your friends help to fill my empty hours.'

'Do you know why Councillor Claverton began his campaign?' I ask. 'Is he responding to residents' concerns?'

'I really don't have a clue, Mr Johnson. It's almost as though he dreamt it up out of the blue. I have heard no complaints about them before. But, of course, people sometimes just need to be given someone else to hate. Look at Hitler – or this horrid American president. I saw the banners for the first time yesterday when I went for a little ride along the river path – quite, quite despicable.' She sips her tea and her beady eyes flick between us like an inquisitive bird. 'Now, please tell me more about this morning's incident.'

I briefly describe Linda's ordeal and our suspicions that it was a deliberate act of early morning sabotage.

'Oh, that poor, poor lady. I did notice that her boat was missing first thing this morning. I often watch her and her children through my camera. From what I have seen, she seems to be a very capable and loving mother?'

'She is,' confirms Nina.

'Do you know anything about Andropov Developments, Mrs Manningham-Westcott?' I ask.

'Ah yes. Well, we all know they have bought the land opposite and we are waiting to hear what their plans are. It's such a shame. My husband and I used to spend hours watching the Tiller & Brown site when it was in full production. It was like having a continuously changing Lowry painting on our doorstep. The men would all arrive for work and leave in their thousands and I would try to capture them on my camera. Of course, my neighbours all found it far too industrial. They are snobs without having anything to be snobbish about. And now, I suppose, we shall have to stare at rows and rows of dreary new homes instead. Some more tea, please, my dear.'

'Do you think Claverton's campaign might be connected with Andropov Developments in any way?' Nina asks as she refills the three cups.

'What an intriguing question,' says Mrs Manningham-Westcott. 'Why should you think so?'

I explain about the woman who has been offering £30,000 to the boat owners to give up their permanent mooring rights.

'Ah,' says the old lady, clapping her palms together and holding them under her nose. 'So that's what she was about, was it? I saw her coming and going in those ridiculous shoes of hers. And, of course, I have seen both of you with the boat people as well. That is why I decided to invite you up here. I don't know them, of course, but I feel as though I do. Are any of them taking the money to leave?'

'Just one boat so far,' I reply. 'The smallest white one.'

'The one with the young couple on,' nods Mrs Manningham-Westcott. 'A shame. I shall miss them. Now please tell me who the others are.'

We give her a brief inventory of the other boats and their owners. She is particularly interested in the immaculate *Nautilus* and its distinguished-looking elderly owner.

'Professor Arthur Chesney, did you say?' She hobbles over to a wall that is covered in bookshelves and pulls out a recent edition of *Who's Who*. She thumps the thick red book down onto a side table and finds the professor's entry, which she bends closely over to read. 'Emeritus Professor, Bristol University,' she says approvingly, 'and he has written an impressive range of books. I wonder if he ever came across my husband.'

Nina has been looking at a large framed black-and-white photograph to one side of the main window. It shows the Tiller & Brown site in full production with clouds of smoke and steam rising above it on a cold winter's day.

'This is very good,' she says. 'Is it one of yours?'

Our hostess nods cheerfully and then she gives a look that is both naughty and sly. 'Would you like to see a secret?'

I notice that she says 'see' rather than 'hear' but, of course, we both nod with encouraging smiles.

'Barnaby had this made for me before we moved here. We had one very similar at our home in India.' She pats the books and I assume she means the bookshelves, which stretch from wall to wall and floor to ceiling. 'He was practising at the bar in Delhi when we met. Of course, English people thought that he had married beneath him, and my parents thought it was the other way around. Then Barnaby became a Crown Court judge in Bristol after we returned to England and we moved here when he retired.' She sees my puzzled expression. 'There's a small work room hidden behind these books,' she says gleefully. 'See if you can find out how to access it.'

Nina and I examine the bookcase closely but there is no sign of a latch or lever of any kind. I recall visiting a National Trust house once where the guide revealed a light switch concealed behind a book about electricity, so I begin studying Mrs Manningham-Westcott's books in more detail. I also calculate that any handle would probably be between waist and shoulder height, to give ease of access, and at one end of the bookcase or the other. As I search, I come across a book that looks more careworn and handled than its neighbours. It is an old leather-bound book about photography. I pull it out and flick through a collection of beautiful landscape photographs by Ansel Adams called *Sierra Nevada: The John Muir Trail*. It appears to be a 1938 first edition signed by the great man himself. Behind me, I hear our hostess catch her breath.

I peer into the gap where the book was resting and see a knob-shaped handle made of brass. I reach inside and turn it. Nothing happens so I try pulling it. There is a click and the whole bookshelf seems to shift minutely. Now I pull, and the entire wall of books begins to pivot on its centre, smoothly turning 90 degrees and opening up to create an entrance on either side into another room with no windows but lots of framed photographs, a large desk, a slim modern computer, a printer and at least ten filing cabinets. There is a little round of applause from both women and I turn, smile and make a small bow of acknowledgement.

'Very impressive, Mr Johnson. You are clearly a born investigator! The book was also a gift from my husband. It is rather rare and valuable now. It set a new standard for photography books at the time. You see, I have always been a passionate photographer and I needed a darkroom wherever we lived to develop my pictures. Now, of course, everything is digital and all I need is a good printer with the correct paper. And thankfully, there are no chemical smells any more either, although Barnaby was very understanding.'

'A precious book about photography hides a secret room for photography,' says Nina. 'How absolutely wonderful.'

I replace the book carefully and walk into the hidden room, followed by Nina and Mrs Manningham-Westcott, who opens a filing cabinet drawer and brings out a brown folder labelled *Tiller & Brown*. She fans out a series of black-and-white photographs that show a line of men, perhaps a hundred long and ten rows deep, who are walking through the factory gates as one single mass of manual labour. She has close-ups of men loading steel from the backs of old lorries and there is another of a crane operator, high above the site, stopping to have a cigarette and unconsciously looking directly at the camera. She undoubtedly has an artist's eye. Her subjects are beautifully framed. There must be thousands and thousands of photographs in these filing cabinets, I think. A life's work capturing other people's movements in spite of her own immobility.

'Can we see your photos of the boat people?' I ask tentatively.

'Of course,' she says, ushering us both towards the table. She opens another cabinet and puts a different brown folder in front of us. 'I'm going to have a sherry,' she says. 'Would you care for one too?' She catches me glancing at my watch – mainly because I have already been given a 'medicinal' whisky for breakfast by the professor. 'Yes, Mr Johnson. It is eleven a.m. – which counts as a pre-lunch aperitif – and besides, when one is eighty, one can bloody well drink when one wishes.'

I mumble an apology while Nina pipes up.

'Ignore him, Mrs W. I'd love a sherry. Thank you.' She nudges me in the ribs with a giggle as I open the folder and fan out the photographs. According to the professor the moorings have only been in place for about two years but there is still a collection of about a hundred photographs. Their quality suggests that they have been taken with the sole aim of creating beautiful images; there is no sense of intrusion or spying to them. The professor features in many, staring into the distance or concentrating on a book, and there are also many of Linda playing with her children or hanging out washing along a line suspended above the roof of her boat. The detail provided by the telescopic lens is extraordinary.

'These are wonderful,' says Nina, as our hostess returns on her sticks.

'I'm afraid I can't manage the tray, my dear. Would you do the honours?'

We sit and sip the dry sherry as we sift the pictures with care. There is a beautiful one of Fred and Esther's largely naked bodies taking a swim together in the dappled sunlight of a summer's evening. Another captures the scene I witnessed on my first visit to the boats: Danny fishing and watching a float on the water while Tammy stares closely at her mobile phone on the roof of their boat, each engrossed in their own separate worlds.

'Please don't tell them about this,' says Mrs Manningham-Westcott suddenly. 'I couldn't bear for them to think I was being nosy or for them to become self-conscious. They are simply my life-models, posing for my art just as a painter might capture people without them knowing.'

I drain my glass, stand and give her a card with my number on it. 'Thank you. It has honestly been a real treat meeting you. Do please call me if you learn anything more about the campaign.'

'Or the plans for the site across the river,' adds Nina. She leans forward and gives the old lady a kiss on one cheek. 'And thank you, it's been marvellous. I love your pictures and your hidden room.'

Mrs Manningham-Westcott takes each of our hands. 'It has been lovely meeting you, too. It is so nice to have some new company for a change.'

Eddie is still loitering in the kitchen, hoping for more biscuits, and as I go to fetch him I take another quick peep through the camera's viewfinder. There is no one moving about on the boats now and, apart from *Nautilus*, they look scruffier and shabbier than ever. From this distance, they also look very small and vulnerable.

CHAPTER SIXTEEN

After lunch on board *Jumping Jack Flash*, both Nina and I are quiet. We both had largely sleepless nights and the early morning trauma of Linda's near-death experience means we are both feeling a bit shattered. I can sense my chin falling down onto my chest and my eyes beginning to droop when a text arrives on my mobile with a ping. I am surprised to see it is from Ben Mockett.

> Last chance! Interview with Mrs Powell fixed for tomorrow at 11 am. You on?

I look across at Nina, who is prone on the sofa with Eddie lying across her stomach.

'Is it about Linda?' she asks.

'No. It's Ben. He's giving me one last chance to do the interview with Mrs Powell.'

Nina sits upright. 'Well. You know how I feel about that,' she says uncompromisingly.

'Yes. I'm in no doubt about how you feel about that,' I say.

She senses that I may be reconsidering my position. 'Have you changed your mind?'

'Not sure. Given what happened to Linda and the kids this morning, I'm wondering if I can trade a story about the residents' campaign for the Powell interview?'

Nina sits up. 'You should. You must, Jack,' she says. 'It's a win-win. You'll give some comfort to that poor lady and you'll help the boat people by telling everyone how horrible this campaign is. Linda, Juno and Noah could have been killed. No one in their right mind will support that kind of action.'

I concede she may have a point but I'm still very reluctant to add fuel to Ben's ridiculous serial killer theory.

'I suppose I can try to do the interview on my own terms,' I say, thinking out loud. Although I suspect that Ben won't be at all happy about the end result if I do.

'Of course you can,' Nina says encouragingly. 'I can come with you if you like.'

'Sorry no, Nina. It's work.'

I wait for the explosion of protest, but it doesn't come. It seems that she is just grateful I have changed my mind.

I text a reply to Ben:

> Okay. I'll do it. But ONLY if you run a piece on the boat campaign in return. Send address.

There is an immediate response.

> Deal. 1,000 words. Her views on Pusher copycat theory non-negotiable. Also need picture of you interviewing her. Copy by Wednesday evening. She's at 15 St James's Square.

I sigh and show Nina the reply. 'I'm going to need you to come after all if he wants an action shot of me interviewing her.'

Nina smiles sweetly but wisely decides not to crow about it.

Then my mobile rings. I assume it will be Ben eager to gloat and supply me with more instructions, but the display tells me it is Will Simpson, my closest and oldest friend and a reasonably successful actor.

'Hi, Will.'

Nina perks up even more. She's met Will before, during last year's adventures in the Midlands, and she likes him. Most women do. I switch on the phone's speaker so that she can hear both sides of the conversation.

'JJ. My man! How are you... and how is the blessed Nina?'

'She's here on the boat with me, listening in,' I say, just in case he is tempted to say something inappropriate.

'Hey, great. Hi, Nina,' he calls out.

'Hi, Will,' she calls back happily.

'Are you still moored up in Bath, JJ?'

'We are,' I say. 'No plans to move on at the moment.'

'Great! I've just been asked to step in at the Theatre Royal next week. *The Importance of Being Earnest*. The guy playing Algernon has broken his leg.'

Nina claps excitedly.

'Nina's very pleased to hear about Algernon's accident,' I tell him. She pokes her tongue out at me. 'When are you arriving?'

'Thursday. Rehearsals Thursday, Friday and Monday, and curtain up next Tuesday.'

'Do you need a bed?' I ask, more out of duty than hospitality. Will can be an exhausting guest.

'No. You're okay. The production company has fixed me up with a decent hotel. It's the least they can do when I'm helping them out of a crisis. But I thought we could maybe get together for the weekend?'

Nina holds a thumb up.

'Yes, great,' I say. And I mean it. I have been thinking of taking the boat out for a weekend trip for some time, and now I think it might encourage Nina to extend her stay even longer. 'Let's take the boat up the canal to Bradford on Avon. We can leave Friday evening and get back Sunday afternoon.'

'Sounds brilliant,' says Will. 'I'll get you tickets for the play too. Send me some directions to the boat and I'll swing by late Friday afternoon, after we've finished rehearsals.'

'Great, see you then.' I hang up and try not to be too jealous of Nina's undiluted pleasure at the news of our unexpected visitor.

'It'll be lovely to see Will, and the weekend trip is a lovely idea. Am I invited?' she asks, although she is one hundred per cent sure of the answer.

'Maybe,' I say. 'If you promise to behave.'

She throws a cushion across the boat at me and Eddie barks with excitement. I check the BBC's online weather forecast for the weekend. It shows unbroken sun, light winds and high temperatures. Then I settle down to make a list of requirements for the weekend trip. The boat hasn't been moved for several months so I will need to do some routine checks and top up with diesel and water.

Nina wanders off to send an email on her laptop to cancel her volunteer shifts at the hospice in Salisbury for the rest of the week and peace descends on *Jumping Jack Flash* again. I look around the interior fondly. The yard did a really good job of rebuilding her and there is not even a hint of the foul-smelling silt and mud that had penetrated all of the wall linings. My heart-stopping decision to wreck the boat in a lock had been ridiculously dangerous at the time. But I couldn't see any other way of seizing the initiative from the men who were holding Nina and me captive at gunpoint. The former hire boat has much more of a homely feel to her now, with more soft seating, a few small pictures, some additional bespoke joinery and my all-important book and bottle shelves, complete with guard rails to prevent the contents moving about in a heavy sea. Needless to say, they are there just to provide a suitably nautical touch as heavy seas don't happen very often on the canals.

Robert comes down the garden to join us as the shadows lengthen into the late afternoon. He has brought a silver ice bucket containing a bottle of Moet & Chandon Imperial in honour of Nina's arrival.

'Let's see if we can clear the canal,' he says, sending the cork flying off the stern onto the towpath opposite. We cheer his achievement and move through the boat to sit in the open bow and toast his generosity. Then I bring him up to speed about the events on the river. He's curious to hear more detail of what Andropov Developments are planning for the old industrial site, but all we can tell him is that, as far as we know, no plans have been announced or submitted yet.

'If they're investing the kind of money I think they are, then they certainly won't want your boating chums spoiling one of the most important entrances to the site,' he says. 'It could put people off buying – or even reduce the value of all the properties they build.'

'And no doubt that's why they're trying to pay them to go away,' I say. 'The timing of this residents' campaign is just too convenient to be a coincidence.'

Robert tops up our glasses. 'I'll put out a few more feelers about these Andropov twins,' he says. Then he changes the subject and begins to tell us about a large, orange trimaran he is having built for himself at considerable expense in South Africa. Robert is a proper sailor who has skippered long-distance ocean-going races in the past and he regards the 4mph limitations and flat calm of canal-boating with wry amusement. He continues chatting comfortably with Nina while I prepare a paella. We finish the champagne and another bottle of wine and eat our dinner in the dusk before he kisses Nina's cheek, gives me a manly hug and ambles back to his dark and empty mansion on the hill.

The Wolf is bending his tall frame into a crouch on the top platform of a fire escape. His brow is furrowed as he looks across the river at the boats on the other side of the pedestrian bridge. A small pair of binoculars is hanging on a cord around his neck and he lifts them to his eyes. There is no sign of any people, but the interior lights of three boats are creating reflections on the smooth surface of the black water. He registers that the smallest white boat, the one with the young couple on, has gone. One down, four to go. Once more, he craves a cigarette but, wary of being spotted on his high vantage point, he will wait until he is back at ground level. Wolves are good at waiting, he thinks. Good at waiting and then pouncing with extreme violence. The Wolf label suits him. He had been given it because of his lupine appearance – high cheekbones, long straight nose, flaring nostrils, coal-black eyes. But it had stuck because it captured his particular way of fighting.

He remembers 1993, in the mountains of Bosnia and Herzegovina. He had been leading a small group of elite soldiers for Karadzic as they tried to secure ethnic Serbian territory. The enemy had eluded his wolfpack for several weeks and so he had simply changed tactics and allowed them to come to him. He had waited patiently for ten days with his men in the freezing high-altitude temperatures above a pass in the mountains. And, eventually, they had come. Like lambs to the slaughter. Not one man or boy had been allowed to survive the ambush and some of them took a long time to die. Yes, he thinks to himself. I know how to wait. And I know how to strike. He had been paid well to strike many times since. In Russia and beyond. The man Powell had upset the wrong people and the Wolf had been the agent of their vengeance.

He remains crouched and motionless on his platform for half an hour, his binoculars trained on the boats below. As he stands to go, he turns to his left and sees movement behind the side window of the top flat in the building opposite him. He shrinks back into the darkness but keeps watching from under his hooded eyes. The white hair of a dark-skinned old woman shines in the darkness. She is gripping the end of a telescopic lens in both hands. It seems to be angled downwards, towards the river and the boats. Then he watches as she walks with difficulty over to close some wooden-slatted shutters behind the window facing him on the side of her apartment. He stretches thoughtfully and makes his way silently back down the metal fire-escape to ground level.

CHAPTER SEVENTEEN

The following morning, Nina and I give Eddie a quick run in the park, lock him on board *Jumping Jack Flash* and set off for our interview with Mrs Powell. But first we take a detour to see how Linda is faring. It is just after nine-thirty when we get to Victoria Bridge. Linda is on the stern platform of *Maid of Coventry*, cleaning Noah's rescued buggy with a scrubbing brush and a bucket of soapy water. The sound of the children playing drifts up from inside the boat. Nina gives Linda a kiss and I give her a hug. She wipes a soapy forearm across her tired-looking eyes.

'How are you, Linda?' asks Nina.

'All the better for a night's sleep – although it took me ages to get the kids off. They were worried we'd go adrift again in the night, poor lambs. And Angus, their kitten, has gone missing, so they've been consoling themselves with your teddy bears this morning. I haven't seen him since before we drifted. He could be hiding, but I'm worried he may have been bumped off the boat when we hit the bridge yesterday. I was a bit sleepless myself, so I put some of the kitten's bells on the mooring ropes and opened a window just to reassure myself in case anyone tried to mess with them again. But I got to sleep in the end.'

I look across at the mooring pins and sure enough, a small chain of little bells has been twined around the rope. Linda shakes herself.

'So, thanks for asking, but I'm tired, grateful and bloody angry all at the same time.' She looks directly at Nina. 'But we would have gone over the weir if you hadn't jumped down onto my roof, Nina. It was very brave. I'm so grateful to you.' She holds both of Nina's hands in hers and squeezes them. She is still holding them when she turns to me. 'And to Danny and Tammy. Danny did brilliantly to get my engine going. But I am so bloody furious that someone did this. With Noah and Juno on board? What could they have been thinking?' Tears well up in her eyes and Nina moves in to give her another hug.

'I see Fred and Esther's boat has gone,' I say awkwardly.

Linda disentangles herself from Nina and pushes a hand through her hair. 'Yeah, they slipped away yesterday teatime. Can't blame them I suppose, after what happened.' We all look up at the residents' signs. There are no more of them, but they look as malignant as ever.

I leave Nina with Linda and wander over to *Nautilus*. The professor is pottering in his galley when I call down through the boat.

'Jack!' he calls back cheerfully. 'Is Nina with you? Would you like some coffee?'

'No, thanks,' I say, moving down through the library to join him. 'I've got to do an interview for the *Chronicle* at eleven o'clock with Rufus Powell's widow. I was wondering... do you think what happened to Linda's boat is connected with the loss of your chimney and Linda's pushchair?'

The professor waves a hand dismissively. 'As I said before, kids. Minor vandalism. Annoying but there it is. Hardly something new. Comes with the territory.'

'You mean this has happened before?'

'Happens all the time,' he replies. 'There's always some petty crime along the river. We're just too tempting a target for some people. Although, untying boats is bloody dangerous, of course. But whoever did it probably just didn't think through the consequences.'

'So what else has happened recently?'

'Oh... let me see,' he says as he pushes the plunger down on the cafetiere. 'Danny had a lifebuoy thrown in the water a couple of weeks ago, but it got snagged up at the weir and he got it back. And I think he also had a fishing rod stolen. Linda had a few little plastic chairs on her roof for the children, but they disappeared. I'm afraid it just happens. I don't think Bill has lost anything – but then he's got that huge tarpaulin wrapped around his boat. I don't store anything on the roof. It's annoying about the chimney, but not the end of the world. That reminds me, I must get around to ordering another one before the weather turns. I'll need the stove working by the autumn.'

Much as I admire the old man's stoicism, I can't help wondering whether this spate of theft and vandalism might also be connected with the setting adrift of *Maid of Coventry* – and whether it really is just the work of local louts. Could it be part of a co-ordinated campaign of harassment and intimidation?

Anxious not to be late for Mrs Powell, I collect Nina and we head off to St James's Square. It is the only complete Georgian square in Bath and one of my favourite places in the city, quiet and slightly hidden behind the extravagant grandeur of the Royal Crescent. It would be number one on my list of land-locked places to live if I ever found myself with a few million pounds to spare. The forty-five Grade 1 listed buildings that surround the four sides of the central green were built in 1793. I always make a point of looking out for number 35, which was once the home of Charles Dickens, another journalist, like Hemingway, who did pretty well for himself as a novelist.

Nina produces a comb and makes me drag it through my curls. She flicks a collar back under my jacket and tuts at the unpolished state of my dusty and rarely used brogues. There is no unsightly electric bell to spoil the glossy black-painted splendour of the front door, and so I lift a heavy brass lion's head and let it bang down three times.

It is a rare journalist who enjoys the so-called 'death knock' and I know many cub reporters have contemplated going back to the office and lying that no one had been in when they called. You never knew what kind of reception you would get – an angry swear word and a door slammed in your face, incoherence and grief-wracked tears, or a courteous invitation to tea and shared memories. This time, at least, I know I am expected.

The door is opened by a slender, elegant woman who is only a few inches shorter than me. She is wearing a brown and white polka dot dress that is gathered by a belt at the waist. Her eyes crinkle above prominent cheekbones as she examines us. There is the slightest blush of rouge on her cheeks and she smells of expensive perfume.

'Mr Johnson?' she asks in a well-spoken and slightly husky voice. 'I'm Jennifer Powell.' We shake hands. I introduce Nina as Angelina Wilde and explain that she is here to take a photograph of the two of us.

'Yes. Your editor asked me if that would be all right.' She shakes Nina's hand and then turns to stride down her hallway with us following. The house feels oppressively cloistered and silent, as though it too is in mourning. The loud tick-tock of a beautiful old grandfather clock in the hall is unmuffled on the wide oak floorboards, which gleam with the polish of ages in spite of the gloom. We follow Mrs Powell into a sitting room at the rear of the house that smells of beeswax and lavender. A small chandelier is suspended from a rose in the centre of the high ceiling and a collection of oil and watercolour landscapes hang from a picture rail that goes around all four walls at head height. The antique furniture, the small side tables and the fireplace are immaculately tasteful and in keeping with the age of the house. A huge display of white lilies erupts out of a crystal vase in the middle of a mahogany drum table.

'Please,' Mrs Powell says, pointing to a small settee, embroidered in blue and yellow silk. She takes a chair opposite, crossing her ankles and moving her knees together and positioning them elegantly to one side. She waves vaguely at a jug of coffee with cups and saucers on a small table between us. 'Do help yourself. I made it on the assumption that you would arrive promptly and thankfully you did. It's still hot.'

I pour three cups and distribute them.

'Firstly, Mrs Powell, I would like to say how sorry I am – we all are – about your husband's death.'

She nods in acknowledgement but doesn't say anything. A piano begins to be played in another part of the house; upstairs, I think.

I don't recognise the music, but it is classical and unbearably sad. Mrs Powell's mouth forms a *moue* of annoyance.

'Our daughter,' she explains. 'Arabella is sixteen and was very close to her father. They are very similar. They were very similar.' She looks at Nina and the door. 'Perhaps you would be good enough?'

Nina moves to the door, closes it gently and returns to her seat alongside me. The piano notes are now muffled, but can still just about be heard. And then, without a single question from me, Mrs Powell begins to speak.

'Rufus and I married when he was thirty and I was just twenty. I was a temporary secretary at his architectural practice and he rather swept me off my feet. My parents thought it was a super match. He was a single child who lost both parents when he was young and so he was independently wealthy. He quickly made a name for himself as a specialist on historic buildings and he was already well connected with many of the families who owned or ran them in London. The business thrived, but he retained complete ownership in spite of many offers. He always refused to contemplate having any business partners. He wouldn't compromise on having complete control of the company. And then, on the day before he was sixty, he came home and announced that he was going to sell up. He had talked about retiring to Bath all his life and so there was no debate or discussion. Rufus was very decisive about everything. We sold our home in Chelsea and moved here, to St James's Square.'

I am scribbling furiously in an attempt to keep pace. It's a long time since my shorthand was one hundred words a minute.

'Arabella adjusted very well to the change of school and I picked up some new charities to support and some new partners for bridge. Rufus, however, became quite bored rather quickly – even though he continued to sit on the bench as a magistrate in Bath. He had been a Justice of the Peace in London for quite a long time and, of course, his experience in the capital meant that he was quickly asked to act as a senior magistrate down here. Anyway, it wasn't enough to keep him occupied so that's when he threw himself into the work of the Georgian Fellowship. He was very critical of some of Bath's more modern buildings and he was determined to do what he could to protect the city's heritage.'

She pauses to sip some coffee and I take the opportunity to get out my phone.

'Do you mind if I record you on this?' I ask apologetically. 'My shorthand is a bit rusty.'

She wafts a manicured hand in acquiescence and continues. It is clear that she has thought through precisely what she is going to say to us in advance and will not be easily side-tracked.

'He was quickly acclaimed as the Fellowship's vice-president and then president. He had the real expertise, don't you see? And he had the time and inclination to devote himself to it. He always used to tell me that there would be no carbuncles built in Bath on his watch.'

'So, he wasn't afraid of a fight?'

'Rufus wasn't afraid of anything or anybody. He felt he had a higher duty to do all in his power to maintain the standards of the city's founding fathers. He had no time for anyone who wanted to take shabby shortcuts or who was dominated by petty commercial considerations.'

'And he was at a Fellowship dinner on the night of his death?' I prompt.

'He was,' she says. 'I was due to go with him, but I had one of my migraines. It's very troubling for me to know that if I had been there, he might still be alive now.' She stares unblinkingly, as if challenging me to disagree. 'If Rufus was out late, he would usually sleep in a spare room or on the day bed in his study in order not to disturb me and so I wasn't aware that he hadn't come home until the following morning – when the police officers came to the door.'

'Why do you think he was killed?' It is a blunt question, but I calculate that Mrs Powell is more than capable of fielding it.

'The police believe someone may have tried to rob him on the way home and it all went terribly wrong.'

'Is that what you believe?' I ask quietly.

'He is dead,' she says with a shrug. 'In the end, that is what matters. Rufus could have lived for another twenty or thirty years. He was fit and healthy and he had a real purpose to his life. Instead, it seems that someone may have killed him for a few pounds and a mobile phone.'

'My editor...' I begin. I am unwilling to go down this path, but I have made a deal. 'My editor believes your husband may have been the victim of some kind of... madman. A serial killer, perhaps, someone who may be copying the Midlands Canal Pusher.'

'Yes, Mr Mockett mentioned that on the telephone. And I believe you have written a book about this man – what was his name, Keith Tomlinson?'

I nod.

'It's possible, I suppose, but it seems highly unlikely to me. The missing wallet and phone would seem to speak for themselves and I am unaware of there being a spate of similar deaths or drownings on the canal or river here.'

I send up an unspoken prayer of thanks for the thoughtful composure and common sense of Mr Powell's widow.

'I also understand that the police are looking back over my husband's caseload as a magistrate. They need to rule out any connection with someone who may have come up before him. Someone who perhaps picked him out for revenge. A convicted thief or violent person, perhaps.'

Interesting. This is a fresh angle for me. 'Anyone in particular?' I ask.

'If there is, they haven't told me. No,' she adds briskly, 'this is all speculation. I am sure the police will do their work properly. My main aim in agreeing to this interview is to put on record how passionately my husband felt about the importance of his work for the Georgian Fellowship and this wonderful city, and how much he will be missed as a loyal husband and a loving father.'

'Was he working on anything in particular before his death?'

'Oh, Rufus always had something on. He was particularly interested in the old Tiller & Brown site on the River Avon.'

Nina and I exchange looks as Mrs Powell continues. 'He said it was one of the very last opportunities for a very sizeable development in the city. He was extremely interested in what was going to be proposed by the new owners of the site.'

'No plans have been announced or submitted yet,' observes Nina.

'Rufus wielded considerable influence,' she smiles with satisfaction, 'and so, of course, they gave him a private briefing.'

'Who did?' I ask quickly.

'The people who have bought the site. They sound most intriguing. Rufus was invited to their offices in London. They sent a chauffeur-driven car to collect him from the house and they took him to The Wolseley for lunch. He entertained Arabella and me over dinner with an account of his day. It was all very amusing.'

'Amusing?'

'The buyers were identical twins, you see. Anthony and Sebastian, I think he said their names were. But he couldn't tell one from the other. He said they were identical in every detail, even down to their watches and cufflinks. He said it was quite extraordinary. He spent a few hours with them, but said he couldn't be sure who was who for the entire time he was with them!' She smiles faintly at the memory.

'And what about their plans? What did he think of them?'

'Oh, Rufus completely and utterly detested them. He said there was a scale model in their offices showing the proposed development, and that it was unspeakably inappropriate. I have no doubt he would have marshalled the Fellowship's resources against the plan.'

'When was this meeting?' I ask.

She moves to a walnut bureau, opens a drawer and pulls out a leather-bound diary.

'Let me see. Yes, two weeks before he died. The Fellowship meets monthly, so he was preparing to address the next meeting on the issue – that would be in another week or so.'

'Well,' I say, my mind reeling to take in this new information, 'I think we've got everything we need, Mrs Powell, unless there is anything else you would like to say?'

'Except the photo,' whispers Nina. I am still distracted by the dead man's reaction to the twins' plans.

'Oh yes, the photo. I was wondering if you might pose with your daughter?' I'm reluctant to play Ben's game by putting myself in the picture.

'Oh no. That was not what was agreed. The photograph is to be with you, I understand. The famous author.' She says the last few words with a hint of a condescending smile.

Nina makes way for Mrs Powell to replace her on the settee and we face each other, with me self-consciously balancing my notepad on my knee and Mrs Powell looking back at me with a calm and emotionless face. Nina takes a few shots of both of us and of Mrs Powell on her own, and then we stand to leave.

'You know, it's funny that the Tiller & Brown site should come up this morning,' Mrs Powell says as she ushers us into the hallway. 'I was just thinking over breakfast this morning that it's such a shame his speech will now go unheard.'

I stop so suddenly that she nearly careers into me. 'Speech?'

'Oh, yes. Rufus put great care into his President's Address for the Fellowship meetings. He often rehearsed it with me and Arabella in the evenings. He wanted to be word perfect.' I vaguely register that the piano has stopped, and I glimpse a slight movement at the top of the first flight of stairs. Mrs Powell is still speaking, 'Perhaps the *Chronicle* might still be interested in what he was going to say?'

'You bet,' I say. 'I mean, yes, of course, it will be an important part of his legacy.'

For the first time since we arrived on her doorstep, Mrs Powell looks genuinely moved. 'Bless you,' she says, putting one hand on my arm. 'Please, wait here just a moment.'

Nina and I exchange significant looks but remain silent. Mrs Powell returns quickly with a bundle of A4 paper.

'It's only a draft with some notes, of course, but it will give you the gist of the thing.'

I force myself not to take the papers out of her hand too quickly and we shake hands. 'One more question, Mrs Powell,' I say, standing on her doormat. 'Did you tell the police about this speech?'

She looks at me quizzically. 'Of course not. It's hardly relevant to his death, after all. Thank you for coming. Goodbye to you both.'

The door swings shut behind us and we walk down the elegant front garden to step out into the perfect square of houses.

'Bloody hell,' says Nina.

'Bloody hell indeed,' I echo.

CHAPTER EIGHTEEN

Nina and I walk back into Royal Victoria Park where we find an empty bench by the pond. I begin to read the speech and, as I finish each page, I pass it to Nina. There are ten pages of double-spaced text. The first half deals with routine Fellowship business, pays tribute to two members who have died and announces the recruitment process for their replacements. Powell goes on to update his colleagues on the progress of a number of planning applications that are being closely tracked by their organisation. Then he moves on to talk about the Tiller & Brown site.

'Ladies and gentlemen, I have to report that four weeks ago I was invited to London by Andropov Developments Ltd to be briefed on their outline plans for the old Tiller & Brown site on the south bank of the River Avon. As you all know, this site is now derelict. In many respects, it represents one of the last significant development opportunities of real size on the edge of Bath's historic city centre. Its importance simply cannot be overstated. This will be one of the largest and most important brownfield regeneration projects in the United Kingdom outside London. The eyes of the country will be upon us and, I am sorry to tell you, they will be as sorely disappointed as I was. I learnt, to my horror, that this company is intent on cramming more than 3,500 homes onto the site in the form of twenty tower blocks. I believe this to be far too many and I also believe that their design will be

a serious disappointment to those, like us, who wish to see the classical architectural principles of the Georgian era respected and echoed in what should be a showcase of outstanding craftsmanship and creative imagination. These discredited and dangerous modern forms of building will loom over our city and quickly deteriorate into an antisocial and alien part of our wonderful landscape.

Any development on this site needs to include more of the wonderful green parks and open spaces which are such a feature of our beautiful UNESCO World Heritage city. It also needs to provide new distinguished and shared public buildings, rather than an arid dormitory of boxes piled on top of each other. This may meet a short-term need for profit and more housing in this city, but it will be condemned as a dreadful wasted opportunity in the longer term. It will become nothing more than a high-rise ghetto.

My briefing, as your president, was in confidence and I am unable to share any further details with you. I was not allowed to remove any plans or images from the developers' offices. However, ladies and gentlemen, I have no hesitation in telling you, within the privacy of this meeting, that when these plans are finally submitted for formal planning approval, I shall be recommending that the Georgian Fellowship makes nothing less than a full-scale public declaration of war on them.'

'Wow!' says Nina, as she comes to the end of the last page. 'He doesn't pull his punches, does he?'

'No. It seems that Ben's got two stories for the price of one. But the real question is, does this have any possible connection with his death?'

'Well, Mrs Powell clearly didn't have much time for Ben's copycat serial killer theory.'

'Nope. Ben isn't going to be very happy with her comments about that.'

'And the police seem to think it might somehow be connected with his work as a magistrate,' adds Nina. 'That was interesting.'

'Yes – we're going to have to ask them about that. They certainly haven't mentioned that in public as a line of inquiry yet.'

'So, if that's the case, how could his death be connected with the Tiller & Brown site?'

'Think about it,' I say. 'Andropov Developments briefed Rufus Powell in confidence about their plans. The Andropov twins have already spent a fortune on buying the site and will need to spend another fortune to get planning permission and then build on it. But the potential profits on construction of an entirely new village of more than three thousand homes close to the centre of Bath will be enormous.'

Nina picks up the thread. 'So, the twins take the president of the Georgian Fellowship out for a swanky lunch to get him onside in advance.'

'And no doubt he tells them precisely what he thinks,' I continue. 'And thanks to that speech, we know exactly what he thinks from beyond the grave. Our friend Rufus Powell was obviously a pretty no-nonsense character. Two weeks later, he's whacked on the head and ends up in the river. A powerful potential voice of opposition to the scheme has been silenced before he's had a chance to go public. That's quite a coincidence and extremely helpful for Anthony and Sebastian Andropov.'

Nina shakes her head. 'It sounds even more, of a stretch than a copycat Canal Pusher. Surely no businessman would take the risk of murdering a magistrate? It would ruin them if it came out.'

'And it's not as though Rufus Powell had the power to stop the plans – just to campaign against them,' I add. We sit thinking in a bubble of our own silence for a moment amid the shouts and laughter of the park-goers.

'But if the residents' campaign against the boat people has somehow been engineered by the twins,' Nina muses, 'they're obviously pretty ruthless about getting their own way.'

'Maybe,' I say. 'But we don't have any proof they're behind that. And they're offering quite large sums of money to the boat people too. Maybe Claverton's campaign really is unconnected with them.'

'So, they're really nice rational businessmen making nice rational decisions?' asks Nina.

I shrug. 'Which brings us back to the reason for Powell's death.'

'Assuming there is one.'

'Well, of course, there has to be a reason – but it could just be a simple one. A random robbery that went wrong.'

'You mean we're over-complicating things?'

'Seeing conspiracies where there are none...'

'And why would the twins invest all these millions of pounds and then risk exposing themselves as ruthless gangsters and ruining it all?' Nina says. 'You're right. It doesn't make sense.'

I gather together the pages of Powell's speech. 'Unless it makes sense precisely *because* so much is at stake. I think we're going to have to try to meet the Andropov twins and find out precisely what kind of people they are.'

We need to get back to the boat to let Eddie out. But as we pass the grand columned entrance of Bath Guildhall, I spot the Statue of Justice on the tall pedimented facade of the building. It jolts me with a sudden idea. The Guildhall is the home of Bath Council, the local planning authority. I tug Nina through the main door, which is flanked by ornate iron railings and old-fashioned lamps.

'What are you doing? Where are we going?'

'We're going fishing,' I say with a grin.

The receptionist sniffs and is less than welcoming when I present my press card and ask to see the council's chief planning officer. She directs us along a corridor and up some stairs to the planning department. Another receptionist, who probably went to the same charm school, is sitting behind a desk in a wide hallway with tall high-backed chairs ranged along its length. I repeat my request and give her my card.

'Can I ask what it is in connection with?' she asks frostily.

'The old Tiller & Brown site.'

'Please take a seat.' We move down the hallway and perch on two adjoining seats made of faux leather with the council's crest on their back-rests. I watch the receptionist talking on her phone. She hangs up and shortly afterwards a trim young man in a slim-cut two-piece suit appears. We are pointed out and he advances towards us.

'You're from the *Chronicle* and you want to speak to Mrs Wilkinson?' he asks. 'I'm her PA.'

'That's correct, if Mrs Wilkinson is the head of planning.'

'It's about the old Tiller & Brown site?' he asks crisply.

'It is.'

'Well, we haven't had any planning application for the site yet so there's nothing really to talk about,' he says. 'And Mrs Wilkinson isn't available right now. I'm sorry, but I'm afraid you'll need to make an appointment.'

The young man doesn't look very sorry, but I've learnt from experience to try to stay on the right side of any bureaucracy's secretariat. 'Of course. Well, I'd still like a little chat with her, so can you have a look at her diary please?' I ask sweetly.

The PA frowns in obvious irritation. 'Just a minute, please.' He walks briskly back down the hallway and disappears through the door behind the receptionist.

'At least he said please,' I mutter. Ten minutes pass. Nina gets restless and starts wandering down the hallway, examining photographs of the current crop of councillors and senior council managers. She points to one photograph in particular and pulls a face at me. I walk over and see it is Robin Claverton, the councillor we tangled with in the park and the scourge of our boat friends. The newness of the photograph suggests that he has been elected relatively recently. Eventually, Mrs Wilkinson's PA reappears and I see he is holding an electronic tablet against the narrow lapels of his jacket.

'As I said, Mrs Wilkinson doesn't see any point in talking to the *Chronicle* when we haven't had a planning application for the site.'

'But she wasn't too busy for you to check if she would see me?' I say. The PA bristles but I persevere, 'Look, is she really saying she won't see me at all? That she won't talk to her local paper, *The Chronicle*?'

'I didn't say that, did I?' he snaps. 'I just said she doesn't see much point in it. Please follow me.'

We follow him to the receptionist's desk and I muse how difficult it must be to get such narrow trousers on in the morning. No doubt the socks are a concession to his workplace and bare ankles are his more usual look. He moves behind the desk, alongside the department's receptionist, exchanges a tut of frustration with her and puts the tablet on the desk. He prods its screen until a diary appears and then swipes it forward onto the following week. It has spaces for seven days spread out across two virtual pages and I can see there are already appointments scheduled on most of them.

'She might be able to see you early on Tuesday afternoon next week,' he says grudgingly. 'Just for half an hour.'

I take out my own phone and pretend to consult my own empty calendar as I lean forward, eyes down. 'Yes. I could do that,' I say eventually. 'That would be wonderful. Thank you very much. It's really, really appreciated.'

He raises one eyebrow, unsure if I am being sarcastic or not. Then he bends forward to type a time and transfers my name from my card into the tablet. Then he straightens and hands the card back to me without returning my smile. 'Two o'clock on Tuesday then, Mr Johnson. Goodbye.'

His brusqueness is carefully judged to be just the right side of efficient rather than rude. We take our time leaving the hallway as I repeat Nina's exercise and scrutinise the head-and-shoulders photographs of the councillors and senior council managers. I particularly search out Councillor Laurence Merton, who is labelled as chair of the planning committee, and the chief planning officer, Mrs Gwyneth Wilkinson, before we move out onto the street.

'Hang on a minute,' I tell Nina as she begins to set off towards Pulteney Bridge. 'I need to write something down.' She watches as I pull out my notebook and write 'Monday. 1 p.m. Saltford Golf Club. Merton and Wilkinson.'

'But your appointment is on Tuesday at two,' she says in a puzzled voice.

I put away my notebook. Like all competent journalists, I have the facility to read upside-down writing and I'd taken full advantage of it.

'And I've just learnt that Mrs Gwyneth Wilkinson, who runs the planning department, and her boss Councillor Laurence Merton, who is chair of the planning committee, are having lunch with a Mr Sebastian Andropov at a local golf club next Monday.'

Nina grins and gives me a high five. Then she goes and spoils it by saying, 'You know, you ought to be a journalist.'

'Now I wonder what business they will be discussing!' I say.

Nina links one arm through mine and we head back to Eddie and the boat in good spirits.

CHAPTER NINETEEN

Vince Porlock takes a swallow of rum out of his pint glass and looks through half-closed eyes at the others sitting at the table in the Archangel's backroom. Adolph, the large German Shepherd belonging to Mad John, his sergeant-at-arms, is stretched across the doorway so that anyone daring to disturb them will have to step over the dog very carefully. Everyone who is there for the lunchtime war council is a senior Full-Patch member of the Bristol Bulldogs. Vince has known them all for years and they trust him with their lives. He trusts them too, up to a point. Bob-the-Prospect is standing guard on the other side of the door. A metal baseball bat is leaning against the doorframe next to him and he has a small wood-chopping axe tucked into the back of his leather biker trousers. He has been told in no uncertain terms that Vince's inner circle do not want to be disturbed.

'Well?' growls Vince. 'What have you got for me?'

The others exchange worried glances. The Big Man has a suspicious mind and a short temper. Retribution has been swift and violent over the years on any member of the chapter who lets him down. He might be aging, fat and lame, but he has plenty who will do his bidding without question. Vince Porlock operates at the top of a rigid hierarchy. They also know he can call on serious sums of money that he has cannily accumulated over the years if he needs to.

Mad John takes off his mirror aviator sunglasses, smears them further on a beer towel and replaces them quickly. He always wears them, inside and outside, to hide his cross-eyes, the result of a pub brawl in the Cotswolds when they had been knocked out of their sockets.

'I've had a good chat with all the lads,' he says, shrugging apologetically. 'But no one is coughing to it, Vince.' One hand drops down to his side where it nervously rubs the handle of a woven leather bull-whip. He carries it mainly as a symbol of his rank and status as the Big Man's number two, but it has been used occasionally during bouts of rough-house bullying of the Prospects. Just for fun.

Vince turns to look at a younger man sitting on Mad John's left. He has 'Wild Child' tattooed across his throat and his head is shaven, in contrast to the others at the table who wear their hair long and with untrimmed beards. 'Did you talk to Clive, like I said?'

Wild Child leans forward and puts both his hands flat on the table, either side of Vince's walking stick. He is wearing two leather wristbands with pointed metal studs on them. 'I rang him last night like you said, Vince. He says he honestly doesn't have a fucking clue who hit the guy in Bath. Says the first he heard about it was when he was taken out of the prison canteen to be questioned. Straight up.'

'D'you believe him?' asks Vince. His eyes are fixed like lasers on Wild Child. He knows the man is a good friend of his son and suspects that if The Idiot has done something really stupid, then Wild Child would know about it.

Wild Child judges his response carefully. If he's proved to be wrong, he knows the Big Man will remember this exchange and suspect him of double-dealing. He looks Vince firmly in his cunning, piggy little eyes for long enough to hope he will be believed. 'Yeah, I think so. Clive'll be out in just a few months. It's not like he went down for life or nothing.'

Snakebite, an older man with a bushy red beard on the opposite side of the table, chips in. 'And if he did order it from inside, there'd be whispers. We'd soon hear who did it – and how much he paid them for the job.'

'Unless...' says Vince. 'Unless he got someone outside the Bulldogs to do it.' There is a momentary silence while they take this in. Would Clive really do that?

'He wouldn't dare,' says Mad John. Adolph gives a low growl, seemingly in agreement.

Vince raps the handle of his stick down on the table. 'The CCTV pictures show there was a biker there. Our marker was left on the bridge. Fresh paint, the cops said. So did someone outside the family do the job? Someone Clive knows from another chapter?'

'He wouldn't do that,' says Wild Child automatically.

'All right – maybe he wouldn't,' says Vince, who privately also wonders how The Idiot would have paid for such a hit. The Big Man deliberately keeps his son on a tight financial lead. 'So, if it's not him, is someone else fucking about with us? Pretending to be us?'

'Causing a bit of mayhem?' asks Mad John.

'But who?' asks Snakebite. They all know that the other gangs operating in Bristol are largely based on racial groupings – mainly the Blacks, the Chinese and the Eastern Europeans. But it doesn't ring true. The city's gang scene has been pretty peaceful and profitable in recent years. They have even worked together on some projects, when Vince felt he had something to gain from it. Gang warfare and violent rivalry was expensive and a distraction and, by and large, Vince chose to steer clear of it whilst also developing good connections with other Hells Angels' gangs across the country.

The fifth man at the table clears his throat, removes a wad of chewing gum from his mouth and rolls the sticky globule slowly between a thumb and forefinger. He is roughly the same age as the Big Man and wears a similar denim waistcoat with Death's Head badges stitched on both sides. They all turn to him. He rarely speaks but when he does, the others listen to him with respect. Uncle Mick is one of Vince's most long-serving and trusted lieutenants.

'Seems to me,' he says in his strong Bristol accent, 'that we need someone over there, asking a few questions of our own.'

Vince nods approvingly, his chins wobbling vigorously in the process. 'Who?'

The Big Man, Mad John, Snakebite and Wild Child all look at Uncle Mick again, who bares his yellowing teeth in a grin. 'It'll need to be someone who don't necessarily look like a Bulldog. Someone who can pretty themselves up a bit and go unnoticed among the civilians.'

Vince looks at Uncle Mick and then at Wild Child. 'Get Bob-the-Prospect in here now.'

CHAPTER TWENTY

That afternoon, Nina takes Eddie off for a ten-mile run along the canal path to the Dundas Aqueduct and back while I head below to meet my deadline. The interview with Mrs Powell virtually writes itself. I listen back to her firm, calm voice coming through the speaker on my phone and marvel at her articulacy and resilience. I dutifully include her comment on the copycat Pusher theory, and I know that Ben will be frustrated by her lukewarm response and suspicious that I am behind it. At the end, I include the following paragraph:

'Mrs Powell says her late husband had been preparing for the next meeting of the Georgian Fellowship when he died. It is understood that he was going to announce his fierce opposition to plans by Andropov Developments Ltd for a huge high-rise housing estate of 3,500 homes to be built on the derelict Tiller & Brown site on the south bank of the River Avon. No plans have yet been formally submitted to Bath Council.'

Nina returns with Eddie just as I am attaching the article to an email. I send it off to Ben along with Nina's photographs of Mrs Powell and me, plus a recommendation that he considers running the last paragraph as an expanded story with a reaction from Andropov Developments if they will give him one. I also suggest he finds the space to run the full text of Powell's intended speech to the Georgian Fellowship. I still need to write up the boat campaign story but decide to take a break and go up onto the stern platform where Eddie is lying, still panting heavily. Nina takes a shower, makes two mugs of tea and joins me by the tiller.

'Story done?' she asks.

'I've finished the Powell interview. Got to do the residents' campaign story next.'

'Won't you need to get a few quotes from them?'

I nod. 'And some photographs. And I'll need to speak to Claverton again, if I can. If not, I'll quote his pamphlet. But I'll have to keep it tight. It's print day tomorrow. The paper will be filling up fast and I can't see Ben giving it a huge amount of space anyway.'

There's a cheery greeting from the other bank just as I finish speaking. We look across and see Danny and Tammy on the canal path. Danny is waving enthusiastically while Tammy, as usual, looks awkward and sulky.

'I persuaded Tammy to come for a walk to see your boat,' calls Danny happily.

'Wait there, I'll come and fetch you,' calls Nina. She shoots off up the garden, slips through the side passageway and quickly appears on the opposite bank where she greets the pair and shows them the way back to our boat. Danny pumps my hand while Tammy just raises hers weakly and mutters, 'Hi.'

I give them the guided tour around *Jumping Jack Flash* and Danny is as full of praise as Tammy is silent. I notice, however, that she has picked Eddie up. She is carrying him around carefully and nuzzling the nape of his neck with her stud-pierced nose and whispering something quietly in his ear. Nina notices this too and I tilt my head sideways at her. She gets the message instantly.

'Tammy, why don't we leave the blokes to their boat talk and take Eddie up to Sydney Gardens? I expect he'd like to share an ice cream after his run.'

Tammy thinks for a moment and then whispers, 'Okay.' She heads off out of the boat with Nina following closely behind.

'Beer, Danny?' I ask.

'Thanks very much, Jack. She's a lovely looking boat, so she is. Nearly as nice as *Nautilus*.'

This is a massive exaggeration, but I let it pass and Danny squeezes his considerable bulk into a chair opposite me while I prise the caps off two bottles of Bath Gem ale and place them between us.

'How's Linda?' I ask.

Danny looks solemn and takes a swig from the bottle.

'Not so good really. That crash into the bridge really knocked the stuffing out of her. One minute she's angry and the next she's crying. She isn't worried about herself but she's terrified that the kids could have been hurt – or worse.'

'I'm glad you're here,' I tell him. 'I think I've persuaded the *Chronicle* to carry a story about the residents' campaign against you. I'm going to write it. I hope the story of Linda and the children's narrow escape will attract some sympathy and make some of the residents, or even Robin Claverton, reconsider what they're stirring up.'

Danny nods slowly, thinking this through.

'I don't suppose it'll hurt. But you should see what Linda, the professor and Bill think first.'

'I'll pop round and see them this evening,' I say. We then spend a couple of minutes agreeing a quote from Danny that he is happy with. But he is much more comfortable chatting about narrowboats and boat trips he has made in the past. I learn that Danny's wife died of a brain haemorrhage five years ago. Without his wife's salary, he could no longer afford a mortgage and so he had sold up, bought a boat with the modest profit and his wife's life insurance, and taken Tammy onto the water.

'All the money went on the boat,' explains Danny. 'And every time we tried to stay somewhere long enough for Tammy to go to school and me to get a job, they kept moving us on. We couldn't afford a marina.'

'So how did you afford the mooring on the Avon?' I ask, genuinely puzzled.

Danny takes another large swig of beer from the bottle. 'Ah well, you see we had a stroke of luck. We'd travelled down the Severn to

145

Sharpness and I found a few weeks of work unloading and loading boats in the docks. Then I followed a boat with a pilot across the Bristol Channel. Scared me witless, it did, specially with Tammy aboard. But we got to the Avon and made our way into Bristol. I thought there'd be a bit of work there. Well, we found a temporary mooring on a pontoon near Prince Street Bridge and bugger me, as soon as we tied up this lawyer appeared. Mr Heath, he was called. Well, it turned out he'd been tracking me across the country because my wife's mother had died. She'd left her bungalow in her will to her daughters, and so some of the money was due to Tammy now. She always had a soft spot for me and Tammy, so she did.'

I clinked his bottle with mine at the news of his good fortune.

'Well, after expenses and all that we had thirty thousand in the bank. Thirty thousand pounds!' Danny clearly thought of this as a miracle windfall, and even now, could barely believe his luck. 'We headed up the river and fetched up alongside the professor just as he was doing the deal with Tiller & Brown. So of course, I handed over twenty grand for the mooring of a lifetime.'

'It was a bargain, Danny.'

'Aye, it was. I was at the end of my tether, Jack, I can tell you. Tammy was fed up living on the boat and being moved on all the time. Every new place we went, the other kids called her a water gypsy and they were nasty to her. We've been happy for the past two years.'

I reflect to myself that Tammy seems far from happy now, but perhaps it's just the usual angst of adolescence.

'Course, the rest of the money didn't last very long,' he adds sadly. 'But I've got a few locals who use me for odd jobs, gutter cleaning and lawn mowing and that kind of thing. But we can stay in Bath for as long as we want. I know Tammy won't want to live with her old dad on the boat for ever. It gets her down a bit.' He squares his chin. 'But I know that if we're settled here, then she has the best chance to get settled on her own – or set up with a nice fella, maybe. So, there's not a cat in hell's chance that we'll be taking that money and shipping out. Not a chance. And we've got our friends, Linda and the professor and Bill. And now you and Nina. It's a shame Fred and Esther chose to go, though.'

I'm not quite sure how to respond to all this. Danny has an almost childlike simplicity and faith in others which, I suspect, is at odds with Tammy's view of life – particularly if she has had such a troubled childhood, losing her mother at a young age, being relentlessly bullied, living in the squalor of the *Otter* and being perpetually so short of cash that she can't enjoy the same things as other girls of her age. It must be lonely for her.

'Er, maybe we should go and see what Nina and Tammy are up to?'

Danny readily agrees so I push another bottle of beer into his hand and we stroll up to Sydney Gardens, where we discover Eddie having the time of his life. He is chasing his red rubber ball along the ground as the two women catch and roll it quickly between them. You would think he'd be exhausted by his ten-mile run with Nina, but the little dog seems to have limitless supplies of energy. He is yapping with excitement and for the first time since we have met her I see Tammy grinning and laughing. At one stage, Eddie leaps up into her arms as the ball hits a bump and bounces high at the last minute. She catches him and rolls backwards onto the ground with a shriek. I notice she is careful to shield him from being hurt when she lands and makes a big fuss of him afterwards. Nina sees us watching, sipping our beers, and runs over.

'Just in time, Mr Johnson. I'm knackered, even if Eddie isn't.' She takes my half-full bottle from me and I take over from Nina while she sits on the bench with Danny. However, Tammy clearly enjoys the game far less with me at the other end and deliberately contrives to let Eddie catch the ball halfway between us and run off with it into some bushes. I know from bitter experience that the terrier in him will now hope to retain it for as long as possible. Even better if he can persuade me to indulge in a fierce head-shaking tug-of-war for it. So, I decide to abandon the game and approach Tammy.

'He was really enjoying that,' I say enthusiastically. 'Thanks, Tammy. Would you like a dog of your own one day?'

Her jet-black fringe hangs down across her eyes as she dips her head awkwardly. 'Dad says we can't afford to feed one,' she says quietly, before slouching back to Nina and her father's bench. Once again, it seems, I have failed in my efforts at intergenerational communication.

I rejoin the others and agree to walk back to the Victoria Bridge moorings with Danny and Tammy, because I need to wrap up the second article for the *Chronicle*. Nina will take Eddie back to *Jumping Jack Flash* and do some cooking. Nina enjoys good food, especially when someone else is at the stove, but whilst I slavishly follow complex recipes, she is much more creative and produces delicious meals without resorting to other people's instructions. Tammy vanishes at some stage on our walk back. One second, she was trailing along behind Danny and me and the next she was gone. This is obviously a familiar trait and Danny doesn't seem at all bothered by her sudden absence. I mention to him that Tammy is great with Eddie.

'Aye well, she'd like her own dog. But she wants a lot of things, does our Tammy. She wanted to stop changing places all the time, and now she wants me to take the money and move on. She wants a dog and a new smartphone and even a laptop. But we all need to live within our means, don't we? She needs to find a job now she's finished school – but she doesn't want to do that.' Danny's voice is full of bewildered frustration.

After we arrive, I call on Linda. The children tell me there is still no sign of their missing kitten. However, their mother is happy to go along with an article for the *Chronicle* and so we quickly agree a few quotes about the banners. She seems much more cheerful at the prospect of 'fighting back' as she describes it. I take a photograph of Linda with Noah and Juno in front of *Maid of Coventry*. The children don't understand why I don't want them to be smiling in the picture and they look worried until their mother bribes them with a sweet each to look serious. Then I head to *Nautilus*.

The professor is reading a novel in his library but puts it down and courteously makes me welcome. I explain why I have called, and we jointly produce a quote for him.

'Now before you go, I have something for you to try,' he says with a chuckle. 'I called into Great Western Wine to pick up a special order. I'm afraid I have rather indulged myself.' He opens a small side cupboard, pulls out a bottle and hands it to me. It is a Highland Park. I am familiar with the distinctive broad-shouldered shape of its bottle and its rich smoky taste because I once visited its distillery at Kirkwall on Orkney. However, I notice with surprise the label: AGED 40 YEARS. I have only ever enjoyed the eighteen-year-old Highland Park before. I have been tempted once or twice to buy the twenty-one-year-old, but backed off, and I just laughed at the price of a thirty-year-old. I have never even *seen* the forty-year-old before. It has a metal motif embedded into the side of the bottle with an 'H' inside a Celtic-looking triangular shape.

'I need a favour,' says the professor. 'And one or two glasses of this exceptional whisky is the fee.'

'I don't care what kind of favour you need doing,' I say. 'It's a deal.'

He chuckles to himself and fetches two glasses with tapered rims above flat bowl-shaped bottoms. Then he opens a small and well-worn leather notebook and flicks through it. 'I've had this only once before,' he says. 'Ah, here it is.' He uses a forefinger to run down some handwritten notes. 'Goodness me, I was just... let me see... yes, just fifty when I last tasted it. Whiskies like this are wasted on the young – present company excepted, of course.'

The professor decides this is the perfect moment to prise the cork from the bottle and he carefully pours some of its golden contents into both glasses. We inhale deeply. It is surprisingly delicate. 'Chocolate?' asks the professor.

'Honey?' I ask in reply. He adds a little water from a glass jug and we both roll the whisky around in our mouths. I had once been told to give at least as many seconds for this part of the process as the whisky has been ageing for in years, but it would be crass to look at my watch and check when forty seconds had expired.

'Mmm...' says the professor eventually. 'Profound. Quite profound.'

'It's sensational,' I say, slightly hoarsely, 'and very complicated.'

'You're right,' says the professor, scribbling something new in his notebook. 'I can't detect any particularly dominant element. But it is wonderful.'

We then give due attention to the lingering after-taste. The finish on this little beauty is more heather-honey sweetness and then there is a final hint of soft smoke.

'Nina will kill me when she hears about this,' I say, eyeing my glass greedily.

'Oh, my boy. She is so delightfully gamine. So utterly charming. And she seems to be very fond of you.'

'But not fond enough,' I say sadly, and immediately regret the spirit-induced indiscretion of the moment. The professor puts a hand on my arm.

'Hmmm... just as I thought. You must give her time. She's worth it.'

'I know,' I say. 'Thank you.'

It would be sacrilege to chat further in the presence of such nectar-of-the-gods and so we sit quietly, appreciating every drop of the special dram. Without asking, the professor leans forward to refill our glasses and adds a further splash of water.

'This is a bottle every whisky lover should try before he dies,' says the professor, holding it up to the light from a porthole. 'Not that I have any intention of doing so imminently. Thank you for not asking its price, Jack. That shows a particular delicacy.'

I bow graciously but make a mental note to look it up later on my computer. 'You wanted a favour from me?'

'Ah yes. I need to get some more diesel from the jetty at Bath Marina. Danny usually helps me, but I think he may have some work tomorrow. And I don't want to ask Linda to go back past the weir after the fright she had. Would you and Nina be good enough to help me with the boat and Weston Lock tomorrow morning? I don't like to keep asking the others all of the time.'

I had planned to work at the *Chronicle* tomorrow morning in order to make sure Ben didn't play fast and loose with my interview with Mrs Powell – and to make certain that he ran my story about the campaign against the boat people. But with an early start, I could probably do both and it feels churlish to make difficulties after the professor has given me the keys to whisky heaven.

'Of course,' I say. 'Shall we do it first thing? Eight o'clock?' He readily agrees, and we clink glasses. I eventually tear myself away from *Nautilus* and the single malt that has been quietly maturing for four decades. As I am passing Bill's boat, I realise I still don't know its name and look on the side for one without success. A faint whiff of coal smoke suggests he may be inside, although there isn't the barest chink of light showing from under or around the edge of the tarpaulin. I knock on his closed hatchway. It won't hurt to get one final quote for my story. There is a scurrying noise down below and then silence.

'Bill?' I call. 'Are you in there? It's Jack. Jack Johnson.'

I hear the hatchway slide back six inches and Bill's shifty eyes and sharp nose emerge from a corner of the tarpaulin covering the stern. 'What d'you want?' he snaps. I thought he might be more friendly after the meeting at the Old Green Tree, but his manner is brusque and unfriendly.

'Oh. Hi, Bill. I'm just writing an article for the *Chronicle* about the residents' campaign against you and thought maybe you could give me a few words? All the others have agreed to be quoted.'

'No.'

'I'm sorry?'

'I said no,' he repeats more emphatically. 'D'you really think I want to advertise myself in a newspaper? Goodnight.'

He vanishes and I hear the hatchway slide firmly shut. I am left standing there with my mouth open. As I wander back to my mooring,

I ponder his reaction. Perhaps Bill has gambling debts that are catching up with him and he needs to remain hidden from his creditors? Or perhaps he has something else to hide? I shrug. The whisky has made me feel fuzzy and I take a huge gulp of fresh air. I hope I've sobered up completely before I get back to *Jumping Jack Flash* where I must try to finish my article with quotes and pictures of all the boat owners. All of them except for Bill.

CHAPTER TWENTY-ONE

It is seven forty-five the following morning when Nina, Eddie and I arrive at the moorings on foot. The faint buzz of rush hour barely encroaches on the peacefulness of the river, which seems to be running much more slowly today. Danny is on *Otter*'s stern, while Tammy is cross-legged on the boat's roof, eating something for breakfast out of a bowl. Linda is also up and sweeping dust and dirt from the roof of *Maid of Coventry*. They all wave cheerily at us – except Tammy, of course – and so I assume it has been a trouble-free night. The professor is already waiting at the tiller of *Nautilus* with a small red lifebelt fitted over both his shoulders and across his chest. He is sipping a cup of coffee and offers us some, but Nina volunteers to go down into his galley and bring up two more cups.

'I did all my checks yesterday afternoon,' he says. 'I checked the prop and I've topped up the oil and radiator and I've tightened the prop-shaft gland. She's good to go.' He disappears back down into his library just as Nina emerges with the coffees. We are sitting, enjoying the fine early morning weather, when the professor reappears with a book.

'I have a present for you,' he says to Nina. 'Jack had some rather good whisky in return for this good deed, and so this is for you, to keep.'

Nina examines the brand-new book, which is a hardback collection of seventeenth-century verse. She looks delighted, although I suspect she was hoping to taste the whisky. I couldn't help singing its praises over our dinner yesterday evening.

'I particularly want you to read "To His Coy Mistress" by Andrew Marvell,' the professor says with an air of mischief. 'I've marked the page.'

Nina thanks him, gives him a kiss on one cheek, and puts the book carefully on a metal ledge that runs alongside both sides of the stern platform. I throw my coffee dregs overboard and we put our empty cups alongside the book.

'There's enough water to turn her here,' says the professor. Nina slips forward to undo the bow rope as the professor turns the ignition key and the engine of *Nautilus* coughs into life. We edge slowly out into the river, where the professor puts the tiller hard over and then juggles between forward and reverse until the boat has pivoted in its own length. The manoeuvre has taken about three minutes under the friendly gaze of all of the other boat owners except Bill. Even Tammy has remained on deck to see us off. Once the bow is pointing downstream, the professor waves to them and we set off slowly. However, we haven't even reached the Midland Road bridge before the professor puts one hand on my shoulder.

'She's feeling very sluggish, Jack; can you check the engine?' I go down the steps and double back behind them. Two ring-pull catches allow me to lift the cover of the engine bay in one easy movement but there is nothing easy about what I see. My eyes and mouth open in horror. Water is pouring in from somewhere at the stern of the boat and it is only a matter of inches before it will be flowing over the bulkhead and into the main cabin. I shout something incoherent, but it is drowned out by the noise of the engine with the cover removed. There is a flash of sparks as the water reaches the engine's electrics and it cuts out immediately. The sudden silence is awful.

'Jack! Jack! What is it?' calls the professor. Nina's head appears in the hatchway above me.

'There's water pouring in!' I shout desperately. The water is now flowing quickly over the bulkhead and around my feet, but I can see no obvious way of stopping it. Even using a bucket to drain the engine bay would fail to keep up with the rapid rate of flow. I rush back up the stairs to the stern where Nina is standing next to the professor. He is still clutching the tiller with both hands and is ashen-faced.

'It's already in the main cabin and there's no way of stopping it! We'll have to abandon her.'

'My books,' says the professor desperately. 'My books.' He pushes past me and almost falls down the steps in a rush. I open a seat lid, pull out two more lifejackets and throw one at Nina. Then I head down after the professor. He is halfway along the boat, frantically pulling books off their shelves with one hand and trying to hold a growing pile of them in the other. Our feet are splashing in ankle deep water now.

'It's no good, we have to go,' I say to him. But his eyes are wild and there is spittle on one side of his mouth. 'My books, I must save my books,' he wails pitifully.

'Jack!' shouts Nina from the stern, and then I hear Eddie barking from somewhere near the bow. I wade forward and find him on a seat in the galley. He is looking down at the advancing water and yapping at it furiously. I grab Eddie by his collar and make my way back towards the stern with the dog draped over my left shoulder. Nina is below now too, both hands gripping the professor's shoulders as she tries to talk sense into him.

'The books will be ruined whatever happens now. Please leave them. You've got to save yourself,' she is saying urgently to him.

But the professor is shaking his head furiously and tears are streaming down his cheeks. 'This is my home. This is my life,' he is saying. His distress is horrible to witness, but the water is now almost at knee level and rising relentlessly. Nina looks at me hopelessly and so I bundle Eddie into her arms and tell her to get out. Then I wrench the pile of books from the professor's hands and deliberately let them drop into the water.

'Jack, what are you doing?' he shouts, but I ignore him, loop two arms around his waist from behind and manhandle him backwards, through *Nautilus* and towards the rear hatchway.

'Jack, Jack! Put me down. This is my home,' he shouts as I bundle him forcefully through the length of the boat. There is a real resistance to my steps now as the water continues to flow through the boat at a frighteningly fast rate. My heart is beating furiously, and I am terrified at the thought of being trapped underwater with a panicking seventy-five-year-old man. The image spurs me to one last physical effort and I push the struggling professor up the steps. Nina helps by pulling him up and onto the stern platform, which has now sunk to almost the same level as the river's surface. Something crashes loudly from the boat's interior and I realise it won't be long before water is pouring through the boat's windows too. I hear a shout from the far bank. The others have seen what is happening and have crossed the bridge. They are clustered helplessly on the path; their mouths open with shock.

'Swim for it!' calls Danny, both hands cupping his mouth. 'Hurry.' His big frame is bent over a large round lifebuoy and he seems to be tying a rope to it. Linda has her little boy in her arms and Juno is clutching her leg. A handful of other people have also stopped to watch the unfolding drama.

I bring my face close to the professor's. His eyes are blank with shock.

'Listen to me,' I say. 'We need to get clear before she goes down. Do you understand, professor?' But he is completely stunned and staring blankly above my head.

'Nina, go for the bank now,' I say. She nods and just walks off the boat with Eddie clutched against her chest. Her head dips under the surface briefly but then she is up and swimming a strong breaststroke towards the bank. Eddie has broken free of her, but he also seems to be swimming strongly with his broad brown otter-like head sticking out of the water.

'Come on, professor,' I say gently, 'it's our turn. Hang onto me.'

I make him sit down on the stern platform next to me, our legs dangling in the cold water and then I push us both off. I can immediately feel the current trying to take me, but I can only paddle with one hand as the other is gripping a strap of the professor's lifebelt. He is floating but doing little else to help himself. I try a one-armed backstroke, rotating my right hand overarm while my left hand pulls him along in my wake. He is coughing and spluttering, waving his head violently from left to right. My backward circling hand hits something solid after about five strokes. I turn to look over my shoulder and see the large circular lifebuoy. Danny must have thrown it out and into the river. I hoop one arm into it. As soon as I do this, I can feel myself being pulled strongly through the water, back towards the bank. But the sudden jolt dislodges my grip on the professor and a gap suddenly widens between us.

'Stop!' I shout, letting go of the lifebuoy. I swim a few strokes of front crawl back to the professor. Now, however, he is flailing his arms violently. I duck under the water and come up behind him in a position where I can get the palm of one hand firmly under his chin and pull him backwards. He continues to flail but I have him now and I kick my legs until we are back at the lifebuoy. I put it over the professor's head and he clings onto it with both hands, coughing and spluttering. Once again, we are forcefully hauled in and many hands reach down to pull us up the steep side of the bank. I look back to *Nautilus*, which now has only about a foot of its upper-structure and the roof showing. Then I see a little brown shape in the water. Eddie. He's doubled back towards the boat instead of the bank, and seems to be swimming around in small circles, confused and unsure of his position. He's still swimming strongly but the current is pushing him further downstream, in the direction of the weir and I can hear a high-pitched whining coming from him.

'Eddie!' shouts Nina. I hold a restraining hand out to stop her, but suddenly there is a splash.

'Tammy!' shouts Danny. The teenager has made a shallow dive into the river and is swimming with a strong front crawl towards the dog. We all watch as she strikes out to the front of the boat and I silently pray that she isn't stupid enough to try to climb aboard its sinking structure. But instead, she reaches Eddie and grabs him by the collar. Then she turns in the water to face us, but the dog is struggling and she is obviously finding it difficult to swim with him. They have already been pushed downstream together by at least another ten metres. Then the bright orange plastic of the lifebuoy sails out over the river once again, trailing its orange rope.

'Grab it, Tammy,' shouts Danny desperately. 'For God's sake, grab it!' There is a sob in his throat.

Tammy uses her free hand to hold onto the hard, plastic ring and keeps a firm grip on Eddie with the other. I join Danny and we both pull the rope fast back through the water. Some early morning commuters reach out their hands and pull Tammy up the bank where she drops Eddie to the ground and folds her arms across her clinging wet T-shirt. Her whole body is shivering. Danny crashes through the growing crowd of bystanders and wraps his arms around his daughter. Nina now also moves towards the pair and wraps her arms around both of them.

'Thank you, Tammy,' I hear her say emotionally. 'Thank you so much.'

I begin to move over to make my thanks too, but Tammy suddenly looks up at me with a warning expression. I see tears fill her eyes before she breaks free of Danny and Nina, turns quickly and strides off, back up the path towards the moorings. Shock, I think to myself. Danny is clearly torn between following her and staying to make sure we are all right, so I give him an encouraging push and he sets off after his daughter.

The professor is sitting on the ground with Linda's arm around him. Her children are loitering in the background, grave and wide-eyed, watching to see what happens next. One of the commuters is coiling the rope of the lifebuoy into tidy circular loops.

'Christ, she went down quickly,' I say in a quiet voice. The old man is almost catatonic. His eyes are filled with pain and fixed on the spot where *Nautilus* has now disappeared below the surface. A small continuing row of bubbles is all that is left to signal her presence. Nina moves alongside me.

'What just happened?' she says quietly. I reflect that the professor's shock will soon make way for grief at the loss of all his worldly possessions, including a lifetime's collection of precious and rare first editions.

'Come on, love, let's get you dry,' says Linda, helping him gently to his feet. The children each take one of his hands and the unbearably sad-looking little group moves off.

'We'll need to report this,' says Nina. 'They'll need to mark her as a hazard to other boats and bring her back up as soon as possible. Let's get into some dry clothes and then someone can go to the marina and fetch some help.'

CHAPTER TWENTY-TWO

Maid of Coventry's interior is much less ordered and tidy than usual as it assumes the role of a disaster recovery centre. The few remaining clothes of Linda's ex-husband have been strewn around the professor and me to select from. He is the first to be ushered into a hot shower and Linda soon has him towelled and dressed with a brisk, nurse-like efficiency. Once we are all showered, dried, dressed and clustered around the table in her galley, sipping hot drinks and trying to take in the fact that *Nautilus* has sunk, I look at my watch and realise that barely forty-five minutes have passed since we set off to refuel her. It all happened so incredibly quickly. The professor hasn't spoken a word since I manhandled him off his boat and I am worried that he will resent me for it forever. But when he eventually turns to me, it is with a huge depth of sadness rather than anger.

'How could it happen, Jack?' he asks in a whisper.

I shake my head in bafflement. Canal boats don't have the type of seacocks that you find on other boats. All I can imagine is that someone has drilled holes in the boat below its waterline. But this is madness. How on earth would they do that without anyone noticing?

'Don't you worry about that now,' says Linda, patting his hand. 'We'll get to the bottom of it.'

The professor's head begins to nod in exhaustion and we move him onto Linda's bed, where he quickly falls asleep. Danny joins us after about twenty minutes.

'How's Tammy?' asks Nina straight away. 'She was so brave.'

'She's pretty shaken up,' says Danny. 'Doesn't want to talk about it. I've left her in bed. I've been down to the marina and they're getting a work party together. They keep a boat there with all the necessary kit on board.' Danny goes on to explain how they'll send a diver down to close the windows and doors and seal the weedhatch, decking, exhaust, sink outlets and air vents. Once this is done, a generator on the workboat will pump air into *Nautilus* and any airholes will be plugged as soon as they appear.

'I'll go back out in a minute and keep an eye on what's happening,' says Danny.

I have my fingers crossed that the boat will quickly rise to the surface – but I know from bitter experience what state it will be in. All the cabin linings and soft furnishings will have been completely ruined, and foul-smelling silt and mud will be everywhere, behind the wall linings and in every nook and cranny of the boat's interior. The engine and gearbox will need rebuilding or replacing, new electrics will be required, and new galley equipment will have to be installed. Even the solid fuel stove will probably be beyond repair. All of this can be fixed with insurance money, I think to myself, but the professor's books, papers, antiques and paintings will be irreplaceable. The gentle and civilised bachelor had built a tailor-made life for himself on the river and now it has been shattered. And if I discover that it was anything other than a terrible accident, I vow to myself, then I won't rest until those responsible are brought to justice. Nina interrupts my gloomy thoughts.

'Jack,' she says quietly. 'You need to go to the *Chronicle*.'

I press the heel of my hands into both of my eyes and take a beat. If I don't go, I'll have no chance of influencing what Ben prints. But I desperately want to stay here. Eventually I raise my head and sigh.

'Yes, I suppose I do. Can you stay here with Eddie? I'll get back as soon as I can.'

As I walk back to the bridge, I take in Bill's boat. Once again, there is no sign of life on board. He has not been out at all this morning, not to witness the mayhem, or just to lend a hand. He had definitely been on board last night when he was so curt to me. Where was he now?

When I arrive, Ben is already in his little corner office at the *Chronicle*. He waves me over as soon as he sees me.

'G'day Jack,' he says, rubbing his hands together enthusiastically. 'Nice interview. It's going to be a great edition this week, mate.'

'I'm sorry I'm a bit late.' I explain about the sinking of *Nautilus* and our swim ashore from the boat. 'I was hoping I might be able to add something about it to the story about the boat people,' I say.

'You're not saying it was deliberate?' he asks.

'I honestly can't say at this stage. But a lot of unpleasant things seem to be happening since this residents' campaign started.'

Ben shrugs indifferently. 'I could only give your piece ten pars – but it's above the fold on page three,' he says in a matter-of-fact way. 'Check over the Powell story first and then you can work in the sinking if there's time. You'll have to keep it to the same overall length, though.'

I settle at my desk to see what damage Ben has wreaked on my interview with Mrs Powell. In spite of being more of a sub editor than a reporter, I get quite protective of my own writing. And I am quite certain that Ben is capable of sorting the wheat from the chaff, and then publishing the chaff.

In fact, I am pleased and surprised to discover that my report about the interview is largely unaltered. Most of it is spread across pages two and three of the newspaper with a small teaser story on the front page. A large photograph of me and Mrs Powell is also on page three with a caption saying: 'Mrs Jennifer Powell (53), widow of murder victim Rufus Powell, talks exclusively to *Bath Chronicle* reporter Jack Johnson, renowned author of *The Canal Pusher*.' I remove the word 'renowned' and then read a small panel of copy that explains how I had been an intended victim of the Midlands Canal Pusher, Keith Tomlinson, and gone on to write the authoritative account of his killing spree before I moved to Bath, where I still lived on a narrowboat. I don't like it but there is nothing factual that I can take issue with and so I turn my attention to the front page story, which has a photo by-line of Ben looking suitably serious.

It's a pretty shoddy piece of work with almost nothing new from the police and no hint of anyone yet recognising the blurry video-grab of the man in the motorbike crash helmet and leathers. Nevertheless, the picture of the hunched figure walking purposefully in the rain is reprinted on the front page under a headline that screams: **'IS THIS THE BATH PUSHER?'**

The main story is full of Ben's speculation that Rufus Powell may have been the random victim of a killer who is now copying Keith Tomlinson's methods, although neither the police nor anyone else had given him any supporting quotes.

I turn away from it in disgust to look at my ten-paragraph story about the boat people. It is headlined: **RESIDENTS CAMPAIGN TO REMOVE BOAT-PEOPLE 'EYESORE'**. I let that go for the moment and get to work rewriting the intro. In the end I come up with: 'A canal boat has been deliberately sunk on the River Avon in Bath amid fears that a residents' campaign is spiralling into intimidation and violence.' I add a few more facts about the sinking of the *Nautilus* and then reduce some of the quotes from Danny and Linda to make room for the new angle.

Lower down in the story there is already a direct quote lifted from Councillor Claverton's campaign leaflet about the moorings and I have included a few choice insults from the sheets hanging out of the windows. Finally, I go back to the headline and rewrite it: **'BOAT SUNK AS FEARS MOUNT ON RIVER.'** I am annoyed that there is no room in the print edition for my photograph of the professor or Linda and her children, but I begin work on an expanded version of the story for the paper's website where space is much less of an issue. This takes me a couple of hours and includes five photographs including one of the residents' signs, more lengthy quotes from the professor, Linda and Danny, and a bit more of Claverton's bile from his leaflet.

The newsroom has filled up in the meantime and Tom comes over to ask if I have made peace with Ben. I glance over at the editor. He is hunched behind his own computer but, as if sensing my eyes on him, he looks up and waves me over. I square my shoulders, ready to defend my copy changes, but he is too pleased with himself to take issue with them and remains largely uninterested in the boat-sinking story. I ask if I can go.

'Yes, sure,' he says distractedly, before adding, 'You can bill us for three days. Two for the Powell interview and half a day for today.' He thinks he is being generous.

'Okay, Ben,' I say. I should have left it there, but after the sinking of *Nautilus* I am still shocked as well as being tired and angry. 'Just for the record, your front page story is pure garbage. I'm surprised you put your name to it – let alone your picture.'

He looks at me furiously.

'We'll see, won't we?' he snaps back. 'You'll be eating your words if there's another body found in the water. You're just worried that your book has created another killer,' he adds nastily. 'And maybe I'll be asking you for a response to that for next week's paper.'

I swallow any further reply and walk out, slamming his glass door with sufficient force to stop several nearby conversations and even stunning Petra into silence as I leave without looking back.

CHAPTER TWENTY-THREE

Back on the *Maid of Coventry*, Linda is bustling around in her galley, heating up soup for everyone, and Nina is buttering bread rolls with Eddie waiting hopefully nearby. The children are on the floor, building something out of a collection of small plastic bricks. I bend down to join them.

'What are you doing, Juno?' I ask.

'We're building a new boat for the professor,' she says quietly. Noah just nods in agreement.

Linda calls everyone to the table. The atmosphere is subdued, and we keep our voices low in order not to wake the professor, who is still sleeping in Linda's bed. However, we are all hungry and Linda is just serving up second helpings when a woman's voice calls from outside.

Linda bangs down the spoon. 'If it's that woman offering money again I'll swing for her,' she says.

Nina puts a hand on hers. 'I'll go and see who it is.' She quickly reappears. 'It's Mrs Manningham-Westcott!' she announces to me with a smile.

Seeing Linda's bafflement, I explain about the elderly lady we had met who lives in an apartment on the opposite bank of the river. Linda automatically bristles and so I add hastily, 'But she's completely on your side.'

'She's lovely actually,' agrees Nina.

'Well, don't leave her standing out there. Ask if she'd like some soup,' says Linda briskly. Nina disappears again, and I join her to help the elderly lady out of her mobility scooter and onto the boat, where it is an awkward struggle for her to descend the steep stairs. Mrs Manningham-Westcott takes my vacated seat and then looks around the interior with undisguised interest.

'Good day to you all,' she says. 'I am so sorry to interrupt your luncheon. But I just had to come. I watched the boat sink this morning from my apartment and I had to make sure you were all right. Especially poor Professor Chesney. He must be quite distraught.'

At that very moment, the door to Linda's bedroom opens and the professor comes out. Linda bustles kindly around him and Nina gets up so he can take her place at the table. His hair is dishevelled, and the borrowed clothes are slightly too big, so there is an overwhelming air of vulnerability about him. Nevertheless, the sleep must have done the professor some good because his voice is no longer quavering. He peers at the newcomer.

'I don't think we have been introduced,' he says in a whisper. 'Professor Arthur Chesney.'

'Rani Massingham-Westcott,' she says and takes his outstretched hand. 'I am so sorry for the loss of your boat. I watched it all happen from my apartment this morning. It was shocking, quite shocking.'

I briefly tell the professor about the ongoing operation to raise *Nautilus* and he voices the thoughts I have already had.

'The boat can be mended, of course,' he says. 'But I shall never recover my treasures.'

'But what on earth caused it to sink?' asks Mrs Manningham-Westcott. 'It all seemed to happen so quickly.'

'We don't know yet,' I say. 'But we might find out when she comes back up to the surface.'

'I spend many happy hours watching the river. I saw you yesterday afternoon making all the preparations for your trip.'

'That's what is so strange,' says the professor. 'I checked the boat from bow to stern yesterday, and there was nothing out of place. All was as it should be. I know I'm not mistaken.'

Just then, Danny's large bulk fills the galley. Tammy is behind him, looking nervous and awkward as usual. There is no more room and so they lean against some cupboards.

'Ah,' says Mrs Massingham-Westcott. 'You must be the brave girl who dived in to rescue little Eddie. I saw it all. Well done, my dear, it was a wonderful thing to do.'

Tammy mutters something inaudible while Danny beams with a proud smile. Then he remembers the presence of the professor and quickly adopts a more sombre look.

'The diver has just come back up,' he says. We all look at him and he looks back at each of us awkwardly before reluctantly fixing his gaze on the professor. 'He says there was no weedhatch cover in place.'

Everyone falls silent.

The weedhatch is a metal box above the propeller shaft. It gives the boat owner access to the propeller to free it from plastic bags, baling twine, barbed wire, leaves or any other bit of debris that get tangled around it. The hatch cover is fixed firmly into place with a bolt and a securing bar, otherwise water will rush into the engine compartment as soon as the propeller starts to turn. It is one of the most basic things to be checked before embarking on a narrowboat voyage of any kind. Now the sudden sinking of *Nautilus* makes complete sense. Why hadn't I thought of it before? But why was it missing?

'But... but... I don't understand,' stammers the professor. 'How can there be no weedhatch? I used it to check my propeller yesterday afternoon. And I remember tightening the bar afterwards because I had to wash some of the grease off my hands.'

The professor is old, but no one doubts his memory.

'Then someone must have removed it last night,' I say.

'First they set my boat adrift and now this,' says Linda, shaking her head in bafflement.

'But how would they know I was going to move the boat today?' asks the professor. There is a momentary silence. Who else, apart from me, Nina and the others on the moorings knew that the professor was planning to move downriver to refuel?

'Maybe they didn't know,' says Nina. 'Maybe they just took out the hatch cover and got lucky. Perhaps we should check on all the boats?'

Unlikely, I think to myself. Even without a weedhatch cover, the boat would have been perfectly safe on its mooring. The boat needed to be underway for the water to flood over as it did. The professor would have been certain to spot its absence after any length of time spent motionless on the mooring.

'Well,' says Mrs Massingham-Westcott. 'If I saw you making preparations to leave from my window, anyone else may have done so as well.'

'True,' I say. 'But whoever took it must have known their way around boats. They must have known what the result would be.'

'That's true,' says Nina. 'It doesn't seem the sort of thing a local vandal would do.'

'And, taking it out completely wouldn't have been easy after dark,' adds Danny.

'They probably didn't take it far,' says Nina. 'It's probably at the bottom of the river.

'Well, one thing is for sure, we need to get the police involved,' I say.

'Good luck with that,' says Linda. 'The two constables who came to see me couldn't have been less interested. They even asked if Noah or Juno could have been playing with the mooring ropes,' she adds disgustedly.

'This is different,' I say. 'There's been a hell of a lot of damage. Deliberate damage.'

'And WE could have been killed,' says Linda angrily.

I raise both hands placatingly. 'I know that, Linda. I'm not saying that setting you adrift wasn't a seriously criminal act. I'm just saying we need to try the police again. Hopefully they'll be more helpful this time.'

Linda harrumphs, crossing her arms. 'I saw them looking at the banners opposite. I think the police are on the same side as the residents.'

'We don't all think the same, my dear,' chips in Mrs Massingham-Westcott. 'I think the signs are quite dreadful.'

'I'm afraid they will think that a doddery old man just forgot to replace the weedhatch cover,' says the professor, 'or that somehow I lost it overboard.'

'That's not fair,' says Danny.

'Ridiculous,' echoes Linda, and Tammy shakes her head as she pets Eddie, her fringe covering her eyes.

'All right,' I say firmly. 'If everyone agrees, I think it's best if Nina and I take the professor round to the police station now. This is a serious crime.' I see Linda beginning to speak. '*Another* serious crime,' I add hastily. 'We were both on board with the professor, so we're material witnesses, and we can try to make sure they take it seriously.'

'I'll get back to *Nautilus*,' says Danny. 'They say they'll try to tow her back to the marina later on and get her up the slipway. Don't you worry, prof. I'll keep an eye on her.'

I reflect that there won't be anything of any real value left to keep an eye on, but I keep the thought to myself.

'Linda, why doesn't the professor move onto Jack's boat?' asks Nina. 'There's a bit more room on *Jumping Jack Flash* and he might be more comfortable there for the moment.'

'Good idea,' I say immediately. 'And some of my clothes should fit him too.'

The professor doesn't show any sign of resentment at being discussed in this way but mutters something about not wishing to be a burden.

'Well, of course, he'd be very welcome to stay on here,' says Linda. 'But the children might disturb him...'

'That's settled then,' says Nina with a smile.

'And we're cruising up to Bradford on Avon for the weekend – it'll do you good to spend some time out of Bath,' I say directly to him. 'Do you need us to see you home, Mrs Manningham-Westcott?'

'No thank you, dear. I'm perfectly capable on my scooter. Just help me get back up those stairs.'

'Right then.' I look around the table. 'Anything else for now?'

The group breaks up. Nina, the professor and I manage to hail a taxi to the city's police station where we spend over an hour waiting in a bleak reception area until a young detective constable appears to take our statements. He pays a little more attention when I tell him the value of the damage may well be more than a quarter of a million pounds. I have calculated that *Nautilus* would easily have cost more than six figures and that the professor's lifetime collection of first editions and original paintings might have been worth just as much again. I tell the officer that the sinking might be part of a co-ordinated campaign of intimidation, and make sure my statement includes a reference to the recent acts of vandalism as well as Linda's ordeal.

The officer, who can't be more than twenty-five, finally shuffles the paperwork together and writes on a piece of paper. 'That's the crime number for your insurance,' he says, sliding it across to the professor. 'I'll talk to my boss and we'll take it from there.'

'Before we go,' I say, taking out my card and laying it on the table, 'what's the latest on the Powell murder inquiry?'

He stiffens and inspects the card, which has the *Bath Chronicle* on it. 'You'd need to talk to Detective Inspector Kerr about that. She's the Senior Investigating Officer.'

'Is she in?'

'No, she's in Bristol. And she's a bit busy running a murder inquiry at the moment, sir. They'll let the press know any developments through the normal channels.'

I nod. 'And it's all gone very quiet, hasn't it? You guys aren't giving much away. Any new leads?'

He stares back at me impassively.

'Look,' I say tapping my card, 'my phone was wrecked in the sinking, but I'll try to replace it with one with the same number. Otherwise I can be reached via the *Chronicle*.'

He still says nothing.

I try again. 'It might be worthwhile for DI Kerr to find time for a chat with me. I've been following this case and I have information she might need. Can you pass on that message to her, please?'

The police officer gets to his feet but picks up my card. 'Goodbye, Mr Johnson.'

We gather together on the street in front of the station while Eddie cocks his leg on a railing. It is now four in the afternoon. The professor looks beaten and dispirited so I suggest a plan to Nina.

'How about you take the professor back to *Jumping Jack Flash* and make him comfortable? I'm going to try to get a new mobile phone sorted out and buy some stuff for dinner.'

Later that evening, sitting around the table after a dinner of steak, mashed potato and peas – most of which has been left uneaten by our guest – the professor grasps Nina's arm with a sudden thought.

'Your book. The poetry. Did you manage to save it?'

It is ridiculous to imagine that anything made of paper could have been salvaged during our swim from the sinking boat, but Nina is gentle with him.

'No, I'm sorry. It went down with the boat.'

He shakes his head miserably and mutters something about being ready for bed. So, I show him to my double berth and settle him down for the night.

I have moved myself onto the narrow little berth opposite Nina's and reflect that I wish we were sharing her bedroom in different circumstances. We have coyly dressed and undressed separately in the tiny bathroom. Our recent tetchiness with each other is forgotten as we whisper quietly about the day's dramatic events and fall asleep trying to make sense of them.

CHAPTER TWENTY-FOUR

I'm up and about early the following morning and so is Eddie who, as usual, has spent the night at the bottom of Nina's bed. The dog and I make a quick foray into town for fresh croissants. I am pleased to see the professor eat a whole one quite quickly for breakfast, before dropping his fingers under the table for the little dog to lick off the crumbs. I push a second at him and the professor takes it after a moment's hesitation. He pours himself a second cup of coffee.

'I am very grateful to you both,' he says. 'But I won't impose on you for very long. I shall try to find somewhere to rent in the city today – after I have been to inspect the damage.'

Nina and I exchange glances. We have already discussed this issue across the gap between our single bunks last night. 'Nonsense,' I say. 'You must stay with us for at least a few days. The company will do you good. As I mentioned, I have a friend arriving today for the weekend and we're planning to make a trip down to Bradford on Avon and back. We'd very much like you to join us.'

'Yes, please come,' says Nina. 'It will give you a little break and help to take your mind off *Nautilus*.'

The professor looks at us both affectionately. 'Very well. If you are sure. I am very grateful to you both.'

Nina claps her hands and I exhale and nod happily.

'We thought you'd appreciate a bit of privacy last night, but with Will arriving I don't think you'll want to share a bed, so is it okay with you if we move you into the single berth opposite Nina? And I'll share the double with Will.' In truth, of course, I would love to remain in Nina's bedroom, or even to share the double with her, but the new sleeping arrangements are quickly agreed by the other two.

'Now, I think I must face the challenge of seeing what remains of *Nautilus*,' says the professor. 'I shall have a walk along the river to the marina, I think.'

'Do you mind if Jack and I come with you?' asks Nina. 'I can try to get myself a new phone in town afterwards.'

Good call, I think. It's going to be an ordeal for the old man and he will need some moral support. But just as we reach Bath Deep Lock, my new mobile phone rings. The others pause as I fish it out of my pocket. It isn't a number that I recognise, but I accept the call.

'Mr Jack Johnson?' It's a woman's voice: crisp, no-nonsense and hard to age. 'Detective Inspector Mary Kerr of Avon and Somerset Police. I believe you told one of my officers that you may have some information for me?'

'Yes,' I reply. 'I told him it might be worthwhile for us to have a chat.'

'Worthwhile for you or for me?' she asks. 'If you're just a reporter fishing for a new angle, then you can forget it.'

'Worthwhile for you,' I say. 'I might have a new line of inquiry for you regarding the Powell murder. No proof. But if it went anywhere... well, I'd hope for some kind of preferential treatment. Maybe an early tip-off on any arrest?'

There is a pause while she thinks about this. I let it continue uninterrupted.

'All right. I'll give you half an hour.'

'When?'

'Now. The station in Bath.'

'It'll take me ten minutes to get there,' I say.

'I'll put the kettle on.'

I briefly relay the call to the others and we agree that they will go on to the marina and that I will ring them when I have finished at the police station.

Detective Inspector Kerr greets me in the station's reception area with a brisk handshake. I guess that she is aged in her late thirties or early forties. She's dressed in a black skirt and jacket, with a white-collared shirt underneath. Her hair is ash-blonde and neatly bobbed around her heart-shaped face. Her eyes are dark with tiredness, but she fixes me with an unblinking stare.

I register that she is astute enough not to allow a newspaper reporter anywhere near the murder inquiry room, where I might see any amount of helpful information posted on noticeboards or walls. Instead, I am steered into a small interview room where a polystyrene cup of machine coffee is waiting for me. It looks like grey dishwater.

'I thought you said you'd put the kettle on,' I say, sipping the drink with a grimace. It tastes even worse than it looks. The chemicals in the polymer of styrene overwhelm the taste of the instant coffee and powdered milk added to lukewarm water.

'I was being sarcastic,' she says. 'So, Mr Johnson, what have you got for me?'

I notice she hasn't bothered to take out a pen and notebook or even sit down in the other chair.

'This could be something and nothing,' I warn her.

'Let me be the judge of that,' she says, leaning against the wall with her arms folded.

'So, you're not getting anywhere fast at the moment, DI Kerr?'

She bristles, and her lips tighten. 'I told you, Mr Johnson, if you're just on a fishing trip, then this discussion is at an end. Anything I say is off the record... not that I'm planning on saying anything. Understood?'

'It's okay. I understand. Right, then. If you're standing comfortably?'

I describe my recent interview with Mrs Powell for that day's edition of the *Chronicle*. Detective Inspector Kerr frowns with annoyance. The police often find it hard to understand why grieving relatives or crime victims might want to talk to anyone other than themselves and, when they do, they imagine it is always the result of intrusive doorstep harassment by the press. However, she keeps quiet and lets me continue.

I tell her that the dead man had been planning an all-out assault via the Georgian Fellowship on a planning application yet to be submitted for the old Tiller & Brown site.

'How do you know this?'

'Mrs Powell showed me a speech her husband was going to give at the Fellowship's next meeting. It pretty well declared war on the developers, Andropov Developments. It's owned by a pair of twins, Sebastian and Anthony Andropov.'

Then I explain about the attempt by the developers to buy the moorings back from the boat people. 'But at the same time, someone is trying to intimidate them,' I say. 'Their stuff keeps being thrown into the river – pushchairs and chimneys, all sorts of stuff – and they've had a boat nearly go over the weir after it was untied during the night. Now another boat, an expensive one, was sunk yesterday.'

'Sunk. How?'

'It looks like someone removed a weedhatch cover in the night and the boat went down as soon as it was moved.'

I doubt the DI knows what a weedhatch is, but I feel a frisson of satisfaction when she pulls out a notebook and unscrews the top of a fountain pen. I imagine that she is scribbling down the name of Andropov Developments Ltd and the Andropov twins.

'What was the name of the site again?'

'Tiller & Brown. It's mostly on the south bank of the Avon, between Victoria Bridge and Midland Bridge,' I reply.

She makes a few more notes and then snaps her book shut.

'Mind if we step outside, Mr Johnson?' she asks. 'I'm gasping for a cigarette.'

I'm slightly surprised. DI Kerr has seemed indifferent and unfriendly up until this moment. We move outside and stand by the railings, where she lights up and inhales deeply.

'So, let me get this straight,' she says. 'Your theory is that these property developers didn't like what Rufus Powell was going to say about their plan and so they knocked him on the head and dumped him into the river?'

'Or had someone do it for them,' I answer. 'He was about to go nuclear on their plan.'

'We're obviously interested in anyone who might have a grudge against Mr Powell,' she says. 'But Mrs Powell didn't mention her husband's opposition to this scheme. It's all a bit far-fetched, though, isn't it? You're saying these millionaire developers are sinking boats, throwing pushchairs in the river and committing murder all at the same time?'

'And setting boats adrift with young children onboard,' I say defensively, but even as I say it I realise how mad it all sounds.

'That's one hell of a conspiracy theory,' she says. 'And presumably you have no proof whatsoever?'

I shrug unhappily.

'Well, do you?' The detective throws her cigarette butt onto the pavement and grinds it into a grey smudge with her shoe. I notice there are some others already littering the area.

'No. No I don't. That's your job isn't it?'

'I had a few inquiries made about you before we met, Mr Johnson. You popped up on our database. I put a call in to a Detective Chief Superintendent Chisholm.' She pauses to let this sink in.

DCS Chisholm was the senior police officer who eventually oversaw the successful prosecution of the Canal Pusher and a professional drugs ring, with a lot of help from Nina and me. I'm suddenly unsure where this conversation is heading.

'He says I can trust you and that I should listen to what you have to say,' she goes on. 'All right, so I've listened. I'm willing to trust you if you swear to keep a lid on it for now. I don't want anything in the *Chronicle* or anywhere else.'

'I swear,' I say quickly.

She gives me a long searching look. 'If you let me down... '

'I won't.'

She looks around us. 'All right. Let's go back inside.'

We move back to the little interview room and this time she sits down opposite me.

'So, I don't buy your complicated conspiracy theory, Mr Johnson, because there's a much simpler and more plausible explanation. As you know, Rufus Powell was a city magistrate. What you probably don't know, though, is that a few months ago he sentenced a low-life Hells Angel to a year in prison for GBH during a right-wing rally, here in Bath. That low-life is called Clive Porlock and his father Vince just happens to be the boss of a big gang of bikers called the Bristol Bulldogs. Well, Clive went down to the cells threatening Mr Powell with all kinds of violence and vengeance and we have good reasons to believe that he managed to deliver on those threats.'

'The biker caught on CCTV?' I ask, remembering that Mrs Powell told me the police had been looking back at her husband's previous court cases. The DI nods. 'But you said reasons plural.'

'The silly sods couldn't help themselves from claiming the credit.' She takes a small bundle of photographs from her inside jacket pocket, shuffles through them and puts one down in front of me.

'Two capital Bs, back to back,' she says. 'It's the tag of the Bristol Bulldogs. It was painted on Pulteney Bridge, down by the water where we think the attack happened. The camera there had been disabled and it makes sense, given where the body was found. The paint was still fresh. They're sending out a message to say don't fuck with us.'

'And you've kept all this out of the press,' I say thoughtfully, 'but you haven't arrested anyone?' I'm rapidly trying to take this all in.

The detective chews one corner of her mouth. She looks like she is already starting to regret opening up to me. 'As you can imagine, Vince Porlock and his guys aren't exactly falling over themselves to co-operate with us and Clive denies any knowledge. Well, as the lovely Mandy Rice-Davies said, he would, wouldn't he?'

'So, what are you doing about it?'

She gathers up the photograph and returns it with the others to her jacket pocket. 'Mr Johnson, I've told you more than I should already. Our inquiries are progressing and that's the one and only thing you can report from this conversation. Understood?'

'Yes, but... '

She cuts me off. 'Thanks for coming in. Please leave this with me now. I've explained why you need to do that. We have a very credible line of investigation, but it's going to take time to crack this.'

'Look,' I say, 'the least you can do is make sure the threats to the boat owners are treated seriously. Maybe there's no connection whatsoever with Powell's death. But this campaign against them is getting out of hand – someone could get killed. You could step up patrols in the area.'

'I'm running a murder inquiry,' DI Kerr says tersely, but then seems to relent. 'I'll talk to my uniformed colleagues about it.'

'Well, you've got my number.'

'Yes, we've got your number,' she says meaningfully. 'So, don't let me down.' She holds out a hand to indicate our chat is over.

I don't particularly like the way she is dismissing me, but I can't think of an appropriate response. 'You might want to read today's *Chronicle* when it comes out,' I say as we shake hands. She may not buy my conspiracy theory, I reflect, but I imagine she'll have even less time for Ben's copycat serial killer theory.

'Oh yes, we'll be doing that. I could do with some light relief,' she says, holding open the door and ushering me through it.

Leaving the station, I exchange texts with Nina and we arrange a rendezvous, but my mood doesn't improve as I slowly wander through the bustling city streets. In truth, I feel like a complete idiot. How could I go blundering into the middle of a murder inquiry with such a ridiculous hypothesis? Of course, Powell's role as a magistrate had to be relevant in some way. It must have brought him directly into contact with a wide range of violent criminals. I wonder to myself what the police's next step will be. Their efforts to track the ongoing movements of the biker on the CCTV must have reached a dead end. And, as the DI said, any kind of confession or leak from within the Hells Angels' gang was highly unlikely. If there was no murder weapon or DNA evidence, how would they even begin to make a breakthrough? Idly, I wondered if they would try infiltrating the Bulldogs with an undercover officer. Rather them than me.

CHAPTER TWENTY-FIVE

Nina and the professor are in even lower spirits than me when we meet for lunch at the Raven, a city centre pub. Even the eccentric metal sculpture of the bird in a top hat riding a bike above its pub sign fails to raise a smile. Apparently, they had arrived at Bath Marina just as *Nautilus* was being towed up the slipway behind a tractor. I had seen *Jumping Jack Flash* in a similar condition and had some idea of the damage that even the briefest time underwater can do to a boat. When I cilled it, I'd hired *Jumping Jack Flash* for less than a month with a view to buying it. I'd barely had time to get acquainted with the boat, let alone grow to love it. But for the professor, witnessing the sopping wreckage of a lifetime's collection of books on his once beautiful wide-beam boat, it must have been a gruelling ordeal. I spare the pair from describing it to me. The speed with which they both empty their wine glasses is a measure of how horrible the experience has been.

I refill them both from the bottle of red on the table and tell them briefly about my morning. They are both interested in my interview with the detective inspector, but I play it down and I don't share the new information about the Hells Angels' gang. I'm embarrassed to have leapt to conclusions about the Andropov twins, and I want to turn it all over in my mind first. Anyway, Nina is distracted by trying to fire up her replacement phone and the professor is still quietly absorbing the damage to *Nautilus* and its contents.

'Well, at least DI Kerr might encourage her pals in uniform to take the campaign against the boat people seriously,' says Nina. 'And your *Chronicle* story may help too.'

The professor, who has been toying with a beef and ale pie, puts his fork down and sighs. 'Even if they find the people who sabotaged my boat, it won't bring back my books or the paintings and furniture. I think I shall start looking for a flat. The insurance money for the boat and what's left of my savings should be sufficient. I think I've had enough of living on the water.'

Nina gives me a worried look.

'You don't need to make any big decisions straight away,' I say, putting one hand on the professor's wrist. 'Just give yourself some time.'

He nods unconvincingly and returns to his pie and gloomy thoughts.

After our meal, we wander the city centre's shopping streets and I pick up some copies of the *Chronicle*. We find a bench on Kingsmead Square to read the paper.

'It's quite a small story,' I say apologetically, as I see the professor reading about his sunken boat on page three.

'At least you tried, my boy,' he says bleakly. 'We haven't known each other very long but you are already a good friend. Thank you for pulling me out of the boat. It would have been very stupid of me to go down with her.'

'I thought you might resent me for it,' I say, anxious to clear the air.

'I did at first – but that was just the shock. There was nothing more we could have done to save *Nautilus*. It made sense to save ourselves. You saw that, and I didn't. Thank goodness no harm came to you or Nina, or even little Eddie. I couldn't have lived with that.'

'You didn't do anything wrong, professor. The person who removed your weedhatch cover is to blame. And we'll find out who the bastard is if it's the last thing we do.'

Back at *Jumping Jack Flash*, the professor's emotional morning has tired him out. He gratefully settles himself under the duvet on a single berth for a siesta and is asleep within minutes. Keen not to disturb him, Nina and I head for a seat in Robert's garden. My phone rings. Linda.

'Hi Jack. I just wanted to say thank you for the piece in the paper. We've all seen it. That should make them sit up and take notice.'

I am dubious about how much it will achieve, but I am pleased that it has raised morale. I update Linda on the professor's state of mind and she tells me that they all plan to visit the marina this afternoon to inspect *Nautilus*.

'Linda, I've tried asking the police to step up patrols by your moorings and to take these latest incidents seriously, but I think they're a bit distracted by the Powell murder.'

'We've been talking about that,' she says. 'We're going to take it in turns to mount a guard during the night, just for the next few days. Bill, Danny, Tammy and me will do two hours each, see how it goes. If that doesn't suit, we'll do a night each, every four days.'

'That's a good idea, Linda. We're taking the professor away for a weekend trip, but we'll be back on Sunday evening so we can help you with your night shifts after we get back.'

'Bless you, Jack, that would be helpful. Love to Nina and the professor.' She rings off.

The afternoon passes quietly; Nina reads and I struggle with a cryptic crossword. We both doze in the sun until the sky clouds over and it becomes too chilly to stay outside.

'At least the forecast for the weekend is fine and warm,' I say as we duck back down into the galley, where the professor is quietly sipping a cup of tea. My phone rings again. Mrs Manningham-Westcott.

'Jack?' she asks in her clear, refined voice. I respond to her inquiries about the professor whilst he looks on at me. Then she continues.

'I have something to tell you, Jack. Two police officers came to my door half an hour ago. They said they were doing house-to-house inquiries and wanted to know if any residents had seen anyone acting suspiciously near the boats. I told them I knew all about the sinking because I had witnessed it. They were very interested in what had happened and we had a nice cup of tea together.'

'That's marvellous, Mrs Manningham-Westcott,' I say. 'It shows that they're starting to take it seriously.'

'But that's not all,' she continues. 'Since they called, I've noticed that some of the sheets with their horrible slogans have been taken down. I'm sure your article in the paper has helped, my dear. No one would want to be part of something nasty like that.'

I grin to myself. It's a small victory but I'm happy to take what I can. I hope Linda and the others will also notice that the tide of opinion might be turning.

'I must be going, Jack. Give my regards to Nina and the professor and have a lovely weekend trip.'

When I pass on her regards and brief the others, it seems to cheer them up a little.

'Well, this calls for a refill,' says the professor, reaching for the teapot.

'No,' I say, 'it calls for something stronger.' I pull an eighteen-year-old Highland Park out of my backpack. 'I know it's not the forty-year-old, and I was going to save it for our trip, but perhaps just a small one?'

'It would be rude not to,' smiles the professor. Nina grins at me, and gets up to fetch glasses and a jug of water. An hour and two whiskies each later, Will Simpson makes his dramatic entrance in a blaze of noise and energy as usual. We can hear the roar of his powerful motorbike on the other side of Robert's house and a text message follows almost immediately:

I'm here.

I quickly climb the slope and slip through the side passage to greet my old chum. He has already pulled off a full-face crash helmet and he gives me a hug, pulling me against his waxed-cotton jacket.

'JJ! Great to see you. Looking good, man.'

Will was my contemporary at school, but still manages to look and act about ten years younger than me. His boyish good looks and trim, muscular frame, combined with an infectious enthusiasm for life, mean he is never short of female companionship. Will has been an actor since we left boarding school and he is still criss-crossing the country on his bike, picking up stage work where he can, doing the occasional TV one-off or mini-series and waiting for his big movie break. I show him a safe spot behind the house to park his motorbike and then he swings a canvas bag over one shoulder and saunters down to *Jumping Jack Flash*, where Nina and the professor are waiting. Nina runs up to him and is enfolded in another bear hug and the professor is greeted with an eager handshake. Then Will rolls around on the deck with an ecstatic Eddie while we all laugh at their antics.

I want to reach our first mooring at Bathampton before it gets dark tonight, but it is only an hour away. I do the final checks of the boat and order Nina and Will to untie the mooring ropes and bring the stakes onboard with them. I have made a particular point of checking that my weedhatch cover is in place and firmly secured.

Nina and the professor stay in the bow and Will joins me at the tiller as we pass through the tunnels and under the elegant iron footbridges of Sydney Gardens. It is a long time since I have had the boat moving and I enjoy the experience as the suburbs glide by slowly in contrast to the trains that run parallel with us. We arrive in open countryside very quickly. The canal runs along a shelf of the Avon Valley that rolls away in a glorious vista of woods, hills and fields below us. I point out Solsbury Hill on the far side of the valley, which prompts Will to begin imitating the guitar opening to Peter Gabriel's hit song. I happily join him with the opening words, 'Climbing up on Solsbury Hill, I can see the city lights, wind was blowing time stood still, eagle flew out of the night...' Nina and the professor look back at us along the length of the boat's roof, laughing at our high spirits.

It's a beautiful summer's evening and I can feel the stress of the last few days easing from my shoulders as we make our way slowly through the glorious scenery. Will argues that the song must have come out when we were in sixth-form as we know it so well. I take issue with this and he is forced to concede, after Googling, that it was released in 1977, when we were both just four years old. As a forfeit, Will ducks below for two small bottles of cold beer and then finds the song on his phone and plays it while we gaze across at the hill that inspired it.

There is an interesting range of boats moored along this stretch of the canal, and most are occupied. Some are neat and tidy, suggesting that their owners may commute to work in the city just as I do. Others are the chaotic-looking refuges of individuals who have chosen to live an alternative, off-grid lifestyle. Some have strange homemade artworks decorating their boats or the banks opposite, and now and then there is even a raft, lying low in the water and boasting a shed or a flimsy looking shelter made of dirty canvas. A whiff of cannabis or coal smoke occasionally drifts towards us as we pass.

Two hire boats come towards us, weaving slightly, one immediately after the other and travelling in the opposite direction, back towards Bath. I push over to the right-hand side of the river to give them as much room as possible. They are the remnants of a stag party, returning their boats at the end of a week of drunken celebrations. Bodies are stretched out, comatose and unmoving on their roofs, contrary to boatyard instructions, and cans of lager lie next to them, slowly broiling in the evening sunshine. A man dressed as a mermaid is at the tiller of the first boat. He's wearing a long blonde wig and his shiny red dress has a large fishtail hem. He cheerily waves a bottle as he weaves past us, going slightly too fast for this stretch of canal. The roof of the second boat is also littered with prone bodies, among them a man wearing a yellow mankini and a Stetson.

'Nice look, cowboy,' Will calls out, and he is rewarded with a lazily raised thumb. I move back into the centre of the canal after they've passed. The long straight stretch continues, lined with moored boats and bisected by two swing bridges, which Nina and Will manage to open and close efficiently. It has taken just over an hour to reach the picturesque village of Bathampton, where road bridges cross the canal and the River Avon and a toll bridge does a brisk business taking handfuls of coins from a continuing queue of motorists. We motor on past the George, where a good-sized crowd is already spilling out of the pub's doors, pass under an old stone bridge and find a mooring gap at the end of a line of boats, opposite the broad expanse of a cricket pitch.

'Kingfisher!' shouts Nina, as she is tying the bow fast, and we all turn to catch a blur of metallic blue skimming along the far bank. I regard this as a very good omen.

During our trip so far, the professor has remained in the bow with Nina and I have seized the opportunity to fill Will in on some of the developments in Bath over the last week, particularly the story of the sinking of *Nautilus* and what it means to the professor.

'So, we all need to be kind to him and, ideally, distract him from thinking too much about what has happened,' I say, as I cut the engine and quiet descends.

'Perfect,' says Will. 'I need someone to help me learn my lines and your prof sounds like he'll be an ideal Lady Bracknell.'

'Good idea,' I agree. 'But first things first – the George.'

As we saunter down to the bustling pub, a family stand to leave their outdoor picnic table just as we arrive. Once again, our trip seems to be blessed. Will and Nina head off to fetch menus and the first round of drinks.

'Your friend Will is quite charming,' says the professor. 'You said he's an actor?'

'Yes, he's just been drafted in to the Theatre Royal at short notice. The curtain goes up on Tuesday so he's up against it a bit. *The Importance of Being Earnest.*'

'Ah yes, I know it well. I taught a course on modern dramatists. Although it's hard to think of Wilde as modern these days.'

'Knowing Will, he'll have told his agent to tell them he's played the part before – and now he'll be frantically scrambling to be word perfect,' I say, slyly.

'Well,' says the professor tentatively. 'Perhaps you could suggest to him that I might help him to learn his lines? I don't want to feel like a spare part if I can assist in any way.'

'Great idea, professor,' I say. 'I'm sure he'll be very grateful.'

CHAPTER TWENTY-SIX

It is already warm by the time we all surface the following morning and feast guiltlessly on bacon, fried egg sandwiches and tomato ketchup. A few early boats have already gone past, but we are in no rush. Bradford on Avon is an easy day's cruising and I intend to use the weekend to regain some much-needed equilibrium. Will and the professor settle themselves in the bow with a copy of the play and their occasional laughter drifts back to the stern where Nina and I are taking turns at the tiller. It immediately takes me back to our journey through the Midlands last year. Today, we're relaxed, but then we were fleeing the press, a drugs gang and, it turned out, a sociopathic serial killer. The experience had drawn us together but the intervening months had increased both the physical and the emotional distance between us. And now Nina is going abroad, I remind myself. But at least we may be able to have a few final cruises together. I study Nina's elfin profile as she concentrates on the speed and direction of the boat. Her hair is just curling off her neck and swept forward at the sides into a short peak at the front. Her nose tilts upwards above well-shaped lips wearing a coat of bright red lipstick. Two elegant gold hoops hang from her ears. She is a picture.

Nina was an experienced canal-boater when she first volunteered to help me on *Jumping Jack Flash*, but I flatter myself as her equal now when it comes to manoeuvring the boat, handling locks, bridges and even aqueducts with ease. She is at the helm when the sharp left turn into Dundas Aqueduct quickly comes upon us. She doesn't manage it the first time, but reverses, pivots the boat slightly and heads straight down the throat of the gloriously high structure that takes us above the Avon and the railway line. We swing immediately right at the end and enter a heavily wooded area where vegetation and tall reeds blur the edge of the canal.

At the end of the wood, the canal opens out onto a bend and there are signs to the various attractions of Limpley Stoke just before a bridge. We find a mooring gap on the other side of it, drive in our stakes, tie up and lock up. We wander slowly across a path mown through a meadow to a bridge that looks down onto the Avon. The river is stunningly beautiful at this point, shallow and crystal clear, fronds of bright green weed waving lazily in the current. A short climb up a steep lane on the other side takes us to the Hop Pole, a traditional village pub built of local stone. I claim some shaky outdoor furniture on the steep slope of its garden lawn while Will fetches beers and lunch menus from inside, and wait for Nina and the professor to catch up and join us.

'How are the rehearsals going?' I ask the professor, when he sits down.

'Hmmm... ' he replies carefully. 'I am enjoying myself immensely, but then, of course, I have the book in front of me. I fear our friend faces something of a challenge in the time available to him. Algernon is a hefty part.'

Upon returning from the bar, Will, however, is his usual cheerful and confident self. 'It's always like this,' he says nonchalantly. 'Then something clicks, and it all begins to flow automatically.'

He soon has us roaring with laughter at anecdotes of recent on-stage disasters and an extra-marital adventure with an enthusiastic drama teacher in Stoke whose lorry-driver husband returned home unexpectedly early one morning.

'Fortunately, I could run faster than the fat bastard, even in my bare feet and carrying my helmet and leathers,' he says cockily. 'It's lucky I'd left my bike at the theatre or he would have trashed it. I immediately baled out for London and the understudy sent me a bottle of vodka as thanks for giving him the break.'

Fuelled with drink, food and good humour, we slowly wander back to the boat and agree on an hour's doze before we get going again. A quiet mooring at this time of day, and immediately after a good pub lunch, is a thing to be properly relished. We rest, reassured rather than disturbed by the murmur of passing boats or the buzzing of a wasp somewhere in the cabin. Eventually, Nina stirs us all into motion, gives everyone a small bottle of cold water and orders me to untie the boat.

When we reach our second aqueduct at Avoncliff, I'm back on the tiller. My sharp right turn is complicated by a crowded boat with at least twelve members of an extended family on board. They are all wearing white sailors' pork pie hats. Two inflatable balloons are dancing on strings tied to the handrail on their boat's roof. They are an eight and a zero, so I assume this is a hire boat and that one of the crew is celebrating a significant birthday. However, they are making heavy weather of leaving the aqueduct and the man at the helm looks anxious. So I nip past on the wrong side and just make it with a slight graze against one stone side of the aqueduct's entrance. This doesn't prevent Nina from holding her finger and thumb in a L-shape to her forehead. Our private code signifies this as 'learner' rather than 'loser', but I have to shrug in agreement.

The next stretch of canal is a great deal more stressful than it was when I travelled down it in the other direction for *Jumping Jack Flash*'s arrival in Bath. The summer traffic is now at its peak and increasing numbers of paddleboards, hire canoes and even swimmers begin to appear ahead. Many seem inexperienced and unsure of how get out of the way, which is disconcerting when you are bearing down on them in sixteen tonnes of slow-moving metal and wood. In the end, I ask Nina to go to the bow, where she sits on the roof and indicates with her arms when I should veer left or right. Occasionally, I hear her advising people on how to avoid being mown down and once or twice I am sufficiently alarmed to sound the horn. Most of these small craft are being hired out to daytrippers who have flooded into the prosperous little town of Bradford on Avon for the weekend. The wool trade, which originally made the town's fortune, has been replaced by tourism and the crowds can be overwhelming even if the architecture is breathtakingly lovely. So, we navigate the only lock on our trip and motor to a steep cutting, where we moor up for the night. It's a nice quiet spot still within walking distance of the town centre behind us and a marina ahead of us. The professor is keen to stretch his legs and sets off on his own to find a Saxon church. The rest of us are feeling too lazy to go exploring. Will opens a Duoro, which was in his shoulder bag, and we sit in the bow, toasting our happy reunion with our glasses of Portuguese red.

'The prof's being a great help,' says Will. 'And he's given me lots of intelligent criticism about the play. I hope I haven't tired him out.'

'Well, it doesn't look like it. He's a tough old bird,' observes Nina. 'It was a great idea to get him away from Bath,' she adds, turning to me.

'I hope nothing else has happened whilst we're away.'

'Linda or Danny would have told us,' says Nina sensibly. 'It seems so far away from all of this.' She stretches luxuriously to expose her flat midriff above the buckle of her belt. Eddie, who has been lying on his back on her lap, gives a little grumble when he is disturbed by her movement.

'I notice you didn't mention Bill,' I say to Nina.

She opens one eye, squinting quizzically. 'Well, I doubt he'd be the one to contact us. He hardly ever seems to be about.' Then she sits up and looks directly at me. 'What's your point?'

'I'm just wondering if he's completely on side. He was pretty rude to me the other night when I asked him for a quote for the *Chronicle*, and I thought it was strange that he wasn't about the following morning when *Nautilus* sank.'

'Go on,' says Nina.

'Well, he's obviously got money worries...'

The light dawns. 'You think he might be getting paid to...?' She sounds shocked.

'Well, it would be easy for one of the boat people to slip out at night and untie ropes or remove weedhatch covers,' I say.

'Or throw children's buggies in the river,' she continues thoughtfully.

'I just think we should keep a close eye on him,' I say. But maybe my imagination is working overtime again.

Nina throws together a mushroom and cheese risotto and when the professor returns we eat in the main saloon as the daylight is fading outside. I light a couple of storm lanterns and put them in the bow with four glasses, a jug of water and the bottle of Highland Park, which is still three-quarters full. The conversation inevitably drifts back to the moorings, the developers and the death of Rufus Powell.

'You two seem to have a knack of finding trouble,' says Will, but then he looks at me seriously. 'Is there any way that it could be someone copying the Pusher?'

'Possible but seriously doubtful,' I say. 'Even if the killer tried to make it look like a random mugging that went wrong, there hasn't been a sudden spate of bodies found in the water.'

'And we know there could be other reasons for people wanting Rufus Powell to disappear,' adds Nina.

I maintain my silence about Hells Angels' gangs for the moment, but glance uneasily at the professor. I hadn't wanted us to discuss all this again with him present, and he has fallen silent now after previously being on his usual fine form, giving us an enjoyable discourse on the merits of Japanese whiskies versus Scottish. Nina catches my thought.

'Do you want to use the bathroom before me?' she asks the old man gently. He is gazing into the darkness and clutching his whisky glass in cupped hands. He swallows what is left and stands.

'I have had a wonderful day. Quite wonderful. Thank you very much. Good night to you all.' He makes his way down the boat while I exchange a grimace with the other two.

'Let's try to keep it light tomorrow,' I say quietly. 'He'll have to confront reality again soon enough.' The drink and the stress of navigating our way through the day trippers has wiped me out. 'I think I'll turn in too.' 'What?' says Will. 'You've got to be joking. The night is young, my friend.' He holds his glass in the air as he says this and a small amount sloshes over the rim.

But I have caught something of the old man's gloominess, and I know I shall have to face the crowded canal again in the morning. Best to do so with a clear head. 'No, I'm off to bed. G'night.'

'One for the road?' I hear Will asking Nina as I move down through the boat. The door to the bow closes softly behind me.

Sound travels easily over water at night and Will has an actor's voice so that even his whisper can project to the rear seats of a theatre. I'm not trying to listen, but as I lie near the bedroom's open porthole on the inner side of the double berth, his words drift in anyway.

'Good health.'

'Cheers, Will,' says Nina.

I put my hands behind my head on the pillow and try to nod off to the sound of their desultory chat, in which Will moans about the idleness of his agent and Nina describes some of her work at the hospice.

Then, after a short silence, I hear Will ask, 'So then, lovely Nina, are you and Jack an item now?' I turn my head sharply towards his voice; every part of me is awake and straining to hear Nina's answer. I know Will has been drinking heavily throughout the evening, but why on earth would he ask such a question? Surely he won't make a pass at her? I lean up on one elbow, my head level with the porthole.

There is a significant pause before Nina answers hesitantly. 'No. No, we're not. Jack and I have become the very best of friends and... well, if I was ever to fall in love again, I am sure it would be with him. But we're not an item. No.'

'So, what's stopping you?' asks Jack, sounding puzzled. 'From falling in love again, I mean?'

'I'm still in love with Alan,' she says quickly, matter-of-factly.

I close my eyes for a brief moment.

'He's dead, Nina,' says Will bluntly. 'Don't you have to leave him behind some time?'

'No!' Now she sounds angry. 'Leave it, Will. You don't know what you're talking about and we've both had too much to drink.'

'Yes. I do, Nina,' says Will, enunciating his words with the extreme care of the inebriated. 'Jack's truly in love with you – it's written all over him. You'd be mad not to be the same. He's a wonderful guy and you're made for each other. I'm sorry, but there it is. Anyone can see it. You'll say it's none of my business but I'm his mate and I care for him and I want him to be happy again after Deb. And I want you to be happy again too.'

I know that it is the whisky talking and one part of me is willing him to shut up and come to bed immediately. But the other part recognises that Will is saying things I no longer have the courage to confess to Nina – and I am desperate to know her true state of mind.

'Alan and I were only married for six weeks before he died,' she says calmly. 'But we had known each other all our lives. I've never loved anyone so completely and utterly as him... and maybe I never will again. If I do, perhaps it will be Jack. But that's as far as I can go at the moment.' She pauses, then adds, 'Did Jack tell you I've been offered a job abroad? In Dubai.'

'What? No. Really? Are you going to take it? Why?'

Good questions, I think, feeling very stupid not to be having this conversation with her myself.

'It'll be healthy for both of us. We can both come up for air and think about what we really want. We're in limbo at the moment. I don't know what I want, and I'm not sure Jack knows what he wants either.'

I sigh heavily to myself in disagreement and Will sighs audibly in frustration. 'Are you sure, Nina? Have you spoken to him about it?'

'I think you'd better go to bed, Will. I need to anyway. Goodnight.'

I'm pretending to be asleep as Nina walks quietly down through the boat to her single berth, but I sense her stop and look down at me. So I open my eyes and we stare at each other for a moment without speaking. Then she moves on through the boat and through the door to her sleeping area. I leap out of bed and hurry to the shower room. I am anxious for Will not to see from my face that I have heard every word of their conversation. It has distressed me deeply. How can she be in any doubt that I know what I want? How can going to Dubai possibly help at all? I stare at myself in the mirror and unexpected tears of frustration and self-pity well up in my eyes. I rinse my face under the cold tap and rub it vigorously with a towel.

As I open the door, I am confronted by the professor, who is standing outside with an empty water glass. It is obvious from his face that he too has heard the conversation. He gives me an unutterably sad but sympathetic look and puts one bony hand on my bare shoulder.

'*Courage, mon brave,*' he whispers as I turn and head back to the double berth which is, thankfully, still empty of Will. My friend staggers to it shortly afterwards, dumps most of his clothes on the floor and collapses onto the mattress beside me without visiting the bathroom. He must have had a pee over the side. He is snoring within minutes while I have many hours of wakefulness ahead of me.

CHAPTER TWENTY-SEVEN

I decide to get up early after a very restless night, but it means I am forced to climb out over Will's body. Luckily, he is still comatose. Eddie hears me and comes through the swing door to say hello and so we both slip out for an early Sunday morning walk. The entrance to Bradford Marina appears after a short while on my right. We cross a wide road bridge and make for the terrace of a restaurant that looks out over rows of moored narrowboats. The smell from the kitchen tells me they are just opening for business and so I go inside, order a full English breakfast and share the bacon and sausages with Eddie.

In some ways, I tell myself, I am heartened by what I overheard last night. It suggested that one day, if Nina ever felt able to move on from Alan, then I was someone she might be able to love. Or am I kidding myself? If she can't return my feelings now, will she ever be able to? If it was even a remote possibility, why is she contemplating a move to Dubai? What if she meets someone else out there? Who is this 'old friend' of Alan's who has secured her the job? But these are exactly the same thoughts and questions that have been going around and around in my head all night, so I try to wash them away with a deep swig of coffee and ask for the bill.

'Hey, here he is,' says Will, looking slightly ashamed of himself as I join the others in the galley where Nina is frying bacon and buttering toast. She avoids my eyes and bends down to give Eddie a scrap of rind. 'Good morning, Jack,' says the professor. But he too sounds subdued. I suspect that he may have quietly told Will and Nina that their late-night chat could be clearly heard by the rest of the crew.

'Would you like some bacon?' asks Nina, pulling out a chair for me to sit down. 'There's plenty to go around.'

'No thanks, Eddie and I shared a full English at the marina.' It sounds more abrupt than I mean it to and an awkward silence follows. 'Well, another coffee then?' says Will, putting a steaming mug in front of me.

'I never have bacon butties for breakfast at home,' says Nina. 'But it seems very wrong to have anything else when I'm on *Jumping Jack Flash* – especially when we're travelling.'

'This is wonderful,' says the professor. 'Pass the ketchup would you, please, Will?'

Their stilted conversation and extravagant politeness are starting to make me even more fed up. I give myself a good mental shake and try to rescue what is left of our weekend.

'Right then,' I say rubbing my hands together with ridiculous heartiness. 'The weather is going to be glorious again – twenty-five degrees, a very light wind and there's already a clear blue sky. We're in no rush to get back, but I'd like to get past Bradford on Avon before the day trippers come out onto the water again. So, buck up, you lot, we need to get the lines in and turn this ship around.'

The others seem grateful for the call to action and bustle to their duties at bow and stern, while the professor joins me at the tiller.

There is only just enough water outside the marina's entrance to turn the boat around, but I manage it with the tiller hard over and after countless alternating reverse and forward thrusts. Finally, we are pointing back towards the city and we make our way slowly past moored boats into Bradford on Avon where we top up the water tank. Another narrowboat is conveniently waiting in the lock to share our descent. As I hoped, we are still too early for the hire canoes to be out and our trip back to the first aqueduct is much less stressful than the previous day. The canal follows the route of the Avon along the steep wooded valley and the pattern of the previous day reasserts itself, with Will and the professor ensconced in the bow with Oscar Wilde, and Nina and I together at the tiller, quietly watching the world go by. At one stage, she puts a hand over mine and quietly asks if I am okay. I give her a smile and a wink, but I don't completely trust my voice, so I remain silent and the moment passes.

I'm keen to keep Nina on the stern alongside me, despite the slight awkwardness that lingers, and so I tell her about my conversation with DI Kerr and how the police murder investigation centres on the Hells Angel gang in Bristol. 'To be honest,' I finish, 'I think she thought I was some kind of conspiracy nutcase. She only told me about the Bristol Bulldogs because Chisholm told her she could trust me – which was good of him. Best to keep it between ourselves for now.'

'Well… ' she starts cautiously. 'It does sound pretty plausible. A gang boss's son is sent down for a year and Daddy wants to get revenge on the magistrate who was responsible – or the son gives orders from prison for it to be done. It might still have been a violent revenge attack that went wrong. They may not have meant to kill him. But it does seem a likely scenario.'

'And it would mean there's no connection between Powell's murder and the campaign against the boat people – if we assume the Andropovs are behind that.'

We lapse into our separate thoughts and, after a while, she drifts forward to see how the others are doing.

Our passage to Dundas Aqueduct passes uneventfully save for when we come across a charming isolated cottage, where an overweight, topless and tattooed middle-aged man is sitting in a folding garden chair. There is another chair alongside him occupied by a blow-up woman wearing a large floppy sunhat and nothing else. Will stands up in the bow to point out the bizarre scene to me. The man gives him a cheery thumbs-up.

'What's your girlfriend's name?' calls Will.

'Dolly,' says the man with a grin. 'And she's not my girlfriend, she's my wife.' I smile awkwardly at him as we cruise past the eccentric – but seemingly happy – couple.

Having crossed the aqueduct again without incident, we find a free visitor mooring and head for a licensed café called the Angelfish at Brassknocker Basin. It will only take another three to four hours to return to Bath and so the afternoon is stretching out enticingly before us. We order a bottle of chilled Provencal rosé to share with our sandwiches, but when they arrive Will suddenly stands up and, in the haughty voice of a young aristocrat, says to the professor.

'Good heavens! Lane! Why are there no cucumber sandwiches? I ordered them specially.'

The tracery of fine wrinkles around the professor's eyes crinkle with pleasure. He stands to attention and bows his head like a well-trained manservant.

'There were no cucumbers in the market this morning, sir. I went down twice.'

Our young waitress is watching this exchange in total bafflement. Others on nearby tables have turned to watch what is going on.

'No cucumbers!' explodes Will loudly. Now everyone is watching.

'No sir. Not even for ready money,' says the professor calmly and gravely.

'That will do, Lane, thank you.'

'Thank you, sir,' says the professor, before sitting down and calmly reaching for his wine glass. Will turns to Nina and puts both hands on his hips.

'I am greatly distressed, Aunt Augusta, about there being no cucumbers, not even for ready money.' Then he sits back down and sips his wine.

'I'm sorry,' says the waitress, brandishing her notepad at us. 'You didn't ask for cucumbers. You asked for prawns and beef with horseradish.'

We all explode with laughter and I reassure her that she mustn't pay any attention to my silly thespian friends. Will rises back to his feet and clinks a spoon on his wine glass. The café obediently falls silent.

'I apologise for disturbing you, ladies and gentlemen, but that was a short extract from *The Importance of Being Earnest,* which opens for one week only at the Theatre Royal, Bath, this Tuesday. I do hope you will come. It will be magnificent – and, as usual, so will I in the role of Mr Algernon Moncrieff.' He gives a little bow and sits down. Someone begins to clap, but it quickly tails away in embarrassment.

'Idiot,' I say to him, as our waitress retreats in confusion. 'I hope you give that poor girl a generous tip. Now, listen up for a moment, I've been doing some thinking this morning.'

I tell Will and the professor how Nina and I have learnt of a lunchtime meeting on the following day, which is to be attended by one of the Andropov twins, the planning committee chair and the council's chief planning officer.

'You crafty sod,' says Will in admiration.

'Well, that is interesting news,' adds the professor.

'I would love to be a fly on the wall at that meeting,' I say. 'But the question is how?'

'They haven't met you before, have they?' asks Will, and I shake my head. 'And you say it's at a golf club?'

'That's right,' says Nina. 'Saltford, at one o'clock.'

'Well, why don't we book ourselves in for lunch as well?' asks Will excitedly. 'I can slip away from rehearsals for an hour, or even two at a push.'

I look at him dubiously. Will's work ethic is something to admire from a distance.

'It might be members' only,' says the professor cautiously.

Nina pulls out her new smartphone and searches for the club's website. 'It says visitors are welcome, but there's a dress code. It looks quite smart.' She passes me the phone and I read some hype about it being 'one of the finest golf courses in Somerset'. Will takes the phone from me, inspects it and grins. Before we can stop him, he's dialled and is speaking in a pitch-perfect American drawl.

'Well, hi there, darling. My name's Algernon Bunbury the Third,' Will says.

The professor covers his eyes.

'Ah'm just visiting your beautiful little country looking for golf clubs to add to mah collection.'

Now it is my turn to cover my eyes.

'Put me through to your restaurant will you, honey? Yeah, hi there, pal. You do steaks? Great. Me and a buddy want to do lunch at your place tomorrow. That's swell. One o'clock, name's Bunbury. Yup, you can use this number. Mah assistant will pass a message on. That's swell, buddy. See y'all tomorrow.'

Will hangs up and triumphantly slides the phone back across the table to Nina. Then he turns to me. 'You do own a jacket and tie, don't you, buddy?'

Our young waitress has reappeared with our bill during Will's performance on the phone and is now staring at him as though he is quite mad. The professor insists on paying for our lunch plus a tip for the bewildered girl. Afterwards, as we stroll back to the boat, Nina demands to know why Will didn't book a place for her at the golf club. I sense she is not impressed at being described as Bunbury's assistant.

'It's a golf club!' protests Will innocently. 'They probably don't even let women over the threshold.'

This is nonsense, of course. The chief planning officer is a woman and she is already booked in for the lunch with Sebastian Andropov and the chair of the planning committee – but I keep quiet. Nina's jaw is clenched in an all too familiar look of stubborn resistance. She hates to be left out of anything and is about to make her feelings known.

'To be honest, it makes sense for at least one of us to stay under their radar, Nina,' I say, 'just in case.' This is just about enough to placate her. I draw her to one side. 'When will you have to get back to Salisbury? You can stay as long as you want, you know that. But... the hospice... ?' I tail off.

I can tell she is calculating whether my question is connected to her night-time conversation with Will.

'It's not a problem. They're covering my shifts and I'd like to stick around until this stupid campaign stops and I know the professor is happily settled. And I'd love to see Will's play. If that's okay with you, Jack?'

'More than fine,' I say, quietly rejoicing as we rejoin the others.

The five-mile route back to Robert's garden passes peacefully. All the visitor moorings at Bathampton are occupied and so we cruise past the George and we are soon navigating our way through Sydney Gardens and below the grand mansions of Bathwick.

Will gives Nina and the professor a hug goodbye. 'Swell weekend, folks,' he says in his fake American accent before switching to aristocratic English. 'And thank you for the help, Lane,' he says to the professor. 'It was invaluable.'

'A pleasure as always, sir,' replies the old man with a slight incline of the head and in plummy tones which remind me of Sir John Gielgud.

I walk with Will up the garden to unlock his motorbike. He gives me a rare bashful look. 'Look, Jack, I'm sorry about speaking to Nina like that. I just think you guys should be together, you know. I blame the drink. But it's none of my business and I'm sorry. D'you really think she'll go to Dubai?'

I look back down at the boat, where Nina and the professor are tidying up the mooring ropes. 'Who knows, Will? I'm nearly fifteen years older than her, I live on a boat and I've just thrown away the only part-time job I had. I'm not a great prospect, am I?' I give him a rueful smile. 'Don't worry about it. Thanks for coming.'

He gives me a hug. 'See you tomorrow for lunch, my friend.' Then he kicks the big engine of his bike into life and roars off.

CHAPTER TWENTY-EIGHT

Another large motorbike is speeding down the dual carriageway from Bristol to Bath at the same time that evening. The rider is in high spirits and, occasionally, on clear stretches, he weaves his powerful bike extravagantly from one side of the road to the other. Bob-the-Prospect enjoys the honour of ferrying Vince around in the side-car, but he is relishing riding solo again on the two wheels of his 500cc Kawasaki. The young man is excited by his imminent adventure and bursting with pride at being trusted for this mission by the Big Man and his uncle, Mad John. The only downside, he reflects, is having to ditch anything that suggests he is a Bristol Bulldog. The Big Man had pressed a fistful of £50 notes into his hand and given him very specific orders. It had taken all of Saturday afternoon for Bob-the-Prospect to get his long hair washed and cut into a short back-and-sides and to buy three new outfits in the menswear department of Top Shop. He had presented himself for inspection to Mad John at the end of the day, feeling like a complete stranger to himself in the skinny jeans, white cotton shirt and blue linen jacket. His boots had been swapped for a shiny pair of black Oxfords and he was clean shaven.

'I look like a fucking squaddie on home leave,' he had complained to his uncle.

'You don't look like a Hells Angel and that's the main thing,' replied the Bulldogs' sergeant-at-arms from behind his sunglasses, throwing him a clean black motorbike jacket that was bereft of any badges or insignia. Mad John had hinted that if his nephew did well over the next couple of days, his apprenticeship could be ripped up: Bob-the-Prospect would become a Full-Patch Bristol Bulldog, something he'd longed for ever since joining the gang just under a year ago.

Bob had been depressed and lonely after losing his mechanic job when the car dealership closed, and so his uncle's suggestion that he join the Bulldogs as a Prospect had come at just the right time. But Prospects were the lowest of the low and treated as such by the other gang members. They were regularly sent on menial tasks and roughed up occasionally until Vince decided that they had proven themselves. Nothing too serious. Just a hair wash in the Archangel's bog or having their bikes kicked from behind when they were riding in a pack, so that they wobbled dangerously. Bob-the-Prospect knew he'd had a slightly easier time thanks to being Mad John's nephew and a friend of Vince's son, Clive. It had been a proper wrench for him when Clive had gone down for GBH. He was certain that Clive wouldn't have taken out a contract on the Bath magistrate. Bob-the-Prospect couldn't imagine his friend having the imagination or the courage to do something like that without his old man's say-so. But if he didn't, then who did? And if the police didn't know, how in hell's name could Bob-the-Prospect even begin to find out?

His room at the modern mid-priced hotel in Bath had been booked in advance by his uncle and the receptionist had shown him somewhere safe that he could lock up his bike. He was relieved about this. He didn't want some skanky low-life trying to steal his pride and joy. You couldn't trust anyone these days. The receptionist was a tidy looker, too; Bob-the-Prospect was sure she'd been flirting with him a bit. In his experience, women were a bit put off by his unwashed Hells Angels' appearance and, he had to admit, he'd quite enjoyed the novelty.

He stood in front of the hotel room's full-length mirror and looked closely at himself. Other gang members had teased him for his slight resemblance to Leonardo DiCaprio; he had even features, slightly narrowed eyes, full cheeks and good teeth. Some had called him 'Babyface' for a while. But this nickname had been shortened to 'Baby' after five of the Prospects had been forced to do one of many impromptu initiation ceremonies. This particular one involved drinking eight pints of lager (cider was also allowed) and racing stark naked from the Archangel to a neighbouring pub and back. He had stood out from the others, partly because he won fairly easily and didn't need to join them as they retched into the gutter, but also because of his total absence of any tattoos. He had promised himself a couple of Death's Heads on his chest if, or rather when, he became a Full Patch. Bob-the-Prospect thought Vince's memory of him as a clean-skinned 'Baby' had probably contributed to him being chosen to pass as a civilian for this mission.

Right now, teeth brushed, closely shaven and with an expensive haircut, he had to admit he felt pretty good about how he looked. He might even try asking the receptionist if she had any plans for when her shift ended. He would base himself in the city for a week, just as he'd been ordered, keep his eyes and ears open and do whatever the Big Man asked him to do. Nice little break really, he thought to himself, stretching out on his hotel bed and helping himself to the biscuits that had been left on his tea tray.

CHAPTER TWENTY-NINE

On Monday morning a text arrives on my phone while I am walking Eddie. It's from Tom, the *Chronicle*'s young property and business correspondent. He knows of my interest in the old Tiller & Brown site but has been unable to give me any further information until now. The text says:

> Andropov Developments. Presser announced.
> Tomorrow – Tuesday 11am Bath Spa Hotel.

I assume that this press conference has been called to announce the details of the company's planning application for the site. I now know where I plan to be tomorrow morning.

On the boat, I iron a clean shirt, buff my shoes and decide I will look sufficiently presentable for a golf club lunch in a light summer jacket and black chinos. The roar of Will's motorbike announces his arrival, but instead of his usual leathers, Will is dressed in a cream linen suit as he saunters down the slope of the garden to the boat. It is only the high, unusual cut of the lapels that gives it away as an Edwardian-era costume borrowed from the theatre. Nina straightens my tie for me and inspects us both.

'Hmmm... I know the dress code says smart casual, but you're a bit too smart,' she says to Will before turning to me, 'and somehow, even with a tie, you're a bit too casual. I'm not sure how well you're going to blend in.'

'We'll be fine, honey,' says Will in his southern American drawl as he gives her a peck on the cheek. 'Don't wait up.'

I wince and shrug my shoulders in apology as Nina frowns in annoyance. 'And I don't think most golf club luncheon guests would arrive on a motorbike – especially if they're pretending to be American millionaires.' She is clearly still miffed at not coming along. 'You should take a taxi.'

'Don't worry. We'll try to keep the bike out of sight,' I say. I climb onto the pillion seat behind Will and he hands me an open-faced helmet from one of the large plastic panniers mounted at its rear. The ride is scary – largely because Will handles it in the same way he approaches most things in life; that is to say with a devil-may-care insouciance and a reckless appetite for cutting corners. We are an odd couple and always have been. His audacity often got him into trouble as a boy, while I kept my nose clean and became the first boy to edit the school newspaper. But his charm meant he was widely liked by teachers and pupils alike and he seldom paid too much of a price for his pranks. The acting life suits his low boredom threshold and his performances often have a dangerous edge which audiences – mostly – find exhilarating. Much like his motorbike riding, I think to myself, teeth clenched in terror as we tip over into another ridiculously acute angle.

The sloping drive to the golf club quickly emerges from an established residential area, which is off the main road between Bath and Bristol. A smart new timber driving range has been erected immediately after the entrance, on the right-hand side, and Will parks the bike behind one end of it so it will be hidden from the clubhouse. We lock away our helmets, smooth down our clothes, straighten each other's ties and stroll up the tree-lined drive.

The clubhouse is a sprawling, modern single-storey building and just inside the main entrance a photograph of the Prince of Wales indicates that it has been built on Duchy of Cornwall land. No one challenges us as we wander through the reception area, peering casually into trophy cabinets crammed with silverware and framed photographs. I open one door to find a snooker table, covered in a plastic sheet and filling the room. Eventually, we find a bar and a young woman in a purple waistcoat and matching skirt who is polishing some glasses.

'Good afternoon, gentlemen,' she says. 'What can I get you?'

I have already briefed Will to try to blend into the background, but he does love to give a performance.

'Hi, honey,' he says softly in his fake-American accent. He passes a hand through his thick black hair and lets her admire his perfectly white and even teeth with a friendly smile of many megawatts. 'What do you recommend?'

A blush rises at the girl's throat. She puts her head on one side, involuntarily returns his smile and is unable to tear her eyes away from his. I groan inwardly.

'Oh... the bitter is nice,' she says.

'Two pints of bitter it is then, honey,' says Will. 'And please have a drink on me.' She stammers her thanks while he continues to watch her every movement behind the bar. 'Say, honey,' he says as he hands over some cash, 'we've booked to have lunch here. The name is Bunbury. But my pal here hates eating in an empty room. Do you have anyone else coming in?'

She punches up a screen at her till, presses a few buttons and studies it. 'There's a party of three and two couples booked on the terrace at one o'clock,' she says. 'And a couple of tables of four at half past one in the restaurant.'

'Great. Hey, Jack, what say we eat on the terrace too?' I mutter my agreement. 'Hey, honey, can you fix that for me and my good friend here?'

'No problem,' she says, without taking her eyes off Will, and suddenly I am reminded of Mowgli's hypnotism by the snake Kaa in the Disney film of *The Jungle Book*. She collects a couple of menus and asks us to follow her out onto the terrace, which overlooks the golf course. It has a modern steel and glass barrier around it and black metal latticework tables and chairs. Will immediately and expertly steers us towards the table nearest to one that is already laid for three guests and before the barmaid can object claims it by sitting down as he thanks her extravagantly for her kindness.

It is ten minutes to one and I look down onto the green and solitary bunker of the eighteenth hole. There is no one in sight and I wonder if our quarry is playing a round or just arriving for lunch. We soon learn it is the latter when a waitress ushers a man and a woman to the table next to ours. I recognise Mrs Gwyneth Wilkinson, chief planning officer, and Councillor Laurence Merton, chair of the planning committee, from the photographs lining the hallway at the Guildhall. Laurence Merton is a small, plump red-faced man in his mid-fifties with a short-cropped fuzz of grey hair. His forehead is damp with sweat and he mops it with a paper napkin as he sits down. Gwyneth Wilkinson looks slightly younger than her boss and more composed as she peers with interest around the terrace. Her maroon trouser suit is perhaps a size too small and she is wearing heavy make-up beneath an elaborate grey coiffure. Will and I pretend to be engrossed in our menus, but that doesn't stop the two new arrivals giving us a long inspection before looking at their watches and whispering privately to each other.

Five minutes pass before Mr Andropov makes his entrance. This time, a restaurant manager has materialised out of nowhere and is obsequiously showing the businessman to his table, accepting the discreetly folded twenty-pound note pressed into his palm as he does so. It's a strange thing for Andropov to do. The restaurant is nearly empty. He must be very keen to secure first class service for himself and his guests. But then, I reflect, as I peruse the distinctly unremarkable menu, the choice of venue is also odd. If he wanted to impress the councillors, there are countless exclusive and expensive watering holes in Bath's centre and many more five-star country house hotels in the countryside around the city. This golf club seems much less grand by comparison. But Andropov was keen for the meeting to be off the beaten track.

Merton and Wilkinson rise to greet him. Sebastian Andropov is tall, at least six foot, slim and athletic-looking with wide muscular shoulders under an impeccably fitted grey pinstripe suit. He is wearing a white shirt and blue tie and carrying a leather briefcase. As he shakes hands, his cuffs shoot back to reveal an expensive rectangular dress watch and black pearl cufflinks. In the flesh, he looks exactly like the photograph in the magazine article I saw on the screen in Robert's study.

From behind my menu, which I am poring over as if it is fascinating, I hear him murmur, 'Good to see you again,' as they shake hands. So, this isn't their first meeting. The waitress arrives to take our orders as the manager bustles around the nearby table with menus and recommendations. As he places his order, I am relieved to hear that Will has dropped his American accent and is now focused on blending in as quietly as possible.

'Smooth-looking bastard,' he whispers, once the waitress has left.

'Takes one to know one,' I whisper back. Then we embark on a conversation of very little consequence in normal tones.

A bottle of champagne arrives at the neighbouring table in a silver bucket of ice on a stand. Below us, a pair of golfers who look like they are father and son are chipping onto the green. I direct Will's attention to them and pretend to watch them with interest, but really I am focusing all of my energy on trying to overhear Sebastian's conversation with the councillors. However, it is hopeless. The group have lowered their voices to a level that fails to travel to our table and we can hear nothing apart from an occasional burst of discreet laughter that betrays their good humour. Our meal proceeds in tandem with theirs, although their service is a great deal more attentive. Sebastian asks the manager to pour the champagne, but after that he takes it on himself to keep his guests' glasses topped up – which he does frequently. Councillor Merton seems to be the least comfortable of the three, constantly shifting in his seat, repeatedly tapping his shoes under the table and occasionally looking around the terrace at us and the handful of other guests who have joined us. His nervousness seems to make him thirsty and his glass is refilled the most often. Sebastian, in contrast, makes his first drink last for the whole lunch.

Will and I are increasingly frustrated. We are learning nothing in return for the price of our three-course lunch and Will is checking his watch with increasing frequency. The rest of the cast will be waiting to rehearse with him again in just under half an hour. He greets our neighbours' order for three brandies with a small groan. Their balloon glasses are delivered while I deliberately spend an inordinate amount of time checking our bill. As I put my card down to signal I am happy to pay, the arrival of the brandy seems to prompt them to relax a little. Suddenly we are able to hear their conversation.

'Cheers to you both. Thank you very much for taking the time to meet me before tomorrow's big announcement,' says Sebastian smoothly, clinking their glasses in turn. 'In fact,' he continues, 'I have a token of our appreciation for each of you.' He bends down to pick up the briefcase from under his chair and removes two small boxes. Both have been wrapped in the same metallic blue paper.

'Oh no, we couldn't possibly... ' Councillor Merton begins, sounding slightly panicked, looking around the room. 'Not now –'

'Nonsense,' says Sebastian quickly, soothingly. 'This is just a very small memento of our lunch; well within the limits of permitted hospitality. Mere tokens of our appreciation for your time. Please, see for yourself.'

Merton and Wilkinson look at each other unhappily and then glance over at the other tables before slowly unpeeling the wrapping paper. They look like naughty children cheating at pass-the-parcel. I risk rising slightly in my chair on the pretext of calling the waitress over to see what appears when the box lids are taken off. Six golf balls, presented in two lines of three in each box. Merton gives a relieved sort of laugh.

'You see – golf balls. What could be more appropriate for our lunch venue? A mere trifle. But we must capture this moment.' Andropov pulls a mobile from an inside jacket pocket, quickly framing both of his guests. Merton looks both startled and worried. 'Please, hold up your balls,' he says. Gwyneth Wilkinson giggles as the two councillors pose awkwardly with their gifts, elbows resting on the table, holding the boxes above their empty brandy glasses.

I whisper an urgent instruction to Will, and suddenly I too am standing.

'Please, allow me,' I say, in my most helpful and polite voice. 'I'm sure you would all like to be in the photo.' I reach a hand out for the developer's mobile.

Andropov fixes me with a hard stare and narrows his eyes.

'No,' he says firmly. 'Thank you, but that won't be necessary.' He replaces his phone in his jacket pocket. Merton and Wilkinson are looking up at me with eyes like rabbits transfixed by the headlights of an oncoming car.

'Aww... c'mon, buddy,' says Will, his American drawl loud and disarming. He's moved quickly to stand behind Sebastian and puts one hand on his shoulder, almost forcing him to stay seated. 'Let's all have a friendly group photo. Y'know –' he beams a smile directly into the twin's face – 'I might just be planning to buy this cute little golf club, so I'd appreciate a memento of our lunch today too!'

I already have my own phone in my hand, recording video of Will, Sebastian, Merton and Wilkinson before anyone can respond.

'That's enough,' snarls Sebastian, sweeping Will's hand from his shoulder and standing as though to square up to him. There is barely six inches between them. Will steps back and away from the table, holding both hands up in the air exaggeratedly as though pleading for calm. I continue to film.

'Hey, fella, no offence, just trying to be friendly. Jesus... you Brits.' Will exaggeratedly brushes himself down while I restore my phone to my back pocket. Then we both back off and rejoin our table. 'So goddamn unfriendly,' Will complains loudly to the room. He looks utterly disgusted and wholly the innocent party. 'Bravo,' I say quietly.

The restaurant manager has materialised out of nowhere and is fluttering ineffectually as Andropov and the councillors busily gather their possessions and shoot angry glances at us as they leave. We do our best to act aggrieved and ignore them, then follow almost immediately. Will and I emerge from the main entrance to see a chauffeur-driven powder-blue Bentley Mulsanne pulling away with Sebastian in a rear seat. The car is the same one that had been parked outside the Royal Crescent Hotel. It is very possible that the twins are staying there during their time in Bath. Meanwhile, Merton and Wilkinson are getting into the rear of a taxi together.

Will checks his watch.

'Bloody hell, Jack! The director will kill me.'

We sprint down the drive to Will's motorbike. 'That was a bloody waste of time,' he says, as he retrieves our crash helmets. 'Couldn't hear a thing.'

'Not necessarily,' I say thoughtfully, as I climb up behind him.

CHAPTER THIRTY

Will ignores several speed limits on our ride to the theatre and I am grateful to walk the final stretch home from Barton Street. As I emerge through Robert's garden door, I see Mrs Manningham-Westcott's mobility scooter parked on the top terrace. Laughter is coming from the interior of *Jumping Jack Flash*. Eddie's warning bark gives me away and Nina's close-cropped head pops out of the rear hatchway.

'Hi, there,' she says. 'We have a visitor. How did it go?'

'Couldn't hear much,' I reply. 'But I'll tell you properly later.'

'How was Will?' she asks. I detect a slight air of jealousy. She clearly still thinks that she should have been there rather than him.

'Surprisingly helpful, actually,' I say. 'Come on, better not neglect our guests.' The saloon table is laid for tea, and Mrs Manningham-Westcott and the professor are tucked neatly side by side on the banquette seat.

'Mr Johnson,' says the old lady. 'How delightful. And may I say how terribly smart you look? I've brought some homemade coffee and walnut cake. Homemade by my housekeeper rather than by me, but quite delicious.' She cuts me a slice without asking and pours me a cup of tea from the pot. 'Isn't this lovely? You have a cosy boat, Mr Johnson.'

'Please, call me Jack,' I say, eating cake and mentally resolving to do more exercise. I am unused to three-course lunches followed by cake and increasingly conscious of the tightness of my trouser waistbands. Walking the dog just isn't enough any more.

'How did the lunch go?' asks the professor. 'Nina and I briefed Rani about what you and Will were up to.'

I smile inwardly at his familiar use of Mrs Manningham-Westcott's first name.

'Frustrating in one way,' I admit. 'Sebastian Andropov met with Merton and Wilkinson – the planning committee chair and the chief planning officer,' I explain. 'They had a tight little lunch together, but their voices were so quiet Will and I could hardly hear a thing.'

'Suspicious in itself,' sniffs Mrs Manningham-Westcott.

'So, women *were* allowed into the club,' says Nina accusingly.

I choose to ignore her. 'At the end, Sebastian gave them a gift. A box of golf balls each.'

'Is that allowed?' asks Nina.

'I don't know,' I say. 'One of them made some kind of reference to being within the permitted limits of hospitality. Golf balls wouldn't have cost much, surely?'

'But with an expensive three-course lunch?' observes Nina.

'Well, I imagine developers and builders are allowed to brief the council in such a way as long as it's all declared in some kind of hospitality register,' I muse. 'Oh,' I suddenly remember. 'We did manage to get a bit of a video of the happy gathering at the end – much to their annoyance.'

I pull out my phone and everyone watches the twenty-three seconds of video. It shows the man and woman from the council seated and looking up at me with startled expressions. They are balancing their golf balls above the remnants of their meal and holding them towards the camera. Sebastian is sitting with Will standing behind him, looking angrily at me, before he snaps 'That's enough.' Then the camera veers away and I stop recording.

'Well,' observes the professor, 'they all look distinctly uncomfortable at being seen together in that way.'

I nod in agreement. 'And it wasn't the first time they had met either. How are Linda and the others?'

'Nothing to report,' says the professor. 'They are mounting guard throughout the night now and there is always one of them there during the day. It was a quiet weekend, but it will be quite a strain on them to keep it up.'

'And I've been keeping an eye on the boats for as long as possible through my telescopic lens,' adds Mrs Manningham-Westcott. 'But it's hard after dark. My eyes aren't what they used to be, and I get tired.'

'It's good of you to do anything,' says the professor and she smiles back at him with genuine pleasure.

'And your boat?' I ask tentatively.

'Again. Nothing to report,' says the professor sadly. 'I need to arrange for insurance assessors to visit the marina this week and then decide whether to restore *Nautilus* or sell her as a hulk.'

Mrs Manningham-Westcott tuts sympathetically.

'There is one other bit of news,' I say, and they all look at me expectantly. 'The twins are holding a press conference tomorrow morning at eleven o'clock at the Bath Spa Hotel. I expect they'll use it to announce their outline plans for the site prior to a formal planning application being made. I'm sure the *Chronicle* will send Tom, their property and business correspondent, but I'm also planning to attend.'

'I'll be going too,' says Nina, with a look that dares me to suggest otherwise.

'I would very much like to see these two gentlemen in action,' says the professor. 'If the sabotage of my home is connected with the development of their site, then they have a great deal to answer for.'

'I agree,' I say. 'But proving it will be another matter.'

'Nevertheless,' the professor says firmly, 'I shall be attending.'

'I suppose we might get a clue about why they are prepared to pay you to leave,' I say.

'Right, then,' Nina says. 'I suggest we call round on Linda and the kids. We haven't seen them all weekend and we can tell them the latest. And we can escort Mrs Manningham-Westcott back to her apartment on the way.'

'Thank you so much,' she says, before adding, 'and I think it is high time, Jack and Nina, that you also called me by my first name, Rani. Manningham-Westcott is such a mouthful.'

'It's a beautiful name,' says the professor. 'I looked it up. Did you know it is the name for an Indian princess? The wife of a Raja.'

The professor stands and gallantly helps Rani to use her sticks to get up and out of the boat. Eddie runs ahead but the rest of us make slow progress as we match her pace up the stepped garden. Back on the mobility scooter on level ground, the professor walks alongside his new friend as Nina and I lag behind them a little on the twenty-minute walk to the moorings. Once again, I am struck with sadness at the gap where the *Nautilus* should have been. There are now only three boats instead of five. The professor peels away to escort Rani to her flat while Nina and I approach Linda's boat. Today it is dark and locked up. As usual, there is no sign of Bill, either, but Danny appears to say hello and I can see Tammy lurking just below on *Otter*'s stern step.

'Good trip?' Danny asks cheerfully.

'Great, thanks,' says Nina, before I can speak. I look at her carefully. The weekend trip was not an unqualified delight for me due to the overheard conversation between Nina and Will. But she seems to be perfectly genuine in expressing her pleasure at the jaunt to Bradford on Avon and back.

'All quiet here,' says Danny. 'We're doing two-hour shifts through the night. It's a bit knackering but it's made us feel a lot safer.'

A thought occurs to me.

'Look. It will be easier with another two people doing shifts. Or even three,' I say, thinking of the professor. 'Why don't I bring *Jumping Jack Flash* down onto the professor's mooring for now? Then Nina and I, and the professor, can take our turns too. With a bit of luck, it'll mean you only have to mount guard every other night.'

'Great idea,' says Nina, enthusiastically.

'Well,' says Danny, using one of his huge workman's hands to ruffle his hair thoughtfully. 'I can't deny it would be a big help.'

I give the professor's new mobile a ring, looking across the water at Rani's apartment window where two shapes are silhouetted. The professor answers and the shapes wave down at us. I tell him my plan and he readily agrees, so I tell him to stay put for the moment as we move the boat. 'No time like the present,' I say cheerfully.

'Can I leave Eddie with you?' I ask Danny. This brings Tammy out onto the stern at speed. She quickly scoops up the dog and takes him back down into *Otter*'s interior without saying a word.

'She loves that little terrier,' says Danny fondly.

'Well, she did save him from being drowned,' adds Nina with equal fondness. 'So, I'm sure he feels the same about her.'

Nina and I jog back to *Jumping Jack Flash*, where I put a brief explanatory note through Robert's letterbox and text Will about our change of address. Then I check my weedhatch again, just to be sure. Our return journey from Bradford on Avon means we are already pointing in the right direction to continue through the city and out towards the canal's junction with the River Avon. We make our way down the small flight of six locks and onto the river, where I swing left and we are soon throwing mooring ropes to Danny and the professor, while Tammy holds Eddie and looks on from the bank. The professor jumps onboard our stern as I cut the engine.

'Excellent idea, Jack. I don't want the Andropov brothers thinking they've automatically got my mooring back – and we can take turns on guard duty, as you say.' I realise he is slightly emotional but he turns his face away from me and up to the apartments. Rani is still in her window and he waves to her. She waves back.

'Nice lady,' I say, meaning it.

'Extremely,' he agrees. 'Now, do you have anything with which we can toast your arrival?'

I head below to open a bottle of red.

Linda and her children reappear in the early evening. She has been doing some Sunday cleaning shifts where Juno and Noah are welcome to tag along. The professor and Linda draw up a new rota of night-time guard duties, which has her, Tammy and Danny sharing three-hour stints on one night from ten p.m. to seven a.m., and me, Nina and Bill doing the same on the following night. Despite his protests, Linda has put the professor on the substitute's bench in case anyone gets too tired or is unable to do their guard duty for any other reason. I reflect that it will be interesting to see if Bill actually turns up at his allotted time.

CHAPTER THIRTY-ONE

The warmth of the day is still lingering in Parade Gardens, where Bob-the-Prospect is out for a pleasant stroll with Tina, the receptionist from his hotel. She had enthusiastically accepted his invitation to get together once she finished her shift. They'd managed to secure two ice creams from a trolley just before its operator packed up for the day. Now they are leaning over the railing by the river and looking upstream at one of the best views of Pulteney Bridge with the horseshoe-shaped weir in front of it. Deckchairs are being noisily stacked behind them and the little brass ensemble that had been using the bandstand has packed its instruments into the back of a minibus and driven away.

Tina lifts her nose into the air and inhales deeply. The sweet medley of smells from the surrounding flowerbeds is powerful; they are a blaze of regimented colours at this time of year. Bob-the-Prospect has learnt that Tina has just graduated in fashion design after three years at Bath Spa University but is staying on in her shared student house this summer to earn some much-needed funds.

'Then I'll be back to Cumbria to live at home for a while and try to get my business off the ground,' she says, looking up at Bob-the-Prospect, who is at least eighteen inches taller than her. He's told her that he is having a bit of a cheap city break, before he begins a new job in a car recycling depot in Bristol. They have also already established that neither is currently in a relationship, but the young man is slightly daunted by his companion's education and middle-class manners. Bob-the-Prospect left school at sixteen with very few examination passes but, he thinks, he's got a street-smart brain. Tina is very different from the women who hang around with his gang at the Archangel – and, of course, none of them would be interested in going out with a Prospect anyway.

'So what kind of business would that be?' he asks, finishing the cone of his ice cream and wiping his mouth.

'Bamboo clothing,' Tina announces excitedly. Her undiluted enthusiasm and ready smile produce two dimples framed by the long blonde curls of her hair. 'It's really environmentally friendly and I want to start a line of nightwear for women. Camisoles, pants, bras and so on.' She blushes slightly as Bob-the-Prospect looks down at her with a grin.

'Now that *does* sound exciting!' he says.

She gives him a playful punch in the chest and they walk on out of Parade Gardens and across the historic shop-lined Pulteney Bridge. Bob-the-Prospect has decided to kill two birds with one stone on this evening walk; he is heading for a specific place. Sure enough, at the bottom of some stone steps, he comes across the painted graffiti of the two back-to-back capital Bs. He puts a hand out to it.

Tina watches curiously. 'What is it?'

'Oh, nothing, really. It just caught my eye.' Bob knows the sign is there because the police had questioned Vince closely about it and the Big Man had told him to make it his first port of call. But he can't see anything strange or unusual about it... other than the fact that it was probably left there by a murderer. But was that murderer a Bulldog?

'Come on,' he says, 'I'm gasping for a pint.'

'And I'll have a G&T, please... make it a large one.'

He shakes his head in mock sadness. 'Students... what a waste of space.'

The Wolf is angry and frustrated. He has visited the hiding place under the bridge, read the note that had been left there, and realises he will have to take matters into his own hands. Once again, he is perched on the fire escape with the light fading as he looks down on the moorings through his small field binoculars. The shutter of the old Indian woman's side window has been closed since he arrived at the vantage point. Nevertheless, he shrinks back into the dark recesses of the metal landing, pulls the peak of his baseball cap down over his eyes and stays as motionless as possible.

Earlier that evening, a new boat arrived at the moorings: Jumping Jack Flash. *He can easily read the name through his binoculars. It is red and black with a picture on the side of a grinning clown dressed in a diamond-patterned jacket and trousers. The painted figure sports a maniacal grin and piercing eyes, which are staring directly back at the Wolf from across the river. There is something deeply unsettling about it and yet it also, somehow, strikes a chord of recognition with him. He, too, is an agent of chaos. But the boat's arrival has worsened his mood. He was making good progress but now, it seems, another canal boat has simply plugged the gap of the one that sank in the river.*

The new boat arrived just before dusk and the Wolf had pulled a digital camera from his small backpack just as it was being tied up. He appreciated the quality of the camera's images compared to those on a phone, which he regularly burned anyway – just to be on the safe side. Using the zoom button to its maximum, a colour picture of the couple at the helm came quickly into view and he rattled off ten pictures in quick succession. He has seen the young woman and the slightly older man coming and going previously at the moorings, usually accompanied by a small brown dog, but he had no idea that they owned a boat. Who were they and where had they come from?

The camera is equipped to allow him to send and receive pictures with texts and so he crouches onto his haunches and chooses a shot of the couple and then two single head-and-shoulder pictures of each of them. He sends the three photos with a short text and waits for a reply.

When it comes, minutes later, the Wolf smiles with grim satisfaction. His bill is increasing with each new instruction and he is looking forward to an excellent payday. This is what all of his military training and experience has made him ready for. It is better that he is now working on his own.

CHAPTER THIRTY-TWO

There is a steady drizzle falling when I wake on Tuesday morning. I heard Nina join someone for a guard duty during the night although we had agreed the new rota would start this evening. So I leave her to a rare lie-in and resign myself to a good soaking as I give Eddie a walk along the river path for the two-mile stretch downstream to Bath Marina and back. I stop to look briefly at the wreck of *Nautilus*. She is a sad sight, resting on huge blocks of wood on a concrete apron, her windows caked with dried mud and silt and her once-pristine paintwork now a dirt-streaked mess. God knows what the interior is like. I assume that no serious work will begin on her until the loss adjusters have paid a visit. Will they try to suggest carelessness by the professor in order to wriggle out of paying compensation? That would be a hammer blow for the poor old man.

Eddie doesn't mind the rain in the slightest and he jogs happily back to the boat with me. We can both smell the bacon as we are crossing the footbridge and, sure enough, Nina is grilling some in the galley whilst the professor is buttering rolls. I pat my emerging belly sadly, but it doesn't stop me tucking in hungrily with a couple of fresh mugs of tea to wash it down. Nina's holiday eating habits do not seem to have any impact on her own trim figure – but then she is a frequent and fast runner. 'I think this will prove to be a fascinating morning,' says the professor, who has begun to wash up at the little sink. 'I haven't been to many press conferences – and none outside the confines of the university.'

'I can't wait to see what the Andropov twins are like,' says Nina.

Guiltily, I accept that I would prefer to go to the press conference on my own. I'm unsure what kind of reception I shall get when Sebastian recognises me from the golf club terrace. I know it won't work, but I try to put them off anyway.

'There is a risk that you won't get in,' I say. 'They might be restricting entrance to bona fide journalists, in which case you'll be turned away at the door.'

'I'll tell them I'm from the *Architectural Digest*,' says Nina determinedly.

'Oh dear, yes...' the professor says. 'I shall be from *Waterways World*!'

My worries are reinforced when, an hour later and dressed respectably, we leave *Jumping Jack Flash* only to find Linda waiting for us on the bank. Beneath a bright yellow plastic raincoat she has on one of her usual voluminous and highly coloured cotton dresses, and she is standing under a very large, orange umbrella. It is not an ensemble designed to blend into the background.

'There you are at last!' she says. 'Come on, shake a leg. I can't leave Tammy with the kids all day.'

'Linda –' I say, giving the professor and Nina a cross look, which they both decline to register – 'I'm really not sure that it's a good idea for us to go mob-handed.'

She squares her jaw, showing the small gap between her two front teeth. 'Aye, well, I don't think it's a good idea to go stirring up trouble and sinking boats,' she snaps. 'And if these people are behind it – and nearly killing me and my kids – then I'll be the first to find out about it. Come on, I'm getting damp waiting here.'

She marches off up to the bridge while the rest of us trail after her. The professor sidles up to me.

'I'm sorry, Jack. Once I told her about the press conference there was no stopping her. You know how she is when her blood is up.'

The Bath Spa Hotel is situated in a lovely old mansion beyond some impressive gates at the end of a long drive on the fringes of Sydney

Gardens. A sign in reception indicates '*Andropov Developments Ltd Press Conference – Admiralty Room*'. Two smartly dressed young women are taking down a list of names at the door but, to my dismay, they don't seem to be asking for press accreditation of any kind. It does indeed seem that we shall be going mob-handed.

I go first and scribble 'Jack Johnson, *Bath Chronicle*' in their book. Nina follows and puts down her name, 'Mrs Angelina Wilde, *Architectural Digest*'. Linda and the professor add their names without bothering to invent a periodical and we make our way to four chairs in a row at the back of the room.

There are five or six others already seated. I recognise one of them as Tom, the *Chronicle*'s young property and business correspondent. He waves at me and gives the others in my group a puzzled look. Then Nina gives me a nudge with her elbow and nods at the door, where the bulky figure of Councillor Robin Claverton is stooping to add his name to the register. As he stands upright, he scans the room and notices us, and shoots an angry look at me and Nina before finding a chair as far away from us as possible.

Our chairs face a table that has been covered with a tablecloth, holding a decanter of water, two glasses and an open laptop. There is a white screen pulled down behind the table, but the projector suspended from the ceiling is not switched on yet. We are ten minutes early. At five minutes to eleven, the two doors are swung back and a television crew bustle in self-importantly with their bags of equipment. The cameraman sets the camera up on a tripod at the back of the room in the walkway next to Linda, runs a cable along the floor to a microphone, and puts it on a stand on the table. Finally, the cameraman pulls a lamp out of a canvas bag, sets it up on a stand to one side of the table and plugs it in. The front of the room is now bathed in glaring white light. The television reporter has sat in the front row, just to one side, so that they can get him in shot if he asks a question. I notice that he already has a microphone pinned to one of his lapels.

One of the two women on the door stands up and presses a remote control. The projector hums into life and '*Andropov Developments Ltd*' in gold writing appears on the screen, alongside a logo featuring an eagle with two heads, its talons gripping the earth's globe. As company emblems go, the only message I'm receiving is one of twin-headed rapacious greediness. The other young woman slips out of the room, the doors swing open again and the Andropov twins make their entrance.

The low murmur of conversation in the room is immediately stilled as people take them in. Sebastian and Anthony Andropov are wearing dark charcoal pinstripe suits, white shirts and red silk ties with matching ruby tie-pins. They give vague but friendly nods to the assembly and take the two chairs behind the desk. The twin facing us on the right stands first. It is quite extraordinary. They are a mirror image of each other down to the last detail. Their facial features are not just similar – they match in every last respect from the high, almost oriental cheekbones and narrow eyes to the thin straight lips, slightly squat nostrils and arched eyebrows above blue eyes that appear both clever and watchful. They must have had their thick, dark hair cut and styled side by side and at the same time, I think, because there is, literally, not a hair's breadth of difference between them. The social diary article said they were twenty-five years old, but they carry themselves with the confidence of older men.

'Good morning, ladies and gentlemen. I am Anthony Andropov, and this is my brother Sebastian. We are the joint managing directors and owners of Andropov Developments Ltd and we are delighted to welcome you here today to present our exciting plans to redevelop a derelict industrial site on the south bank of the River Avon in Bath.'

He nods to one of the women holding a remote control and an aerial picture of the site appears behind him.

'The former Tiller & Brown site is more than thirty acres of astonishing potential on the edge of the very centre of this wonderful city,' continues Anthony smoothly. 'We have worked with our award-winning architects, Napton and Mosse, to prepare a scheme which, we believe, will truly make the most of this amazing opportunity.'

The picture behind him now replaces the big old industrial buildings, gas holders and warehouses with a cluster of twenty or so rectangular-shaped tower blocks. They have different modernist designs on their cladding but, apart from this, appear as identical as the twins, with the top two floors of each block fronted completely in glass.

'This design will provide more than 3,500 badly needed homes for the city in a radical design that can be afforded by people on a wide range of incomes.'

The display changes to a cross-section of one of the tower blocks, showing car parking on the basement and ground floor levels, followed by small studio and one-bedroom starter homes packed together on the first two floors, two-bedroom apartments making up the bulk of the building and then three- and four-bedroom homes on the twenty-first and twenty-second storeys.

'As you can see, as well as affordable housing, we are delighted to present design-led luxury accommodation for those who can afford more space on the upper storeys, including four splendid new double-storey penthouse apartments,' Anthony Andropov goes on, 'using glass 360-degrees around the properties to provide astonishing floor-to-ceiling views across the whole vista of Bath. Our buyers could stay in the same block for all of their lives, moving up through the building as their income rises.'

'I've read the book by J.G. Ballard,' the professor whispers in my ear. 'It's called *High-Rise* and it ends *very* badly!'

Anthony chooses this moment to sit down but he continues to speak. He is obviously the public voice of the pair and I remember the magazine article referring to Sebastian as the 'strong, silent type'.

'At the moment,' continues Anthony, 'the site is somewhat of an embarrassing eyesore for a UNESCO World Heritage city, as I know many would agree. But we are determined to take those derelict buildings and transform them into something that is both practicable and prideworthy.'

'...and profitable,' hisses Linda, none too quietly. Sebastian is scanning the audience to see where the comment has come from and registers my presence. He clearly recognises me from the golf club and narrows his eyes, giving me a long cold stare as his brother continues to speak.

'We will be lodging an application for outline planning permission with Bath Council later this week. We have already invested many millions of pounds in the purchase of the site and, of course, we are prepared to invest many more millions of pounds, and create many hundreds of local jobs, during its construction over the next five to ten years. My brother, Sebastian, and I are here to work harmoniously and in partnership with everyone to make this happen and deliver our vision for the future of this wonderful city.'

This rousing promise is the cue for the lights to dim and both twins to move to the side of the room. A video begins playing on the screen. The stirring tune of Elgar's 'Nimrod' accompanies sweeping virtual reality images of the tower blocks filling the screen. The camera moves effortlessly in and out of windows, showing state-of-the-art minimalist interiors with cool leather furniture, marble worktops and a great deal of glass and steel. At one stage, the sonorous commentary even says the tower blocks have been inspired by the medieval towers of the Italian town of San Gimignano. The professor sucks his breath in disbelief at such hyperbole.

The film ends and the brothers now move back to their previous positions. However, as they walk the short distance, I notice that they also cross over in order to swap places before all of the lights in the room are back on. The one on the right, who I take to still be Anthony, speaks again although I suspect that most people in the room may now believe the speaker to be Sebastian. They have just pulled off a human version of the two-card trick.

Anthony, who is now sitting in Sebastian's chair, continues. 'I would like to add that this development is wholly consistent with the Canal and River Trust's strategy to improve run-down waterside areas. The CRT is a major landowner in its own right with a unique portfolio of land and property worth more than £500 million. The Trust's own research suggests that restoring a derelict waterside site increases the value of existing properties in the same area by no less than twenty per cent. So, in short, our scheme is also very good news for local residents.'

'Hear hear,' says Councillor Claverton enthusiastically.

'Unless you live on a boat,' hisses Linda.

'Well, that concludes our presentation, ladies and gentlemen. You will all be given an information pack and a press release as you leave, as well as a memory stick with the film and other imagery on it.'

I have to concede that it has been a short and well-produced session with slick visuals. But I am shocked at the chutzpah of anyone who is set on building twenty 24-storey modern-looking tower blocks close to the centre of Georgian Bath. These guys must think that they are truly invincible. I suspect some of my doubt is shared by the other journalists in the room as there is a lengthy silence before Councillor Claverton raises a hand.

'Please say who you are and who you represent before your question,' continues Anthony in a tone of utter reasonableness. Claverton looks slightly miffed, as if the world and particularly the Andropov twins should already know precisely who he is. Nevertheless, he darts a quick and hungry glance at the television camera and gets to his feet.

'I am Councillor Robin Claverton and I am responsible for the ward in which this site is situated,' he says pompously. 'And I would like to put on record, even at this early stage, how strongly I support this excellent scheme.' He alternates between addressing the camera and the brothers. 'It will bring badly needed new homes and jobs to our area and make a vast improvement to a site which, frankly, is a carbuncle on the face of an old friend – as His Royal Highness might say.' He is clearly very pleased with himself and his carefully pre-rehearsed comment, and sits down beaming.

'Thank you, Councillor Claverton,' says Anthony, displaying his perfect teeth in a broad smile. 'That is very kind of you, and I am sure your welcome words of support will be duly noted by our friends from the press and media who are here today.'

Tom holds his hand up and identifies himself and the *Chronicle*. 'Have you had any indication from the council whether they will find your scheme acceptable?' he asks.

'We have had preliminary and informal discussions,' says Anthony easily. 'And, of course, we now look forward to taking that forward formally, and in much more detail.'

'But did they give you any encouragement?' presses Tom.

'I think I've said as much as I can,' continues Anthony with another smile, 'although I can certainly say that we have not been *discouraged* in any way.' Sebastian smiles at his brother's remark but his eyes keep drifting back to rest on me.

A radio reporter lifts his hand and asks exactly how much the twins intend to spend on the site. Again, Anthony deflects the question smoothly, saying the amount is commercially confidential but 'very substantial'.

A young woman from a specialist construction magazine now asks what other schemes the twins have been involved in, and receives another expertly delivered non-answer.

'My brother Anthony and I established Andropov Developments Ltd to deliver this unrivalled and unique once-in-a-lifetime opportunity. We are assembling a team of extremely experienced architects, interior designers, builders and, of course, a sales team in order to guarantee the success of our considerable investment.'

They clearly don't have experience themselves, I think.

Someone else asks what price the most expensive penthouse apartments are likely to be and Anthony smiles with satisfaction as he answers: 'More than two million pounds each.'

Finally, the television reporter looks over to his cameraman and points to himself as he raises a hand. Both twins look back at him with broad, confident smiles, yet sit up slightly straighter. They are aware that this may be the key moment from the press conference: television will reach the largest audience of potential buyers. The reporter identifies himself as Clinton Garmston, adding the name of the regional BBC TV news programme, *Points West*.

'There is likely to be fierce opposition from conservation groups to the idea of modern tower blocks close to the centre of Bath,' he says. The twins fix serious looks on their faces and nod slightly, more in sadness than in anger. 'Can you tell our viewers how you will deal with that opposition?'

'We'll meet it head on,' says Anthony. 'That isn't meant to sound combative. I mean to say that we will discuss our plans in detail with all parties and provide all the answers and explanations that we can. However, in the end, the final decision must be taken by duly elected councillors and we are confident that they will see the enormous advantages such a substantial investment and such an exciting scheme can bring to the city.'

'And just for the record,' adds Clinton Garmston, 'can you remind our viewers which one of you is which?'

The twins readily join in with the laughter that greets this request. Then Sebastian replies, 'I'm Anthony,' and Anthony says, 'I'm Sebastian.' They both put a hand on each other's shoulder and there is a small glint of triumph in their eyes. I know they have just lied, and I suspect it is something of a habit for these two. Anthony has spoken for the whole of the press conference but everyone else thinks they have shared the burden equally.

'Well,' continues Anthony smoothly, 'if there are no more questions then, thank you so much for coming and we look forward –'

I stand and raise one hand in the air. 'I have a question.'

CHAPTER THIRTY-THREE

Sebastian leans over to whisper in his brother's ear. Anthony gives him a puzzled look and then looks directly at me without smiling. 'Please don't forget to introduce yourself.'

I hesitate for a second. Do I want this pair knowing exactly who I am? But it's too late now. I have already signed the register on arrival and others in the room like Tom know exactly who I am. Giving another name would prompt too many awkward questions. 'Jack Johnson, *Bath Chronicle*,' I say.

'Goodness,' says Anthony, glancing at Tom, then smiling around the room, 'two of you from the *Chronicle*? And I thought local newspapers were supposed to be hard-up and short-staffed these days?'

No one laughs, and Anthony looks mildly annoyed. 'What's your question, Mr Jack Johnson?'

I am pleased he has used my first name as it gives me a chance to use his and spoil the silly little game being played by him and his brother. 'Well, Mr *Anthony* Andropov,' I say, 'is it true that you gave a private briefing about your plan to the president of the Georgian Fellowship, Mr Rufus Powell? And did Mr Powell, who has recently been murdered, tell you that he was strongly opposed to it?'

The twins both stiffen at the deliberately provocative implication of my question; there is silence in the room. They both must have registered that I know precisely which twin I am addressing. That's good. I want them to wonder what else I may know. However, Anthony's voice is calm and level when he replies.

'Mr Powell was, of course, entitled to his personal opinions although, as far as we know, they were not made in public before his demise and therefore sadly must remain a matter of conjecture. I should add that my brother and I were very upset to learn of his death and we extend our deepest sympathy to his widow, his family and his friends at the Georgian Fellowship.'

I am still on my feet and the BBC cameraman has swivelled back to me.

'So, you're saying that there is absolutely no connection between the sudden and violent death of the president of Bath's Georgian Fellowship and his opposition to your scheme?'

Sebastian is now staring at me with a look of barely suppressed hatred. He puts both hands flat on the table as if he is about to push himself upright. Anthony puts a calming hand on his brother's arm as he replies.

'None whatsoever. How could there be? The mere suggestion is deeply offensive to my brother and me.' To be fair, Anthony does look genuinely baffled and hurt. He looks slowly around the room before settling his gaze on me again. 'I am afraid your line of questioning could be regarded as damaging to our reputation, Mr Johnson. My brother and I would have no hesitation in suing you for libel should it be repeated in print. And, as a journalist, I am sure you appreciate how expensive that would be for you and your newspaper – or for anyone else tempted to repeat this suggestion. As I say, Mr Powell's thoughts about our scheme have not been aired in public and sadly, now it is too late for them to be heard.'

The threat is left hanging in the air. Heads turn to see if I am going to come back for more. I open my mouth to tell them about Powell's pre-prepared but unwritten speech, but Nina suddenly joins me on my feet.

'I have a question, if I may,' she says. 'What will happen to the canal boats that are moored on the river at the entrance to this site? I see they aren't on your artist's impressions of the new development and yet the owners of those boats have permanent moorings – for life.'

'I'm sorry, I didn't catch your name?' says Anthony, and he pauses expectantly. His tone is still calm and polite. My questions don't seem to have rattled him in the slightest. He is either a consummate actor or the Andropov twins have nothing to hide. The silence stretches out. Nina folds her arms in front of her.

'Will you answer the lady's question?' demands the professor with the considerable authority and projection of a lecture hall voice. Sebastian again leans over to whisper into his brother's ear. Anthony gives him a puzzled look, shakes his head very faintly and then finally responds.

'We believe the aesthetic quality of the pedestrian approach across Victoria Bridge and into our development is crucial to achieving healthy sales and making the whole scheme a success. And so, we have offered the current owners of boats on that particular mooring a very generous relocation package. Indeed, I understand that the owners of one boat have already taken up our offer.' He pauses slightly, before going on smoothly. 'Of course, we do recognise that riverside moorings and boats are an essential part of Bath's heritage, as well as being something of a tourist attraction, and we would hope to offer some of our penthouse buyers the additional opportunity to purchase a luxury mooring, should they so wish. And if they remain unsold, well, then we would be willing to contemplate more short-term moorings for people visiting their friends or family who are living on the site.'

'Very reasonable. Very reasonable indeed,' says Councillor Claverton loudly from his seat.

'Thank you, councillor,' continues Anthony. 'And so, as I say, our lawyers have advised this very small group of boat owners that we are happy to compensate any of them who wish to sell their mooring rights to us. Indeed, we are offering them much more than the price they originally paid for the moorings and discussions are ongoing.'

'You bastards!' Linda is on her feet now, red-faced, red-haired and pointing a red-painted fingernail accusingly at the twins. 'It's you that's behind all the trouble we've been having,' she says in a half-shout, before pointing sideways to the professor. 'This poor man's boat was deliberately sunk. And me and my children were nearly drowned.' Linda's voice is starting to crack with emotion. 'It's you, isn't it? You're trying to get rid of us in any way you can. Well, you can stuff your money because we aren't budging and you can't make us.'

One of the two public relations assistants has begun making her way across the front of the room. I'm still on my feet alongside Linda and Nina. Sebastian stands too now, his eyes blazing with anger. He stabs an angry finger at Linda. 'You need to sit down and shut up,' he snarls furiously.

Now Anthony is standing too, but only to whisper in his brother's ear. Sebastian darts a look at the television camera, takes a deep breath and sits back down. Anthony looks slowly all around the room before refocusing on Linda.

'I'm sorry,' he says. 'It sounds as if there have been some upsetting incidents. But your accusations are quite unfounded and completely untrue. We have no knowledge of the incidents you describe.'

Nina has her arm around Linda and we all sit down. The public relations woman whispers in Anthony's ear.

'Yes... I think so,' he says, once more fixing a wide smile on his face and looking directly to the camera.

The woman stands to face the room, while her partner stations herself at the door again. Her smile couldn't look more artificial. 'That brings our press conference to an end, ladies and gentlemen,' she says. 'Do please take one of the press packs with a brochure, press release and a copy of the film as you leave.'

But Linda isn't finished yet. She shrugs off Nina's arm and swiftly pre-empts the exodus to the door, where she snatches a thick pile of press packs from the table and hurls them into the air. An avalanche of A4 paper falls over the heads of the journalists and fans out across the front of the lens of the television camera. 'You bastards!' she shrieks. 'You leave me and my children alone!'

The journalists immediately gather around Linda. The twins take in the chaotic scene and quickly walk out of the room, their jaws clenched tight in anger. Claverton follows them. The public relations women, sensing they have lost any influence over the audience, stoop to regather as much of their literature as they can. The professor, Nina and I join Linda.

'What the hell was all that about?' the regional television news reporter asks Linda. But she is sitting back down now, all emotion spent, and quietly sobbing into the palms of both hands.

'Jack?' asks Tom.

I calmly explain how a co-ordinated campaign against the boat people has seemingly spiralled into vandalism, theft and violence. I tell them to look at the *Chronicle*'s website, which details Linda's lucky escape and the sinking of *Nautilus*.

'It's all terribly convenient, don't you think?' adds Nina. 'You heard what Andropov Developments think of the boats on their precious site.'

'How much are they offering to buy the moorings?' asks Tom.

'Thirty thousand pounds each,' I say, and the others scribble the figure in their notebooks.

The TV reporter pipes up. 'Look, Mr Johnson, you say you're a journalist with the *Chronicle*? You know the form here. We can't even begin to hint that these guys are connected to this vandalism and violence unless there's any proof. Is there any?'

I feel the others' eyes on me as I shake my head.

'No. No proof. Not yet.'

Linda throws down her hands in disgust. 'Proof? What proof do you need? My children's drowned bodies?' She gets up, pushes her way through the throng and stomps out of the room. The TV reporter holds me back from following her.

'And what was all that about the dead magistrate, Rufus Powell?' he asks. 'That was pretty full-on. Have you got any leads on that?'

'His widow told me that her husband had been privately briefed by the Andropov twins on their development plans and that he was going to campaign strongly against it,' I say. It sounds weak even to me.

He shakes his head. 'Even if that's true, you connected it with his murder with no evidence whatsoever?'

I shrug. He's right. And, unknown to him or anyone else, the police have a much more plausible alternative line of inquiry. I've been a bit of an idiot in the heat of the moment.

'Sounds like you've been on quite a fishing trip, my friend – but there's not much bait on your hook, is there? Shame, we've got some great footage of the end but I'm not sure we can use any of it. I'll need to talk to our lawyers.' He shakes his head again and begins to help the cameraman pack up their equipment.

I follow the others out through the hotel's reception and into the car park. The drizzle has stopped now and the sun is coming out. Linda, Nina and the professor are replaying the press conference among themselves.

'Well?' says Linda belligerently as I join them. 'I don't regret a word. It's about time people knew what was going on.'

'You were magnificent,' says the professor. 'An Amazon warrior in the corporate jungle grappling with two identical snakes.'

'How much do you think will be reported, Jack?' asks Nina. I explain that without any proof, the accusations are too serious to repeat – even with the twins' denials. I anticipate that it won't be long before the Andropovs' lawyers are issuing threatening warnings to the relevant editors.

'So, all in all, something of a Pyrrhic victory?' says the professor sadly. 'However, it was interesting to see more detail about their awful plans. And I did enjoy Linda's performance.'

Nina has linked arms with Linda as we walk down the hotel's long sweeping drive. 'Well, libel laws or no libel laws, I won't be pulling any punches in my write-up for the *Architectural Digest*!' she declares. The others burst out laughing but we are interrupted by a car horn behind us.

The enormous, powder-blue bonnet of the Bentley purrs alongside me. I chose the opposite side to the others and am separated from them by the car. A rear window glides down next to me. One twin is glaring out at me while the other peers over his shoulder. I have no way of knowing who is who.

'Repeat any of that crap again and you're fucking dead,' spits the twin nearest to me. The contrast between the smooth salesmanship of the press conference and this crude threat is shocking.

'Dead like Rufus Powell?' I challenge back, but there is no reply and the car accelerates to the end of the drive before turning away into the traffic. There is no doubt that we have made two very powerful enemies this morning.

CHAPTER THIRTY-FOUR

Lunch, clustered around a small metal table under the high canopy of Green Park station, is a high-spirited affair for the others. They replay their questions at the conference and the Andropovs' answers to each other and describe their amazement and amusement at Linda's closing outburst.

'My God,' says Nina. 'Did you see their faces when you threw all their lovely press packs into the air?'

'I don't know what possessed me!' says Linda with a wide grin.

'Tower blocks!' says Nina. 'They'll never get them approved. It'll be a bloodbath.'

'Indeed,' says the professor, 'the Bath heritage lobby will be marching on the Guildhall with sharpened sword sticks!' But as the others join in the laughter, he now registers that I have been quiet for a while. 'Penny for them, Jack?'

'I was just thinking about the twins,' I say. 'It's the first time that I've seen them both together in the flesh.'

'Enough to make your flesh creep,' says Linda with a shudder. 'Slimy, slippery bastards.'

Nina puts a restraining hand on Linda's arm. 'Go on...' she says to me.

'Well, two things really. Firstly, although they tried to muddle people up by switching positions at one point, it was Anthony who did all of the talking. The only time Sebastian opened his mouth was when he lost it with Linda and told her to shut up.'

'Are you sure?' says Nina.

'Why would they do that, Jack?' asks the professor. 'I must confess I missed that. I thought they shared the speaking.'

'No,' I say firmly. 'They made it look like that, but in reality, they switched places just after the film, when the lights were still dimmed. It was slick and fast. So it was only Anthony talking to us all along. And if you don't believe me, there's another way of proving it.'

'How?'

'I noticed it at the golf club. Sebastian gave two boxes of golf balls to the pair from the council. He called them a "trifle", but he actually pronounced it as "twifle". And then today, when they passed us on the drive and wound down the window to talk to me, one of the twins said, "Repeat any of that crap again and you're fucking dead" – only he actually said "cwap" instead of "crap". That must have been Sebastian. He pronounces W instead of R. It's called rhotacism. Anthony doesn't show any sign of it at all.'

'So,' says Linda, 'Sebastian doesn't know his Rs from his elbow!'

After the laughter subsides, the professor says, 'And yet they are identical in every other respect. Fascinating.'

'If you're right, you can tell them apart as soon as they open their mouths,' says Nina.

I shrug. 'But I'm not sure where it gets us. Maybe Sebastian just doesn't like public speaking. So what?'

'Strange they should go to such lengths, making themselves indistinguishable from each other and switching positions to confuse people, just to shield him from... what did you call it? Rhotacism?' observes Nina.

'It must be about the exercise of power,' the professor muses. 'They swap themselves around to keep people guessing. It's just another way of exercising control and keeping others on the back foot. I imagine it might come in useful during business negotiations. The old good cop/ bad cop routine – except people are never quite sure which twin is on which side.'

'Possibly.' I'm unable to think of a better explanation.

'Well,' says Linda. 'As far as I'm concerned, it just goes to show that you can't trust them. Now then. I've got to get back to the kids. Poor Tammy will be tired out by them. I'll let her and Danny know how it all went this morning – and Bill, if he's shown his face yet.'

'Jack and I have an appointment with the chief planning officer at the council,' says Nina. 'We want to see what the chances are of the plans being approved.'

'Among other things...' I mutter.

'Well, in that case I shall come back with you, dear lady,' says the professor to Linda. 'Jack, perhaps I can have the keys to your boat so that I can have a little lie down? I'm feeling quite exhausted by this morning's excitement.'

I give him my spare key and we part company.

'How are you going to play this?' asks Nina, as we approach the Guildhall's ornate ironwork lamps. 'She's obviously going to recognise you from the golf club.'

'I've been thinking about that,' I reply. 'At the moment, all I can think of doing is to keep rattling the cage and hope they make a mistake. I doubt that the twins will have thought to warn Gwyneth Wilkinson about me yet. I doubt they even know that we're due to see her. I'll play it by ear.'

'Just keep rattling the cage? Play it by ear? Yes, Jack, that sounds like a plan,' says Nina sarcastically. But she just shrugs hopelessly when I ask if she has any better suggestions.

We wait on the tall upright chairs in the planning department's reception hallway, and we are fetched on the stroke of two o'clock by the same fashionably dressed young man. Gwyneth Wilkinson's office is wood-panelled and spacious, with a generous allocation of oil paintings from the council's art collection showing various views of the city. She is sitting behind a well-polished mahogany partners' desk when we enter, and rises to greet us.

'Mr Jack Johnson from the *Bath Chronicle*,' says the PA, 'and Mrs Angelina Wilde.' We clearly aren't going to be offered drinks as he pivots briskly and leaves.

Wilkinson reaches across her desk to shake Nina's hand first and then clasps mine. She barely misses a beat as she recognises me from yesterday's lunch.

'I think we met yesterday, didn't we, Mr Johnson? At Saltford Golf Club? You offered to take a group photograph of our little lunch party. Am I right?'

We take our seats opposite her. 'That's right,' I say evenly. 'Funny coincidence. I was interviewing an American billionaire over lunch there. He's thinking of adding the course to his collection.'

Wilkinson laughs easily. 'Really? What is it with these Americans? Even their president collects golf courses over here, doesn't he?' She looks at Nina for approval and is rewarded a little smile in return. 'Well, I hadn't heard any rumours, but we'll certainly be interested if an American billionaire does decide to invest locally. What's his name?'

I flounder momentarily, but Nina comes to my rescue.

'Algernon,' she says quickly. 'Algernon Bunbury the Third.'

'Really? How very strange! Such an English-sounding name. So, Mr Johnson, you're with the *Chronicle*. And you, Mrs Wilde?'

'Angelina is shadowing me, learning the ropes,' I say quickly. 'We hoped you wouldn't mind if she sat in?'

Nina gives a little frown at the idea of being my apprentice but keeps quiet.

'No, no. That's fine... although I'm not sure how I can help you, to be honest. This is about the old Tiller & Brown site, isn't it? We haven't had an application yet so there's not very much I can say.'

'But you must know quite a lot about it already,' I say evenly. 'After all, you were having lunch with one of the developers yesterday, Sebastian Andropov.'

Wilkinson shakes her head and smiles at Nina.

'You see that, Mrs Wilde? A good reporter doesn't miss a thing! So, you know the twins, do you? Their likeness is uncanny, isn't it? I never really know which one I'm talking to. Yes, no mystery there. Developers often have informal discussions with us in advance of making their planning applications. It can save a lot of time and aggravation later. We can brief them on the city's overall planning strategy and local feelings in advance of the formal process. The other guest was my boss, Councillor Laurence Merton, who chairs the planning committee.'

Nina sneaks a sideways glance at me. She was clearly expecting Wilkinson to be much more evasive than this. I have to admit, so was I.

'We went to the Andropov Developments press conference this morning,' I tell her. 'Quite a surprise, really. Twenty 24-storey modern tower blocks on the edge of a World Heritage city centre? What are their chances?'

Wilkinson spreads her palms upwards and shrugs. 'Who knows? It'll be up to the elected councillors and, as this one is so important, I expect it'll be considered by the full council after the planning committee expresses its view.'

'But as chief planning officer, you'll be asked to say what you think? You'll be asked to make a recommendation to the councillors?' I press.

'Yes of course. But we still haven't seen all of the finer details or received any representations.' She glances at the notebook balanced on my knee where I am scribbling a few shorthand notes. 'Like all of our planning applications, we shall play this one by the book. Yes, it's a very big scheme, but it'll go through the formal processes, just like any other.'

'So, there's nothing about this plan, as you understand it, that is already worrying you? Nothing that contravenes the city's long-term development plan as it stands?'

Wilkinson smiles. 'Such as?'

'Oh, I don't know,' I say in exasperation. 'Such as its impact on the city's skyline?'

Wilkinson puts both index fingers onto her high-gloss lipstick and looks at me thoughtfully. 'There will be pros and cons to any scheme of this size,' she says. 'The strategic city plan also calls for new homes and for them to be a social mix ranging from starter homes to high-end. That could be a plus. I'm not saying it is, just that it could be. We all need to wait and see the details, then have a proper debate.'

'What about the moorings on the Avon at the front of the site? The Andropovs are trying to get rid of the boats there. D'you agree with that?' asks Nina more challengingly.

'Oh, really?' says Wilkinson. 'Not really an issue for us. It's between the developers and the boat owners – and the river authorities, I suppose.' She returns a bland smile at Nina.

I can see that we're struggling to penetrate her glib defences and so I decide to switch subjects and go up a gear. I flick over a page of my notebook.

'Okay, moving on. I was surprised to see you and Councillor Merton receiving gifts from the twins at the end of your expensive lunch yesterday. Is that permitted within the council rules on gifts?' The challenge of my question and the sudden change of direction doesn't seem to ruffle the council official one iota. She puts both elbows on the leather surface of her desk and clasps both hands in front of her.

'Of course there are rules, Mr Johnson. And we always abide by them, otherwise suspicious people like you end up putting two and two together and making five.' She buzzes through to the PA. 'Andrew, bring in the hospitality and gifts register, please.'

She smiles at us while the young man delivers a large leather-bound book, flicks through it and then swivels it to face me. I go to the latest entry and Nina brings her head alongside mine. Underneath yesterday's date, it says:

'Lunch/hospitality. Saltford Golf Club. Gwyneth Wilkinson and Lawrence Merton as guests of Andropov Developments Ltd (Sebastian Andropov) – approximate value £70 per person including drinks.'

Then underneath it is another entry, which reads:

'Gifts. Two boxes of six golf balls to Gwyneth Wilkinson and Lawrence Merton from Andropov Developments Ltd (Anthony and Sebastian Andropov). Approximate value £6 each.'

'Of course, we usually have to make an educated guess about the value of such gifts, but I don't think I'm too far out. I play a little golf. Anyway, they're well within our individual twenty-pound gift limit and anyone – any councillor or member of the public – can inspect the register whenever they wish. We must be like Caesar's wife, you know – wholly above suspicion.'

I look up at her and I guess my own smile must look slightly sickly because she decides to hit me while I'm down. She pulls open a drawer of the desk and puts a box on the table in front of us. She removes the lid with one hand to reveal six ordinary-looking golf balls in two rows of three.

'I've still got them here in the office, but I must take them home and put them in my bag. I haven't played with this particular brand before, but I doubt I'm good enough to notice the difference. Perhaps I'll just save them for putting practice. Do you play, Mr Johnson?' I ignore the question, which was accompanied by a supercilious little smile. 'Do you mind?' I ask, pulling the box towards me and taking out a ball.

'I asked if you played golf?' she repeats, with a hint of steel in the question.

I meet her eyes without blinking. 'No,' I say. 'I agree with Mark Twain.'

'Ah yes,' says Wilkinson. 'A good walk spoilt. Is that it? Well, we shall just have to disagree on that one.'

I roll the ball in the palm of my hand. It appears to be a perfectly normal, white, round, dimpled golf ball. I replace it in the box.

Wilkinson decides this is a signal that our conversation is over. She gets to her feet and checks her watch.

'Now, I'm afraid I have a full afternoon of appointments and so, if there is nothing else?'

We are back out on the street by twenty past two, ten minutes short of our allotted half hour. I am cross with myself for failing to use all of the available time and frustrated by the woman's stonewalling.

'It was like bowling to Geoffrey Boycott,' I complain to Nina. 'She could have stayed at the crease all afternoon, playing forward defence strokes. She's probably been on a bloody media training course. Come on, I need a pint.'

We head to the Old Green Tree, which is conveniently nearby. Nina buys the first round and we retreat to a corner table.

'You have to admit, she was very plausible,' says Nina unhelpfully.

I dig out my mobile phone and replay the video from the end of the golf club lunch.

'But look at her yesterday,' I say. 'She looks as nervous as hell sitting there after a slap-up lunch with Sebastian.' It is hard to equate Wilkinson's anxious demeanour of the day before with the confidence we have just witnessed.

Nina agrees with me. 'But she had an answer for everything, Jack. So where do we go from here?' she asks.

'For another pint,' I say grumpily, heading to the bar.

CHAPTER THIRTY-FIVE

My mobile starts ringing as I am waiting at the bar. I'm surprised to see it's Danny and accept the call, but it is too noisy so I head outside, waving my phone at Nina in explanation. Has another disaster happened at the moorings during our absence?

'Hi, Danny. Problem?'

'No, Jack, no, not at all...' he hurries to reassure me in his lilting Irish brogue. 'But I have a man here who wants to meet you. I was having a cup of tea with a chap moored down by Green Park and this chap came along with your picture from the paper. He was asking if anyone knew where your boat was moored. Says he wants a chat with you.' Danny lowers his voice conspiratorially. 'Says he might have some information for you about Mr Powell, may he rest in peace.'

Suddenly, I am very alert. Information about Powell's death? Who is this person? And can they be trusted?

'Jack? Jack, are you still there?'

'Hi, Danny, yes.' I quickly calculate that there can't be much danger if we meet this person in a crowded public place. 'Yes, I'm here. I'm with Nina in the Old Green Tree. Can you see if he knows where that is?' The phone goes quiet for a moment. Then, 'Yes, Jack. He reckons he can use his phone to find it. Says he'll be there in ten minutes. He's just set off.'

'Wait a minute. Danny, did he say what his name is?'

'Oh, yes,' says Danny. 'Says his name is Bob. He seems a nice enough lad.'

I collect our drinks, return to Nina and let her know we are about to have a visitor. Sure enough, ten minutes later, the door to our little ante-room swings open and a tall good-looking young man pokes his head around it. He appears to recognise me and advances with a newspaper in one hand and his other outstretched.

'Mr Johnson?' he says politely. He is slightly taller than me, broad-shouldered, broad chested and clean cut. He's well groomed and he's clearly had a recent haircut. 'Bob Dimond. Pleased to meet you.'

We shake hands and I introduce him to Nina. 'Can I get you a drink?'

'No, no. I'll do that. Same again?'

I accept a half but Nina declines. I see her watching his back at the serving hatch.

'Nice-looking boy,' she says.

'Behave… you're nearly old enough to be his mother.'

Nina feigns outrage. 'And if that's true, you're old enough to be my —'

Bob turns to us just as Nina is about to poke two outstretched fingers in my eyes, which I am pushing away with a palm of my hand. We're still hand-wrestling and laughing as he sits down at our table with a pint for himself and a half for me.

'Danny told me you'd be here,' he says, somewhat redundantly, before taking a long swallow of his lager. 'Last week's paper said you were living on a boat, so I started trying to find you after breakfast this morning. I expect you're wondering who I am.'

'Hmm… yes we are,' says Nina, in a way that sounds mildly naughty.

Bob puts his newspaper down on the table. It's last Thursday's edition of the *Chronicle* and it is open at my interview with Mrs Powell. He takes a moment to collect his thoughts and then begins to talk.

'I'm a Hells Angel,' he says.

Nina is sipping her beer at the time and splutters in surprise.

'And I'm an archangel,' I say.

The lad, who I estimate to be in his early twenties, furrows his brow in concern. 'No, straight up. I am. I'm dressed as a civilian, though. While I'm here in Bath.'

Nina's wiped her mouth now and is shaking her head beside me in disbelief, but then the penny drops for both of us at the same time.

'You're with the Bristol Bulldogs?' I ask.

'The ones who are suspected of killing Rufus Powell,' says Nina.

Bob gives a beaming smile, showing film-star teeth. 'That's right. The Big Man – that's our boss, Vince Porlock – he's sent me over here to try and find out what's going on. He's more than a bit pissed off. Just because it was a biker on the CCTV and our BB sign was left on the wall by Pulteney Bridge, the police seem to reckon that his son Clive ordered the attack on Powell. Or maybe they think it was Vince. It definitely wasn't, though.' Bob spreads his hands in innocence. 'He doesn't know anything about it. None of us do.'

'So why have you been trying to find me?'

'Well, the Big Man read your story in the *Chronicle*. We can't go talking to the police, can we? So, he told me to track you down and see if you knew anything more that could help me... er... him... er... us.'

I take a swig and study Bob carefully over the top of my beer glass. Hells Angels gangs have a nasty reputation and are often mixed up in a wide range of criminal activities. But this lad couldn't sound more straightforward or innocent. Was I being naïve? Could Bob be a dupe being used by this Vince Porlock or his son to throw the police off their scent?

Nina seems to be having similar thoughts. 'How long have you been a Bulldog, Bob?'

'Bulldog Bob,' he laughs. 'A bit less than a year. But I'm only a Prospect.' We must look puzzled as he continues, 'An apprentice, like. I won't get Full Patch till they think I'm ready for it. My uncle's very high up in the gang, though,' he adds proudly. 'He's Vince's sergeant-at-arms, Mad John. He's got a dog called Adolph.'

I shake my head in disbelief.

'It's true, honestly,' he says.

I hold both palms up at him to signal that of course it is, I don't doubt him. Of course, I believe that he's an apprentice Hells Angel, a 'Prospect', who has had a civilian makeover and wandered in off the street to quiz me about alternative theories for the murder of a magistrate.

'Right then,' Bob says, rubbing his hands together enthusiastically. 'Who do *you* think did it?'

I look at Nina. Nina looks at me. She shrugs.

And so, I give Bob a quick precis of my suspicion that Powell's death is linked to his opposition to the Tiller & Brown site planning application, and that the Andropov twins are also behind a campaign of intimidation to force the boat people off their moorings.

He listens attentively. I'm not sure how much he has really registered, but then he surprises me. 'That all makes sense,' he says thoughtfully. 'Course, I read the story about the residents' campaign in the newspaper. But you couldn't connect it with the planning application or Powell's death. Not in the paper. No proof.'

'That's right, Bob,' says Nina. 'It might just be a coincidence. Or it might just have been a random mugging that went wrong.'

'What about all this other stuff in the paper about a copycat serial killer? Somebody who's doing what that bloke in the Midlands did – the Canal Pusher, was it?'

'That's all bollocks,' I say bluntly.

It's Bob's turn to laugh out loud. 'Good enough for me,' he says cheerfully. 'Right then, I'd better report back to the Big Man and Mad John. And then,' he adds, with a grin, 'I've got myself a date.' He grabs a beermat. 'Got a pen?'

I pass him mine and he scribbles a mobile phone number on the cardboard disc. 'That's me. I'll be around at least until the end of the week. Vince will be really grateful if you hear anything else. Really, *really* grateful, if you get what I mean. Nice to meet you Jack, and you, Nina.'

After the door swings closed behind him, we both burst into laughter.

'He has to be the nicest Hells Angel I have ever met,' says Nina.

'Have you met many then, Mrs Wilde?'

'Well, he certainly seemed to be straightforward, and friendly, and rather handsome actually.'

'You heard,' I say chuckling. 'He's already got a date.' I transfer the number from the beermat into my phone's contacts.

'But seriously, Jack. I think I believe him. Why would their gang send someone to ask questions if they really did it? Surely they'd keep a very low profile? So, if the Bristol Bulldogs didn't kill Rufus Powell...'

'Then the police are wasting their time,' I finish for her.

'And that means someone else did.'

Back at the moorings, Nina and I knock up the other boats and invite everyone onto *Jumping Jack Flash* for a catch-up. Everyone is present, even Bill. I hand two cartons of fruit juice to Linda's children, as the others all take a bottle of beer or a cup of tea. It is still mid-afternoon, but rather than go up on deck it feels more private to have this meeting inside. I've switched all the wall lights on and the interior of *Jumping Jack Flash* is bathed in a cosy yellow glow. Linda has already told the others about the press conference but now that we're together again, there is a bit more of a post-mortem and I learn that the woman from Andropov Developments reappeared at the moorings at lunchtime, repeating the twins' financial offer to move on.

'We all told her the same again,' says Linda, looking around the small group for confirmation.

'That's right,' says Danny. 'You know how I feel.'

'I informed her that I was sub-letting my mooring to you, Jack, and that I would be resident once more on *Nautilus* as soon as she was repaired,' says the professor. 'Although, to be frank with you all, I am wondering whether I have the energy.'

'If you decide you don't want to repair *Nautilus*, none of us would blame you if you took the money,' Bill says. 'It's a lot of cash,' he adds, a wistful expression replacing his usual slightly furtive air.

I study Bill's face. If he does have gambling debts, it's strange that he hasn't jumped at taking the money himself. But there is a murmur of general agreement with him. The professor's eyes, which are often watery, seem to moisten even more than usual.

'Thank you, Bill,' he says. 'As Virgil says, *Haec olim meminisse juvabit*. One day, it may be pleasant to remember even this.'

Everyone retreats into their own thoughts for a moment before Nina breaks the silence. 'So, the question is, what else can we do?'

'Jack's article seems to have prompted a few residents to take down their signs, at least,' Linda says.

'That's true enough,' says Danny, peering out of a porthole. 'There are still about five or six of them up there, though.'

'We should keep the guard duty going overnight and make sure there's always at least one person around during the day,' I say.

'Be nice to get a full night's sleep tonight,' says Linda. 'I'm exhausted.' She has one eye on Noah and Juno. They're on the floor with Tammy, who's helping them fuss Eddie, to the small dog's obvious delight.

'Well,' says Nina, 'you were full of beans at the press conference!'

Everyone laughs. Linda blushes.

'I did get a bit carried away,' she admits. 'But they were so bloody smug, sitting there in their fancy suits with their fancy plans and calling us an eyesore. It's their bloody tower blocks that will be the eyesore. I'm more convinced than ever that they're the ones behind all our troubles.'

'There's one other thing,' says Bill. He seems to be avoiding my eyes, but then he seems to avoid everyone's eyes most of the time. 'When that woman came to my boat, she said the money wouldn't be on the table for ever.'

The professor nods. 'She said the same to me, but when I asked how long she wouldn't be drawn.'

Bill gives a cough. 'If they *are* behind those signs, and the cutting free of Linda's boat, and the sinking of *Nautilus*, then it's also possible they had the magistrate killed,' he says. 'And if that's the case, then the violence will continue, especially if we've all turned down their money again. They'll be very angry about you guys disrupting their conference today.' Then, he adds, slightly lamely, 'so we, er, all need to be on our guard more than ever.'

It's the most I've ever heard him say. In that moment, I realise that – as far as I know – Bill is the only one of the boat owners who hasn't been targeted so far. His words haven't provided much comfort to anyone. Was his contribution aimed at ratcheting up the pressure on the others? It certainly hadn't been very reassuring.

'Well,' I say, 'Nina's doing the first shift tonight, from eleven till one, I'm doing one o'clock till three and Bill's doing the graveyard shift, three a.m. till six.' I throw Nina a whistle liberated from a surplus lifebelt. 'If you hear this in the night, it's the alarm being sounded.'

'Yes well,' says the professor, giving a meaningful look at the children, 'I'm sure there will be no need for that.'

Linda takes his cue. 'Bedtime, kids,' she announces loudly. As she bustles Juno and Noah out of the boat and the others follow her, I notice Bill swipe a full and unopened bottle of beer as he goes. I let it pass, but I'm still not sure what to make of him. Linda, Danny and the professor clearly trust him, but as far as I'm concerned, he's shown me nothing to earn that trust.

Setting my worries aside, I rustle up Spanish omelettes and make a mental note to restock the fridge and larder in the morning. During dinner, the professor once again protests that he hasn't been included in the rota for guard duty but then tells us that he is thinking of going to visit a niece in Hampshire for a few days.

'I don't want to impose on your hospitality for too long,' he says. 'The change of scene will give me a chance to think things through.'

Nina tells him she thinks it's a good idea, and I reassure him that he is welcome to stay for as long as he wants.

'No, no,' he says. 'I've always believed that house guests are like fresh fish. They go off after three days. And that's even more true of boat guests.'

'Well, I'm not on guard duty for another couple of hours,' says Nina. 'I think I'll go for a run while the light lasts.'

'Do you mind if I tag along?' I ask her. 'I know I'll slow you down, but I need to do something about this.' I pat my stomach.

She laughs. 'Come on then, old man.'

CHAPTER THIRTY-SIX

We head upriver towards the Boating Station, a Victorian rowing clubhouse overlooking one of the prettiest reaches of the River Avon. Its restaurant, the Bathwick Boatman, with its quaint wooden balcony, is a great place to eat and enjoy watching people hire wooden skiffs from the jetty below. Our plan is to jog through town, stop for a rest at the clubhouse and then duck under the main railway and return on the towpath. Just as we are setting off across Victoria Bridge, two men emerge from the gathering gloom. 'Excuse me,' says one.

'Sorry to trouble you,' says the other, with the exaggerated politeness of a bouncer who is about to deny you access to a nightclub with the sweetest of smiles. 'Can you help us?' They are standing directly in our path. The men are similarly dressed in jeans and jackets with heavy boots. They are polite enough, but there is something about their chunky build and no-nonsense demeanour that suggests they are graduates from a school of hard knocks.

'What is it?'

'We're looking for a bloke called Bill Francis. We were told he lived somewhere around here. Any ideas?'

Nina is jogging on the spot, keen to get away on our run. She's about to respond helpfully but I cut her off. 'No. Sorry. Never heard of him. Good luck. Come on, Nina.'

I set off and Nina follows but as soon as we turn a corner she asks, 'Jack, what was that about?'

'Unofficial debt collectors, I think. The professor told me that if anyone came asking, Bill told the others to deny all knowledge of him. I didn't want to get him in trouble.'

It is probably two miles each way for our planned run and I know Nina has deliberately slowed her usual pace, but I'm struggling to keep up. The light is now falling nearly as fast as the air in my lungs, so I opt for a rest on Cleveland Bridge, with its attractive metal balustrades with a floral motif on each upright, under the pretence of admiring the view.

Nina stops with me and a very elegant wooden motorlaunch comes into view as we look back towards the city centre. A small 'V' of white water at its bow is being pushed backwards in the gathering gloom. I've seen this boat before. It's a beautifully restored leisure craft from the Edwardian era and it has both an open area and a closed wooden and glass cabin where well-heeled tourists can shelter from the rain if necessary. I think it has some kind of connection with the very best hotels in Bath; no doubt the concierge desks book it on behalf of their customers.

As it passes under the bridge, I grab Nina's bare arm. 'Look,' I say urgently. 'Isn't that –?'

'One of the twins!'

We wait for a car to pass then rush over to the other side of the bridge just as the launch emerges from underneath. Sure enough, seated in the middle of the boat is one of the Andropovs. Whichever twin it is has both arms outstretched expansively and is alone on the boat apart from a helmsman, who is sitting in front of him at a wheel towards the bow.

'Come on,' Nina urges. 'Let's see where he's going.'

We run off the bridge and head left but there is no river path here, just large houses with gardens running down to the water. We work our way along the residential roads, stopping to peer at the river whenever there is a glimpse of it, but it's useless. We soon end up at the Bathwick Boatman and dash to the river where its hire skiffs have been lined up for the night. We see the rear of the launch disappearing upstream.

'Oh well. Time for a drink, maybe?'

But we've both come out without wallet or phone. Shared pint of tap water it is. We find a curved and slatted bench under a large tree where we sip our water and enjoy the peacefulness of the setting. Mature trees line the bank on the other side of the river and it is impossible to see anything beyond them.

The prospect of Nina's job in Dubai still looms uncomfortably between us – undiscussed but ever present. I steel myself to take advantage of this quiet moment and ask what her latest thoughts are.

But Nina speaks first. 'Oh, look. He's coming back.'

Sure enough, I can see the bow of the motorlaunch making its way towards us from upstream. Perhaps Sebastian or Anthony, whoever is onboard, has decided to call it a day. Or maybe they will return for a drink or a meal at the riverside restaurant? Nina and I would be out of sight if they tie up at the jetty by the skiffs, but, as the boat gets closer, we see it head for the far side of the river, where it slows to a stop. The helmsman loops a stern rope around the stout branch of a tree to keep the launch from drifting forward, then bustles into the little wooden cabin at the rear and turns the lights on. The cabin's glass windows are tall and rectangular, and we can see the man pottering about, pouring a large glass of white wine and filling a bowl with something. He delivers the refreshments to his client before returning to sit quietly on his own at the boat's stern.

'Come on,' I whisper to Nina. 'Let's get out of sight.'

We move quietly away from the bench, behind a small row of trees and shrubs.

'Which twin do you think it is?' whispers Nina, looking at the figure on the deck.

'God knows,' I say.

It's getting pretty dark now and flimsy running gear isn't much protection from the evening chill. Nina gives a little shiver. 'Don't forget I'm on guard duty tonight, Jack,' she says, looking at her watch.

'Just wait a minute,' I say, watching the Andropov twin, who has taken out a phone and started speaking into it. It's impossible to hear what he is saying across the river, but it quickly becomes clear from his body language that he is not in a good mood. He has the phone clamped to his right ear, but his left hand is making repeated and emphatic chopping movements. Then he stands up and we can hear that his voice is raised, even though we can't make out the words.

'Wait here,' I urge Nina, yanking off my trainers and socks.

'No, Jack, you're not going to –'

But I've already gone. I stoop low along the jetty, through the moored skiffs, and then slip down into the water as quietly as I can. It may be midsummer, but the cold water takes my breath away. I use a gentle breaststroke as I set out across the river, keeping my eyes on the launch, helpfully lit up by the bright yellow lights of its cabin. Luckily, there is hardly any current and I am across and under the far bank's canopy of trees after about fifteen strokes.

I can't feel the river's bottom, but it is relatively easy to drift on the gentle current to the rear of the launch, where I wrap an arm around its rudder. Immediately above me is the back of the helmsman. He's sitting in the rear of the cabin and a few yards forward of us both, the Andropov twin is speaking loudly on his phone.

'Not good enough,' he says. 'I'm paying you good money and we're getting nowhere. What are your plans? What will you do next?'

Sadly, I can only hear one side of the conversation.

Across the river, on the far bank, I can just about make out the white blur of Nina's face. I know she'll be anxious. It's bloody cold and I'm getting stiff, so I give my arm a rest and swap to use the other one to hold on. Only my arm and my head are above the water. The noise and clatter from the warmth of the restaurant on the first floor of the lovely old boathouse seems a long way away.

'No, no, no, no, NO!' says the twin angrily. 'You cannot do that. You really are an imbecile.' There's a pause. Then, 'We need to meet. Tomorrow. I will text you where and when. Okay. Let's go.'

The last few words were directed at the helmsman. I push myself backwards from the rudder, roll over onto my front and swim back under the trees. The boat's engine coughs into life and I realise I was probably only seconds from being mangled by its propeller. The yellow of the cabin at its stern moves smoothly into the midstream and back towards the Cleveland Bridge. I abandon caution and use front crawl to swim back across the river as quickly as possible.

Nina is on the jetty and helps to pull me out onto its rough wooden boards.

'What the hell, Jack?' She seems furious.

'Christ, I'm freezing,' I mutter. I'm not sure what to say to smooth this. I can see people on the clubhouse balcony looking down at us curiously.

'You're an idiot,' says Nina, softening slightly as she takes in my chattering teeth. 'Here – put your shoes on and let's get back for a hot shower.'

We cross under the railway bridge and turn to run back along the Kennet & Avon's towpath. It's a distinctly uncomfortable run in my sopping vest and shorts, but I breathlessly tell Nina about the brief snippet of conversation that I overheard.

'Could be someone he was paying to do his dirty work,' I pant, as we pass my empty mooring at the bottom of Robert's garden. The lights of his house are ablaze and the insistent beat of dance music drifts down from an open window.

'But he could have been speaking to anyone,' replies Nina, evenly. 'He could have been talking to his lawyers about the bribes. He could even have been talking to his brother about another bit of business entirely.'

She's right, of course. Wild swimming in the dark has been for nothing.

'Well, there is one thing I know,' I say stubbornly. 'It was Sebastian Andropov and not Anthony on that boat. He said "You weally are an imbecile!"'

This makes Nina laugh so hard she has to stop jogging for a moment – it's a victory of a sort, I suppose.

CHAPTER THIRTY-SEVEN

At eleven, Nina puts on warm outer socks, a jumper, quilted jacket and woollen hat to prepare for her first night shift. I prepare a flask of coffee for her to take up on deck. Just as she is about to head up the steps through the hatchway, whistle round her neck, there's a loud knocking outside. Will's cheery face appears. 'What, ho!' he says. 'Permission to come aboard?'

I'd completely forgotten it was Will's opening night at the theatre. He kisses Nina, gives me a bear hug and shakes hands vigorously with the professor.

'Well? How was it?' I ask.

'A spectacular triumph,' says Will.

I suspect that this has been his verdict for every single one of his opening nights, but I am happy to go along with it.

'Word perfect, of course, thanks to the prof here,' Will says, clapping the older man on a shoulder. 'Good turnout by the press and I think we'll get some pretty decent reviews. The rest of the cast aren't bad too.'

'Excellent. Congratulations, Will,' says the professor, with genuine pleasure. 'I must get a ticket to see it before I leave.'

Will digs into his shirt pocket.

'Here you go,' he say, fanning out tickets onto the table. 'Five seats for tomorrow. Bring some of your friends. And I found this waiting for me in my dressing room.' He pulls out a bottle of Champagne. 'The rest of the cast have buggered off back to their digs – so boring! But I'm far too wired to sleep. Anyone want to join me? It's nice and cold.'

'Well,' I say awkwardly, 'we're on guard duty tonight. Nina was just about to go up.'

'C'mon,' he says, rootling in a cupboard for some glasses. 'We can join Nina for a bit. This'll help to pass the time.'

'Not for me, Will, I'm afraid,' says the professor, standing. 'Champagne gives me heartburn and I need to go to bed – but you all go ahead.'

There's no point trying to argue with Will when he's in this kind of mood and so Nina and I take a full glass of fizz from him and sit on the boat's roof, facing the opposite bank with our legs dangling over the water. Will chatters away about the play for a while but the chill of the night eventually silences him. Only a handful of lights remain in the windows of the homes facing us and the noise of the city's traffic has fallen away. I'm resigned to staying up now until the end of my shift at three a.m. and so I duck down below and bring some thick blankets up on deck. We each wrap one closely around us. The bottle is empty within an hour and Nina opens her flask of coffee. Will starts to demand more booze, but Nina is adamant.

'You've got to do it all again tomorrow, don't forget,' she chides.

'True,' Will laughs softly. 'I always forget about that on opening night.'

'Silly bugger,' Nina says fondly, handing him a cup of coffee, its steam misting into the night air.

The light is on in the boat's saloon, shining out from a porthole between our legs onto the dark surface of the water. There's hardly a breath of wind, and the river's surface is a shiny mirror disturbed only occasionally by a twig or leaf flowing past on the current.

I wonder to myself whether Nina and Will might be attracted to each other if they did not have me to consider – or even if they did. They certainly seem to get on well. Will has some of the same square-cut good looks that I saw in the newspaper photographs of Nina's ex-husband, Alan.

I glance across at my oldest friend. Nina is quietly trying to persuade him to head back to his hotel and bank what remains of a good night's sleep. I feel a pang of jealousy. Will's 'little-boy-who-must-be-mothered' act, combined with his fit, muscular frame, handsome actor's face and reckless attitude to life means he is consistently successful with the other sex. Would Nina fall for him too?

I'm just about to join Nina in urging Will to return to his hotel when a loud bang shatters the quiet. The glass of the porthole beneath us explodes into fragments.

'What the fuck?'

'Get below!' I yell.

As we scramble down the steps, Nina blows on the whistle. Its shrill, piercing note stops when I take it from her mouth.

'First-aid box,' I snap to Will, 'in the bathroom.'

There's a gash in one of Nina's trouser legs and blood is seeping down her leg. I can see a small triangular-shaped shard of glass embedded just below her knee.

'Sit down.'

I gently prise the glass out. Nina is white-faced, but her voice is steady. 'Help me get my trousers off,' she says.

The movement causes a steady trickle of blood to pool at the wound and run down either side of her leg.

The professor joins us. He's wearing a dressing gown and looks horrified when he sees me bending over Nina's bloodied bare legs. 'Good god! What on earth has happened?'

'Keep still,' I tell Nina, and I pull another small piece of glass out in one clean movement. I pat the wound with an antiseptic pad that Will has handed to me from the first-aid box. I register the anxious faces of the other boat people crowding behind the professor, alerted by the bang of the window or Nina's whistle.

'What the hell happened?' Linda is hovering at the swing door to the twin-berth bedroom. She's also wearing a dressing gown and peering worriedly along the boat, torn between wanting to join us and the anxiety of leaving her children alone onboard *Maid of Coventry*.

'I could be wrong,' I say grimly, 'but I think someone has just shot at us. We're all okay but Nina's got a flesh wound from some glass. You'd better call the police and an ambulance – and stay inside the boats.'

'Oh my god!'

'I'll call 999,' says Danny, moving back along the boat and ushering Linda in front of him and back to her children.

Once I have cleaned Nina's cut I tightly bandage it as she sits on the banquette with both legs stretched out in front of her. Her face has turned from grey now and her lips are trembling slightly. The professor presses a small whisky into her hands and makes her take a sip. We have all been stunned into silence. I look out of the jagged remains of the porthole and see that many of the flats opposite have their lights on. No doubt they too have been disturbed by the bang, the breaking glass and the noise of the whistle. Was one of them already awake and now frantically trying to conceal a rifle or a gun of some kind? I can see the silhouette of Rani Manningham-Westcott in her window. She appears to be hunched over the telescopic lens of her camera.

About ten minutes later we hear the sound of approaching sirens, and then flashing blue lights illuminate the river. Unsurprisingly, a report of gunfire has prompted an immediate and urgent response. Two uniformed officers jog over the bridge with crackling radios and I meet them outside the boat and quickly brief them. One goes on deck and the other makes way for a paramedic who carries a large shoulder bag. Down below, she undoes Nina's bandage with her gloved hands, explores the wound for any remaining fragments of glass, cleans it again and rebandages it.

'It'll soon heal up, love,' she tells Nina reassuringly. 'No need for a trip to hospital tonight. Come to Minor Injuries tomorrow to get it checked and rebandaged.' Nina nods her head. 'Keep an eye out for nausea or chest pains, dizziness or even fainting,' she says.

I escort the paramedic to the stern platform where she pauses before stepping down. 'She's got signs of minor shock – not surprising. Give her some painkillers and try to get her to bed. If she takes a turn for the worse, bring her in to be seen.'

I nod. As I turn to go back to Nina I pause and look up across the river. There are more figures watching from the apartment windows. I give them all a long and raking stare and a couple of lights go out immediately. Back down below, Will and the professor are quietly murmuring to Nina, who looks tearful and vulnerable. 'Aspirin and bed as soon as possible,' I say quietly.

Behind them is the damaged porthole. Its top half is almost completely gone and there are triangular shards of glass poking upwards from its bottom half. I closely examine the sheets of varnished wood that clad the wall. If someone had been firing from high up on the far bank, and if the bullet had gone through the top of the porthole, I calculate that it would have entered the boat at an acute angle. Sure enough, there's a small metal slug embedded in the wood just a foot above the floor. I can't tell whether it's the remains of an air rifle pellet or the head of a small bullet. I resist the temptation to dig it out and turn to the stern, where someone is coming down the steps. I immediately recognise the blonde, bobbed hair of Detective Inspector Kerr at the same time as she recognises me.

'Mr Johnson,' she says. 'Is this your boat?'

'Yes. You'd better come in.'

She motions the uniformed officers behind her to stay where they are and follows me. I introduce her to Will, the professor and Nina. She takes in Nina's bandaged leg and then turns back to me.

'The reports say a gun was fired?'

'This way.' I show her the shattered porthole and the remains of the bullet or pellet, and then take her out through the bow to show her where all three of us were sitting on the roof.

'And these are the moorings you were telling me about?'

'Obviously,' I say. I'm tired, frustrated and angry. I suspect my own shock at Nina's wound is starting to hit home. I point to the opposite bank. 'And those are the homeowners who are campaigning to get rid of these boats.'

'I didn't realise you were moored here too.'

'Does it matter?' I ask. 'I've temporarily taken over the mooring of the boat that was deliberately sunk. We've been sharing guard duty between us through the night – trying to protect ourselves in the absence of any official police interest.'

She chooses to ignore the pointed dig. 'Talk me through it again, Mr Johnson,' she says calmly.

I usher DI Kerr back to the table in the galley and, this time, she writes everything down in a notebook as I go back over the sudden appearance of the slogans, the vandalism, the setting adrift of *Maid of Coventry*, the sinking of *Nautilus* and, finally, the shooting and Nina's injury. Will makes everyone fresh cups of filter coffee while I am talking.

'And you still think all this might be connected to Mr Powell's death?' the detective says, sipping on her drink.

'Yes,' I reply, this time through gritted teeth. Then, 'Well, maybe,' I concede. 'Rufus Powell was against the scheme to develop the site behind us. The owners of the site also want the boat people to leave. They can't bribe them to go, and so maybe they're trying to force them.'

'And maybe they wanted Mr Powell to be quiet too?' she says, looking me square in the eyes.

'You said it.'

'Pretty serious allegations, Mr Johnson,' she observes coolly.

'They're exactly the same ones I shared with you at the station,' I say firmly, 'although now that someone's out here with a gun on the river, you seem to be taking them a bit more seriously.'

DI Kerr looks across at Nina, Will, the professor and Bill, who have all been closely following our exchange.

'I'll need the three of you who were up on deck when the shot was fired to come into the station tomorrow and make some statements,' she says. 'I'll leave a uniformed officer outside until dawn, so you can all get some sleep. I'll also be sending a scenes of crime officer around at nine a.m. to retrieve the slug for further examination. We'll be running checks on the residents who live opposite to see if any of them have got gun licences, and we'll start up house-to-house inquiries again.'

'What about Andropov Developments?'

She drains her coffee. 'Thanks for the drink. I needed that. I was working late at the station when I was alerted to your call.'

'What about Andropov Developments?' I ask again, but more emphatically this time.

DI Kerr gets to her feet. 'We'll take it from here, Mr Johnson. Shall we say ten a.m. for your statements?'

I sigh heavily with frustration, but the detective ignores it and makes her way back along the boat. I follow her up onto the stern and watch her swing the tiller aside to step down the gangplank and onto the path. DI Kerr turns to look up at the fencing, and beyond it at the derelict site; its open spaces beginning to be reclaimed by nature, the big buildings with broken glass windows. A fierce anger is now swamping my exhaustion. I look down at the small group of police officers. Linda's face is peering worriedly back at us from the stern of *Maid of Coventry*.

'Look,' I snap, 'there could easily have been a lot more deaths on this river over the past few days in addition to Rufus Powell. You people need to start taking this very seriously. And you should start by asking Anthony and Sebastian Andropov some questions, because that site, which they own, is the one thing that connects the people on these boats and Powell.'

'Um, excuse me...' Bill has been loitering behind me and gives me and the DI a frightened look as he scuttles past, back towards his boat.

DI Kerr takes the opportunity to leave and I slam the hatchway shut and stomp back down the steps. The other three look equally exhausted. It's one a.m. I look outside through a porthole to check that a policeman has been left on guard, and check my phone. There's a text message from Rani asking if we are all right. I can see the light in her flat is still on, so I text back: 'Everyone is safe. Explain tomorrow.'

It seems that Will is staying on board for the rest of the night. I help Nina limp to her bunk, where she curls up tightly under her duvet. The professor, sitting on the edge of the bunk opposite, nods to me quietly and says, 'Goodnight, Jack. Well done and well said.' I head back to my double berth, where Will crashes alongside me without getting undressed.

'It's always a drama with you, isn't it, Jack?' he says quietly.

'Says the actor,' I reply.

Today began with a press conference, featured a meeting with Gwyneth Wilkinson and a Hells Angel called Bob, and ended with a swim in the river and a gun attack. Will's right, today was a drama, but any further thoughts are lost in instant, deep and exhausted sleep.

CHAPTER THIRTY-EIGHT

It is after eight a.m. before anyone stirs onboard *Jumping Jack Flash* – unsurprising given that we didn't go to bed until the early hours of the morning. A quick check through the porthole above my bed tells me that the constable from the Avon and Somerset force has left. I lie back with my arms behind my head whilst Will, who is still fast asleep, sucks in air through pursed lips and exhales each breath with a little puff of air. He has faint traces of make-up on his cheeks and a tiny smudge of eyeliner from the previous night's performance. The Theatre Royal tonight will be fun: a much-needed distraction from the threat of being drowned or shot at. Will begins to stir, turns onto his front and throws one arm across my chest. I remove it gently and slide out of the bottom of the bed to avoid disturbing him further. I poke my head through the door of the twin berth. Nina looks up at me from the bed with a tired smile.

'How are you feeling?' I whisper.

'Okay, thanks,' she whispers back, careful not to disturb the professor. She swings her legs out of bed and tentatively puts her weight on the one that is bandaged. 'It's all right. Still a bit sore but that's all.' She follows me to the galley with only the barest hint of a limp, Eddie following faithfully, and sits up on the banquette.

'Do you think the gunman was actually trying to shoot us?'

'I honestly don't know,' I say, busying myself with the kettle. 'It was pretty dark. If they were aiming at the porthole, just to scare us, then it was a very good shot. If they were aiming at one of us, and missed, then we were pretty bloody lucky.'

'So,' she sighs. 'What's next?'

'Scenes of crime officer at nine, statements at ten. Then we should get a new dressing for your leg, and tonight we're going to the theatre. But I've got an idea of something to do this afternoon.'

'Which is?'

'We pay another call on Councillor Claverton.'

'Rattling the cage?' asks Nina.

'Rattling the cage,' I confirm, placing a mug of tea in front of her. 'We'll need to find out his home address, I suppose,' I say as I head off with two more mugs of tea for the others.

There's a steady stream of visitors to *Jumping Jack Flash* over the next hour to check on Nina and swap anecdotes about the events of the previous night. They're all shocked when I show them the scrap of silver-coloured metal embedded in the wall opposite the broken porthole. Bill, Linda, Danny and Tammy also have a discussion among themselves over who should use the two spare theatre tickets and finally settle on Danny and Tammy.

'I'll stay,' volunteers Bill. 'I can keep an eye on everything – theatre's not really my thing.'

'And I'd better stay with Noah and Juno,' Linda says. 'I won't enjoy it for worrying after all this.'

As she is leaving, Linda turns to me. She's feisty and independent, but the constant feeling of being threatened is obviously beginning to take its toll. 'Jack,' she says quietly to me. 'That could have been me on guard duty last night and the bullet could have gone into the boat where the kids were sleeping. That's twice they could have been killed in a few days. I'm not sure I can take much more of this.'

'Don't worry, Linda,' I say. 'We're going to catch these bastards.' But I know I feel less confident than I sound.

She bites her lower lip, nods worriedly and heads back to *Maid of Coventry*.

The SOCO is a portly, white-suited individual who arrives promptly and cheerfully admires the boat. 'Always liked the idea of having a go at one of these,' he says. 'But the wife isn't very keen.'

I watch him use a tiny pair of pointed pliers to extract the metal slug and place it in a plastic container. He puts a metal lens to one eye to look at it.

'.22 rifle bullet,' he says confidently. 'Although I didn't tell you that.'

Then he takes a thin metal rod out of his bag, extends it to a length of about three metres, slots it into the hole in the wall and pokes the other end out of the shattered porthole. He looks along its length but shakes his head sadly. 'Too much glass missing to pinpoint its origin,' he says.

Nevertheless, he takes out a camera and shoots some pictures of the buildings clustered at the other end of the rod and another of the hole in the wall. Then he takes several close-ups of the bullet, which he handles with close-fitting latex gloves.

'That's it. Ta very much,' he says, whistling as he leaves.

Will, Nina and I walk to the police station, where a detective constable has been delegated to oversee our three statements. It takes less than an hour for him to amass the paperwork and show us back out of the door without further comment. There has been no sign of the detective inspector. Will heads off for his hotel and 'a bit more sleep' while I join Nina in the back of a taxi. I wait outside the Royal United Hospital's Minor Injuries Unit, but Nina emerges after less than an hour and tells me there is nothing to worry about. She is experiencing no pain when she puts her weight on the wounded leg, and so we walk slowly back down the hill into the city centre, where we head to the Guildhall. She makes me stay outside again and re-emerges after ten minutes. She is holding a piece of paper with the home address of Councillor Robin Claverton on it: Flat 6, Prince Albert Apartments, Carriage Terrace.

'I couldn't find anything online before we had to leave, but I seemed to remember they have to supply their home addresses when they stand for election,' she says smugly. Nina types the address into the map app on her phone and it tells us how to get there on foot. As we walk, we realise we are heading directly back towards the moorings. Sure enough, we discover that Councillor Claverton lives in the converted Victorian pile that stands next to Rani's more modern apartment building.

'Flat 6?' I ask Nina.

'Flat 6,' she confirms. But I stay my hand before ringing the buzzer. 'What is it?'

I know she won't like this but I press ahead.

'Look, Nina. You wound him up a lot in the park. It might not be good tactics to go in mob-handed.'

My heart sinks as I see her jaw set in stubborn defiance. I know only too well how much Nina hates to be excluded and I suspect she is still resentful at missing out on the golf club lunch. But I'm saved by the bell. Well, a horn, actually. The tinny little sound makes us both turn and there is Rani, sitting on her mobility scooter and smiling up at us.

'Ah, there you are. I've been looking for you everywhere,' she says. 'I have something very urgent to show you.'

I take my chance. 'Excellent. Urgent, you say? Nina, why don't you go to Rani's flat and tell her all about last night while I pay a call on Councillor Claverton?'

Rani wrinkles her nose in disgust at her neighbour's name. 'Claverton is such a silly man. Yes, I want to hear all about last night and the police. Join when you're free, Jack. Come along, dear, you can help with the door.'

Nina narrows her eyes at me but trails reluctantly in Rani's wake while I ring the bell for Flat 6.

'Who is it?' says an impatient metallic voice.

'It's Jack Johnson from the *Bath Chronicle*, Councillor Claverton. Can I have ten minutes of your time?' There is a lengthy pause. 'Councillor Claverton?'

'I've got nothing to say to you,' comes the reply.

'Okay,' I say, more calmly than I feel. 'That's up to you. But someone fired a gun – a rifle – onto the moorings last night. Someone was hurt. Someone could have been killed. The *Chronicle* will be running this as a story tomorrow and you might like to disassociate yourself and your residents' campaign from attempted murder?'

I hold my breath and wait for this to sink in. Then the front door buzzes and I lunge to push it open before the buzzing stops. Claverton is waiting in the doorway of his flat as I emerge from the stairwell, breathing a little heavily, onto the fourth floor landing. His school bully demeanour has gone; now he appears more like a sulky teenager. I smile to myself as he suddenly reminds me of Tammy. He doesn't extend a hand. In fact, he keeps both thrust deep into his trouser pockets and stands squarely in his front doorway.

'A shooting, you say?' the councillor says disingenuously.

I can't imagine that he wasn't disturbed by the police car lights and the noise of the events of the previous night, or wouldn't have been alerted to it by his neighbours, but I play along.

'That's right, Councillor Claverton,' I say, more respectfully than I feel. 'It seems that someone used a rifle from a building on this side of the river to shoot at three people who were sitting on the roof of a boat last night. The police are taking it very seriously.'

He visibly blanches. 'Well... that's nothing to do with me or any of the residents here. Some of them were a bit upset about your piece in the *Chronicle* last week – about the boat sinking. It implied that we might have been responsible.'

'No, I don't think it did. Although perhaps it prompted some of them to take their banners down. But last night's gunman could still be a resident who has got a bit carried away by your campaign. Very carried away. A woman on one of the boats needed hospital treatment this morning.'

'Hospital treatment?' he stammers worriedly. 'Someone was injured?'

'Nasty wound to the leg,' I say grimly, neglecting to mention that it was caused by flying glass.

'Good god.' He passes a hand across his eyes.

'Unofficially, the police say it was a .22 rifle,' I add. 'A lethal weapon.'

'I wouldn't want anyone to get hurt,' he says a little pitifully.

'Or even killed,' I add helpfully.

The councillor just swallows hard and shakes his head.

'Maybe I could come in and get some quotes from you, for the paper? Just to set the record straight, Councillor Claverton?'

He swallows again but nods this time and opens the door for me to enter the flat.

Claverton shows me into a large and comfortable drawing room; light floods into it through tall arched windows framed in carved stone. I immediately go to them. There is a sweeping view, stretching from the four moored boats on the other side of the little suspension bridge, across the long expanse of the Tiller & Brown site's river frontage and downriver to the road bridge.

'I had no idea that you lived opposite the moorings and the development site.'

'Yes, well,' he coughs. 'Those boats are as much of an eyesore for me and my wife as my neighbours. Although I'm organising the campaign as their representative councillor, of course, and not in any private capacity.'

'Of course,' I say, taking out a notebook and a biro. I begin to stroll around the walls of his apartment. He follows close behind me. I inspect some of his paintings and the knick-knacks cluttering his shelves.

'So, Councillor Claverton,' I say, picking up a glass snowball with a plastic model of the Royal Crescent inside. Winter immediately descends on the sweep of its façade and I replace it carefully. 'What would you like to say to the *Chronicle*'s readers about last night's attempted murder?'

'Attempted murder? Yes, of course... attempted murder...'

I smile at him, pen poised. He gathers himself together.

'Well, of course, I am shocked.' And, I am surprised to note, he does indeed look genuinely shocked. 'I repudiate violence of any kind and I condemn it in the strongest of terms. I find it hard to believe that anyone connected with our campaign against the canal boats would stoop to such, such extreme tactics.' He watches me scribbling. 'Such *detestable* tactics,' he adds. 'Please use the word detestable.'

'Of course,' I say, poking a tongue out of one side of my mouth as I write detestable and say the word simultaneously. 'De-test-able. There we go.' I set off again around the edges of his room and he plods awkwardly behind me. I'm enjoying this.

'Did you know Rufus Powell, Councillor Claverton?'

The sudden change of topic throws him.

'Rufus P-Powell?' he stutters. 'Yes, of course, everyone on the council knew Mr Powell. The Georgian Fellowship. A distinguished magistrate. Very active, very influential...'

'And now he's dead. Murdered,' I say.

'Yes, I know. Sad business. Terribly sad business. You interviewed his widow in last week's paper, didn't you?'

I am interested that he has read it with sufficient attention to register me as the writer. No doubt he recognised me from the accompanying photograph of me and Mrs Powell. 'Yes, that's right,' I say, with a smile and I plonk myself in the centre of one of his huge squashy sofas. I generously wave him to take the armchair opposite me. 'Charming lady. Stricken with grief, of course.'

'Of course,' he says, sitting down with his big feet splayed out and his hands hanging down awkwardly between his legs. With his funny side parting and short-sleeved white shirt and tie, it is easy to imagine him in a similarly sorrowful pose in front of a headmaster after beating up another kid in the playground. 'I... I've never met Mrs Powell.'

'Did you know that Mr Powell was about to declare outright war on the plans by Andropov Developments for the site opposite you?' I ask pleasantly.

'No,' says the councillor, a little too quickly. 'I didn't know that. Although you mentioned it at the press conference.'

And yet, I think to myself, I had first touched on it in the article which he says he had read. I make a mental note to try to persuade Ben to run the whole of Powell's speech now that the planning application is in the public domain.

'And now he's dead,' I say. 'Dead before he could make his opposition public and organise a campaign against the plan.'

He just looks at me frowning, unsure how to respond. I decide to press my point home.

'Councillor Claverton, the Andropovs clearly don't want the boats on their doorstep any more than you do. And they probably didn't want Mr Powell speaking up against their plans. And Mr Powell is dead – murdered – and now it seems like someone is also being very careless with the boat owners' lives, wouldn't you say? First a boat was untied and nearly went over the weir with two young children on board. Then another was deliberately sunk. And now someone is firing a gun at them. That's a pretty serious charge sheet.'

Claverton looks winded; his jaw is slack and his eyes wide with alarm.

'For the record, Councillor Claverton, have you ever met Anthony and Sebastian Andropov, the owners of Andropov Developments – other than at their press conference yesterday?'

'Umm... I... er... yes. Once. They took me for a walk around the site to explain their plans – as a local councillor, of course.'

'And as a resident, overlooking the site?' I remind him helpfully.

'And as a resident, overlooking the site,' he parrots back at me, before realising what he has said. 'No. No. Not at all. I visited the site in my official capacity.'

'And during your visit, did the Andropovs express any views to you about the canal boats?' I ask evenly, my pen poised above the notebook.

He coughs. 'They might have mentioned them in passing,' he says cautiously. 'Yes, I think they said they would be offering them generous financial terms to leave. They were very critical of the deal that Tiller & Brown did with them in exchange for permanent moorings.'

'And so, you began your campaign,' I say.

'Now, look,' says Claverton, rising to his considerable height. 'My campaign has nothing to do with them. It's a local campaign supported by local residents –'

'And organised by you?'

'Yes, run by me. There's no law against it. It's my job.'

'Really?' I reply sharply. 'I thought being a councillor was a vocation, a civic duty – a calling, rather than a job? You usually get paid for jobs.' I rise to my feet too. 'So, again, just for the record. There's no connection between your campaign and the Andropov twins?'

'None. None whatsoever,' he says.

'And no connection that you know of, between the murder of Mr Powell and the attempted drowning and shooting of the boat people?'

'None. None that I know of...'

'None that you know of?' I repeat slowly. 'And you haven't been paid anything by the Andropovs? Any kind of... consultancy fee?'

'No... no... of course not.'

I flick my notebook closed. 'Well, I suppose that's all we can say for the moment.'

There are small beads of sweat on Claverton's broad expanse of brow. I calculate that his cage has been well and truly rattled.

As I turn to walk to the door, something catches my eye. On a shelf at waist height is a single golf ball balanced on a small silver egg cup near the edge of the shelf, as if on display like a miniature trophy.

'Do you play golf, Councillor? It seems to be very popular among the civic dignitaries of Bath.' Something compels me to pick up the ball and I am immediately struck by how heavy it is.

'No, I don't. That's a paperweight,' says Claverton hastily, snatching it off me and replacing it on the egg cup.

'Oh, I see, well, I think that's covered everything. I'll make sure the article disassociates you and your residents' campaign from last night's shooting. Thank you for seeing me.'

The hand that shakes mine is limp and damp, unlike the door that shuts quickly behind me, which is firm and emphatic.

There are just too many coincidences, I tell myself as I walk down the stairs. They are gnawing away at me and causing the most frustrating kind of knowledge – the knowledge that comes when you know something for a fact, but you can't see a way of proving it.

CHAPTER THIRTY-NINE

I check my phone for messages as I descend the stairs. There is one from Nina, urging me to call in at Rani's flat as soon as I possibly can. I immediately head for the neighbouring building and Nina opens the door for me.

'You've got to see this!' she says, pulling me urgently across the threshold. The bookcase has been swivelled open and Rani is sitting at the table in her secret little studio-office.

'Ah, there you are, Jack. Come here behind the desk and have a look at this.' I do as I am told and bend down next to her to examine an image that fills the large, flat screen of her computer. It shows a muscular-looking man standing on the top of the fire escape of the neighbouring building; the building I have just come from. He appears to be tall and is wearing a dark waist-length jacket and a baseball cap. Most of his face is in profile; he's sharply featured with an aquiline nose, high cheekbones and a small slit of a mouth. The man is holding a compact digital camera in front of him, which is pointed down and across the river, in the direction of the moored boats.

'I noticed him late on Monday evening,' says Rani. 'I was dusting the plantation shutters, when I saw him through the slats on the side window. They're angled so I can see out, but no one can see in. We had them in India. So, I turned my lights out and opened the shutter a tiny bit in the middle. I took quite a few shots without him noticing but this is the best of the lot. Do you think he might be connected with the shooting last night? I'm so silly. I should have told you about him yesterday. And poor Nina with her leg wound.'

'May I?' I say, taking control of her mouse. I use it to zoom in on the man's face, but the image becomes blurred. Then I zoom out so that the man appears quite small on top of the metal platform and the countryside stretches away into the distance above the rooftops.

'He reminds me of someone I've seen,' I say. 'It's his build and the way he's standing.' Then it hits me. 'It's the image from the CCTV on the night of Powell's death!'

I call up the *Chronicle*'s website and find the grainy image of the man walking in the rain. His features are hidden but there is something similar about the tall, muscular build and the way he is bending his head with his shoulders hunched.

'What do you think?' I ask the others, looking at the two images side by side on the screen.

'It could be the same man,' says Nina excitedly.

'I'm not sure,' says Rani, more cautiously. 'You can't see this man's face.'

I fish out the card that Detective Inspector Kerr gave me and ask Rani to open an email using the DI's address. Then I ask her to attach both images to it and dictate a brief explanation.

'Have the police been around yet this morning?' I ask. 'They were going to do more house-to-house inquiries after the shooting last night.'

'Not yet,' says Rani. 'If they come, shall I show them this?'

'Yes, it won't hurt. But tell them that you've also sent it to DI Kerr.'

'Of course, I saw all the activity last night. The blue lights woke me up. But there was no one on the fire escape that I could see at that time, Jack. It could be a coincidence.'

'If it was the same man, he wouldn't have hung around,' I say. 'Look, Rani, it's the *Chronicle*'s press day tomorrow and I'd like to get something about the shooting in the paper. Do you mind if I sit in here for an hour and do some work?'

Rani readily agrees and uses her sticks to vacate the desk. She and Nina head for her little kitchen while I begin to work up a story about the shooting. I use the quote from Councillor Claverton, calling it a 'detestable act'. Then my mobile goes.

'Mr Johnson?'

'DI Kerr.'

'I've just seen the email from your friend.'

'What do you think?'

'It could be the same man,' she says cautiously. 'I want to speak to the lady who took it.'

'We're with her now,' I say. I pass the phone over and hear Rani say 'Yes, that will be convenient' and give her address before placing the phone back on the desk. 'She says she will be here within half an hour.'

DI Kerr arrives with a young sergeant in civilian clothes in tow. Like us, she is running on very little sleep from the night before and her eyes betray extreme fatigue. She must be under a huge amount of pressure from more senior officers to find the murderer of a magistrate. The two officers gratefully accept a cup of tea from Rani and look at her hidden office with undisguised interest. The DI settles herself in front of Rani's computer and Rani shows her about ten shots of the man on the fire escape.

'And what time was this?' DI Kerr asks.

'It was just starting to get dark on Monday. Just after nine o'clock, I think.'

'We brought *Jumping Jack Flash* round from the canal at about eight-thirty,' I say. 'And it looks like he's taking a photograph of something going on at the moorings.'

DI Kerr peers closely at the screen and then holds a paper print of the CCTV picture of the biker next to it. 'If only his face was clearer on this one,' she complains.

'There's something similar about their build,' I say.

She remains cautious. 'Possibly. I don't think there's enough to say this is definitely the same man. But we may not need to for now. He's certainly a person of interest given that he was on the fire escape twenty-four hours before a gun was fired from roughly the same position. That's reason enough to get this new photograph out to the public.' She turns to her sergeant. 'Go and have a good look around the roof and the fire escape next door,' she orders. 'See if there are any cigarette stubs or cartridge cases. And get this picture into the hands of the door-to-door guys. Let's see if anyone round here knows him. We don't want to start a manhunt if he turns out to be some kind of amateur photographer or local bird-spotter.' The sergeant heads off to fulfil his brief.

'If you want it in the *Chronicle*, you'll need to make a decision early tomorrow at the latest,' I tell her.

'You're writing about the shooting?' she asks.

I nod. 'Yes, and an article will be on the paper's website shortly.'

'Okay. If we can't find anyone who knows who he is, then we'll release the picture this evening along with the usual stuff about needing to eliminate him from our inquiries. Thank you for being so vigilant, Mrs Manningham-Westcott. And thanks for the tea.'

I escort the DI to the door. 'If it is the same man,' I say to her quietly, 'then he could be the connection between Rufus Powell's murder and the campaign against the boat owners. I wonder who he might be working for? Have you questioned the Andropov twins yet?'

She hesitates by the door and then turns back to look at me. I can see her wondering how much to tell me and then she shrugs to herself.

'Yes, we paid them a call at their suite in the Royal Crescent Hotel – although I'm still not sure who was who. They were still pretty wound-up about their press conference being ruined and talked about making some kind of complaint. They said you stalked one of them to a private lunch the previous day. They absolutely denied any knowledge of the murder or the campaign against the boats and I've had a stroppy note from their lawyers since then.' She looks behind me at the Tiller & Brown site. 'I hadn't realised how big this site is. You get a good view of it from up here.'

'Yep. There's a huge amount of money at stake,' I say.

'If we release the photograph, it'll be on our website,' she says. 'But if we don't, I don't want to see it on your website, or in the paper. Understood?'

'That may not be my call,' I reply straightforwardly. 'It'll be up to the editor whether it goes in or not.' And if I know Ben, it'll be going in whatever the police think.

She narrows her eyes at me, nods and turns to go down the stairs.

'Oh, there's one more thing.' She stops on the landing and turns back. 'The Bristol Bulldogs.'

'What about them?'

'I don't think they were involved in Rufus Powell's murder.'

'Oh? And why is that may I ask?'

'Let's just say they're making their own inquiries. They'd hardly be doing that if they were guilty.'

'If you're having anything to do with them Mr Johnson, I would be very careful if I were you. Very careful indeed. And they'd better stay out of my way unless they've got something helpful to add – like maybe a confession.' The detective inspector then turns and descends the stairs out of sight.

I immediately return to Rani's office and send the shooting story through for Ben's approval along with a covering note, which explains that there is a photograph of a man on the fire escape, but that the police want the rest of the day before releasing it.

I avoid telling Ben about any possible resemblance to the man on the CCTV, as I know his immediate reaction will be to label our man as his serial-killing Pusher and prepare a screamer of a front page. I don't attach Rani's photo. Instead, I send one from my phone of the smashed porthole. It's still a strong story for Ben. Gun crime is very rare in Bath and a rooftop sniper should keep him happily occupied for a while. Only the police and I have the photograph of the man on the fire escape, and if the police don't release it, I calculate I shall have some useful leverage over my ex-employer.

CHAPTER FORTY

Nina and I stroll the short distance back to *Jumping Jack Flash* and Eddie rushes to greet us as we come down onto the riverside path from the bridge. He wouldn't have been welcome at the police station or at the hospital and so we left him in the professor's care. Noah and Juno also run up to greet us.

'Hello, you two,' says Nina. 'Has there been any sign of Angus?' Angus is the name of the kitten who vanished when *Maid of Coventry* slipped her mooring.

They both shake their heads sadly. 'But we've been throwing sticks for Eddie,' says Juno.

'We didn't throw them in the water,' adds Noah seriously. 'Mummy told us not to.'

Linda emerges from her boat and waves us over. She looks strained and nervous. 'A young man came looking for you about ten o'clock,' she says. 'Said his name was Bob. Do you know who he is?' The visit has clearly unsettled Linda and I remember her overprotective anxiety when we first met in the launderette, and afterwards when she thought I was following her.

'Yes, we know who he is Linda. It's okay,' Nina reassures her.

I deliberately didn't tell Bob where we were moored when we met him in the pub, but he must have found out somehow. He had also given me his phone number, but I hadn't done the same. I'm not sure how happy I am knowing that a member of a Hells Angels' gang now knows where I am living.

'Well, he left a message for you, Jack,' continues Linda. 'He said to tell you that Vince wants to speak to you at the Archangel in Bristol and he'll pick you up from here on his bike at two o'clock.'

The professor is on board *Jumping Jack Flash* and I briefly tell him about the police investigation into a connection between the Bristol Bulldogs and Powell's death.

'I don't think you should go with Bob,' says Nina firmly. 'Not on your own anyway. Who knows what you'd be walking into?'

'I think I agree with Nina,' adds the professor. 'It might not be safe, Jack.'

'I don't know,' I say slowly. 'I'm not sure what I can tell this Vince character – but it'll be a chance for me to weigh him up. If he was behind Powell's death, I don't think he'd have sent Bob over here to sniff around. He'd have wanted to keep a very low profile. I think it'll be okay.'

'Let me come with you, then,' demands Nina. 'It'll be safer with two of us.'

'No,' I say firmly. 'If it is risky, then there's no point in making it worse. And if I'm being taken somewhere on the back of Bob's bike, there's no way of you getting there as well.'

'Oh, for God's sake!' says Nina crossly. She gets up, then walks up and out of the boat without saying another word.

'Can't be helped,' I shrug.

'Oh dear,' murmurs the professor. 'Are you absolutely sure about this, dear boy? I'll just make sure she is all right.'

There's an hour before Bob is due to pick me up and so I make some sandwiches for our lunch but neither Nina nor the professor reappear before five minutes to two. I walk across the bridge and, sure enough, there on the road at the far end is a very large idling Japanese motorbike with Bob astride it. He is clutching a spare helmet and looking cheerful.

'What does Vince want?' I ask loudly over the noise of the bike's engine.

'Who knows?' says Bob, with a grin. 'Hop on.'

The ride into Bristol through the city's usual traffic gridlock is much easier on two wheels than the last time I was there in a car, and I notice Bob, unlike Will, is reasonably respectful of differing speed limits. Nevertheless, I am too used to travelling on water at four miles per hour and I'm relieved when we slow to a stop outside a pub in a rundown suburb of the city. Appropriately enough the sign outside announces it is the Archangel, although I suspect there is nothing particularly angelic about its clientele. I suppose the line-up of twenty or so parked motorbikes, including two with sidecars, is a bit of a giveaway too. Some are low to the ground with chopper handlebars and a few have Death's Heads or the BB logo painted on their petrol tanks.

Bob cuts his engine and pulls off his helmet. 'Come on. Doesn't do to keep the Big Man waiting.'

I take a deep breath and head for the frosted front doors. Inside, I am instantly greeted by a wall of cigarette smoke and silent hostility. The air is fetid with a combination of male sweat and stale beer, spiced with an undercurrent of petrol. The hubbub of conversation dies away as everyone in the room swivels to look at me intently. I try to avoid anyone's eyes but get the general impression of a lot of denim, leather, hair, badges and crash helmets. The scrape of a chair leg breaks the quiet.

'Well, if it isn't Bob-the-Prospect? Nice haircut, Prospect,' says a gruff Bristol accent from one corner. 'Brought your boyfriend, 'ave you?'

This witticism is greeted by general laughter. Bob ignores it, grabs me by one arm and steers me to another frosted door to the side of the main entrance. A younger man is standing in front of it. He nods at Bob, opens the door and inclines his head as a signal to enter.

Inside is a smaller room with a window looking out on to the pub's frontage. Sitting at a round table with a walking stick laid across it is one of the fattest men I have ever seen. He has a denim waistcoat hanging each side of an enormous belly and his receding grey hair is combed into a ponytail. The generous flesh of his face almost hides his little, piggy eyes but, nevertheless, I can see enough of them to guess at the crafty intelligence that lies behind them. He's alone.

'Mr Vince Porlock? I'm Jack Johnson.'

'I know who you are. You stay,' he says to Bob. 'Get out and shut the door,' he orders the other man. 'Sit down,' he says to me. 'Drink?'

'No, thanks, I'm fine.'

'What does he drink?'

'Bitter,' says Bob.

'Fetch him a bitter then.' Bob leaves for the bar. The fat man purses his lips distastefully. 'What's it like then, living on a boat?'

'Cheaper than living on land,' I say. 'And if you get bored somewhere, you just move on.'

He sniffs. 'Don't think I'd like it. The damp would play hell with my chest.'

He smells of strong spirits – rum, perhaps. I imagine a dodgy chest is only one in a long litany of health issues afflicting this man. I nod at the opened pack of cigarettes next to his pint glass. 'They won't help either.'

He ignores my comment. 'Bob-the-Prospect told me about your theory. About the Powell murder.'

'And Bob told me you didn't have anything to do with it. Is that true?'

'I didn't,' he says matter-of-factly. He looks at me whilst scraping the dirt from under one fingernail with another.

'Did your son?'

'Did my son what?'

'Have anything to do with it?'

'You ask a lot of questions.'

'I'm a journalist.'

He coughs a few times. 'Yeah, well, you write about this meeting and the boys'll come calling for you. We know where you live now and it won't be pretty,' he says, with a nasty smile on his delicate little rosebud of a mouth. I open my own mouth to reply, but he continues. 'No. I don't think Clive ordered the attack on Powell.' He shrugs. 'I call him "The Idiot". Sometimes he does stupid things. But I'd know by now if it was him. I run a tight ship.'

Bob reappears with a glass tankard of bitter for me and Vince indicates with an upward tilt of his head that he should leave us again. 'So, these property developers...'

'Anthony and Sebastian Andropov,' I say.

'Russians?'

'English mother. Russian father. He's loaded. One of Putin's cronies who did so well out of the former state-owned industries.'

He nods knowingly. 'Gangster economy and a gangster government. No fucking law and order – that's their trouble.'

I take a sip of beer to cover my amusement.

'What proof have you got?' Vince asks.

'None,' I admit. 'But someone with a gun took a shot at my boat last night.'

He raises an eyebrow in surprise. 'Bob says someone's had it in for you and your mates.'

'Yes. And whoever it is, they aren't afraid to use violence. We're lucky no one has been killed. The Andropovs want the boats gone. Maybe the same guy attacked Powell for them. They had good reason to want him gone too. He was about to declare open season on their plans.'

'They'd be pretty bloody stupid,' he says.

'Or just desperate to make their first big business venture a success. To prove themselves to their rich Russian Daddy.'

'Sons and fathers,' says Vince sadly, shaking his head. 'Sons and fathers.'

'Or...' I begin.

'Or what?'

'Well, I think one of the twins has some serious anger management issues. One of them threatened to kill me after their press conference. Maybe it's just one of them who's cutting corners.'

'So, we find the shooter and see if he's connected to the Andropovs,' says Vince. 'Ten to one it's the same guy who attacked Powell and tried to stitch us up.'

'Easier said than done. Although we may know what he looks like now. An old lady we know may have got a look at him – and she took a photo.'

Vince leans forward as far as his belly allows him. 'Show me.'

I get out my phone and show him Rani's photograph of the man on the fire escape. 'It'll probably go public later today – just waiting for the police to say so.' 'Let me see,' says Vince, snatching my phone and holding it close to his nose. He grins. 'Don't mind if I have a copy of this do you?' Without waiting for a reply he stabs repeatedly at the screen with both his thumbs, no doubt forwarding it to his own number.

'If it was him who killed Powell, then he also left our BB sign on the bridge.'

'And he made the effort to dress like a biker for the CCTV. It hid his identity.'

'And put the blame on us,' adds Vince angrily.

'Clive's case was reported in the newspapers,' I say. 'It must have been very tempting to disguise the attack on Powell as revenge by someone who he sent down as a magistrate.'

'Which is why the pigs have been running around in circles, trying to pin it on us and making things difficult for my business interests. Useless sods.'

It's hard to feel much sympathy for this man but I am more convinced than ever that he and his gang are innocent of Powell's murder – although, I have no doubt, they are guilty of many other things.

Vince Porlock pokes a podgy and heavily ringed forefinger on the table. 'All right, Johnson. I want you to tell Bob-the-Prospect if you hear anything else.'

I take a deep breath. 'No.'

He tilts his head backwards and stares at me. Even in this pose, his multiple chins overlap each other. 'No?' he says quietly. Then he starts prodding the table increasingly hard to reinforce his point. 'This bastard has taken serious liberties with me and the Bristol Bulldogs,' he says, his voice rising. 'And if he's been put up to it by these Russian bastards, then they've got it coming too.' Now he is shouting. 'AND

THEY'LL FUCKIN' WELL LEARN NOT TO MESS WITH ME AND THE BRISTOL BULLDOGS. IS THAT UNDERSTOOD?' He has worked himself up into a towering rage and now he stands up, his face beetroot. There's spittle in one corner of his mouth. 'I SAID, IS THAT UNDERSTOOD?'

I just stare up at this human volcano without speaking and shake my head slightly. This turns out to be enough to cause an eruption.

Vince curls his hand around my pint glass and hurls it at the half-frosted window. The heavy tankard smashes through the glass window. It must be fragile old glass dating from the pub's construction because it explodes, sending big triangular shards crashing to the floor. It leaves a gaping man-sized hole as though someone has been physically thrown through it. The door flies open and Bob and the other young man rush in just as Vince picks up his walking stick and smashes it down onto the table, sending his own pint glass flying. 'I SAID, IS THAT UNDERSTOOD?'

I calculate this man is moments away from a self-induced heart attack. I have never witnessed such naked fury before. Others are crowding around the door.

'Fuck off,' he tells them and the door closes quickly again. I wipe some of his rum off my face with my sleeve and pray my voice doesn't waiver. 'If I find anything else out, the police will be the first to know, not you.' I'm not going to help them to create even more mayhem, and I won't lie.

'Get him up,' snarls Vince. Bob hesitates, but the other young man puts two hands under my armpits and hauls me to my feet. He pivots me so that my back is up against the shattered remnants of the window and then he stands back.

Vince waddles over to me until his belly is pressed against mine. His face is as close to mine as it can get – which is about a foot away. The smell of strong rum coming off his breath is almost overpowering. His voice is now menacingly quiet. 'You'll do what I say or there will be very unpleasant consequences – for you and your woman.'

I don't learn exactly what those consequences will be as our one-sided conversation is interrupted by an almighty crash of metal from behind me, on the forecourt outside the pub.

'What the –'

'The bikes!' says Bob.

We are all speechless with shock. About ten bikes are now lying against each other at an angle of forty-five degrees. They have toppled over like dominos and it is only the stability of one of the three-wheeled bike-and-sidecars preventing the whole line from crashing over. Behind them, I see a green Morris Minor with its door open, its engine running, and I am horrified to see Nina at the wheel. I don't imagine the Bristol Bulldogs will have many scruples about visiting violent retribution on her as well as me. Fortunately, I react seconds before Vince, Bob and the young sentry, and I am already standing closer to the window. I just twist, duck my head, step through the jagged hole and sprint between two of the bikes that have remained standing. Nina already has the car in gear and we shoot forward as I yank the passenger door closed. I give a quick look back as we accelerate towards the junction at the end of the road. All I can see are blurred white faces clustered in a line behind the pub's remaining windows and figures emerging from the front doors. Then Nina swings left onto the main road and we are gone.

'Jesus, Nina! What the hell are you doing here?'

She looks at me sweetly. 'I thought it was rude of you not to invite me,' she says. 'And it's becoming something of a habit. So, I borrowed the professor's car and followed you. Well, I tried to, but I got stuck in traffic. Luckily, there's only one pub called the Archangel and the phone got me here. So, I waited outside. When the window smashed and it all seemed to be kicking off, I thought you'd like a bit of help. Those bikes are heavy, aren't they? But once the first one went over, so did the others.'

I shake my head in wonderment.

'Now,' she says, stopping at a zebra crossing to let a mother with a toddler and a pram go across, and checking her lipstick in the rearview mirror. 'Are you going to tell me what he wanted or d'you want me to take you back there?'

The Wolf had been feared for his towering rages during the war, and afterwards when he worked as a bodyguard in Moscow. He did not shout or swear when he was in such a mood. Instead, he became very quiet and still, his slit of a mouth clamped shut and his jaw muscles clenched over grinding teeth. No one ventured near when he was like this and there was always widespread relief when the storm clouds passed. Up until that point he could be even more dangerous and unpredictable – even with men who had served with him for the longest time. Now, a similar rage was suffusing his whole body so that it almost quivered with tension. He must have pulled his phone from his back pocket and viewed the picture almost twenty times. It showed him on the fire escape, looking down on the moored boats with his camera. He was easily recognisable. His frustration and anger doubled every time he looked at the photograph. How could he have been so stupid? He knew that the crippled old woman in the flat opposite had a camera, and yet he had failed to see her take his picture. He was certain the shutter on the old woman's side window had been closed, and he had been there for barely ten minutes, watching the new boat arrive on the moorings and doing a recce for his return later the following night with the rifle. The fire escape hadn't even given him the angle he needed anyway. He'd moved to the roof of another building further along that had a stone parapet he could hide behind. He spat into the gutter in disgust at himself.

His phone vibrated as yet another text or voice message arrived on it. He had been receiving at least one every half hour since the first one which contained a link to the police website. 'Do You Know This Man?' said the caption alongside some words about needing to eliminate him from police inquiries about a night-time shooting incident on the River Avon. Only a few people would have seen it yet, he thought, but what *if the newspapers reprinted it tomorrow? He had already dumped his jacket and baseball cap in a skip behind a department store and was now wearing a flat cap and a long raincoat with the collar turned up. He had picked them both up for a handful of coins in a charity shop. He felt safe from recognition as darkness fell, but he realised time was running out fast. The messages on his phone made that very clear. But he wasn't going anywhere until he was paid – especially now that he knew another boat was leaving and he could claim a second bonus. The newspaper would be on the city's streets at lunchtime the following day and if they carried the photograph, he would be unable to leave his rented flat during daylight hours. He had to act tonight.*

He knew that the old woman who had taken the photograph would be able to identify him. She could not be allowed to become a witness against him.

He narrowed his eyes, peering again through a hole in the building site hoarding, and then checked his watch. It was now two and a half hours since he had heard the group leave together in high spirits, talking about the Theatre Royal as they passed by within a few feet of him. The lights were still on in one boat and the woman he knew was called Linda was sitting low down on its stern with a flask and a cup. It was clear that she was keeping guard in the absence of the others. The Wolf spat again. They would all have left the moorings by now if that reporter and his girlfriend hadn't interfered. He glared at their boat with its painting of the grinning jester on the side. It still seemed to be looking directly at him and its manic grin now seemed to be mocking him. He shook himself. Enough. I am a soldier, he said to himself. I have been in much worse situations and always I have been victorious. I must be clever and ruthless. I must be like The Wolf.

It was then that he heard the high electronic whine of a battery-powered scooter. It reminded him of a mosquito that needed to be squashed.

CHAPTER FORTY-ONE

The play is a real treat for all of us after the anxieties of the past few days. The enormous chandelier and the jewel-box details of the theatre's interior are a world away from the basic and utilitarian design of our boats. Nina looks amazing. She has dressed up for the occasion in a light summer dress with thin shoulder straps and a high bunched hem, elegant heels and is carrying a chic pink leather clutch bag. Even Tammy, who shyly admits that she has never been to the theatre before, is soon laughing at the imperious Lady Bracknell. During the interval we all agree that Will is commanding the stage and thoroughly enjoying himself in the process. We also feel spoilt: as Will's special guests, free drinks and canapés are waiting for us at the bar. Afterwards, as we cram excitedly into Will's tiny dressing room, the professor leads the praise.

'Wonderful, quite wonderful, my boy,' he says, while Nina gives Will a congratulatory kiss on both cheeks. Nina begs a passing stagehand to take a photograph of us all standing in front of Will's make-up mirror and passes her phone around for us to take a look. It's a good photo. Tammy seems to have an adoring look in her eyes as she gazes at Will, who is beaming to the camera, still dressed in his Edwardian suit, cravat and spats with a red carnation in his buttonhole. Danny, however, looks awkward and is clearly feeling out of place. He shakes Will's hand in turn, thanks him for the experience and then tells me he and Tammy are going back to relieve Linda and Bill from guard duty. Tammy tentatively proffers her complimentary programme to Will and he signs the cover with a grin and a flourish. I am amused to see her flush with embarrassment and laugh like a child as she follows her father, gripping her prize tightly. She's at a tricky age and confused about what she wants from life – neither the uncertainty of endless travelling nor the boredom of a permanent mooring. Frustrated with her father, and yet clearly very close to him. Poor Tammy.

There is room now for the professor, Nina and me to sit down and we chat as Will unselfconsciously strips down to a vest and pants and starts to remove his make-up.

'So, what's been happening?' he asks cheerfully. We bring him up to speed on our discussions with the police since the shooting and Rani's rooftop photograph of someone who might be the shooter. Before we can tell him about the bikers in Bristol, the attractive actress who is playing the Honourable Gwendolen Fairfax appears at Will's door. Her hair is still wet, and it is very strange to see her in a T-shirt, jeans and trainers instead of her splendid period dress and jewels.

'Oh, hi!' she says in a decidedly transatlantic accent. 'I didn't know you had company, darling.'

We all tell her how marvellous she was. She accepts our compliments graciously before turning her big blue eyes, retroussé nose and pearly white teeth in Will's direction.

'Are we still on for supper, Will?'

Will gives us a panicked look.

'Oh?' I say with amusement. 'I thought you'd be coming out with us, Will. You're not double-booked, are you?'

'What? Uh... sure. Well, I...' His eyes are flicking between his attractive co-star and me.

'Oh, stop it, Jack,' says Nina with amusement. 'You're all right, Will. We'll get back to the boat now. Have a nice evening, you two.'

The actress smiles in quiet triumph and Will smiles with relief.

'Yes. It's time we went,' I say to the others, and we leave in a flurry of theatrical hugs, kisses and luvvie endearments.

'That was fun,' says Nina, as we stand outside the theatre's three arched front doors.

'Quick pint in the Garrick's Head?' I ask.

Nina links one arm through mine and does the same with the professor on her other side. 'Nope. Home, please. I'm tired.'

As we walk, the professor gives us an impromptu lecture on Wilde's dramatic canon and, not for the first time, I appreciate what a clever and civilised man he is. Nina and I have become very fond of him and I feel sick with despair whenever I think of his ruined library and boat. He is still planning to leave in his ancient little car tomorrow to stay with his niece and I wonder if we will see ever him again. My attention has wandered but his words drift back into my consciousness as we walk past the end of Norfolk Crescent and a small triangle of grass known as the Recreation Ground to approach Victoria Bridge and the moorings.

'I think it was Tynan who said Noël Coward owed very little to earlier wits like Oscar Wilde,' he continues. 'He said Wilde's best works needed to be delivered slowly, even lazily – while Coward's plays need to be delivered at machine gun speed. I do think our young friend got the pace correct tonight. He was appropriately languid, don't you think?'

'Yes, he was,' I murmur in reply. But in truth, I am remembering a line from the play: 'the truth is rarely pure and never simple'. Will's character Algernon invents a poor invalid friend called Bunbury while his friend Jack disguises himself as 'Ernest in town and Jack in the country'. The confusion of identities is comic, but there doesn't seem to me to be anything funny or innocent about the Andropov twins' deliberate attempt to baffle people. What is the motive for their carefully cultivated identical appearance? And why should they use it to confuse others in such a calculated way? It might give them some kind of an edge in business negotiations I suppose. I return to the sudden thought I had in the Archangel pub. Could it be that in spite of their identical appearance, they have very different characters, and that Anthony is shielding the world from seeing his brother's short fuse and violent temper?

'JACK!' The shout from Nina cuts my thoughts off abruptly and whips me to attention. She is pointing down to the river where a small metal pontoon is tied to the steep, stone-clad side of the bank. I have previously seen fishermen using it. Lying sideways on the platform, with its front wheel bent at a crazy angle, is Rani's distinctive red mobility scooter.

'Good God,' says the professor. 'Rani!'

Nina's already running and I race after her, around a slight bend in the path where we both stop in our tracks, shocked by the tableau that confronts us.

A tall man in a black raincoat and a flat cap is holding Rani under one arm. She is almost off her feet, struggling and whimpering. He sees us at once. He raises his head, staring with black eyes. He looks for all the world like a wild animal with its prey, suddenly sensing a new danger. It's the man Rani photographed on the fire escape, I am certain of it. Barely five metres separates us, and I begin to move forward, whilst holding an arm out across Nina to warn her to stay back.

'Rani!' shouts the professor from behind me. The man in the raincoat bends slightly and scoops the old lady's legs up in his other arm so that she is now held horizontally across his chest. She's lost her glasses and her sari is unravelling in strips of cloth. He steps quickly over to the metal railing and hurls Rani out and down into the water like a rag doll.

'No!' I shout. Shock at the violence of the act temporarily roots me to the spot, but there's a blur of movement to my side and Nina is climbing barefoot over the railing one second and jumping down in the next. I register the splash of her hitting the water.

'Jack, look out!' The professor's voice sounds querulous.

The attacker has not hesitated to close the distance between us and one of his hands reaches into a pocket of the raincoat, before swinging out wide to his side, accelerating towards my brow in one single sweeping movement. There is an explosion of pain followed by darkness.

The next time I open my eyes, I am immediately blinded by a yellow sun that flicks away just as quickly, leaving me unable to see anything but dancing stars. The light reappears. I lurch onto my side to escape it and vomit copiously onto the ground.

'He's back with us,' says a man's voice.

'Thank goodness,' says another, female this time. A sharp, stabbing pain, worse than any hangover I have ever suffered, is slicing its way through my forehead. I close my eyes tight to try to deal with it, but the agony continues. I retch again and can feel several hands lifting me off the cold ground and onto something firm. I risk opening one eye and the blur eventually settles to show a middle-aged man in a high-vis vest bending over me. He seems to be wrapping something around my head, but it isn't doing anything to numb the pain. I feel a hand take one of mine.

'Hang in there, Jack, you're going to be fine,' says a quiet voice.

Nina. I look sideways and see her crouched by my side. She's wrapped in a large silver foil blanket and her short hair is spiky and wet. There are black smudges of mascara under her eyes. I try to talk but my tongue seems too large for my mouth.

'Right, let's do it,' says the high-vis man and I feel myself being lifted up and carried a short distance. Every step sends another hot needle of pain across my forehead. A corridor of white faces is looking down at me on either side, but I can't place any of them. I close my eyes and keep them closed to shut out the light, which I can sense all around me in the back of the ambulance.

Now we are moving. My hand is once again being held and I hear Nina's voice close to my ear. 'We'll soon be at the hospital.'

'Rani?' I croak back at her.

'Already there,' she says. 'The professor is with her.'

'Is he okay?'

My words are slurred. I sound drunk.

'He's fine. The man ran off after he hit you. Now shut up.'

I nod and immediately whimper with the additional pain that the movement causes. 'One more thing...' I whisper. I can sense her moving her head closer to mine and I recognise her Jo Malone scent in spite of her swim. 'Tell them to turn that fucking siren off.'

At the hospital I am put into a backless white gown, wheeled down long linoleum-covered corridors under harsh strip lighting, X-rayed, rebandaged, drugged and finally wrapped tightly under cold white sheets in a bed in a room of my own. A young male nurse hovers nearby while a brisk woman in a white coat looks at my notes before hanging them back on the end of the bed.

'Nina?' I ask them woozily.

The doctor looks quizzically at the nurse.

'His girlfriend,' the nurse explains. I automatically go to correct him but then decide it isn't worth the effort. My head feels as though it is the weight of a ten-pin bowling ball and my neck is about to snap.

'Don't worry, fella. She'll be back in the morning.'

CHAPTER FORTY-TWO

In fact, it isn't Nina whose face is hovering over me when I wake the following morning. It is Detective Inspector Mary Kerr.

'Water,' I croak and she hands me a glass. I glug it dry. She refills it from a clouded plastic jug on a bedside table and I empty it again. The young nurse is still on duty and he puts a strong arm behind me to help me sit upright against some additional pillows. Having checked that I don't need to relieve myself immediately, he takes my temperature while the DI looks on, feels my pulse, scribbles something on my notes and leaves the room.

'Morning,' I say quietly. I'm afraid that if I speak any louder my head might explode.

'Good morning, Mr Johnson,' she says, and although her voice is pitched at a normal level, I flinch involuntarily. She gets the point and lowers it fractionally. 'We took a statement from Mrs Wilde and Professor Chesney last night.'

I'm not in a state to do much talking myself and don't fancy risking a nod, so I just blink in acknowledgement.

'Mrs Manningham-Westcott is out of danger, but she swallowed a lot of water and she has a broken wrist. She's obviously badly shaken-up. It was a very nasty attack. But your girlfriend did a great job getting to her so quickly.'

Why does everyone in uniform seem to think Nina is my girlfriend? But there are worse things in the world and I decide to let it pass, again.

'So, even if your attacker wasn't the sniper – or Mr Powell's murderer – he still attempted to murder Mrs Manningham-Westcott last night and committed grievous bodily harm, maybe attempted murder, on you too. Every officer on the force has been sent his picture; there's an all-out alert for him.'

'But why attack Rani?' I ask in a whisper.

'Good question. Maybe he was worried that she also witnessed him firing the gun? Or maybe revenge for taking his picture – perhaps he's just a violent psychopath who holds life pretty cheap? We won't know till we find him. Did he say anything to you before he hit you?'

'No, nothing,' I say. 'Nothing that I can remember.'

'Shame,' she replies. 'Even an accent of some kind might have been useful. The doctors think you were hit with some kind of cosh – which is consistent with Mr Powell's head injury. Good job you seem to have a thicker skull than him.'

I imagine this is what passes for humour from detective inspectors and give a weak smile. 'The Andropov twins?'

'We've already asked them if they recognise the man on the fire escape and they say he is a total stranger to them. We're concentrating our efforts on finding the man himself. The *Chronicle* already has the photo on their website and the newspaper will have it splashed across its front page today. The BBC have picked up on it too on their local website. And we're stepping up foot patrols around the city.'

Of course, it is Thursday – press day. I quietly worry about the hash Ben will probably make of all this. Then the doctor reappears at my door. She has a quiet conversation with the detective inspector who leaves the room with a small wave to me. The doctor checks my pulse, temperature, eyes and reflexes.

'You're a lucky man, Mr Johnson,' says the doctor. 'There's no sign of a fracture on the X-rays and everything else seems to be returning to normal. However, I think we ought to keep you in for observation for twenty-four hours.'

'No,' I say. 'I need to get back to my boat.'

She frowns. 'Do you have anyone who can look after you? Will your girlfriend be there?'

'Yes. Yes, she will. I'll be fine.'

'All right, let's wait and see how you feel by lunchtime,' she says reluctantly.

I don't feel hungry but nibble on some cold toast before sinking back into a deeply comforting and restful sleep. When I wake and look at my watch, I see that two hours have passed. I tentatively pull back my blankets and swing my bare feet onto the cold linoleum. I can stand without feeling dizzy but ditching the backless gown and getting dressed is a very slow process. It also takes me twenty minutes and at least three lots of directions to find Rani's ward. I am relieved to see her sitting up in bed. She looks much older and more frail without her immaculate coiffure and wearing no make-up, but she is smiling at me kindly.

'Ah, there you are, Jack,' she says, putting a magazine to one side. 'How are you?'

I wave the inquiry to one side. 'No, how are *you*, Rani?'

'Fighting fit to live another day,' she says bravely. 'All thanks to Nina, of course. Such a brave thing to do – jumping in after me. Although this wretched wrist will make life difficult for a while.' She holds up her right hand, wrapped in plaster, with her left, then places it gently back onto her lap.

'What happened?' I ask.

'Well,' she begins, pulling a quilted dressing gown more tightly around her, 'it was quite late when I realised that I had run out of milk for the morning. I wasn't tired, though. If I'm honest, my mind was still buzzing about the shooting and the man I had photographed on the fire escape. Anyway, I thought I'd pop round to the supermarket at Green Park. I was on my way there when that dreadful man suddenly appeared from behind those hoardings. He didn't say a thing. He just put his arms around me and lifted me off the scooter. I was so shocked. It was all so sudden. The scooter ran on into the turn in the path, so he just left me on the ground and tipped it through the gap in the railings, down onto the pontoon. Of course, I was unable to run away. Then he came back and picked me up again – it was as though I weighed no more than a leaf. And glory be, that's when you and Nina suddenly appeared. Well, you know the rest. Obviously, Nina and I didn't see you being attacked because we were in the water. Arthur alerted some people and they helped to get us out onto the pontoon. He also called the ambulance and the police, bless him.'

The professor appears in the doorway of the ward exactly on cue. He is in the same clothes as the previous evening and I realise he hasn't been back to the boat yet. He must have dozed in a hospital chair all night. Nevertheless, there is a new vigour and sense of purpose about him.

'Jack, my boy,' he says heartily, putting an arm on my shoulder. 'How are you feeling?'

'They think I'll be able to leave around lunchtime,' I say determinedly.

'Oh, that is good news,' says Rani. 'Arthur stayed here all night. He's been a great comfort, but I keep telling him to go home and get some rest.'

'Plenty of time for that,' says the professor. 'I want to make sure you are as comfortable as possible before I go. And when you're back home you will need more help, Rani. It won't be easy with that wrist of yours. Even when you get a new scooter, you won't be able to use it for a while.'

We briefly discuss the latest update from DI Kerr and they tell me that a uniformed officer was stationed outside Rani's ward all night and another will be posted at her flat until our attacker is caught. The professor promises to keep me up to date on their movements and I shuffle back to my room.

After another hour lying on top of my bed, I think I am sufficiently compos mentis to make my way to a bathroom, where I undress and ease myself onto a seat under a very hot shower. I am careful not to get my bandages wet but the water helps to soak away a fraction of my exhaustion. I manage to towel myself dry and get dressed again.

It is now twelve noon. I am surprised that there has been no sign of Nina. But I suppose that she had a very late night herself and the river rescue will no doubt have taken it out of her. She has probably slept in and then needed to give Eddie a walk or a run. Nevertheless, I am surprised when one o'clock passes and there is still no sign of her. I try her mobile but there's no answer. Perhaps she had it on her when she jumped into the river? Waterlogged phones are becoming an occupational hazard for both of us. Or maybe she is just out for a late morning run with Eddie.

An unappetising and lukewarm lunch arrives on a metal tray and I toy with it until a new doctor arrives. All of the tests are repeated and my head wound is examined and re-bandaged.

'I hear you want to discharge yourself,' says the doctor dubiously.

'I don't *want* to. I am going to,' I say stubbornly.

'Okay... as long as you get someone to come and pick you up.' I wave a hand in vague agreement. I can get a taxi. 'Keep taking the pain-relief tablets and come back into A&E at once if you get any nausea or start vomiting.'

There is a small shop in the hospital's reception area and I make for it after using a freephone to order a taxi. A small cardboard box with copies of this week's *Bath Chronicle* is waiting to be unpacked by the door and I take the top one.

A banner headline shouts: '*HAS THE PUSHER STRUCK AGAIN? MANHUNT UNDERWAY.*' Rani's picture of the man who attacked us both is spread across six columns. Looking at his facial features again, I am forcefully reminded of the keen, angular look of a wild animal – a big cat like a panther, perhaps, or a wolf? The text, beneath a by-line photograph of Ben Mockett, licks its lips and salivates in the details of the violent attack on an eighty-year-old disabled widow who was callously thrown into the river the previous evening, along with her mobility scooter. It describes how the attacker went on to smash the skull of her have-a-go rescuer, *Chronicle* reporter and the famous authority on the Midlands Canal Pusher, Mr Jack Johnson. The manner of the double attack, writes Ben, has all the hallmarks of the murder of Mr Rufus Powell – a blow to the head and immersion in water. Then, to add further grist to the mill, he speculates on whether the same man carried out a night-time shooting on Mr Johnson's boat when Mr Johnson's close friend, Mrs Angelina Wilde, suffered a leg injury from flying glass splinters. There is also fleeting mention of a boat at the same mooring having been deliberately sunk.

Finally, there is a front-page opinion piece, also by *Chronicle* Editor Ben Mockett, which expresses shock and outrage at the most recent attacks. It promises unwavering support for the police investigation and manhunt, but also demands that they deliver a quick and speedy resolution to the fears that 'are now widespread throughout the city'. Page three is a rehash of previous details and includes a photograph of *Jumping Jack Flash* with her broken porthole. There is also a cross reference to an inside feature on 'A History of Bath Murderers'.

Once in the back of the taxi, I flick through the rest of the paper and find a meagre inside page devoted to the plan by Andropov Developments Ltd. It includes an aerial view of the derelict site and the artist's impression of what it will look like with twenty identical tower blocks on it. I read Tom's copy closely but find no mention of Linda's protest at the press conference or any reference to the twins' comments about the narrowboats and their offer to pay for them to move. Nor is there a reminder of my previous reference to Rufus Powell's objection to the plan. The chair of the planning committee, Councillor Laurence Merton, is quoted as saying: 'This represents a very considerable investment in our city and it is to be broadly welcomed. However, we shall make sure that everyone's views are properly considered before making our final decision on the planning application.'

I look up. The taxi is crawling along behind two enormous coaches bringing tourists into the city for a few hours of gawping. 'Change of plan,' I say to the driver. 'Take me to the *Chronicle*, please.'

The Wolf has been watching the mooring for most of the morning. This time, however, he has hidden in a roofless outbuilding on the Tiller & Brown site, on the same side of the river as the boats. He had approached the site across Victoria Bridge under cover of darkness and used a key to unlock and then re-secure the padlock on the heavy chain that held the gate tightly closed. The early July sun did little to warm him as he crouched in his hiding place behind a partly broken window. The boats were less than twenty metres away, on the other side of the perimeter fence. He had watched as the journalist's woman was the first to emerge. She was wearing shorts and a singlet, and she kicked her heels high, her ponytail bouncing, as she and the little dog set off for a run along the far bank's river path. Then the big man and his daughter Tammy had emerged. He was carrying a toolbag and they also set off over the bridge and turned downstream. Finally, he watched as Andropov's lawyer arrived at the boat called Maid of Coventry. *She was not on board very long. A little later the woman who owned it locked her hatchway and walked upstream, in the direction of the city, holding her children's hands.*

There was no sign of life on the remaining boat. It was still completely covered by its huge and grubby piece of canvas.

He had registered all of these comings and goings seemingly impassively but his mind was in turmoil. He knew, from checking his phone, that the old woman's photograph of his face had been published on the internet by the police and that the Chronicle *and the local BBC had quickly picked it up and put it on their websites. He assumed it would also be printed in the newspaper later today. His attack on the old woman had been pure instinct. He couldn't believe it when he saw her advancing on his hiding place on her mobility scooter. The old bitch could never give* evidence against him if she was dead. It would have been the work of a moment to tip her and her scooter into the river if that bloody journalist and his woman hadn't appeared. He still did not know if the old woman was dead. He'd seen the blue flashing lights of the emergency services from a distance and assumed they were dealing with the journalist too. Interfering bastard. He hoped he was dead. Why wouldn't he be? He had hit him hard, and with the same cosh that had despatched Powell – even though that had been a mistake. He hadn't meant to kill him – only frighten him, or send him to hospital for a while. But the wet and slippy blood had made it impossible to find a pulse. If he'd known the man was still alive, he'd have left him unconscious on the stone ledge. It had been a split second decision to tip Powell into the water. And everything had unravelled from that single moment.

And now he was a hunted man. He knew it made sense to obey his instructions and leave the city as quickly as possible, return to Russia. But he wasn't going anywhere until he was paid. He needed that money badly – for his escape and for his flight, but also because he deserved it. He had exhausted his cash reserves in the packages under the bridge and there was no money left in his bank account to call on. No. He had done his job. The man Powell could no longer cause trouble and the boat people were leaving, one by one. In fact, he had exceeded expectations. He had also taken out the troublesome journalist and the old woman, who was a key witness. But he had still not been paid and that was wrong. Very wrong indeed. And instead of praise he was being subjected to a barrage of abuse and criticism. He would show them that they could not take the Wolf for granted. Wolves can be very dangerous when they are cornered, he thought to himself grimly. He shifted his own broad, muscular back against the corrugated iron behind him in an attempt to get more comfortable. His legs in particular were stiffening.

The journalist's woman had returned after about an hour and disappeared with the dog into the boat with the clown on it. Attractive woman, he thought to himself. Too young and attractive for the journalist. But if the journalist... what was his name? Jackson? If Jackson was dead, then surely she wouldn't be out jogging with their dog? Maybe he wasn't dead? Maybe he was just detained in hospital? Another potential witness against him? With a bit of luck, the man had suffered brain damage, he thought grimly. He'd struck him hard with the cosh. It was a possibility.

What should he do now? Of course, he had to get away from Bath as quickly as possible. But he needed money. And to get money he needed leverage. How could he obtain leverage? His thoughts raced. He was angry and confused. He had been honoured to be chosen by Papa Andropov to support his sons in the UK on their first big business venture. Had he let the old man down? Would he be angry too? No, he thought defiantly. I have done my job. They owe me.

The woman reappeared on the stern of the boat. Her cropped hair was still wet from the shower and she had a pair of black jeans and a black halterneck top on. She wrung out her vest and shorts and laid them to dry on the roof of the boat before going back inside. Her appearance gave the Wolf an idea, and he spent the next thirty minutes turning it over in his mind. It was risky, but it might work. He would have to move fast, he thought to himself, once again checking that there was still no sign of movement on the other boats. He had not seen the old man yet, the one whose boat had sunk. Could he be on board with the woman?

Too much thinking, he said to himself. Not enough action. If the old man was still on board, he would handle him and a small woman easily enough.

The Wolf stood, stretched both legs and went into a crouching run to the metal door in the fencing. This time he left the chain unlocked and the door ajar. Watching the woman's boat, he loped across the short distance to it, mounted the stern platform quietly and looked down into the interior. There were two single beds either side of a steep flight of wooden steps and a door between them. He moved silently down them. A radio was playing music softly on the other side of the door.

Remember the dog, he said to himself. He fingered the cosh in his coat pocket but left it there for now. Pushing the swing door open an inch, he pressed his left eye to the crack. A central walkway stretched down the length of the boat. He could just make out another larger bed on the left beyond an open door into a bathroom and then a kind of cooking and sitting area. He could see the back of the woman's dark hair as she rested on a sofa, her legs curled sideways under her. There was no sign of the dog.

He pushed the door open a little further, enough to slip through the gap onto the other side, where he carefully closed it without making a noise. Then he began to make his way forward, slowly at first and then faster as he drew level with the double bed. The dog was also on the sofa, hidden from view, and it saw him first. It began barking loudly, little white teeth bared, its tail suddenly erect like a flagpole. But it did not attack. It backed into a corner of the sofa and continued to protest.

The woman, however, was immediately on her feet. They stared at each other for a second or two before she lunged across the narrow width of the boat towards a little side table and grabbed a mobile phone. He leapt forward, his large frame crowding in on her and knocked the phone flying out of her grasp. Now they were at close quarters he expected her to scream but instead, there was a focused and furious intensity to her. She tried to kick him between the legs, but he grabbed her foot at the top of its arc and twisted it forcefully so that she flipped sideways, hitting the floor in front of the sofa with a thud. She thrashed her body so that he was forced to loosen his grip as a lamp, the radio and cushions went flying.

Now she found her voice. 'You bastard!' she shouted. 'Let go of me!'

He bent down and hauled her upright and off her feet. She was half his size and ridiculously light. He pinned both her arms to her sides and pushed her back against the wall of the boat. He put one palm over her mouth to prevent further shouting, but she immediately bit it hard.

'Bitch,' he said, removing the hand and using it to punch the centre of a painting that was hanging just inches from her face. It crashed to the floor; the dog kept barking. She winced at the deliberate near miss but didn't look cowed. He moved his face close to hers and snarled, 'Come with me quietly, and you won't be hurt.'

The woman redoubled her efforts to struggle free of his grip. He spun her around and pushed her back down onto the sofa. One hand held the back of her head and pushed her face deep into the sofa while the other levered all of his strength and weight onto the small of her back. He felt her body begin to shake in panic as she realised he might be about to suffocate her. Then he replaced the hand on her back with one of his knees and pulled both of her hands behind her. Her nose and mouth were still being pressed forcefully into the fabric. She couldn't inhale. Good. It would weaken her. But he wanted her alive. He released the pressure on her head for a moment and she bent her head upwards, gasping for air with her mouth wide open. At exactly the same time, he fished into his pocket, brought out a plastic tie, looped it over her wrists and pulled it tight. Then he manhandled her into a seating position with her arms pinned behind her and he knelt down in front of her. She was trying to kick him but he clamped her ankles together between his knees and brought out another plastic tie. She tried to pull her feet free but he looped one arm tightly around her ankles, lifted them up and expertly looped the tie over them with his other hand.

'Help! Help me, help!' she screamed as he pulled it tight. Then he raised the back of his right hand and swatted her cheek so that her head spun and she was stunned into momentary silence.

'Be quiet,' he spat, pushing her in the chest so she was forced to lean back onto the rear of the sofa. He quickly looked around him, spotted a green patterned scarf on a side-table and swept it up. He held it at both ends, flicked it over a few times and then firmly pressed the tight roll of silk into her mouth. She kept her teeth clamped shut but he forced it so tight that it pulled the corners of her mouth backwards. Then, he pushed her neck down so that he could tie the scarf tightly behind her head. It had taken him less than a minute to overpower the woman, but the dog had been barking furiously for all of this time. It had backed itself into a corner by the door, blocked from making a run for the stern by the thrashing bodies and flying furniture. The Wolf now turned his attention to shutting it up.

The woman was making muffled noises of distress as he advanced on the little dog. It tried to make a dash past his feet, but he was onto it in a flash, lifting it off the floor by a fistful of the loose skin at the nape of its neck. The dog's barking turned into a frightened squeal as it hung suspended in the air. Then he used his other hand to yank open the doors of a little cupboard under the sink in the galley, scooped an armful of plastic bottles into a jumble on the floor and threw the dog into it before slamming the cupboard shut with a click of the catch.

The woman's eyes were wide with fright as he advanced back towards her, breathing heavily. But he simply scooped up her mobile phone from the floor and put it into his back pocket before bundling her over his right shoulder, her head against his chest and a strong arm looped across the small of her back. He turned to make his way back to the stern hatchway. She struggled and wriggled furiously, sending crockery on the draining board flying and dislodging more pictures and books, but she was powerless to stop him hoisting her up through the hatchway. He was fully committed now and the woman's phone was ringing and vibrating in his pocket. He ignored it and barely bothered to check the other boats as he ran across the short distance to the gate in the fence, where he dumped the woman briefly on the ground to re-secure the padlock and chain. Then he hoisted her up onto his shoulder again, turned and moved quickly into the disused site. He had to get out of sight with her, and then he had an important text message to send.

CHAPTER FORTY-THREE

Petra is around the desk and fussing about my bandaged head as soon as I enter the reception area. But the newsroom falls silent when I open the door and all eyes are staring at me. Of course, they all know about the attack and I must make a strange sight.

'Jack!' shouts Ben from his glass corner booth. He has today's edition of the *Chronicle* open on his desk. 'Come on over here, mate,' he says, in a manner intended to be generous and friendly. He shoos me into the chair opposite him and looks me up and down. 'Jesus, Jack! How's your head?' He doesn't wait for a reply. 'Seems like you're being targeted by another serial killer, all right. First the shooting and now this. D'you think he's pissed off because you helped to catch the other one? Great bloody story, though,' he adds, rubbing both hands together in glee. 'And we've actually got a photograph of the bastard! Amazing. Could you do a first-person account for the website this afternoon? "How I cheated a second serial killer's attempt to murder me." We'll need a photo of you with your bandage.'

I shake my head in disbelief – but only briefly because it hurts – and turn the pages of the newspaper in front of him to Tom's story on the housing scheme.

'I must have been at a different press conference,' I say, stabbing a finger at the page.

'Bloody hell... you're never satisfied, you know that?' he protests angrily. He slams the glass door shut and turns to me with both hands on his hips. 'We had their lawyers on the phone within an hour of that press conference ending,' he says. 'And believe me, they played rough. They threatened to sue us if we even mentioned Powell's murder or the boat campaign in the same sentence as their planning application.' Ben shuffles through his in-tray and pulls out a document. 'Look. Five pages of threats. Damages to be sought in their millions if their clients are defamed in the slightest way. See who the lawyers are – recognise the name?'

I push the papers away with the tip of a forefinger. 'You could just have reported the facts, Ben,' I say. 'I've already written that Powell was planning to fight the planning application before he was killed. I've got the text of a speech he was going to make. And it's an undisputed fact that Andropov Developments are trying to pay the boat owners to go away.'

'Yeah, and Tom told me about your question at the press conference,' he snaps back. 'It was bloody provocative, Jack. And, let me remind you, you weren't there representing the *Chronicle*. I never told you to go. Tom was there for us. You used the paper's name without permission. And, what's more, you dragged a load of your boat mates along and hijacked it. How do you think that looked? There isn't a shred of evidence that connects Andropov Developments to the murder or the attacks.'

I laugh at his bare-faced cheek.

'Wow... so you *do* care about evidence, after all? I can't remember you worrying too much about it when you wanted Powell's murderer to be another serial killing wannabe Pusher on day one,' I snap.

'Yeah, well. Sorry, mate.' His voice is now raised, and I can see his young staff staring through the glass of his office. 'It's my job to sell papers and avoid bankrupting the business in the libel courts at the same time. I happen to think *I'm* pretty good at doing both those things and *you're* just a bloody liability. So why don't you just piss off before I give you another bang on the head!'

Ben flings open the door and I take the hint. All this shouting isn't doing my head much good anyway. I roll his copy of the paper under my arm and walk back out through the silent newsroom. As I reach the end of the room, I stop, but keep my back to everyone and hold an arm out straight. You can hear a pin drop. Then I let today's edition fall into a waste bin. It is empty, and the thud is gratifyingly solid. Then I go back through reception to the street outside. It was a silly gesture, I confess to myself, and it has no doubt ended any chance of returning to the *Chronicle* to earn money. But it made me feel better and, I reflect, I can still afford to buy myself a new paper if I want one. But only just.

I check my watch. It is now two p.m. and Nina still hasn't been in touch. I try to call her but again there is no response. Maybe her phone is at the bottom of the river. If our journeys to and from the hospital have crossed she would know by now that I have been discharged, so she will probably be waiting for me at the boat. But why hasn't she borrowed someone's phone to call me? I make a detour to a chemist's to pick up my prescription painkillers and a bottle of water. It's going to be quicker walking back to the boat than trying to find another taxi and the air might be good for my head.

I hear the children's voices before I see them as I walk past the triangle of grass bordered by Norfolk Crescent, Nelson Place and the river. Linda is by the playground, watching Noah and Juno play an excited game of tag, running up and over the slide and around the swings and a sandpit. She waves me over, so I make my way to her and she gives me a hug before we sit back down on the metal bench.

'How are you, Jack?' she asks, staring at my bandaged head. 'You did a very brave thing last night. And Nina was amazing. We all heard the commotion and we were there when you and Rani went off in the ambulances.'

'I just got hit on the head,' I shrug. 'But Rani would have drowned if Nina hadn't gone in after her so quickly. What kind of evil bastard throws a disabled old woman into a river?'

Linda shakes her head in bafflement and bites her bottom lip. I can see a copy of the *Chronicle* sticking out of a shopping bag on the

313

ground beside her. When I look back at her, tears are beginning to roll down her cheeks.

'Hey, hey,' I say, moving to put an arm around her. 'What's the matter? No need to cry. Everyone's okay now.' But she turns her body in towards mine and convulses with emotion. Juno and Noah are now standing in front of us, their eyes wide with concern. Linda sees them, pulls a tissue out of the voluminous folds of her dress and wipes her nose and eyes.

'Mummy's all right, my darlings. I'm just sad that Jack here has banged his head.' They stare at her and then at my bandage. 'Run off and play, my lovelies,' she says. I smile at them reassuringly and they move slowly back to the slide, but the bounce has gone out of their game.

'It's no good, Jack. I can't take this any more. It was really difficult when I escaped from the children's dad. He came after us and we had to hide in a women's refuge in Devon for a while. We had no money and I was constantly scared. I haven't taken a penny off him since, because I don't want him to know where we are. He's a violent drunk and I had to keep the kids safe.'

So that's why she was so suspicious of me when we first met, I think. She must have thought I'd been hired by her ex-husband to track her and the children down.

I look over at Noah and Juno. They're taking it in turns to slowly climb the ladder of the slide. As Juno gets to the top she looks anxiously over at us. Noah is watching his sister, then staring back at us too.

'But this is worse,' Linda continues, wiping her eyes with the back of a hand. 'I really thought we were going to die that night, you know? If the boat hadn't turned sideways and hit the bridge, we would have just rolled over the weir and drowned. I'm still having nightmares about it.'

I tighten my arm around her. 'They'll fade with time.'

'No, Jack!' She turns to face me. 'I'm sorry. I feel I'm letting you and the others down, but I've had enough. I've told that lawyer woman that I'll take the money and go. The shooting was the final straw. If they can fire bullets into your boat, they could fire them into mine just as easily... and the kids could be hurt.' I shake my head sadly as she goes on quickly. 'And I'm sorry to you, too. You and Nina have been there for us but look at you. You were nearly killed last night, and Rani too. It's evil, that's what it is, pure evil.'

Linda begins to sob again, and I see Juno and Noah cautiously approaching out of the corner of my eye. She disentangles herself from me and pats her lap to invite the children to jump up. Juno sits on her first, and then Noah sits on his sister's lap. She wraps her arms around both of them and looks up at me.

'You do understand, don't you, Jack? I borrowed every penny I could to buy *Maid of Coventry* and the mooring. The professor lent me the money, bless him. And I've been working bloody hard ever since to pay him back. It wasn't just about repaying his money. It was about repaying his trust in me. I've been skivvying and cleaning other people's homes 'til all hours. But I've loved having the security of a permanent mooring and Juno's just started school. I don't want to disrupt them again, but I just don't feel safe. I can't go through it all over again. I can find another mooring somewhere else with the money they're offering – after I've paid the professor what I still owe him. For a while, anyway.'

'Of course, I understand,' I tell her. 'But the police are close now. They know what this guy looks like and they'll get him eventually. Just give it a few more days, Linda. Don't let them win.'

'It's too late, Jack,' she replies quietly. 'I signed the papers this morning and the money was transferred straight away. We have to leave by this afternoon. I'll find a fourteen-day mooring somewhere on the Kennet & Avon for now and then I'll try to get a job and a school for Juno and we'll settle somewhere else. I've already told Danny, Tammy and Bill. And I've left a letter for the professor. I hope they catch the bastard... of course I do. But what if he's not on his own? What if there are others? I know what it's like to spend my life looking over my shoulder and I'm not going to go through all that again. These two deserve better – and so do I.'

'It's your call, Linda,' I say with real regret. 'I hope it all works out for you. Please stay in touch.'

She leans forward awkwardly from behind the children and gives me a kiss on the cheek.

'Thank you, Jack. And you take good care of yourself and that woman of yours, too.' I begin to protest but she cuts me off. 'Oh, yes, I know... she isn't your woman, that's what you say. But she will be one day, you wait and see.'

I scramble to my feet. I am temporarily overcome with emotion but manage to whisper a strangled goodbye before turning to leave the playground. Linda and the kids are still watching as I turn onto the riverside path where I look back and wave to them. They wave back, and I take a deep breath to steady myself before heading back to meet Nina on *Jumping Jack Flash*.

CHAPTER FORTY-FOUR

From across the river I can see the cardboard circle that I have temporarily placed over the smashed porthole on *Jumping Jack Flash*. There's no sign of movement on any of the other boats. In fact, at this moment, there are no other people in sight at all. No fishermen. No joggers. No dog walkers. It all seems unusually quiet. I cross Victoria Bridge and step down onto the path, where I see the hatchway and doors are open at the boat's stern. I breathe out with relief. Nina must be home.

'Come on then, get the tea on, Wonder Woman, I'm gasping,' I say as I step down into the boat. But the words die in my throat as I register the mayhem inside. Cushions are scattered around the cabin, broken plates, cups and glasses are strewn across the floor and several pieces of furniture are turned over. A rack of books has been swept bare, a couple of paintings have had their glass smashed and one canvas seems to have had a fist punched through its centre. The radio lies quiet on the floor with its batteries spilling out. The thought leaps into my mind: is there someone still on board?

I grab the spare windlass and edge slowly forward through the boat towards the bow. I try desperately hard not to make a noise, but the broken glass is crunching into smaller pieces under my feet. Has Vince sent his lads over from Bristol for a visit? Is it revenge for the damage Nina wreaked on their bikes? Is he reinforcing what could happen if I don't help him find the person who incriminated him and his gang for Powell's murder? The wrecking of my home lacks subtlety and I can easily imagine him giving the orders with relish. But where the hell is Nina? Then I think, with a sense of dread – was she here when they came calling?

I hear something; it's a tiny whimper coming from somewhere forward of me. 'Nina?' I call in a whisper. The whimpering stops. 'Nina? Is that you?'

The windlass is poised over my shoulder in readiness as I creep forward cautiously. I am in no hurry to be cracked over the skull again, but my primary thought is for Nina. I am now in the galley. Cushions are strewn across the floor alongside the kettle, which is lying on its side, next to a dark damp patch. Blood? I bend down, wipe my fingers in it and inspect them. No, just water that has spilled out from the kettle. If there is anyone still on board, then I have either passed them in the bathroom or they are outside in the bow's seating area. I double back to check the bathroom, but it is empty and undamaged. I hear the whimper again. The noise is coming from the bow. I rush back along the length of the boat, stand in the saloon and listen intently. I trace the sound to the tiny, fitted cupboard under the sink. I wrench both doors open and there, cowering in the darkness, is Eddie. I start to breathe again and reach inside with both hands to carry the dog up and out of the cupboard. He is shivering, his ears are back as far as they can go, and his tail is clamped down between his rear legs.

'Eddie!' I say, nuzzling his neck with my nose. 'What the hell are you doing in there? Where's Nina? It's okay, boy, it's okay. Good boy.' He begins to lick my face furiously, but he is still whining and looking extremely sorry for himself. I keep him in my arms as I make for the stern. I bang on Danny's boat and then Bill's, but no one is home. *Maid of Coventry* is shut up and locked, just as I would expect with Linda and the kids away in the park.

What the hell is going on? I ask myself. *Where are they all?*

My priority is to locate Nina and make sure she is safe. Nothing else matters at this moment. I pull out my mobile and put Eddie on the ground for a moment, where he stays very close to my feet. I try Nina's number again but there is no answer. I dial another number.

'Professor, it's Jack. Do you know where Nina is?'

'Jack? No. No I'm, sorry. We haven't seen her here at the hospital. Is there a problem?'

'It's all right,' I say, although of course it is not. 'I just need to find Nina. Talk later.'

Was she on board when Eddie was shut in the cupboard? I know there is no way Nina would have left him there and just walked off the boat voluntarily. If she was taken off the boat against her will, where the hell is she now?

I try calling Danny but there is no reply. I know Tammy has a smartphone as her nose is rarely more than a few inches from it. But I don't have a number for her. Or for Bill – I don't even know if he has a phone. What else can I do? Who else can I call? I feel as though I should be thinking all of this through more clearly, but I still feel fuzzy-headed and blind with panic about Nina. Then my phone rings.

'Jack? Did you call me?' It is Danny ringing me back.

'Danny. I'm trying to find Nina. D'you know where she is?'

'No, sorry, Jack. I've been down the marina all day helping to clear out *Nautilus*.' He must sense the urgency in my voice. 'What's the matter?'

'My boat has been wrecked and Eddie was locked in a cupboard. I'm worried that Nina might have been on board at the time. I haven't heard from her all day.' I hear him repeating what I have just said to someone in the background. 'Danny!' I say loudly.

'Sorry, Jack. I was just telling Tammy. D'you think it's the guy from last night? D'you think he's taken Nina?'

I realise my thoughts about Hells Angels have only been disguising an even worse fear. One that has just been voiced by Danny.

'I don't know. I can't reach her on her phone.' Her phone! Of course! An idea occurs to me. 'Danny, do you know if her phone was damaged last night, when she went into the water?'

'I... I don't know, Jack. I didn't see her using it when she came back from the hospital. But she only called in briefly to say how you were... you and Rani. Hang on... '

Someone is talking urgently in the background.

'Jack, Tammy's asking if Eddie is okay.'

'What? Yes, yes, he's scared but he'll be okay. Look, I've got to find Nina. Can you and Tammy come back to the boats as quickly as possible?'

'Yes, of course, we're on our way. But where's Bill?' asks Danny. 'He should be there.'

I glance over at Bill's boat, but it looks quiet and unoccupied. I remember the two men asking after him on the bridge. Could they or Bill be connected with Nina's disappearance in some way? 'No sign of him as usual,' I reply. 'Just please get here, Danny.'

I end the call, scoop Eddie up and rush back into my boat. I know Nina usually keeps her iPad in the cupboard under her bunk and I find it there. Nina and I may not have swapped undying love for each other yet, but we have swapped our computer passwords. I kneel at her bed with the tablet in front of me and send up a silent prayer that her phone is still working, and she has updated it recently. My prayer is answered as the tablet pings into life and grants me access. I frantically search for the 'Find My iPhone' icon and type in her email address and password again.

Incorrect.

Swearing, I do the same again, but this time more slowly and deliberately. The big squares of a heavily pixelated map slowly begin to appear.

'Come on, you bastard,' I say to it. 'Faster.' I'm horribly familiar with this app after using it to track my ex-wife's whereabouts during the dying days of our marriage. It would have almost been a relief to discover that Deb was having secret meetings with a lover – but the truth was much more mundane. It turned out she didn't need a reason to ask for a divorce, other than that she'd fallen out of love with me.

The pixelated squares eventually resolve themselves into a map of our immediate area with the big blue line of the river going through the centre of it. At first, I assume it's telling me the last location of the phone before it went into the river with Nina last night. And then I think it must be indicating that the phone is somewhere in the chaos of the interior of *Jumping Jack Flash*. But I look more closely as the map fully resolves itself and see that the little circular icon is grey rather than green, and a key tells me that this means the phone is now turned off. Why would Nina turn it off? She wouldn't, not with everything going on. But it wouldn't be at all surprising if it had been turned off by someone who had abducted her. The little grey circle isn't on the boat or the far bank of the river at the spot where she rescued Rani. Instead, it is on the Tiller & Brown site, on my side of the river. It appears to be near the site's far perimeter, almost as far along the river as it extends, and inland, close to the corner of Windsor Bridge Road and the Lower Bristol Road. It also indicates that the phone was active until forty-five minutes ago. It must have been safe and dry in her clutch bag when she dived into the river. And now it was telling me where to go – and quickly.

I know I should stop and try to think through my next steps, but my every thought is swept aside by the overwhelming need to get to the location of that little grey circle on the screen. Minutes, or even seconds, could be the difference between life and death – just as they were last night for Rani.

I remember that Danny's boat has the long aluminium ladder strapped to its roof. Eddie is shadowing my every move but I know I'll have to leave him. The poor little dog has already been traumatised, but he'll be safe on the boat now. I grab Nina's tablet and run for the hatchway, shutting Eddie inside despite his high-pitched whine of protest. Then I untie the long ladder and clumsily manoeuvre it against the tall wire fence on the other side of the path. My climb up the rungs is made awkward by the tablet and the effort is making me nauseous – or is that just my anxiety about Nina? I balance one foot on top of a post, hold the tablet protectively to my chest and jump down onto the other side. I let my legs buckle slightly as I land and throw myself forward into a roll. No limbs are broken and nor is the tablet. It is still showing the map and the little grey circle that I need to aim for. However, the end of my head bandage has come loose during the fall and is now trailing in front of my eyes. I quickly unroll it and pitch it into a nearby buddleia.

I adopt a crouching run and begin to make my way diagonally across the site, heading for its far corner. I know that I need to head for the building nearest to three circular gas holders, one large and two small. It is easy to fix my bearings on them, but the ground is rough and uneven, scattered with old bits of metal and brick, chunks of wood and large stone boulders. I stumble occasionally, but quickly arrive at a road that bisects the site. To my right is the padlocked door in the fence directly in front of the classical stone archway that leads onto Victoria Bridge. I look in the other direction and see the main vehicle entrance to the site. It seems to have a small white portable building near it and I assume this houses some kind of security presence – although, looking around, I can't imagine there is much left of any value to steal or vandalise. Vegetation is quickly reclaiming the redundant site. I cross the road, keeping my eye on the security cabin, and run alongside a long building. I am breathing hard now.

At the end there are another three buildings at right angles to it. These are huge industrial sheds of some kind, with their ends open to the elements and a train track running into the central one. I assume that my target destination is at the other end of them and so I jog close to the right-hand wall of the central building. Its walls are made of square stone blocks with a pillar jutting out every few metres. Graffiti has been sprayed in each of the bays between the pillars. There are no windows in the walls, just glass skylights above metal beams, orange with rust. I stop when I reach the big open space at the end and look at another vast red-brick building side-on in front of me. It must run along the perimeter of the site and the main road. It appears to be three storeys high and has windows running along its flank. The lower line of windows is much larger than the higher one. But it isn't the industrial architecture that is grabbing my attention.

Parked off to the left, at the far end of the building, is a powder-blue Bentley Mulsanne.

CHAPTER FORTY-FIVE

There doesn't appear to be anyone in or near the car. I look carefully along the length of the building. It continues for about another hundred metres to my right and so I am roughly opposite its mid-point. I activate Nina's tablet again; the grey spot is almost exactly in front of me. This building is her phone's last location before it was switched off. Was Nina still with it then? Is she here? I creep warily forwards, across a small service road, and crouch under one of the huge windows. Now I can hear raised voices coming from inside. The lower sill of the window is rotten and crumbling and, more problematically, about ten feet off the floor. I spot a metal dustbin nearby and remove the lid. Luckily, it's empty. As carefully as I can, I tip it over and lift it quietly into place below the window. When I climb on top of the bin, it gives me about an extra three feet but the filthy glass is still a foot or so above me. I look around again to see if there is anything I can balance on top of the dustbin, but there is nothing except an old railway sleeper that looks too heavy to move. Then I have an idea. I tap the camera icon on the tablet, press video-record and slowly raise it in both hands high above my head, careful to make sure it doesn't touch the window. I rotate it from left to right, all the time praying that no one inside is facing the window and looking up. I lower it after about a minute. Then I tap the video to view it.

The image is distorted by the dirt on the window and the slight shaking of my hands. However, I can still make out a wide expanse of concrete floor, well lit by the windows that stretch down both sides of the building and its open ends. Just to my left, in the centre of the floor, are four indistinct figures. One of them seems to be lower than the others, sitting perhaps, with their head slumped forward at an angle. One is standing to one side of the sitting person and the other two are facing them, standing side by side. As I watch the video, one of the standing pair raises a hand and points at the other one. My heart is beating rapidly. I'm certain that the slumped figure must be Nina. And the parked car suggests the Andropov twins are present. The other must be the man who attacked me and Rani last night.

Is the twins' driver lurking somewhere? I look in both directions along the side of the building but cannot see anyone. What I do see, approximately twenty metres away in the direction of the parked car, is a slightly open side door.

I climb down from the dustbin and move towards the door. My anxiety to avoid being seen makes me crouch, even though the bottom level of the windows is still four feet above me. The door is open about two inches and I can hear men shouting. But the words are indistinct. I kneel, open the door another few inches and peer through the gap.

This door leads directly into a little wooden cubicle. There is no furniture in it. Large glass panes run above waist height around its internal walls. It must have been some kind of supervisor's or foreman's office. I tuck the tablet into my waistband, drop to the floor on all fours and push the door open to the bare minimum that I need to crawl through. Once inside, I can see a further door immediately to my right that must lead out into the cavernous workspace of the main building. I crawl over to the door and peer through its glass panel. In front of me there's a stack of wooden pallets about fifteen feet high, hiding the door from the space beyond. The large space to my left stretches emptily away to the far end of the building where the Bentley is parked. I'm dripping with sweat. But my fear of discovery is swamped by the idea of what they might do to Nina. I need to get closer.

I risk pulling down on the handle of the office door and then, ever so gently, I bring it towards me. Thank God, it isn't locked. However, there is a tiny scraping noise and the door sticks after opening just a few inches. Now, I can hear the voices much more clearly. A man is shouting.

'Have you any fucking idea of the stakes involved in all this, you fucking stupid bastard?'

A low, guttural voice responds with something I don't catch.

I can see that a small spiral of metal has caught under the bottom of the door. I tug it free, swing the door open further and crawl on all fours to the base of the pallets. They have been stacked alternately and every other one gives a letterbox-shaped view through to the space beyond. The twins have their backs to me. Between them, slumped on a metal chair and facing me, is Nina. Her ankles are secured with cable ties to one of the front chair legs, her arms are pinned behind her back and she has some kind of green gag in her mouth. Her eyes are wide, fixed on the twin who has been speaking. Behind her is the man who Rani photographed on the fire escape. His eyes are glowering, black and hooded. His broad shoulders are hunched, and his neck is thrust forward, as though he is about to pounce. I pull the tablet from under my shirt, press video record again and hold its camera up against the gap in the pallet. The picture is clear on the screen; the pallet is framing it like the pillarbox effect of a widescreen movie.

'You're a Neanderthal,' continues the twin. 'Your face is plastered all over the internet. I tell you to get out of Bath fast and instead you nearly drown an old woman, attack a journalist and now you kidnap this bitch!'

I register that the twin has said 'dwown' instead of 'drown'. Unsurprisingly, it is Sebastian who is raging.

'And then you summon us here,' he continues. 'Just who the fuck do you think you are? The so-called Wolf? Hah! That's a joke. You'll be lucky to be a fucking club doorman if you ever get back to Moscow.'

'And what about you?' Now it is Anthony who is shouting, but at his brother rather than the other man. He pokes Sebastian in the chest.

'You're the fucking idiot! You brought him over here. You told him to scare off Powell. You told him to get rid of the boats. Why didn't you tell me? If this gets out, the whole deal goes down the pan and we go to prison.' The brothers' faces are now inches from each other.

'I was trying to clinch the deal,' shouts back Sebastian. 'You're a pussy, brother. You don't have the guts to do what needs to be done.'

'Oh yeah? Because it's all working out really well your way, isn't it? Why did Papa lumber me with you?'

'I keep telling you both,' interrupts the other man, loudly. 'I just want my money.' His accent sounds East European; I register that Sebastian called him the Wolf and there is a low growl in his throat. 'Two boats have now gone and third is sunk. You owe me the money.'

'Yes. And a man he told you to scare off is dead and our press conference was totally ruined,' says Anthony. 'You're a one-man wrecking ball.'

'I just want my money. Then I go.'

'You don't deserve a fucking penny!' shouts Sebastian. 'Just tell me why you brought her here?' Nina is moving her head, following the exchange. At least she doesn't appear to have been drugged, I think to myself.

'She is insurance,' says the man. His icy matter-of-factness is in direct contrast to Sebastian and Anthony's loud outrage. 'You pay me, I get rid of her. You don't pay me, she stays alive and goes back to her journalist man with lots of information about you while I disappear. Your big house scheme will be dead. Your money wasted.'

'Oh, that's just great. Great! Now he's trying to blackmail us,' Anthony says in disgust. 'And if we co-operate, we've got another body on our hands. This is truly brilliant, brother.'

'This isn't fucking Bosnia,' yells Sebastian. 'If there's anyone who needs to disappear it's you, you imbecile.'

I am still watching this exchange unfold on the screen of the tablet. Now, the man takes an angry step forward and Sebastian takes a step back.

'Do not ever threaten me,' says the Wolf in a raised voice. 'Just give me my money. I have paid out. I want that money back and the money you promised me. Give it to me if you want this woman to quietly go away.'

I make a quick calculation. Then I slide the tablet horizontally into the gap of one of the pallets but let it keep recording. It's time to call in the cavalry. I reach for my phone, but the back pocket of my trousers is flat and empty. Shit! Where is it? Did it fall out when I jumped down from the ladder? No. I can picture it now, all too clearly, lying on the table onboard *Jumping Jack Flash*. I must have left it there when I rushed out of the boat, distracted by the thought that the little grey circle on the map was Nina in trouble. *You stupid bloody idiot*, I tell myself, returning to watch the unfolding scene.

Sebastian turns to his brother and shrugs. 'She's the only person alive who has ever seen us with this cretin.'

The Wolf begins to move forward towards him aggressively, but this time Anthony tries to calm the situation. He holds out a hand, palm first and the Wolf stops.

'Okay, just hold it. It's not too late to salvage this mess. Let me talk to my brother.' The twins take a few steps away from the Wolf and talk into each other's ears. Sebastian is nodding. After a minute or so, Anthony turns back.

'All right. You're going to get your money. Go on,' he says to his brother. I retrieve the tablet and hold its camera back up to the slot. It is still recording to video and the camera is still on zoom. I turn the screen slightly to focus on the twins. Sebastian has dipped one hand into the side pocket of his three-quarter length brown leather coat and pulled out a small white ball. He holds it between finger and thumb and proffers it to the Wolf. It's another golf ball.

'Is this some kind of joke?' snarls the Wolf.

'This is solid 22 carat gold. Each ball is worth approximately £20,000 at today's spot prices. You get this one now and four more later,' says Sebastian.

'When?' demands the Wolf. He has pulled a long, thin, evil-looking knife out from somewhere on his body and is scratching the outside of the golf ball. He seems to like what he discovers.

'When you are back in Moscow and our little problem here has disappeared,' Anthony says, nodding down at Nina, 'are you sure the girl will keep quiet?'

The Wolf shrugs. 'Who cares? She has never seen me.'

'Okay. Good. We don't want this one found on the site. Put her in the trunk of our car. You can lie down in the back. We'll have to take you to your car. Leave the bike here. Then you can get out of the city with her. Take care of her somewhere quiet on the way to Heathrow and then text us before you fly. We'll get you the rest of the gold via Papa. But you never tell him anything about this mess. Now get her out of here.'

The heaviness of the golf ball 'paperweight' in Councillor Claverton's home now makes sense to me. He must have been bribed to stir up the residents' campaign against the boat owners. The other two were given six balls at the golf club by Sebastian – a total of £120,000 each – presumably to deliver approval of the planning application. Gwyneth Wilkinson must have switched them for the ones which she retrieved from her desk and showed us. But then, she was a golfer, she'd said; she would have had easy access to real golf balls.

I slide the tablet back into its hiding place in the pallet and crawl silently backwards into the office, where I make my way to the door that leads outside. I crawl through it again on all fours and then sprint along the length of the building towards the Bentley. There is still no sign of a driver. The twins must have come on their own and in a hurry when they were summoned by the Wolf.

I search the ground and quickly find what I'm looking for: a rusty old nail. Then I move quickly around the car, unscrewing the dust cap from the valve of each tyre and pushing the head of the nail into each one. Air rushes out of them in quick succession and the heavy car is soon resting on four big flat rubber tyres. Now what? They aren't going anywhere fast with Nina in their car and they clearly don't want to kill her on their own land. But what about the Wolf? Will he now take matters into his own hands? Maybe I can make them switch their immediate attention to me once they realise that it isn't only Nina who has seen all three of them together? Maybe I can trick them into thinking they can buy us off instead?

I turn and run to stand in the vast open space at the end of the building. Walking towards me, side by side in their matching leather coats, are the twins. The Wolf follows with Nina carelessly slung backwards over one shoulder. They are approximately fifty metres away and see me immediately. There is a moment of stunned silence.

'Interesting conversation, gentlemen,' I call out to them. 'Put her down and maybe we can do a deal.'

But it seems that they aren't in the mood for any negotiation. One of the twins points at me and shouts at the Wolf, 'Get him, you idiot!'

CHAPTER FORTY-SIX

Three against one. Not great odds. I sprint to the wall nearest the road where a metal ladder is bolted into the brickwork. It stands proud of the wall and rises up into the roof rafters. I begin climbing it quickly. I look down behind me. The Wolf has dumped Nina on the ground and is giving chase. She doesn't seem to be moving and I briefly wonder if they have drugged her for the journey. But there's no time to think. The ladder stops at a horizontal metal beam, one of many spanning the width of the building. Two much larger metal rails rest on top of these beams. They are about two metres apart and stretch the entire length of the building. They are level with the top of the smaller second windows and the ground looks a long way down.

Nina's body is still curled up on the floor and the twins' identical faces are looking up at me. A grunt of effort from below tells me the Wolf is following me up the ladder. There's nothing for it but to step out onto the narrow horizontal beam. The larger central rail looks easier to walk on if I can get to it. I hold both hands out wide to give me additional balance and step out over the void. One slip now and it will be a three-storey fall onto the concrete floor below. I would be lucky to escape with a broken back. I place my feet carefully, one step in front of the other with my eyes fixed determinedly ahead of me. Don't look down.

'Get after him!' urges one of the twins from below. Eventually, I reach the first of the two larger rails, which is at least double the width of the beam I have just been on. But when I turn to look back, I see the

Wolf inching his way towards me. On the plus side, he is wearing large ankle length boots with combat trousers tucked into them. This means he is having to take even greater care than me when he places his feet on the beam. On the downside, he hasn't had a bang on the head and he is still holding the evil-looking stiletto knife in one hand.

I turn and set out along the main rail, moving more quickly and confidently now thanks to its extra width. It's probably the size of a small garden path, which I wouldn't hesitate to run along, but it is amazing how a ten-metre fall on either side makes it seem much narrower and far more dangerous. I'm conscious of the twins tracking my progress from below and pray that one of them doesn't get the bright idea to climb a ladder further ahead and cut me off. The next horizontal beam has two diagonal cross braces meeting the rail in its centre. I hold onto one of them, step across to the other side and pause to get more control of my ragged breath. The Wolf is on the bigger rail behind me, and advancing quickly.

As fast as I dare, I go on into the building's interior. It is only marginally darker as I move away from the big open end of the building because light is continuing to flood in from the huge windows on both sides. I traverse two more horizontal beams and realise I am approaching the halfway point, above the chair which held Nina, the stack of pallets and the supervisor's cubicle. I have the same distance again in front of me before I reach the other end of the building. Perhaps by then Nina may have struggled free and fled to raise the alarm? It's a slim idea to hang my hopes on. The twins are still below me, time is running out and ahead of me is the grey bulk of something blocking my escape. As I get nearer, I realise it is an enormous engine block, the size of a small van. Its wheels rest on the two rails and a massive link chain seems to be coiled around part of its mechanism. It must be heavy-lifting gear of some kind, which could traverse the shed and carry huge weights along its length.

I look quickly over my shoulder. The Wolf has closed the gap between us and he is just crossing through the junction with the beam immediately behind me. The big engine is in front of me and the Wolf is at my back, still carrying his knife. Should I risk jumping? One quick look down dispels that thought.

Fuck it, I think to myself. *If I can't go around it, I'll have to go over it.* I turn and begin to climb the face of the engine.

'Another twenty thousand pounds if you get him,' shouts one of the twins desperately. I am now on top of the engine and panting from my climb. I turn to face the other side and begin to edge my way down. This is much harder; I cannot see where to place my feet. The Wolf's head appears across the top of the engine just as my own comes level with it. He crawls forward on all fours, almost snarling in his determination to reach me, and so I throw caution to the wind and scramble down to the rail again. But as I hurtle down the side of the engine block, both of my feet slip out from under me. My hand catches an outstretched gear lever at the last moment and my fall is arrested with a wrench of my right shoulder. It's cost me precious seconds and the Wolf's head now appears above me, looking down as I set off again along the next section of rail.

And that is when I hear them. The wailing banshee sound of police sirens in the distance. I stop and turn again. The Wolf is standing on top of the engine with his feet apart, looking back over his shoulder. He's heard them too. He turns towards me, measures the distance between us and shakes his head at me. My heart leaps at the thought that he is abandoning his chase. But then, in one lightning movement, his arm is bent and the knife is flying through the air towards me.

I freeze, which probably saves my life as I feel the rush of air as the blade flies past my head. A fraction to the left and it would have buried itself in my face up to the hilt. It clatters onto the concrete below. When I look up, I see the Wolf's broad back retreating.

The sirens now sound very close. I climb back up the engine block, which gives me a good view down the length of the building. The twins are running past the prostrate form of Nina and the Wolf is edging along a narrow horizontal beam to another ladder.

It seems to take an age for the police cars to squeal to a halt in the wide-open gap of the factory shed. I can no longer see any sign of the twins or the Wolf. The sirens are ear-splitting as the sound is funnelled towards me. Black-uniformed figures, some with guns, stream out of the vehicles. A number take cover behind their open car doors, whilst three begin sprinting along the building. I see one stop to bend over Nina.

When I get back to the first beam, it looks even narrower this time and even though I am no longer being chased by a man with a knife, my head is throbbing, and I can feel a distinct tremble in my legs. I am beginning to feel more than a bit sorry for myself. But I have no choice. I step out over the void once more.

I reach the ladder after what seems an age and grab onto it gratefully. Then, hand over hand, foot over foot, I descend painfully slowly to the floor, where DI Kerr and her sergeant are waiting for me with some of the black-clad officers, who I assume to be part of an armed response squad. I note that she has some kind of thick padded vest on over her civilian clothes. I drop down to my haunches. My head is swimming and I think I'm going to be sick, but the moment passes.

I stand up and look back into the shed. Two paramedics are bent over Nina and before the police officers can say anything to me I quickly make my way over to her. The plastic ties and scarf have been cut loose and she is sitting with her knees drawn up in front of her as I approach. Then, gratifyingly, she leaps to her feet, runs towards me, wraps both arms around my neck and kisses my cheek. I squeeze her back.

She puts her mouth close to my ear and I stoop to listen.

'You are one stupid brave bastard, Jack Johnson.'

CHAPTER FORTY-SEVEN

'Did you get them?'

When Nina and I break free, DI Kerr has joined us.

'Yes, it wasn't hard,' she says with a smile. 'Their car wasn't going very fast. Someone appears to have let down their tyres.'

I shake my head in mock sadness. 'You have a terrible vandalism problem in this city, Detective Inspector. Did you catch all three of them?'

She looks at me seriously. 'Three? We've arrested the Andropov twins. They were still in the car when we arrived.'

'What about the Wolf?'

She looks at me as though I am mad. 'Wolf?'

'The man from the fire escape. He was here. He abducted Nina and tried to kill me. Where the hell is he? He had a knife.'

DI Kerr urgently summons the sergeant in charge of the armed police team and he quickly starts organising a systematic search. But the site is vast and has multiple hiding places. I also suspect the Wolf had his own transport hidden away somewhere. Did the twins mention a bike? My head is fuzzy; I can't quite concentrate.

'Bloody hell,' I say in frustration. Nina is looking at me with newly frightened eyes and I realise she won't ever feel safe again until her abductor is behind bars.

'Don't worry. We'll get him,' says DI Kerr grimly.

'But how are you here?' Nina asks the police officer. 'Did Jack call you?'

'No. It wasn't me,' I say. 'I left my phone on the boat.'

'We had two calls,' says the DI. 'One anonymous, and one from Tammy Fairweather. She said your boat had been ransacked, you were both missing, and her dad's ladder was propped up against the fence into the Tiller & Brown site. The anonymous call was from a man who said you were both on the site and in serious danger. Both calls were referred to me at once and, of course, in light of the shooting incident I scrambled the armed response team.'

'I'm glad you did,' I say.

'Thank goodness for Tammy once again,' says Nina. 'But I wonder who the anonymous caller was?'

'No idea,' the detective inspector says briskly. 'However, I have two prominent citizens screaming for their lawyers, so I need to know exactly what's been happening here.'

'Come with me.'

DI Kerr, her sergeant and Nina all follow me to the stack of wooden pallets. I pull out the tablet and fiddle with it, emailing myself a copy of the latest video file before giving it to DI Kerr, who's been watching me curiously.

'If you're sitting comfortably,' I say, 'just turn the volume up and press play.'

Our heads lean forward over the screen. Then the two police officers watch it a second time, scribbling furiously in their notebooks.

'We're obviously going to need to get full statements from you both.'

I explain the significance of the golf balls and suggest that DI Kerr might also like to search the homes and offices of two councillors and a senior council planning officer before news of the Andropov twins' arrest reaches them. I am fighting off waves of pain, nausea and total exhaustion now that adrenalin is no longer coursing through my body.

'We'll need to keep this as evidence,' says DI Kerr, indicating Nina's iPad, which she is holding tightly against her stab vest. 'Let's get you to the station for some statements whilst it's all fresh in your minds. Then we'll run you home.'

The four of us turn to walk back towards the police cars, which have been joined by an ambulance and some kind of custody van. Anthony and Sebastian are in the process of being loaded into its rear, with officers on either side of each of them. Their hands are cuffed in front of them and they no longer look like masters of the universe. They both shoot me looks of pure hatred.

'Remind me to explain how to tell them apart,' I say to the two officers.

'It's weally vewy simple,' giggles Nina.

But we cannot leave yet. We are forced to wait as the search by armed officers continues across the site for the Wolf. The head of the armed response unit is worried that their quarry may still have his rifle and that our exit route from the site may be unsafe.

Suddenly, there is a far-off roar of multiple engines, like cars on the starting grid of a Formula One race. The noise increases and is multiplied by the cavernous tunnel we are standing in. It is ear-splitting. Suddenly about fifty large motorbikes swing into sight. The remaining police officers are standing and staring, or looking back at DI Kerr for instruction.

'Ah,' I say to her, raising my voice above the noise. 'It looks like your prime suspects for the Powell murder have arrived!'

Vince Porlock is sitting in a sidecar at the head of the group and they follow him as his bike swings left and stops in the centre of the shed's opening. The bikers are ranged in one straight line on either side of him. He waves his walking stick in the air and all of the engines are switched off, except for two that keep turning over. The Big Man points his stick forward and the sidecar moves towards us, another bike guarding his left flank. They stop in front of us and cut their engines.

'Mr Porlock,' says DI Kerr, folding her arms. 'What brings you here?' I remember that he has already been interviewed by the detective inspector as part of her misdirected inquiries.

Vince smiles nastily. 'Heard you could do with some help.' He looks at me, narrows his eyes and nods. 'Johnson.'

I nod back. 'Porlock.'

The biker on Vince's left takes off his helmet. 'Bob!' exclaims Nina.

Vince glances up at him. 'Bob-the-Prospect here has been doing his civic duty,' says Vince. 'He's been keeping an eye on love's young dream after all the excitement of last night. You two should be more careful. You could have been killed – again.'

'Get to the point, Porlock,' says DI Kerr with obvious impatience.

This just makes him smile again. Or it could be wind. I can't imagine how he has squashed his twenty-stone bulk into the sidecar, let alone how he will get back out again. He looks like Buddha squeezed into an egg cup.

'Well, now, Bob-the-Prospect saw this lady here being carried on a man's shoulder across from the boat and into the factory site, and it didn't look like she was too happy about it. So he gives me a call like a good boy and I scramble the lads. Then, about an hour later, he sees our hero here, Mr Johnson, go in after her, using a ladder. So, he alerts me again, and I tell him to call 999 – because we're good law-abiding people.'

'The anonymous call,' I say.

'Well, just as we're arriving in Bath, he tells me that one of the nasty men has made off on his motorbike and that he's following him. I call that very public-spirited of Bob. Turns out the baddie was heading for Bristol Airport, having been allowed to escape by the police.' Vince shakes his head sadly. 'Must be the cuts. You just can't get good people when you pay peanuts, can you? I'm a businessman. I know it's a fact of life.'

DI Kerr sighs with exasperation next to me, but stays quiet.

'So, me and the lads head off there too and we cut him off, don't we?'

The Big Man waves his walking stick in the air again. An engine is kicked into life and another bike and sidecar rolls around the end of the line-up and moves slowly towards us. The Wolf is sitting in it, his head lolling backwards. He has blood around his nose and one of his eyes is swollen shut and already turning a shade of purple.

'I'm afraid he put up a bit of a fight and injuries were sustained,' says Vince. 'Call it a citizen's arrest,' he adds, smiling sweetly. Bob-the-Prospect surreptitiously raises a gloved thumb and grins broadly at me.

CHAPTER FORTY-EIGHT

It's mid-afternoon before the police car drops Nina and me off at Victoria Bridge. We have spent more than a couple of hours telling our stories again and signing statements. And in the waiting times in between, we have drunk more horrible machine-made coffee and swapped our accounts of what happened. I'm dosed up on painkillers and Nina is nursing a bruised cheek where the Wolf backhanded her. As we cross the bridge, we both immediately register that *Maid of Coventry* has gone. I tell Nina about my meeting with Linda, Juno and Noah in the park, and Linda's decision to take the money and leave.

'But if the Wolf and the twins are in custody, she didn't need to go,' says Nina.

I look at the empty mooring and shrug helplessly. 'She'd made up her mind. She must have got back before Danny and Tammy and just decided to leave straight away, without any fuss. She was in a bit of a state. My boat was locked up – she wouldn't have known that it had been trashed and that you'd gone missing.'

'I suppose the money will help her find a new permanent mooring somewhere else,' Nina says. 'In a way, she's lucky. I don't imagine that the money to leave will be on the table for much longer, if at all.'

When I get to *Jumping Jack Flash*, I find Danny, Tammy, Bill and the professor all on board, trying to bring some order to the mess. Tammy is on her knees sweeping pieces of glass and crockery into a dustpan and Eddie has been watching them from the banquette. The little dog rushes to greet us both excitedly, followed by the others, who are full of questions.

'I came back for a shave and a change of clothing,' says the professor. 'Danny and Tammy were already here and told me they'd called the police. Eddie was barking so I let myself in and we saw the mess. Then we heard all the sirens, but we didn't know what was going on.'

'Yes, Jack. What's been happening? Where did you both go?' asks Danny. 'I didn't know what to do. It was Tammy who insisted we call the police. Did she do the right thing?'

'Yes Danny, she very much did the right thing.'

'Thank you, Tammy,' says Nina, pulling the girl up off her knees and giving her a big hug. 'You saved our lives.'

It has been a very long day after a very eventful night, but I know that I must steel myself for one last effort.

'Let's get some drinks,' I suggest to Nina, 'and I'll tell them what happened.'

Nina and I distribute beer or whisky in the glasses and cups that have survived her one-sided fight with the Wolf and we all sit around the dining table. Eddie settles himself on Nina's lap while she gives a brisk account of her abduction. I watch her closely as she talks and marvel at her calmness. She has been beaten and trussed up, and listened to men planning to kill her in cold blood. But she is totally in control of her emotions now, lucid and heartstoppingly attractive in spite of her ordeal.

After she finishes, I take up the story, telling them how I'd returned from the *Chronicle* to find the boat wrecked and Eddie shut in the cupboard. Then I explain how I tracked Nina onto the Tiller & Brown site. 'He'd obviously turned her phone off, but he didn't realise that I could still see its last location.'

Then I pull out my own laptop and access my email with the attached video. The group gathers around to watch the conversation between the twins and the Wolf unfold in front of them. I tell them about the rooftop chase, the arrival of the police and the Hells Angels. This is the fourth or fifth time I have told the story in the same afternoon, but I am ridiculously touched by the round of applause from the others, and particularly the squeeze of my thigh by Nina. There is nothing I would like more than to turf the others out of the boat and head to my bed for a fifteen-hour sleep, but I know there is one more task – however much I am dreading it.

'There is one more thing,' I say, helping Nina and the professor to another stiff glug of whisky. I'm sipping water, both out of respect for my head and the painkillers I have been swallowing in industrial quantities. Danny opens three more bottles of beer for himself, Tammy and Bill.

'For some time now,' I continue, 'I have believed that the Wolf was being helped by someone. It seemed to me that there had to be another person involved, someone who knew their way around canal boats. How else would they know how to remove a weedhatch and get away with doing it? I guessed that it was also someone who was close enough to the moorings to quickly slip out and follow the Wolf's orders without being seen. It was also someone who knew there was a plan to move the professor's boat on the following morning.'

There is silence while my words sink in.

Bill is the first to respond. 'Now hang on a minute! Are you saying one of us is to blame for what's been going on?' I watch him closely. His furtive, ferrety eyes are swivelling around the table. 'That's a liberty, that is. What proof have you got?'

'Are you really sure about this, Jack?' asks the professor. 'I find it hard to believe.'

'I also think it was someone who saw the chance to make some quick money,' I go on. 'Someone on the inside who was being paid by the twins, or the Wolf, to do their dirty work,' I add.

Danny bangs the table with his fist, making the drinks jump. A beer bottle spills over and Nina quickly puts it back upright. 'No, Jack, no. You've got to be wrong. None of us would have helped those bastards.'

I open the laptop cover again, move the slider along the timeline of the video to a point I have already memorised and press play.

One of the twins is answering the Wolf's question about when he would receive the balance of his gold.

'When you are back in Moscow and our little problem here has disappeared. Are you sure the girl will keep quiet?'

'Who cares? She has never seen me.'

Nina's hand has tightened on my arm. She has understood. Danny, Bill and the professor are looking at me in bafflement. Tammy is just staring back at me with her head shaking infinitesimally.

'It was you, wasn't it, Tammy?' I ask quietly. 'He says, "Are you sure the girl will keep quiet?" Not the man. Not the woman. Not Linda. The girl. And he wasn't talking about Nina. They'd already told the Wolf to keep her quiet permanently. To murder her. You were taking money and instructions from them, weren't you? It was you who tipped stuff overboard during the night. You untied Linda's boat and you took the professor's weedhatch out. You were ideally placed to sneak out during the night. You've been giving them information about us all along.'

Danny's simple honest face is bewildered. He is looking between his daughter and me in undisguised horror.

'Oh, Tammy,' says Nina in a whisper. 'Why?'

'Tammy? Tammy? What does he mean? What's this all about?' her father pleads.

I had expected flight or fight from Tammy, a rapid exit or a furious denial, but she surprises me. There aren't even tears. She puts her thin white hands flat on the table in front of her, fixes her eyes on her father and begins to talk quietly without looking at any of the rest of us.

'Yes. He's right, Dad. A boy on a bike stopped me about a month back and said he'd been paid to give me a message. It was a map showing a hiding place under Midland Road bridge. I went there and found a thousand quid bundled up in a plastic bag with a note. A grand, Dad! The note said to come back a week later for more money. So I did, and there was more money – the same again. But this time the message told me to dump some of our things in the river, and Linda's pushchair – and the chimney from *Nautilus*.'

'Tammy,' groans Danny in a pained whisper. 'No... you didn't.'

'Don't you see?' she says urgently. 'It was money to fix our engine – or to pay for me to get out of this dump. I couldn't believe you weren't going to take their money to leave.'

'And the money and the messages kept coming, didn't they, Tammy?' I ask.

She hears my question and nods, but her eyes stay fixed on her father.

'I didn't know Linda's boat would drift downstream. I thought it would just float out into the river and everyone would get a bit of a scare. But the current must have got stronger during the night after the storm. I never thought that Linda or the kids might get hurt. I thought they'd just find the ropes untied in the morning.'

It's a good job Linda isn't still around to hear this, I think to myself.

'My boat and my books,' says the professor in a horrified whisper.

Again, Tammy's eyes are fixed unswervingly on her father as she answers.

'I didn't think *Nautilus* would sink. I swear I didn't. I just thought some water would get in and they'd notice it before they set off.'

'That's why you jumped in and saved Eddie,' says Nina wonderingly.

'But I told them I wouldn't do anything else after that. I left a message telling them to stuff their money. I didn't know who they were. I never saw no one. But then it all went mad.' Tammy turns to look at me for the first time. 'They shot at you and attacked you, they attacked Rani and then they kidnapped Nina. That's why I called the police. I knew the same people must be behind it straight away.'

Tammy now looks slowly around at all of us. She is still in control of her emotions – but only just. She nervously pulls on the silver ring through her lip.

'I'm sorry.'

The apology hangs in the air. No one moves. No one speaks. She tries again.

'It was a lot of money, Dad, and I didn't think anyone would get hurt. I just wanted us to get away from here.'

Tears are now coursing down Danny's cheeks and Tammy can no longer look at him. She just stares down at the table, her jet-black fringe hanging down in front of her eyes. Danny puts one arm around her bony shoulder and looks at us all.

'I'm so sorry. So sorry. It's all my fault,' he says in a wavering voice. 'I knew she was unhappy. We'll leave, of course, we'll leave and Professor, we'll try to make it up to you. You can have the money Tammy was paid and you can have the money they'll pay us for our mooring.'

Tammy has now turned her head inwards and is pressing her face against her father's chest. We can all tell from the movement of her back that she is silently sobbing. I exchange a look with the professor. We both know that there will be no more financial inducements from Andropov Developments to leave the moorings.

'It wasn't your fault, Danny,' says Bill. But Danny just stares red-eyed back at us, too stunned and ashamed to say anything else while his daughter sobs into his chest.

CHAPTER FORTY-NINE

A week after the arrest of the twins and the Wolf, a selfie attached to a text arrives on my phone. It shows a picture of Bob with his arms around an attractive young woman of about the same age. They are beaming at the camera.

> I've moved to Cumbria with Tina. Living above her studio at the bottom of her mum and dad's garden. (Don't tell Vince or my uncle!) Come and see us sometime. Bob.

An emoji of an upraised thumb is attached to the message. I noticed that he no longer referred to himself as Bob-the-Prospect. I suspected that his prospects were much better than they had been.

After months of delays, and a long trial, some of the most expensive criminal defence lawyers in the land were unable to prevent the twins from being given the maximum sentence of ten years' imprisonment for attempted bribery and corruption of a public official. The golf balls, or 'gold balls', as the prosecuting barrister insisted on describing them, were found in the homes of the two councillors, Merton and Claverton. Five of Claverton's were found in a wall safe at his home and the sixth was on his bookshelf, where I had seen it. He stupidly couldn't resist trying to hide it in plain sight. The police also discovered a sizeable deposit in a newly opened bank account belonging to the planning officer Gwyneth Wilkinson. She was caught on CCTV visiting the premises of a rare metals dealer in Bristol, where she had traded her six balls for a bank transfer. The trio were also sentenced to long periods in prison. The bribe money, which totalled some £360,000, all found its way back to Her Majesty's Treasury.

The prosecution's task was made much easier after the Wolf, who was still furious with the twins for not being paid, filled in many of the blanks in the police investigation. However, that didn't prevent him from getting life for the manslaughter of Rufus Powell, the attempted murder of Rani Manningham-Westcott, the kidnapping of Nina and causing grievous bodily harm to me. In mitigation, his defence counsel argued that he had been brutalised while fighting for the Serbs as a young man. But evidence emerged that he was one of the most feared soldiers in that awful conflict, and, during his sentencing, the judge remarked on his wartime nickname of 'the Wolf'.

The video evidence from the tablet was incontrovertible and, although it was Sebastian who had commissioned the attacks on Powell and the boat people, both twins were given life sentences for commissioning Nina's murder. Andropov Development's plans for the Tiller & Brown site were stillborn and the company was wound up. The brothers were desperate for a major payback on their investment – and to impress their father who had bankrolled them so heavily – and so Sebastian had decided to leave nothing to chance, including the planning process and the unsightly moorings at the site's most photogenic entrance. They had been banking on selling the moorings at a considerable profit to the owners of their new penthouse flats. In the event, it was desperation that destroyed them. Some newspaper columnists speculated that they had employed methods which were commonplace in Russia and expressed satisfaction that British business operated to higher standards.

Tammy's part in the matter could not be hushed up after the Wolf named her in his testimony. But she escaped with suspended prison sentences and a community service order after all of the boat people, including Linda, spoke up in her defence. However, Danny was a changed man. His friendly openness was replaced by a haunted and guilty look, and often he would scuttle away when any of us came across him. Bill stepped up to help Danny repair *Otter*'s engine and, after the end of the trial, the father and daughter quietly motored away into the early autumn mist and onto the canal network. We haven't heard from them since.

Rani's wrist mended in time but by then she had grown dependent on the professor for conversation and companionship. The dependency was mutual and so when she gracefully invited him to stay more permanently, he gratefully accepted. The distinguished-looking elderly couple are now a regular sight in the city, Rani on her scooter and the professor walking alongside, stooping courteously as they chat together. They can often be seen enjoying the Theatre Royal, browsing in a bookshop called Mr B's Emporium of Reading Delights or sharing an occasional restaurant supper. But they are most content, when the weather is warm, to take a couple of books into Royal Victoria Park and simply read, side by side.

Nautilus was restored but never regained her former glory and she looked forlorn and empty without her library and other treasures. The professor sold her shortly afterwards and also traded his Morris Minor for a more spacious vintage Bristol motor car, which he refers to as his 'gentleman's express'. Rani and the professor both enjoy its stately comfort and the aroma of the old leather seats as he helms it carefully into the Somerset countryside for weekend pub lunches.

I moved *Jumping Jack Flash* back to the bottom of Robert's garden, leaving Bill's boat as the sole occupant of the Victoria Bridge moorings. Robert seemed genuinely delighted to have me back and hosted a dinner party to celebrate my return with some of his dashing young friends from London. Over coffee, he told us that another property company had secured the Tiller & Brown site and that it was already consulting on the details of a much more acceptable scheme for well-designed housing, green open spaces and a smattering of restaurants and shops. The firm had also declared its intention to provide 24-hour visitor moorings besides the bridge. Bill, of course, is still legally entitled to stay for as long as he wishes. I suspect that he will eventually negotiate a lucrative payment to remove his canvas-wrapped hulk from its mooring.

The remaining protest signs hanging from the residents' windows vanished overnight after news emerged of the arrest of Robin Claverton, their councillor and neighbour. Rani's key part in the investigation gave her moral superiority over the whole issue, and established her as the queen of her neighbourhood. I believe she is even considering standing for election to the council – or perhaps encouraging her new flatmate to do so instead.

I received a brief email from Linda last week. She is in Wiltshire, where the children have settled at a new school. She has a job as a teaching assistant and her wages, combined with the Andropovs' money, means she can just about afford her new permanent mooring. She has paid the professor every penny she owed him.

To say that the national press enjoyed the trial of the Andropov twins and the Wolf would be an understatement. The twins, who were denied bail, were forced to disclose their real identities by wearing nameplates while they were in the dock. Their identical looks, parentage and high-flying luxurious lifestyles made great copy, as did the brooding menace of the hardman who Sebastian Andropov had hired to do their dirty work.

One national newspaper headline, above a picture of the three of them being escorted into court, shouted 'RIVER RATS' and I smiled at the memory of a crudely painted sheet calling the boat people the very same thing.

Nina and I became momentary celebrities once more after my clandestine video was screened to the court. The judge praised my courage and quick thinking, but it was clear that he was much more smitten by Nina, going out of his way to praise 'the extraordinary bravery and tremendous pluck of this young war widow'. Nina had been forced to postpone any idea of going to Dubai while her presence was demanded as a witness at the trial. But the gloomy prospect still loomed over most of my waking hours.

The *Chronicle* dedicated acres of space to the unfolding story, of course, and Ben even made a trip to our mooring where he offered me my shifts back. I gave him a beer and declined – but he didn't seem too disappointed as he had already secured a new job with the local ITV news programme. I continued to work on a longer account of the whole saga. My agent secured another book deal and sold serialisation to a Sunday newspaper, which appeared with many previously unseen photographs as soon as sentencing had been delivered. Detective Inspector Kerr also co-operated a great deal with my writing and was subsequently promoted to another force.

At the end of the trial, Rani and the professor – or Arthur, as Rani insists we must now call him – invited Nina and me to dinner at her apartment. The portrait of her husband still had pride of place above the fireplace, but it was clear that Rani now doted on another man and that the feeling was mutual. After shrugging off our coats, the two women took their flutes of champagne into the kitchen and I stood in the window, looking out over the redundant factory site. 'This is yours,' I said to the professor, returning his collector's copy of *The Old Man and The Sea*.

'The only book to survive the sinking,' he said sadly. He flicked through its pages to an illustration of the old man trying to harpoon sharks, which were taking bites out of the huge marlin that he had caught after an epic struggle and tied along the side of his skiff.

'The marlin is stripped bare by the time he makes it back to land,' I said to him.

'Yes, Jack,' replied the professor, looking across at Nina and Rani. 'At least we managed to salvage something from the sharks. In fact, I think we did rather well.'

Just as we were leaving that evening, the professor presented Nina with a book. It was a replacement for the copy of *The Oxford Book of Seventeenth-Century Verse*, which went down with *Nautilus*. I came across it later, onboard *Jumping Jack Flash*; it had a scrap of paper sticking out to mark the place of poem number 495. Two lines had been underlined, whether by Nina or the professor, I do not know.

The Grave's a fine and private place,
But none I think do there embrace.

CHAPTER FIFTY

A month after the trial, Nina and I have arranged to meet at the National Trust's gardens at Stourhead in Wiltshire. The extraordinary scarlet and orange display of autumn colour, reflected in the still waters of the lake, is now over and the hordes of visitors have drifted away with the leaves. Bare branches of acers, hornbeam, chestnuts, maples, oak and beech trees reach up into an unseasonably clear blue sky. Nevertheless, the cold air steams our breath and even hints at the arrival of snow in the next few days.

Nina has one arm hooked in mine as we walk on the circular track, which is occasionally dignified by a grotto, temple or folly. Eddie is on his lead, trotting happily along on the other side of Nina after a ridiculously excited reunion in the car park.

'You know, I should be insanely jealous. I feed him, water him, walk him three times a day, give him shelter and even love – and yet it's patently obvious that he'd prefer to be with you.'

She laughs delightedly and bends to reward the little dog with a ruffle of his head. 'Ahhh, that's because he's a sweetheart with impeccably good taste. Aren't you, Eddie? Who's a good boy?'

'He's a two-timing little –'

'Jack!' she says. 'Behave. Anyway, as I said before, if you have someone to look after, you're more likely to look after yourself.'

We both go quiet while a prosperous-looking middle-aged couple walk past us. They have their hands full with two lively miniature

351

Schnauzers and a wire-haired dachshund, who they call Basil. I wait until they're clear of us.

'Talking of looking after me... perhaps it's time that you did?' I say, teasingly. I can't help hoping that the events of our summer in Bath, the risks we have once again taken for each other, our shared perils, shared disappointments and our shared satisfaction at the outcome have drawn us together more closely. Perhaps now, at last, she may be able to return some of my feelings for her.

Nina stops and looks up at me. Her short hair is growing out again and is swept back at the sides, where it is fastened by two elegant black grips. Her big eyes are unblinking. 'I do have something to say to you, Jack. Let's find a seat.'

My heart is pounding as we make our way towards the Pantheon with its round roof and classical columns. It sits on a smooth bank of grass just above the lake. There's no seat outside, but there is an elegant wooden one inside with two marble sculptures flanking it in the security of their semi-circular alcoves. We are alone, but there is something about the space and the moment that makes us talk in whispers.

I cough with nerves. 'So, what do you have to say, Nina? You know how I feel about you.' Brilliant Jack, I think. Why can't I articulate the depths of my feeling to this woman?

'Yes, Jack, I do know,' she says quietly. 'You heard what I said to Will that night on the boat and I meant it. I do love you – in a way – and there's nothing I would like more than to make you happy. Make us both happy.' She bites her lower lip and pauses.

'Tell me your next word isn't going to be "but",' I say, equally quietly.

She smiles sadly. 'But... I do need more time, Jack. Alan died less than a year ago. It still seems so wrong to just shrug my shoulders and move on.' She holds one of my hands in hers. 'I can give you one bit of good news, though. At least, I think you'll like it.'

'Go on,' I say cautiously. In truth, I am mildly encouraged. At least the one-way nature of our relationship seems to have become slightly more balanced after her most recent words. I can give her time if I have hope.

'I've decided not to take the job in Dubai. I would miss the seasons – days like this and the English countryside.' She waves through the open door to the view across the lake. The elegant stone bridge by the garden entrance is creating five perfect circles with its arches reflected in the water. 'And,' she adds, 'I've realised I would miss you too.' Then she laughs. 'And Eddie, of course.'

I nod and swallow. I am ridiculously pleased that Nina isn't going to live and work abroad. There is no way my meagre resources would have stretched to regular flights to the Middle East and I believe our relationship is still too fragile to survive that kind of distance.

'Good call,' I say, as cheerfully as possible. 'So, basically what you're saying is that I come somewhere between the English weather, the English countryside and Eddie?'

'Oh no, Eddie comes before you,' she replies, laughing. 'But seriously, let's keep things as they are for now. Can you do that for me, Jack?' She reaches up and pecks me on one cheek. 'There is one more thing, though.'

'Here it comes...' I say grimly.

But it can't be too bad as she laughs again and swoops Eddie up onto her lap. 'It's Anna.'

Anna is Nina's niece and she often talks about her very fondly. She is nineteen and on a gap year, travelling in the Far East and preparing to go to university. I haven't yet met her but the photographs on Nina's phone show a vivacious young woman with long wavy blonde hair in a side parting, a ready smile and big, blue eyes. I remember Nina's overwhelming pleasure and pride when she told me that Anna had secured a place at Oxford. The girl has been very close to Nina ever since her parents' divorce five years ago. Anna has had nothing to do with her father, Nina's older brother, ever since he announced the separation from her mother, who had just been diagnosed with breast cancer. Sadly Anna's mother died when she was sixteen, but she categorically refused to live with her father, and when home from boarding school spent holidays with her grandmother, Nina's mother, instead. Nina clearly feels very protective of the girl and regularly has her to stay and the two women seem to have become more like sisters than aunt and niece.

'I want to rent out my flat and find somewhere in Oxford for Anna's first year,' she says. 'I know she'll want to find her feet without me breathing down her neck, but I also want to be around, just in case she needs me. I might as well try to find some kind of job there, instead of Salisbury, except for... '

'Except for Salisbury being closer to Bath – and me.'

'Well, yes, that's the downside of my little plan.'

'Not really,' I say, giving Eddie's ears a fondle. 'That's the whole point of living on the canal. Have boat, will travel.'

'Really?' she says, her mouth cracking into a huge grin.

'Really,' I say. 'I'll see you on the Isis.'

Author's Note

Just as *Canal Pushers* was inspired by newspaper coverage of a spate of drownings on Manchester's waterways, the idea for *River Rats* also came from real tales of the towpath and the riverbank. The vast majority of waterside residents rub along very well with boat owners, but occasionally there are tensions and a mooring trial on the River Avon at Saltford – a few miles downstream from the setting of this book – seems to have gone badly wrong.

This may be, in part, because a fourteen-day mooring limit hasn't been strictly policed. These continuous cruising restrictions continue to cause disputes across many parts of the canal network. The Canal & River Trust interprets the rules to mean boaters must be on a continuous journey, mostly in one direction, from one place to another and must travel at least 15–20 miles a year. But the National Bargee Travellers' Association disputes this, because the British Waterways Act of 1995 does not specify any distance or travel pattern.

Meanwhile, what some see as the 'gentrification' of the canals continues, with new homes and housing estates constantly springing up along the edge of the country's canals and rivers. These new developments can bring new tensions as residents, pedestrians, joggers, cyclists, anglers and boat owners all jostle for their own space and their own interests.

While these real issues form some of the backdrop to *River Rats*, it remains entirely a work of the imagination as far as plot and character are concerned. The setting, however, remains mostly faithful to reality as indicated by the map at the front of the book, kindly designed by Michael Pearson of J.M. Pearson & Son Ltd. Once again, I have relied on their excellent 'Canal Companion' series of guidebooks, specifically the Kennet & Avon edition.

I must particularly stress that Tiller & Brown is an invented company occupying the former Stothert & Pitt site in the city and that Bath Council is a fictional authority which should not be taken to refer to the current Bath & North East Somerset Council or its predecessor Bath City Council. The developers, councillors and council officials are, like all of the characters in *River Rats*, wholly fictitious.

Huge thanks are again deserved by the excellent crew at Orphans Publishing – specifically the skipper (and director) Helen Bowden, publishing manager Joanna Narain and editor Debbie Hatfield, who once again supplied outstanding edit notes, tactful guidance and enormous encouragement. My thanks also to proofreader Anne Haydock, and the wonderful design team.

I am again grateful to Jeremy Clapham, Stuart Makemson and Matty Smith for their feedback and expertise on all boating matters in the book. My Border Terrier-owning neighbour David Birt provided diligent additional proofreading support, as did Sally Webbs, my wife Helen and Paul Deal, a former *Bath Evening Chronicle* editor who still lives near to the city. I hope the *Chronicle* will forgive my outrageous and wholly fictional depiction of its editor and its journalism. I spent two incredibly happy years on its payroll. It was, and remains, a very professional operation and I am eternally grateful to the *Chronicle* for giving me the chance to meet Helen when she worked there as its theatre critic, a reporter and subsequently a sub-editor.

Thank you also to my friends and family for their unstinting encouragement, and particularly to Guy Hinchley for advice on the law (and mobility scooters) and to Chris Palin and Mike Mockett for their gold bullion calculations. Thanks also to Dr Jerry Luke for his medical input.

I must also apologise wholeheartedly to friends and family for all those times I have been a braggart or a bore about my new writing career. I shall try to contain my excitement more sensibly from now on.

This book is dedicated to my son and daughter, Will and Ella. I am more proud of you both than I can say and I love you very much.